The Pearl Thief

Fiona McIntosh is an internationally bestselling author of novels for adults and children.

Originally from Brighton, Fiona McIntosh moved to Australia in her teens and went on to co-found an award-winning travel magazine with her husband, which they ran for fifteen years while raising their twin sons.

She now roams the world researching and drawing inspiration for her novels, and runs a series of highly respected fiction masterclasses. She calls South Australia home.

FIONA McINTOSH
The Pearl Thief

EBURY
PRESS

This edition published by Ebury Press in 2019
First published by Ebury Press in 2018

1 3 5 7 9 10 8 6 4 2

Ebury Press, an imprint of Ebury Publishing
20 Vauxhall Bridge Road,
London SW1V 2SA

Penguin
Random House
UK

Ebury Press is part of the Penguin Random House group of companies
whose addresses can be found at global.penguinrandomhouse.com

www.penguin.co.uk

A CIP catalogue record for this book is available from the British Library

ISBN 9781529103786

Printed and bound in Great Britain by Clays Ltd, Elcograf S.p.A.

Penguin Random House is committed to a sustainable future
for our business, our readers and our planet. This book is
made from Forest Stewardship Council® certified paper.

In memory of a beautiful and loyal reader, Julie Fry

PROLOGUE

* * *

PRAGUE

August 1939

Petr Kassowicz would not be going to safety. Instead, together with his sisters and parents, he would be taking his chances when the troubles arrived. And they would arrive. Of this his father, Samuel, was convinced.

Within months, winter not yet out, in a frozen March of 1939, Samuel and his countrymen had heard the intimidating sound of German boots marching on the cobbled streets of Prague. Their country was called a 'protectorate' of Hitler's; essentially, all Czechs were now servile to the Germans.

Samuel had campaigned throughout spring and summer for his wife to allow their twins to leave on the hastily arranged *Kindertransports*. He broached the topic once more as she arrived with a tray in the garden room of their small city dwelling. As he tried to find the right words he considered their situation. They'd already left the grand family home, preferring the relative security of being closer to the other Jewish community in the city. The children could walk to school, though attending would likely be banned shortly. An educated guess by Samuel, a student of history, privately whispered that they would have to leave this house too and move in with a few other families: quiet time would become a luxury; food would be scarce and regulated. He sighed at the grim picture of their future he had in mind. He had to try harder for the children.

The toasted nut smell of the alchemy of shattered coffee beans with hot water had wafted into the sitting room and the fruity notes would dance in on the steam from the pot soon. His mouth salivated; the morning cup was his favourite and he wondered when that small pleasure would have to end as well. Samuel tried not to let his maudlin thoughts overwhelm him. Instead he watched his wife laying out the china for their coffee; his beloved, petite Olga with her normally ready smile no longer dressed in fine clothes, no longer sang, danced or listened to music – he could hardly blame her, though. There was no occasion for any celebration. He had loved her on sight when their parents had first been introduced to each other one Shabbat at a family friend's. As a fifteen-year-old he'd looked across the table and seen the candlelight reflected, twinkling back at him from a fourteen-year-old's eyes that he compared to the colour of roasted almonds. His father had caught his gaze and Samuel had lowered it for the blessing being recited but his heart was already dissolving with desire to know the shy girl whose mother was admonishing her with a similar frown.

They'd been required to wait until he was eighteen; grown to his full height, past six foot like his father, and filled out to lose some of the scrawniness his mother had fed him against. But she'd not won that battle; his body shape was broad but helplessly hollow . . . like his grandfather's. And, like his forebears, his face was narrow. His mother accused him of being gaunt but he surely ate enough for his other brothers too, and in time his appearance would become elongated by the beard he grew after their joyous marriage and the birth of their first child. Their new daughter they named Katerina; Samuel, being a lover of history, had particularly liked its links to Ancient Greece and its meaning of 'pure'.

He regarded Olga now with a fresh charge of affection; she really hadn't changed so much since they first met, although the weight of sadness of Occupation had drooped her shoulders and the dimples he adored rarely showed themselves now. Her hair was still lustrous and wrapped loosely up behind her head; it wasn't yet shot through with a single strand of silver and while her skin was not as taut, she had lost none of the radiance he admired in her complexion. Her wide mouth and full lips that used to laugh a lot and that she had liked to paint red were now bare but they still kissed him tenderly. He had felt loved each day of their twenty years of knowing one another, seventeen of them as husband and wife.

Now, when they should be enjoying the best of their years with their family complete, there was so much pain of regret. Still, he risked her precious affection with his next breath.

'Olga, I want you to consider allowing Hana and Ettel to go to England on one of the rescue trains. They've got each other, my love. And they won't separate twins, which means we can at least get two of our little ones to safety.' He recalled the thousands of parents lined up outside the newly established office of British stockbroker Nicholas Winton, the architect of the rescue. So many were applying for their children to be taken to the haven of England. He would gladly queue too. 'I can walk us to the Winton office this moment. We can register the girls for —'

Olga interrupted him with a sob and the angry sound of china being clattered. She clutched her heart and her breathing became shallow, her words so staccato they made no sense. They were simply sounds of bitterness.

He waited, not daring to push further, until she found her voice. 'I will not give up a single one of my children!'

'Do you think I want to send any of our children away from us? Olga, there is no future here for them – surely you can see that now? At least if we can send them out of Europe there is a chance for them to survive the inevitable war.'

She came back at him so fast it was like the crack of a whip. 'I'd rather we all died together than be separated!'

It was a severe error in judgement, Samuel was sure, but he did his utmost to understand. Olga was a born mother. It was all she had ever wanted to be and she was the best sort of mother: firm but kind with a generosity that put him to shame. She loved each child differently, promoting their individualism; encouraging Lotte's natural need to be the centre of attention: 'She'll be a performer, mark my words!' Olga would say. And she would never criticise Katerina for her interest in fashion – a topic he despaired of especially, as secretly she was his favourite child: gifted in music, highly intelligent, and with a rare poise for one so young. 'She's our most beautiful child,' her mother would boast to him, 'a natural canvas for exquisite clothes. She'll design her own one day, you'll see.'

'My darling . . . please.' He risked a desperate final pitch. 'If they've made us give up our bicycles, radios, furs, even our skis, you can see how they're already beginning to imprison us through denying us basic necessities. Food will be next. They're unlikely to allow us to remain together long. At the very least, allow baby Petr to go. Give him a chance. Soon there will be no way out, not for anyone. He can grow up safe and —'

And that's when Olga snarled at him; he'd never seen hate in his wife's face previously. She had been the sweetest young woman that all his peers fell in love with, and he was the lucky suitor she had loved in return. Their marriage had been one of equanimity; he couldn't recall a cross word. Instead, there was always a smile for her husband, her children, her neighbours. Affection was Olga's character constant. And so to feel bitter rage from her was shock enough – but to see a mixture of despair and contempt being levelled at him, and in a voice he didn't recognise, was more than he could bear.

———

That had been the last time he'd mentioned their children being involved in the *Kindertransport* to her but Samuel was at the railway station for each train of hope – as he thought of them – to bear witness. And today, 2 August, felt auspicious. This Wednesday was the afternoon that the eighth *Kindertransport* would leave Prague.

The rest of the Kassowicz children were staying with friends. These regular visits were a highlight in their lives and he knew Katerina at twelve could marshall her three sisters. It had traditionally given him and Olga quieter days and a chance for an evening out, but since the arrival of sickly Petr that avenue of pleasure was no longer theirs to walk down. He didn't mind; time alone with Olga, when their son finally slept and no other children needed their attention, was enough.

'Why don't you come with me to the railway station?'

'Why?' She frowned, touching the cheek of Petr, who gurgled from his high chair.

Samuel shrugged. 'Young Pavel is on it. I thought we could be there together, show some strength for our closest friends. Anna will be —'

'No, Samuel, forgive me,' she said, suddenly wringing her hands as her gaze dropped with shame. 'I can't face all those farewells, all those tears. And Anna, a mother saying goodbye to her only child . . .? It's unbearable,' she explained.

Samuel grasped an element of fear nagging beneath her excuse that perhaps she had not made the right decision when the opportunity had been there.

He readied for his departure and called back in to the parlour where Olga was poring over a meagre list of groceries that needed

5

to be fetched by the next day. She scribbled beneath the din of Petr's sobs.

'Give me the list,' he offered. 'I'll be glad to pick up some of the items you require while I'm running my own errands.'

'No need,' Olga said, an apology carried on her smile. 'Wear your overcoat, my love,' she suggested, sounding the most wearied he could recall.

'It's a lovely day,' he replied, glancing out of their window past the kitchen gardens he'd helped their gardener peg out and plant for Olga.

'And still autumn's early nip is riding on that wind and I don't want you having another bout of bronchitis.'

He smiled, fetched his coat and returned, buttoning it up as he kissed his wife and child goodbye. Petr was red-faced and upset, his eyes tightly closed as he took another long gasp, ready to hurl it back out to deafen the neighbours.

'He's poorly today.'

Olga sighed. 'He's in pain, poor little mite. Perhaps some weak chamomile? We'll go out into the garden and pick some; sometimes that helps the wind in his tiny belly.'

'You're sure about not coming today?'

'I'm sure, Samuel. You go, hug them and kiss little Pavel from me. They're braver than I.' She was rocking a whingeing Petr as she gave her husband a wan smile. He knew she hadn't slept and was likely half asleep on her feet still trying to comfort their son.

'Olga, you look exhausted. Why don't you wrap up Petr and I'll take him in the pram; give you a chance to rest? A change of scenery will do him good.'

She tried to shoosh him, get him on his way, but her efforts were half-hearted and he could tell she likely needed him to insist. 'My love, you will be refreshed if you get a few hours of sleep. And all the children will be home soon.'

She nodded, no doubt imagining the enthusiastic voices and activity as four children returned to their home and she had to help them get ready for a week of school.

'Are you sure?'

He gave her a look of mild exasperation but filled with affection and added a soft hug. 'I shall walk him until the fresh air drugs him to sleep.' They shared a soft smile. 'The rhythm of the pram wheels on the cobbles alone will soothe him. I'll be home within the hour; I won't stay long at the station – it tends to be chaotic, anyway. I just want Anna and Rudolf to know they're in our thoughts.'

He was surprised when Olga acquiesced. 'I'll get him ready. Give me a couple of minutes.'

And so Samuel Kassowicz, former well-known glass manufacturer, art collector and historian, found himself wheeling a pram out of his house headed for the railway station. First, however, he decided to take Petr past the Prague *orloj*. This astronomical clock was mounted on the town hall in the square and he never tired of observing its mechanism in action on the hour when wooden figures would emerge – 'The Walk of the Apostles' – while a skeletal figure representing Death would strike the hour. Petr was already calming at being out in the cool air, seeing activity, colours and hearing new sounds, and Samuel hoped the clock would enchant his son as it had all his sisters.

The pram wheels bumped over the damp cobbles as he angled their path towards the southern end of the large square that dated back to the twelfth century and to its early-fifteenth-century clock, which promoted various myths. One circulated that if the clock was not kept in good repair by the folk of Prague, a ghostly figure mounted on the *orloj* would nod at the residents and put them in peril. Legend said that the only way to counter the town's endangerment was for a boy to be born on New Year's night. Many legends swirled around the magnificent clock with its rich blue dial, from some believing the original clockmaker was blinded so he couldn't make another, to him sabotaging his own work beyond repair. Samuel had enjoyed researching the clock down the centuries and its many periods of repair and additions, the most recent in the middle of the 1800s.

He paused, taking his son from the pram to hold him so he could direct the boy's attention to the clock when it would move any moment. 'You see, Petr,' he pointed, knowing the boy didn't understand but was distracted entirely from his tears nonetheless. 'The inner ring depicts the signs of the zodiac – you are Libra, if we follow that thinking. I am Pisces, your eldest sister the Aquarius and the twins are appropriately Gemini.' He chuckled at this. 'Lotte is like your mother, both Virgo. Now those golden numbers shown at the edge? They're called Schwabacher numerals and they mark off Old Czech Time – these days, Petr, we count our hours from midnight but back centuries ago when this clock was made they marked the hours from sunset. It's connected with the Roman Catholic holy bells that mark the hours of the day and commences from the Angelus bell, a half-hour prior to dusk. This form of counting the hours helped the workers – particularly those outside – to know how much daylight remained for their toil, and of course for each season this changed, noon sometimes being in a different hour.'

Samuel continued talking gently to his boy until the *orloj* chimed its bells and the two doors slid open above the clock face to allow the figures to rotate. People smiled at him and his child as they passed, some also pausing to admire the figures of prevailing prejudices, from Vanity to Greed, and Philosopher to Angel. Samuel cleared his throat quietly and shifted Petr back into his pram as the figure of the Jew with his bag of money circulated clearly. 'Shall we continue?' he said conversationally to his son, who gave him a bright smile to warm him.

8

Samuel steered the pram around the fringe of the town square. 'You know, Petr, this used to be the most significant marketplace. Why?' he asked and then proceeded to answer his own question. 'Well, you see, its history can be traced back to the tenth century, long before the clock was designed and installed. And in those days it was considered a main junction – a crossroads, if you will – between the east and west so it was a vital trading place, and in fact the building just behind here' – he nodded – 'is the former customs house where all the goods brought through by the foreign merchants were cleared. This used to be a thriving centre of shops, some fixed, some that just seemed to set themselves up in the moment, and all around here' – he swept his hand vaguely, sounding enthralled – 'were more than a dozen stone cots where the most expensive imported cloth was sold.' He smiled to himself, continuing talking as they moved down into the main boulevard along New Town's south-eastern border. 'Bakers stood alongside potters who jostled for space with herbalists and other craftsmen, from wood products to leather. And where we stood near the clock, the vendors of food tended to gather . . . butter, cheese, grease, fruit and vegetables, including our famous mushrooms and other forest gatherings. But fish' – he waggled a finger in the air – 'Prague had special privilege for fish sellers. They had their own market by the north-western part of the town hall. And the annual markets, I believe, were a sight to behold. Everyone came from all over the region.'

Father and son made their way down the main artery of Prague, which ran perpendicular to Wenceslas Square and was host to the National Museum, the main theatre and the impressive neo-Renaissance train station, his destination. Samuel was sure that Petr enjoyed the walk – the unfamiliar sights and sounds had dried his tears, and if there was still pain in his small body, he was distracted from it. But as the coiling pressure of Petr's crying and

Olga's fatigue and fears began to ease in Samuel's chest, a fresh tension replaced it. He felt it each time he came to bear witness to another trainload of children leaving their homeland. And this would be the worst one of all because it might be the last transport of hope. Who knew if others would get through?

Soon he was standing in the main hall beneath the grand half-domed ticket hall that looked out towards the station's triumphal arch. It was flanked by towers topped with glass globes that were meant to symbolise the gateway to this grand city. Normally this was a place of happy welcomes, but now it was the chaotic scene of people preparing to hand over their most precious belongings.

Samuel had parked the pram at the entrance, and carrying his becalmed ten-month-old son he found himself turning misty-eyed with his friends as they gave a final kiss to the rosy-pinched cheeks of their own infant son, barely weeks older than Petr. Pavel cried when lifted from his mother's arms and she had to be physically supported by her husband, stoic midst his wife's misery, as a man ticked his son's name off the list of children headed for London.

'Why won't they let us onto the platform?' Anna groaned, leaning heavily against her husband who wore a masklike expression.

He could see Rudolf was feeling emotion as a physical pain and when his friend didn't answer, Samuel obliged.

'They believe it makes the parting harder,' Samuel said softly, also knowing from his network of contacts that the Germans were searching all the outgoing children's suitcases for valuables once out of sight of their parents. Even if Pavel's tiny suitcase had nothing of value to Hitler it would be an abiding and painful memory to his parents watching his clothes and favourite toys being rummaged through and flung around.

'It couldn't be harder,' she wept, 'and it's a few minutes more with him.'

The first whistle blew and a gasp rippled through the station as parents felt their hearts collectively breaking to its shrill sound. Samuel knew there would be two more yet, but even so, he began to urge his friends to leave.

'You won't be able to see anything,' he murmured to Rudolf.

'We'll watch the last billow of steam take our child from us,' his friend replied through a clenched jaw.

Samuel nodded, squeezed Rudolf's arm and looked back into the rare, smiling face of his son. He looked so like his eldest sister, Katerina, it hurt. Petr was made in her image . . . including the curious 'cat's eye' of one pupil. The striking flaw he recalled from his grandfather had endeared him to both children. Petr giggled and the sound was a balm to his father; Samuel kissed his son's tiny forehead and regretted once again the decision that prevented Petr from having a life of freedom. He would have to suffer all the indignities and restrictions that were surely coming their way. No amount of wealth, it seemed, could protect his children from a madman's hate.

He shook himself free of the dark thoughts and hugged Anna. 'Come visit when you feel up to it,' he said, giving her a gentle but lingering peck on her cheek. 'Olga will bake her famous poppyseed cake.'

Anna gave Petr a teary smile and nodded at Samuel, unable to reply.

He had to get away. The farewells hurt but still he wished it was Petr leaving alongside Pavel; he had a momentary daydream of their two boys growing up alongside each other in some kind stranger's home in England. Samuel had only just turned to shoulder his way out when a cry went up. A voice on a loudspeaker began to yell. People strained to look, their voices rippling into one murmuring sound of enquiry. Samuel returned to where his friends stood.

'What's happening?'

'They can take another baby, if I'm understanding correctly,' Rudolf said.

They listened to the next announcement but couldn't hear all of it above the din. Samuel didn't pause to wonder at what propelled him. He simply moved on instinct, pushing his way to the front of the temporary barrier where an official with a clipboard was fielding questions.

Samuel's tall stature and his expensively tailored clothes helped attract attention. 'Excuse me, sir? Please, my name is Samuel Kassowicz,' and he could see by the lift of the man's eyebrows that the well-known name registered with the fellow. 'What is this about an additional baby?'

The man shook his head in soft exasperation. 'A mother has panicked at the moment of handover and now she refuses to send her infant.'

'Every parent here would surely understand.'

'It's no surprise, but with respect, I am disappointed that the child is missing out on this rescue attempt that everyone here has been working so hard to bring about.'

'There are no words that can convey how grateful the Jewish community is . . . but it doesn't help the pain of separation.'

'What this means is that we have a critical space and it would be short-sighted to waste the opportunity.'

'Take my daughter, please?' a father suddenly cried, elbowing his way through.

'Sir, please, we can't take another girl.'

The man's exclamations and further enquiries were lost as another woman reached the front, breathless, bullying her way past Samuel, who fortunately stood a good head taller so he still had a clear view. 'Well, I have a son,' she pleaded, 'he's three, old enough to be no trouble. I want you to take him.'

Other parents muscled through, offering their children. Samuel felt only heartache for them all. They would each have had the same opportunity as his family and, for various reasons, like Olga, had opted against it but now, faced with the dilemma, caught up in the excited terror of this potential last chance, who could blame them for thrusting their beloved children at this man?

The official put his palm in the air. 'Please,' he began, but the cacophony only got louder.

Samuel joined in with the official to quieten the folk around him. There was an atmosphere of new desperation but they knew and trusted Samuel Kassowicz, a prominent member of the Prague Jewry. They listened to his plea for calm so the official could explain.

The man tried again. 'What you need to understand is that there is a family in England that is expecting to receive a baby. They've prepared for an infant. They've got clothes for a boy. It probably suits their life to have a son growing up. They may not want a daughter, or a three-year-old, or a seven-year-old.' He gave a look of deep apology to those parents who had offered those children. 'I'm sorry for you all. But we have to be grateful to these people at the other end and we want your children to be safe and cared for and, above all, cherished while they're with them. So we need to deliver what we've promised . . . what they believe they're getting.' Samuel hated how their children sounded like commodities. He watched the official scan the worried faces. 'Forgive us, please, but all we can take is an infant boy.' As a father held up what looked to be a deeply upset newborn he said hurriedly, 'A child who is sitting up, on solid food.' He glanced now at Samuel holding a solemn Petr, who regarded the crowd from beneath his blue cap and the crook of his father's arm. 'Mr Kassowicz, how about your boy?'

Samuel swallowed in shock. He dared not admit to himself that it was the reason he'd forced his way to the front of this horde of desperate people. He tried to pretend to himself in this moment that he was simply an interested observer. Rudolf arrived at his side.

'Samuel. Really? Are you going to do this?'

'Sir, I shall have to press you to make a decision, or I will search elsewhere.'

'She'll never forgive me,' he murmured to himself, feeling spangles trill through him like a phosphorescence of private, disbelieving horror as he began to shift his son from his comfy cradle. He was doing it. It was as though the father of Petr, who loved this tiny child, and the rational manufacturer that was Samuel Kassowicz, who could make the toughest of decisions, had suddenly parted company. The father stepped back while the colder, rational man stepped forward. 'Take him to safety,' he said in a voice that sounded equally disengaged. It had a gritty quality, as though it had fought its way to his lips, pushing past the gatekeeper of his conscience and all the protests that told him not to do this.

'Very good, sir. This is an awkward situation, a brave decision. Your wife, is she —?'

'His mother will understand,' he lied. 'This is what she would want,' he pushed on, searching for the truth that finally emerged. 'I regret deeply that we didn't formalise this when we had the right opportunity.'

'Then the angels are certainly taking care of him today, Mr Kassowicz, because he can leave with us in a few minutes.'

'I have nothing to send with him,' he said, looking around, feeling the drag of nausea clawing its way to his throat.

Rudolf pulled at his arm. 'Samuel! Olga . . .' He didn't need to finish. His voice was laced with shame, echoing how Samuel felt.

Samuel nodded nonetheless. 'Our son will be safe, Rudolf, like yours. That's what matters.'

The official answered his query. 'The parents of the child not going will donate his case and its contents. I'm afraid your son must travel on his documents.'

Samuel frowned. 'Why?' But even as he asked he knew what the answer would be. It was obvious.

'Because all the paperwork is complete and there are barely minutes now before the train departs – no time to prepare fresh details, no time to even change these. In fact, it makes no difference that he is not . . .' The man consulted the pages, flipping through them until he found what he needed. 'Hersh Adler. He's a boy of the right age and the family at the other end will accept him as such.' He shrugged. 'No one will care.'

Samuel bristled, the bile arriving in his throat. He had to swallow. 'I shall care.'

'Forgive me, Mr Kassowicz, sir. I hope you know I meant no offence.' A woman arrived at his side with enquiry in her expression.

'Have we a substitution?' She looked anxious, clearly in a hurry. 'We leave in two minutes.'

The official – he didn't even know the man's name – searched Samuel's face. 'Sir?'

Samuel held his breath and kissed his son one last time, tasting the soft baby skin, smelling his mother's perfume on it like a guilty wraith. 'We will not forget your name, Petr,' he promised, and without allowing himself another second to renege on the terrible decision that he already knew was going to have far-reaching consequences, Samuel Kassowicz handed over his son.

Petr let out a wail immediately as the square-jawed woman grabbed him. She didn't mean to be rough, Samuel could see that, but her hands were larger than Olga's and perhaps held Petr too tightly. He looked lost in her arms as he squirmed and protested.

'He suffers colic,' Samuel ground out. He knew he sounded pathetic.

'We'll take care of him,' she said, and her smile changed her features to the kindest of expressions. She was indeed one of the angels looking out for his son. The angel looped a cardboard sign around Petr's tiny neck; it carried a number and Samuel could only make out the first two . . . a six followed by a three. And then Petr was gone. She had turned and walked briskly away, probably deliberately not giving Samuel any opportunity to change his mind or shout any more instructions.

'Goodbye, sir,' the official said, and although Samuel distantly heard the words, he couldn't tear his gaze from the broad, squat back of the woman who carried his son from him . . . and he knew in his heart it was forever.

Samuel followed the wail of Petr, distinctive enough until it was lost to the piercing sound of the train whistle and a vast billow of steam that accompanied a jolt of the train and a screech of wheels. The crowd reached a feverish excitement that was all fear. Rudolf and Anna were at his side behind the barrier and Samuel hadn't realised they had all linked hands, all collectively holding their breath until the third whistle sounded. Then all the families pressed forward, a single moan of despair lifting to the ceiling of the Art Nouveau hall as their children eased out of Prague's main station within the carriages of the *Kindertransport* that the Germans were likely glad to be rid of.

Samuel watched from the distance until there was nothing but empty railway tracks, until all the other parents, including his friends, had drifted away. He stayed until there was not a soul left on the platform, and it was only then as a cold wind blew through the empty glass and steel canopies and against his cheeks that he realised he was silently sobbing.

1

* * *

The neat angles that ordered the planes of Severine's face looked as though they'd been drawn in determined strokes with a sharpened pencil. Yet the keen points that usually held her figure so finely poised, from the wide triangle of her shoulders tapering to the slant of her ankles, seemed to pleat, shrinking her as she backed away from the glass cabinet. Swooning for a heartbeat, she reached blindly behind for a nearby seat into which she folded.

The tailored two-piece she wore, with its Parisian designer's label stitched to the satin lining, folded with her. Nevertheless, it maintained its hauteur and thus her envied *chicness* that her female British colleagues referred to with wistful envy. Perched on the chair, though, she resembled a fragile bird, ready to startle; she didn't register others, not even when her colleagues descended making collective clucking, worried noises.

'Mademoiselle Kassel!' her companions cajoled, but it was as though she could no longer hear them.

In these moments of terror, Severine couldn't touch the present because she was transported. Today, suddenly, she was no longer standing on parquet floors surrounded by burnished timber and glazed bookshelves in the King's Library of the British Museum. In her mind it was no longer morning in London's Great Russell Street of 1963 that was rife with traffic and people sniffling with the tail end of their spring colds. All those human sounds and today's innocent landscape had dispersed in her mind and coalesced into the vivid scene of 1941, a memory she had bullied over the past decade into hiding.

In these protracted moments of rekindled terror, the nightmare escaped from the prison in which she kept it, unleashing the recollection of blood, so powerful she could feel its damp stickiness once again clinging to her skin. On her lips was the taste of it . . . like the copper of the Czech korunas that used to tang on her childhood tongue when she hid them in her mouth on the way to the sweetshop.

She had pushed the horror of 1941 so far away inside, buried it so deep, that there were some days – the rare, shiny ones – when she did not think on the evil that had changed the course of her life. Severine did, however, feel the burden of it inside like a viscous poison trying to erode its way out to consume her again with all its toxic, terrifying reality. But she had taught herself to be the ringmaster of those demons, and that circus was not allowed to play in the big tent of her mind – unless she chose to let the beasts out.

That disciplined control meant for many years she'd led a quiet, regimented life of exacting routine in order to keep evil corralled, to keep her thoughts occupied and tidy. And particularly to keep her emotions cooled. It meant, though, that she – once an effervescent and precocious child – had become someone for whom neither unbridled joy nor genuine laughter was likely.

But today she'd shown no control. It was the sight of the Pearls that had triggered her.

Her day had started without any clue of the drama about to unfold. She'd woken at the usual time of nearing five-thirty to a frosty spring dawn. Early sunlight slanted through her Bloomsbury flat on the top floor of the red-brick mansion; she wasn't sure whether it was neoclassical or baroque. English architecture's fluid styles down the centuries confused Severine and she reminded herself once again to check with her colleagues at the museum. Nevertheless, she liked the tall and brooding symmetry of her building – called Museum Chambers – which she presumed was Victorian by its austerity but it was countered by decorative details of scrolls, window dressings and a portico in white stone. It was her temporary home and a mere stroll from her work at the British Museum. Her apartment in France had tall French windows and these English sash versions with pretty boxes of tumbling flowers during spring and summer were, in Severine's opinion, a happy substitute. Her balcony encased by wrought iron would be ideal on a balmy summer's evening, although she would never know. Her contract was only for six weeks.

She gave a soft sigh as she looked down into Bury Street, already moving with people at first light with a street sweeper and a couple of pedestrians hurrying in opposing directions. They were featureless huddles of clothes insulating their owners against the icy feel of the morning.

'Past three weeks now,' she calculated in whispered French, her mind reaching to Paris and the realisation that she'd be heading back to France soon. She nodded, guilty at feeling torn because she was enjoying this London sabbatical and all its challenges, especially using the local language. 'Maybe they'll extend it,' she murmured, this time in English, liking how it rolled easily off her tongue. Her late father would be proud if he could hear her using the languages he'd insisted she master.

'French, because there's none more beautiful; English, because there's none more relevant; and German, because there's none more practical right now,' he'd counselled back in 1934 when she was seven. 'But always be proud of your Czech and Hebrew . . . because that's who you are,' he'd added, tweaking her nose playfully.

Severine had shaken her thoughts free and focused on her life now – it never helped to rekindle even the good childhood memories for too long. Did she really want to stay longer in London? Live here? She was prepared to entertain the notion. To remain in England . . . permanently? It would require organisation to sell up in France, set up a proper home; maybe a bedsit in the city and a cottage in the countryside . . . York, perhaps, which she liked so much . . .

She'd bathed and considered wearing her favourite trapeze dress – a copy of Yves Saint Laurent's daring silhouette that had not just taken away the collective breath of French designers but had sent a tremor through fashion houses worldwide. She could remember her own sigh of pleasure at seeing the clean, stark lines that appealed so strongly to her tidy mind and neat ways. The 'young Turk' who'd taken the helm at the death of her design hero, Yves Saint Laurent, had borrowed from the master's design and inspired her to claim a style of her own. She realised that breakthrough design had opened the door to the baby-doll dresses that so many modern Londoners today embraced as their own invention. 'But it was all French.' She smiled to herself as she said it. 'Perhaps I *should* have gone into fashion,' she added. She knew it was eccentric to talk aloud when no one else was present, but put it down to years of self-inflicted loneliness.

Rather than think on the reason why she had chosen antique jewellery as a specialty, she distracted herself by rifling through her small wardrobe of outfits. Each of them had been saved for diligently because she preferred the sharply reliable cut of the more expensive designers and was prepared to have fewer options as a result.

Severine reached for a two-piece dress that she hadn't worn yet in London because it hadn't warmed up enough for ballet-length sleeves, but the frost would pass quickly and she'd have her coat. Memories of the Thames freezing over during the winter just gone were still fresh in people's minds, but the thaw was well and truly past. There had been photos of children playing on the ice covering the great river in all the British newspapers, which had been picked up and run in Paris too. It had happened on the Seine in years gone. Right now, it was time to think only spring, she decided. Severine pulled the Parisian-designed mid-grey double-knit skirt over her slim hips, which the unfussy outfit enhanced. The simple round-necked top had elbow-length sleeves and her only adornment was a silk scarf in deep marine that she didn't deliberately choose in order to set off the colour of her eyes, but glancing at her reflection critically, she accepted it did just that.

No rings on slender fingers, no brooch at her collarbone, not even a watch around her narrow wrist did she adorn herself further with. But she liked lipstick for a kiss of colour. Now in her mid-thirties, Severine Kassel had admitted to this same mirror that she didn't consider herself young enough for the *ingénu* look of hip London and its pale-faced, pastel-lipped youth. While a sweep of vermilion was close to being mandatory for a Parisian, she chose instead a duskier cousin and dragged it carefully across her bottom lip first. 'Moroccan Rose is perfect,' she said, pouting at her reflection to admire the choice. '*Très bon*,' she admitted to her image staring back and attended to her top lip with even more care to get the line of colour exact.

Severine rarely ate breakfast and today was no exception. A cup of coffee filled her belly mostly for its warmth and particularly because she enjoyed the ritual of brewing that allowed her to recreate the smell of Paris in London. While she could never embrace the fascination that the British had for tea, she knew how important it was to sip the beverage with colleagues for purely social reasons. Every problem was solved over a pot of tea, it seemed. But here, in

Bury Street, the top floor smelled of darkly toasted beans where the acidic notes had been roasted out to leave the signature bittersweet note of Costa Rica percolating on a tiny stove.

Despite its intensity, Severine took her coffee black, short, unsweetened, and standing up at the small kitchen counter. She swallowed her morning caffeine in no more than three sips, just as she would if she were calling into a French café on the way to her office at the Louvre.

She pulled on coat and gloves, ignoring a hat, in favour of a thick extra scarf, before picking up her glossy, dark tan crocodile leather handbag that she'd bought a decade earlier in the flea markets north of Paris. It reminded her strongly of the one her mother had carried for special occasions just before the German occupation of Czechoslovakia. She briefly wondered who carried that exquisitely structured design of polished reptile skin now – it would be worth plenty – and immediately sifted the dangerous thought away. She hung the gleaming bag she helplessly admired on her elbow and with a single final glance at the mirror, she departed her flat.

Severine left Bury Street almost to the minute each working morning. Neighbours she wouldn't be around long enough to learn names for would lift a hand in welcome and she would return the gesture with a smile.

'I could set my watch by you, miss,' the local pub owner said with an appreciative wink. He and his lads were restocking their cellar for another day as she approached the corner into Great Russell Street.

'Morning, miss,' his three helpers chorused, lifting caps.

They never could get their tongues around 'mademoiselle', although she'd tried to teach them. 'Morning, handsome boys.'

One put his hand on his heart as if swooning; another gave her a cheeky whistle. 'Will you come dancin' wiv me tonight, miss?'

Their elder flicked his cap at the lad. 'Cheeky blighter! Watch your manners around a lady, Billy.'

She threw a careless grin over her shoulder, aware the daring one was young enough to be her son, and waved as her heels clicked her away across the damp London pavement towards what had been in the eighteenth century a grand mansion purchased from the Montagu family by a body of trustees. Mid-century that house had been reinvented as the British Museum through an act of Parliament to which King George II gave his formal assent in order to house the tens of thousands of objects, books, manuscripts, drawings and specimens that formed the cabinet of curiosities assembled by Hans Sloane and bequeathed to the nation. By the turn of that century explorers from Captain James Cook to collectors of antiquities donated or sold their collections until the museum began to bulge with everything from gems and coins to the famous colossal marble foot of an Apollo. And still it had grown, as Victorian and Edwardian archaeologists and collectors had plundered the ancients from Greece to Egypt through the Ottoman Empire.

Severine stood at the grand gates and considered the vast expansion that had occurred over the decades with new buildings, new floors and new acquisitions from all over the world. The war had meant enormous disruption at the Louvre, which was more about theft than destruction. It was a shadow, though, in comparison to the scale of reorganisation and cunning of the chiefs at the British Museum. She'd listened with no little wonder at her colleagues' descriptions of shifting priceless antiquities to secure basements around London, to an old quarry in Wales, to tube stations like Aldwych, where – she couldn't help her delight at hearing – the famous Elgin marbles from the ancient Parthenon frieze had been stored for the duration of the war. According to her older colleagues, they'd begun their ambitious arrangements for the dispersal of important pieces as early as 1934. Transfixed, she'd listened to how various people involved with the nation's treasures had gauged the dangers of war ahead and had begun stockpiling packing cases five years before the first shot was fired.

'Oh yes, indeed, when the order came in the summer of 1939 from the Home Office, dispersal was fast and efficient,' Mr Partridge had explained, enjoying her interest. 'Material of first importance left directly after dawn on the following day and roughly one hundred tons of material was packed and despatched within a fortnight, including all prints and drawings.'

She'd given a brief but audible low whistle at hearing this. 'What about the larger sculptures?'

'They required equally heavy sandbagging, and those of global importance, such as the Elgin marbles, were given special treatment and removal at great expense and effort,' he'd assured her.

For all their quirkiness, she liked the British people enormously, especially for their determined preservation of history. She had been enchanted to learn about Sir John Forsdyke, former director and principal librarian, who was the mastermind behind the evacuation. According to colleagues, he possessed an eccentric personality, walking around the museum through the war years wearing a tin helmet with *Director* stencilled on it, and was one of the main architects behind what became known as the 'suicide exhibition'. This contained duplicate antiquities, models, casts and various reproductions mounted in various galleries.

'It served the dual purpose,' the eldest librarian had explained to her in the tearoom, 'of giving education and entertainment for wartime visitors but could serve as a sacrifice to the perils of war.' If that were not astonishing enough, Severine learned that the first of six high explosive bombs fell on the museum roof on 18 September 1940. It passed through the Prints and Drawings study room, its floor and four other concrete floors below that to land unexploded in a basement. And in further irony, a second, smaller bomb had arrived, miraculously passing through the hole created by its predecessor, to land harmlessly on the mezzanine.

The third unfortunately ripped through the King's Library – now the Room of Enlightenment – to destroy one hundred and fifty or so precious volumes. A fourth shed its oil outside the copper sheathing of the room and the emptied Duveen Gallery was hit by a small bomb that damaged its architecture but no artefacts. The newspaper library was all but destroyed with a further bomb and lost its thirty thousand volumes of nineteenth-century British provincial newspapers.

The old man with a rheumy gaze and an egg stain on his tie had sighed. 'Luck ran out in May 1941. Incendiaries rained down and the fires burnt uncontrollably, racing through so many of the display rooms, and the suicide exhibition fulfilled its destiny.' He had given Severine a smile of resignation and she could feel his sorrow as she watched him limp away, back to one of the library rooms, presuming he would have been one of those quirky, diligent staff who had been instrumental in the preservation of the antiquities.

Now that all the precious artefacts were returned and the museum had begun the long restoration from damage sustained during the Blitz, specialists had been called in to help, particularly those, like her, with expertise in Jewry.

She recalled the day the senior team at the Louvre had spoken to her of this.

'Your heritage is precious; the world is relying on survivors to help with art and all manner of items stolen from the Jewish people during the war.'

'How does London know about my knowledge in antiques?'

'My fault,' an older colleague had admitted with a smile of soft apology. 'I told them provenance is your area of expertise.' He'd stepped closer and squeezed her hand as tenderly as her father had in years gone by. 'We're still emerging from the darkest of times and commerce is on everyone's minds, my dear Severine. You know as well as any how the market has been flooded with fakes alongside genuine articles.' She had nodded as he'd wanted her to. 'Our friends at the British Museum are equally determined not to acquire stolen pieces. We have agreed to lend your expertise.'

'For how long?'

'A short secondment. Six weeks, maybe. Just help where you can; it's a start. Help with the curation of some of the jewellery in particular, but give an opinion on the backlog of Jewish items they've either acquired formally or that have somehow come into their sphere.'

'Whatever you can do is a boon, Sev,' a younger male colleague had encouraged her. 'We're proud to offer such expertise out of the Louvre. Your weekends would be free to visit the city of York you enjoy so much.' He'd winked.

She'd smiled and nodded. She couldn't deny it was a genuine opportunity for her. And it was true: she did love York for so many reasons, not least for the city's addictive history. But, more importantly, she might even get to Durham and spend time around the university, for one or two weekends. That sealed it.

'I've said you could be there at the beginning of April.'

She sighed now at the British Museum gates. There had been trepidation about coming to London and now here she was feeling sentimental about leaving this great city after such a short time.

'Missing home?' said a voice she knew.

She smiled. 'Morning, Catherine.'

'Gosh, I love the way you say my name. Growing up I thought it was so common. Every fourth girl in my class was Kathy or Kate, or spelled with a C like my version, but you make it sound exotic and regal.'

Severine fell in step with a dismissive grin . . . if only Catherine knew her truth.

'No, really. You do know you could read out the museum's guidebook to most of the men who work here and they'd think you were making love to them.'

'Stop it!'

'Well, you are the mysterious French expert that everyone's lost their marbles for. To be honest, I think half the women are in love with you too.'

Severine laughed. 'And the other half?'

'Hate you to bits.' Catherine grinned, adopting a catty tone. 'That figure! That coiffed hair! That simmering gaze! That accent. The aloofness – so bloody French and rude!'

Severine cut a glance of dismay. 'Really?' It didn't bother her to be a mystery or indeed even to be disliked for her distant manner, but she needed no hostility in her life.

'Of course!'

'Well, I can't help that you're all peasants,' she said with a light sarcasm intended to amuse.

Her friend tipped back her head to enjoy the laughter. Severine had to shoosh her, for the sound of her amusement echoed loudly around the museum's courtyard. Catherine, a few years younger than Severine, was one of the bright women she'd met and might even call a friend. She was also helplessly pretty in all the non-artificial ways that counted; she needed no make-up to improve on a flawless complexion and was apple-cheeked, had hair the colour of summer straw and a donkey laugh that was hilarious.

'So, *are* you missing home?'

Prague? Always, she thought to herself before she replied. 'I was just thinking that I was going to miss London a lot more than I imagined I could,' she admitted.

Catherine laid a friendly hand on her arm. 'Oh, good. Not

much to miss about France, then?' she said with a cheeky grin.

Severine reached for a lighthearted response. 'Not the clothes, not the food, not its beauty, not its bakeries and patisseries, not its perfume . . . no.'

Catherine was clearly enjoying the soft sarcasm, grinning as they wound their way around the forecourt to one side of the museum.

'I do miss my walks through the Paris Tuileries and the Luxembourg Gardens, though. They're easier than having to walk to Regent's Park for my exercise.'

'Well, Severine,' Catherine said, still unable after all her practice to pronounce her companion's name in the correct way. 'Oh, blimey, I have to learn to say that properly before you leave us. It's a beautiful name and I'm buggering it up.'

'I don't mind, honestly.' Severine smiled. What she really wanted to say was, *It's not my real name, so I don't care.*

2

They entered the grand building through a side entrance for staff, kissed each other farewell and moved to their respective working areas. Catherine was part of the Duveen Gallery restoration team, so Severine didn't expect to see her friend until that evening when she'd reluctantly agreed to have a drink at the nearby pub. She headed for the museum's Reading Room, the most beloved of spaces in the museum. It sat in its centre, a grand construction of iron and glass that had taken her breath away the first time she had entered the chamber. It was Catherine who had accompanied her, delivering her to Mr Partridge who would show her around.

A small gasp had escaped at first sight. 'This is perfection,' she had breathed. 'Nothing short of circular glory.'

'Everyone craves working from here – most of us find a reason to walk in at some point in each day, Mademoiselle Kassel. But you will be here for most of your working hours, so you will be the envy of many museum staff,' Mr Partridge had said. 'It is within these walls that notable writers found . . .' She remembered now how he had considered the right phrase before smiling benignly,

'. . . a peaceful mind, including Rudyard Kipling, Mark Twain, Conan Doyle, of course, Orwell, Shaw . . .'

She'd read none of the writers he mentioned, although she knew their names, but Severine didn't need to know their work intimately to understand that the Reading Room was like a place of worship for any researcher.

'Three miles of bookcases in all, and I believe we have calculated twenty-five miles of shelves.'

'A lot of books, Mr Partridge,' she'd remarked, not merely impressed. She had felt a fresh awakening of excitement to be within this chamber of vast knowledge; the pulse reached back to childhood, connecting her to her father's teachings and later – even as young as she had been – to the museum they had worked in together. As the world had tumbled into madness and despair, their determination to preserve for posterity what their invaders wanted to destroy had felt vital. It had kept a measure of lucidity in a life of increasing insanity. She had blinked away the memory.

Each morning when she entered her quiet working chamber her spirits soared, all the way to the oculus at the apex of the Reading Room. Daily, she allowed her gaze to sweep across the vast circular bookshelves with their thousands of books full of secrets. Severine preferred the day overcast so the light streaming in was muted. It gave a dreamy quality to a chamber painted duck-egg blue and the colour of freshly churned cream that already felt ethereal – to her, anyway. Forty or more French-style double windows stood like a row of sentinels at the base of the glass dome, which could be opened to let in air, while the gilding that shone from the dome's laced iron structure added a sense that one had entered a heavenly space. She believed it. Outside its round walls the museum shifted with a restless river of people. People, footsteps, sounds of delight and curiosity in hushed tones. But in her workspace there was a stillness where a single cough or the rustle of a turning page could puncture a weighty silence that was enclosed by the papier-mâché ceiling interior.

'It reminds me of the Pantheon,' she'd once remarked, but Catherine had smirked.

'Blimey! Listen to you. When did you visit Rome, then?'

'As a child. Er, my father travelled in his work and took our family to visit the great city.' Fortunately, Severine had not been required to elaborate.

This morning passed like most other mornings: her settling down with a comfy sigh at her chosen station before moving to the cabinets containing the index cards. Here she scanned for the subject that was inked onto a small card tucked into the handle. 'Every librarian should nod daily to Melvil Dewey,' she murmured barely above her breath, always grateful to the American who devised a method for classifying library books. Despite its constant revision, the Dewey system held true to the librarian who designed it in the final quarter of the nineteenth century.

Her father had taught her the system, by which time they were using the fifth abridged edition. Severine remembered how the fourteenth full edition had been released not long after her family had died. 'Were murdered,' she corrected in a whisper as she tugged on the brass handle of the drawer she chose, liking the smooth feel achieved by years of similar researchers making the identical motion to reveal the knowledge within. The gesture allowed her to lose the thought but not the sense of it. She never wanted to let go of the truth.

'The Dewey organises the contents of a library into disciplines,' her father had explained, and at her frown, elaborated. 'Fields of study. So, choose something,' he'd challenged her.

She'd considered, remembering her mother arranging flowers that morning and let that guide her. 'Roses,' she'd answered.

Her father had given her a smile. 'Good. Let's imagine that

you were especially interested in historical information about roses, so you'd first move to the number 635, which is for Horticulture . . .'

And her fascination with research had begun that day, aged eight, in the Klementinum, a library in Prague that could potentially rival this Reading Room, she thought.

The morning passed quickly as she lost herself in her work. She had recently opened a box containing gemstone earrings. She guessed amethyst and seed pearls, but design appreciation was merely a passing thought in her work. Severine first noted the jeweller named on the satin lining of the box lid. This already led her mind to Western Europe because she recognised it. She lifted the velvet pad from which the earrings gleamed to see markings that told her this jewellery had already passed through the hands of Sotheby's auctioneers twice in their lifetime. 'Good,' she murmured, mimicking her father. Now it was time to discover their provenance and she was about to stand to head back to the index card cabinets when she noticed a familiar figure stepping quietly across the floor. Severine glanced at her watch; it was already nearing ten.

'Miss Kassel?' he whispered.

'*Bonjour*, John. *Comment ça va?*' she mouthed, not needing to say it aloud.

He blushed as he answered, barely above a whisper this time, and not attempting to reply in French. 'Very well, thank you.'

She pointed to the exit and he nodded. It only took her a few moments to tidy up the desk. She placed the earrings back into a box and locked it, before standing in a fluid movement. A break to stretch her limbs was necessary. She signed the locked box back into the care of the young assistant, who countersigned. She was careful not to let her heels click loudly across the floor as she made for the doors. Outside she found John.

'I'm needed?' She hoped so – it would be a welcome interlude.

'Sorry for the interruption, but Mr Partridge asked if you would help with an item.'

'Of course. His office?'

'Er, no. They're in the Enlightenment Room.'

Even better. She enjoyed every opportunity to stroll through the large space of disconnected curiosities from around the world. 'All right.' She straightened her spine and heard it crack neatly into place. Still holding her notebook and pencil, Severine glanced at the clock to be sure the museum was still yet to open to the public. She headed for the small passageway – they all referred to it as the secret tunnel – that would take her into the Enlightenment Room. They emerged from where the door was cunningly concealed amongst the sweep of bookcases; most museum-goers never learned of its existence, unless by chance or accident.

She was greeted by four colleagues, one other woman amongst them, and Mr Partridge, the most senior, beaming at her.

'Ah, here she is. Mademoiselle Kassel,' he said. 'Thank you for coming.' He waved the pipe he habitually carried but never lit in the public spaces. 'We have something special to show you and would appreciate your opinion.' He peered kindly at her through horn-rimmed glasses.

'I'd be delighted,' she said, moving closer. 'What have you got for me?'

'It's the most exquisite piece of antique jewellery. It's not a necklace; I'm trying to work out what it is,' her female colleague murmured in a breathy tone of admiration. 'Frankly, I'm not sure I recall a piece of jewellery I've encountered that is more breathtaking.'

'Now I'm intrigued,' Severine admitted, not for a moment anticipating what would be lifted from the velvet bag.

She stepped closer to the glass cabinet they stood around, which contained a noose and a whip used on African slaves in the

Caribbean. When she'd looked at those objects on the second day of her secondment, she had read the small card that explained they had been collected in Jamaica during the seventeenth century. It had occurred to her, as she read the matter-of-fact wording, that the objects had been acquired not out of moral concern for the evils of slavery but out of pure curiosity. It was the way of the world. Had anything changed over the centuries? Hadn't the Nazis collected Jewish religious objects to put in their private museums out of curiosity and the hope they could visit those museums of an extinct people they had decided to obliterate?

'Middle Ages, we believe?' one of her colleagues murmured, recalling her thoughts to the present, 'but we don't quite know what it is, to be honest.'

Severine watched as a supple, oddly shaped length of lustrous pearls was lifted to uncoil from the bag in which it lay. From that first glimmer it felt as though someone had suddenly reached into her chest to squeeze her heart. Instantly it was difficult to breathe and with her body moving into shock she was aware, only vaguely now, of blinking fast as if to deny the presence of what she watched emerging, serpent-like, through a rapidly misting lens, of pearl jewellery, heavy and sinuous in its gleaming glory.

Despite her shock, she'd had a couple of heartbeats to register that their lustre had not dimmed. They had been first worn in the eleventh century, so the story went, and certainly the radiant iridescence of their nacre had not dulled over the years since she'd last seen them . . . despite the touch of the treacherous hands that had stolen them.

Her vision tunnelled and she could listen in on the normally silent but now angry rush of her blood, feel her lungs straining for oxygen when she was usually unaware of a single breath unless it steamed out of her mouth on a frosty day. Her senses were shutting down fast. She was blindly reaching behind herself to prevent a fall.

The beast was out . . .

Drenched in blood . . . some of it hers from a head wound, though most of it belonged to others. What last remnant she had of sensibility – perhaps whittled down to base animal survival instinct – had kept her still, silent and looking like another corpse that bitterly cold night. She'd wished she were dead when she later stood at the loose edge of a mass grave that had been hastily dug and quickly filled. The deceased were all those she loved, alive just hours earlier. Strangers had ruthlessly killed them, but only one monster had taken aim at her with his pistol, and worse . . .

Her head snapped back as the pungent vapour of lavender laced with ammonia dragged her from 1941 to 1963. The memory wobbled and dissipated, her vision cleared; she could see the small bottle of Crown smelling salts still waving nauseatingly strong in front of her and she pushed it away. Severine noted a row of worried expressions peering at her from behind the secretary who stood before her and who had presumably brought the salts in a hurry. She watched her screw the purple crown-shaped lid back on the bottle.

'Are you feeling better?' she asked.

Severine nodded. 'Thank you.'

'Should I leave the salts?'

'No, no. I'm fine now, thank you, again,' she said. 'I'm sorry.'

The secretary was bundled aside as the others crowded in.

'Mademoiselle, you gave us a scare. Are you ill?'

'No, Mr Partridge, apologies. I felt dizzy for a moment, that's all. I'm perfectly fine now,' she lied, standing and smoothing her skirt self-consciously, feeling exposed. Her colleagues stepped back. 'Please don't worry yourselves.'

Awkward silence lengthened; clearly she wasn't fine and no one seemed to know what to say or how to proceed after the drama. Severine filled the difficult pause with the truth, once again grateful for her command of their language.

'I can tell you about this piece.' She didn't need to so much as touch it to explain more. 'It is believed that these pearls date back to the thirteenth century and they are said to have been commissioned by the sultan of the Ottoman Empire for his newest and from thereon most favoured wife. The story goes that at just fifteen she was chosen from his harem, plucked from the obscurity of the odalisques to become his sultana, and this was his wedding gift.' She cleared her throat, noting the silence had changed character, thickening around her, filled with anticipation as much as captivation. They were waiting for her to take the Pearls. She preferred not to but the polite and expected words slipped out anyway. 'May I?'

'Of course,' Miss Baker said, gesturing to the Pearls, which were still mesmerising to Severine in their creamy lustre that nonetheless shone metallic, almost mirror-like. She stepped closer, showing no inclination to take hold of the jewellery yet. Severine could view her reflection in each unblemished orb as she leaned in and noted her lips were now a line, her gaze as thorny as the rose their colour imitated.

She still wasn't ready to touch the Pearls so she continued speaking. 'We have no proof of what I've just told you, but they were once known as the Ottoman Pearls, a title coined by a Russian royal – the Grand Prince Alexander of Tver – during the Middle Ages. Don't ask me how a Russian prince came to have them in his possession, but he gifted them to his wife, Anastasia, who famously jested that the chief eunuch of the imperial harem stole and sold them on as far east as he could. I'm not sure I can believe that but the Pearls next surfaced, we understand it, in the Slovakian aristocracy.'

'Good grief,' she heard Partridge say into what had become a now spellbound silence.

She swallowed, knowing she must now finish what she'd begun. Severine finally reached for the Pearls and lifted their heavy, serpentine beauty. Her colleagues all sighed with pleasure at their shimmering iridescence, even in the low museum light. The most dramatic part of their design was yet to clear the box.

'This grand piece of jewellery is meant to be worn like a garment,' she explained. 'Originally it was designed for a slim, tall woman.' She gestured to a loop in the strand of the Pearls. 'See, here is where the new bride would put each arm.'

'Ah,' breathed Miss Baker in a sound of delighted dawning. 'And she'd wear this over what?'

Severine twitched a smile, although there was no warmth in it. 'Over her skin, Miss Baker. She would come to her sultan naked, wearing only this strand of enormous natural pearls like a tiny bolero.' She lifted the piece free of the box to view the jewel it suspended. 'And this exquisite sapphire is said to be of the finest cerulean hue and likely from Kashmir of the middle centuries.'

Everyone sighed at the sparkling teardrop gem. She remembered the weight of the Pearls, their chilled but silken feel, recalling how her mother had curiously rubbed one against her teeth and exclaimed, *That's how you know they're real, when you can feel the grit from the oyster and its waters*. Severine breathed away the memory of her mother, especially the final one that had stuck in her mind of a birdlike woman, huddled, terrified, unaware that she was preparing to die. Severine held the Pearls against herself. 'As you can see, when I hold up the entire piece to approximate the way it would be worn, the sapphire would sit at the woman's navel as a final tantalising encouragement.'

Partridge cleared his throat, looking embarrassed.

Too erotic, she wondered? Perhaps she wouldn't mention, then, that the whole piece was entirely designed to encircle the nubile young wearer's breasts and point the gaze of her husband between her legs, newly shorn by slaves using hot, pliable sugar. The young bride would stand nakedly submissive and welcoming, awaiting his pleasure and hopefully his seed because only a child – a son – could ensure her position, never to be toppled. She held back on that detail but continued with less confronting information. 'If, or rather when, the sultan chose his wife over newer, younger, perhaps more beautiful odalisques, the sultana would wear this piece to show any pretenders who was truly the most powerful woman in his harem.'

'I thought the sultan had many wives?' Miss Baker chanced.

'Yes – as many as he chose. However, there was only one first wife, and these belonged to her alone. The pearls and sapphire were also believed to bring luck to their union, the blue of the sapphire suggesting a son might be made whenever she wore it.'

Poor old Mr Partridge was now blushing furiously at her words. She should stop. She did, returning the extraordinary piece to the box, watching it lie against the midnight-coloured velvet bag she recalled as if she'd seen it just moments ago.

Severine only just caught the sob in time and forced it back down; to those watching it looked like little more than a hiccup. She turned it into a soft cough. 'Excuse me,' she said and took a low, long breath as she faced them. 'I'm so sorry about my swoon earlier. I missed breakfast.'

They seemed to accept her explanation easily enough.

'You . . . you said the piece emerged in the aristocracy of Slovakia. Do you know any more about its provenance?' It was one of the younger men who spoke. 'I'm David Johnson, by the way,' he introduced himself. 'The piece found its way to my office.'

'Hello, David. Er, yes, I do know more,' she admitted. *Time for truth, then.* 'Bringing it up to date, it was finally acquired by the Goldstein family of Bohemia in the 1800s. This stunning piece that so few people know about remained in that Czechoslovakian family for five generations and was passed down through the maternal line from eldest daughter to eldest daughter.'

'Mademoiselle Kassel, am I to understand that this incredible item of jewellery most recently belonged to a Jewish family?' Mr Partridge now looked astonished.

'Correct, Mr Partridge. It did and still does belong to the same Jewish family, although through marriage it came into the family called Kassowicz,' she said carefully. 'It was stolen from them during the Nazi occupation, in 1941. October, in fact, from their country house about an hour out of Prague.'

'My word,' her boss replied, beaming at David Johnson. 'I told you she's frightfully good.' He cut her a sharp look. 'And you're absolutely sure of that?'

Years of torment erupted into rage but of the cool, wintry kind that could burn slow and steady. People said she possessed a simmering beauty but only Severine knew from where the controlled heat originated.

Her tone was even; she had had years of practice masking the pain. 'I am sure. And I can be this accurate because my real name is Katerina Kassowicz and I am the eldest daughter,' she explained, keeping it matter-of-fact, 'and this piece of jewellery is mine, given by my mother to her firstborn daughter.'

There was a collective gasp from her colleagues.

'And what I want to know – need to know from you, please – is precisely who has brought this piece to the British Museum?'

3

JARDIN DU LUXEMBOURG, PARIS

Katerina drew back on the cigarette, watching absently as the tip of the Pall Mall Long burnt orange while she inhaled. It felt odd to have released her name again in public after so long being known as someone else. She held the smoke in her lungs for a moment longer than was usual for her and gradually exhaled while she pondered her situation. She was addicted neither to the nicotine nor to the so-called 'sophisticated look' that many of her female colleagues believed cigarettes provided. Instead she lit one only when she needed its calming drug and the soothing action that lifting the cigarette to her lips brought.

'I didn't know you smoked,' remarked a gentleman who had sat down nearby perhaps two minutes earlier to share the bench she'd chosen on this icy day. He had read his newspaper in silence, not so much as clearing his throat while she smoked.

She had been deep in thought, recalling that morning of just over a week ago in London, and become lost in her musings over its dramatic revelation that had led her to return to Paris disappointingly ahead of her planned return. It was the phone call with the solicitor that had spooked her, causing her to run away from the Pearls and take some time to think through her next step.

At first she hadn't realised the man was addressing her; it took a moment to register that there was no one else nearby he was speaking to. She turned to regard him properly now. The overall impression was of an indeterminate man whose most obvious feature was being dark of hair and eye. Beyond that he was neither tall nor stocky, not thin or paunchy. He was hard to age, too. She guessed late thirties, possibly into his forties, although unwrinkled skin belied that. He regarded her steadily, did not dip his gaze with the embarrassment she hoped she could prompt with a morose, cat-eyed stare at being interrupted. 'That's a coincidence,' she replied in her best sardonic tone, 'because I didn't know something either.'

His expression turned into a quizzical frown.

'That we've even been introduced,' she finished. She looked away once more and inhaled on her cigarette again; it was meant to be smooth but it was tasting bitter, and matching her mood.

'Forgive me, mademoiselle,' he said, not sounding injured but clearly hearing her warning.

She plucked a piece of tobacco from the tip of her tongue, accepting belatedly that she'd heard no intention in his approach; no flirtatious agenda, anyway. Now that she concentrated on it, he had merely stated a fact rather than trying to inject charm or win a smile. She'd looked away, irritated, but now she returned her gaze with a frown. 'Do we know each other?'

He shook his head briefly and the smile, though not much more than a crease at the corners of his mouth, felt genuine to her, and in that heartbeat she glimpsed humility. It had taken courage for him to speak to her, she decided, and Katerina felt the guilt turned on her when he dipped his head. 'Not formally, no.'

She pulled back on the wariness that had become so much a

part of her that every new face was a potential foe. 'And how do we connect *informally*?'

He folded up his paper, tucking it beneath his arm. 'You slipped on the ice over by the pond a couple of winters ago. You were not the only one unsteady. I lent you an arm to the nearby railings. It was all very amusing for everyone.' He blinked. 'I'm sorry,' he added, as if realising that she likely never spoke to strangers or that he'd intruded. 'You've probably forgotten.'

'I don't forget much.'

'Barely registered it, then.' He grinned. 'It was of no consequence.'

She gave her Pall Mall a final chance to impress, watching him carefully through the smoke she blew upwards. No, still astringent. *Blimey!* – she liked that English saying – what she needed was coffee on this frigid day. It was true, she couldn't bring to mind the encounter he spoke of, but she didn't want to be deliberately rude again. 'And why didn't *you* need help?' she asked, glad it didn't come out in English.

He lifted a shoulder. 'I suppose because I don't make a habit of wearing high heels,' he said in the same soft tone.

'Maybe you should try it,' she continued. 'It is the true mark of control to navigate Paris on heels.'

'Perhaps I will in private,' he replied.

She lightened her tone. 'Your wife may not approve.'

They both found awkward smiles. 'Well, fortunately, I'm not married.' He lifted his fedora from the thick, blue-black thatch that revealed a precision parting, combed to one side like a schoolboy's. 'Daniel Horowitz.'

'I hope I thanked you properly back then?'

'You were in a hurry, but your smile was enough.'

'Then allow me to thank you now, Mr Horowitz.'

'Daniel, please.'

She nodded. 'So . . . you're right, I don't normally smoke, hardly ever in recent times. I discovered these extra-long cigarettes in London recently. They are good for at least three, maybe four, full minutes of deep thought when there is a problem to sort through.'

Her companion nodded. 'Then I hope you will untangle it successfully.'

Her gaze narrowed; she was impressed he hadn't pried, especially when she'd inadvertently given an opening.

He surprised her further by standing to make his departure. 'Enjoy your contemplative Sunday, mademoiselle. Again, forgive me for interrupting you.'

She was unused to men taking their leave of her; most liked to hang around and forge a pathway into conversation. She realised she was staring and he seemed eager to leave. 'You didn't.'

'Didn't what, mademoiselle?'

'You didn't interrupt me.' His expression said he would argue that. She gave a nod. 'Or, if you did, I am glad of it.' She lifted a shoulder. 'It gave me an opportunity to thank you for your kindness of the past.'

'A trifle,' he dismissed gently. Horowitz gave a small bow. His gaze was serious and it was as though the other two dozen or so people she could see, just in her peripheral vision alone, were not in the Luxembourg Gardens today, as far as he was concerned. He was oblivious to all but her. 'I hope you can navigate your dilemma,' he said.

Dilemma? What a lovely, mild word to describe the fresh trauma that had come at her without warning in London. She could hardly believe it was she inviting companionship. 'I'm Severine Kassel,' she said, the lie still coming easily. She swapped the smouldering cigarette to her left hand and her right was still ungloved from smoking. She extended it.

He kissed it. 'Enchanted.'

It was a feather's touch, gone so fast she could believe it hadn't happened. 'You walk in the gardens often?'

'Daily.'

'Ah, so we must pass regularly.'

'Daily.' He grinned.

'Are you watching me, Mr Horowitz?' Again, no embarrassment at the truth that stared out from behind eyes the colour of a depthless umber, like those Rembrandt used to create the backgrounds of complex browns on his masterpieces. 'You are,' she said, with dawning. She was the one who sounded unsure now. 'Whatever for?'

'Why does any man watch any woman?' As she startled, he held up a hand. 'You have nothing to fear from me, mademoiselle. I have lived in Paris since the end of the war and I have moved through this park each day since I shifted to the 6th.'

Sixth arrondissement? Katerina was impressed: arguably the most coveted of neighbourhoods on the Left Bank, perhaps in all of Paris. He was either wealthy or served a wealthy family.

He smiled. 'I notice your arrival and departure from the park every day, and while I have no idea where you live and no idea where you head – or even what time of the day you may retrace your steps, because it varies – I admit to looking out for you when I'm here.' He sighed. 'It's simply a personal ritual. Your walking through is another safe day.'

'Safe?' She blinked, intrigued.

He shrugged. 'After the insanity of war, I like my world to remain the same these days, mademoiselle. The repetition of daily rituals – including your passage through the gardens – is reassurance that all remains unchanged and well. I make time now to sit in the gardens each morning and late afternoon, sometimes into the early evening; I like to watch people walking around with life on their minds rather than death.'

Nevertheless, she thought, Left Bank, attired so smartly? It snagged in her mind but then he seemed to eavesdrop her thought and answer it.

'I was left money by family so I could choose to do anything I wanted.'

'How fortunate.' She tried to keep the disbelief out of her tone but chose not to pry.

If he noticed her scepticism, he didn't show it. He continued talking in an even voice. 'I like the peacefulness here. I am reassured by gardens that flourish with a little care – they can be depended upon too; they can come back from the dead, they can reinvent themselves, they can be young and flirty again or they can be majestic.' He paused. 'That was a long speech to explain how it is I am able to look for you at the beginning and end of most days.'

She half smiled, half frowned. 'I'm not sure whether to feel confused by you, Daniel, or charmed by your simple routine. Why me?'

'I suppose I noticed you because you are always – how shall I say – distracted, not part of this world, in a way. I'm enchanted by your mystery and where your mind is when you stride with your tall, elegant gait past here. You don't notice anyone, it seems, and the only indication that you're aware of the changes around you is by the clothing that you shift into, depending on the season.'

'Is there a word for what you do? Should I be talking to the police?' She was only half jesting.

He shrugged. 'Let me buy you a coffee to warm you. You can ask me any question you like and I shall answer with only the truth.'

She showed she believed him by nodding; she didn't imagine he was capable of a secret. 'All right,' she agreed, her body needing the caffeine. This was a day of surprises: smoking again, and now agreeing to have coffee with a stranger. But then, this was a month of drama and change, so as she had nearly two decades ago, she followed her instincts.

They didn't have far to move to. The café had only a few hardy drinkers seated outside, and even indoors it was barely one quarter full. She sensed that he was taking careful stock, intrigued that he gestured to an outdoor table at the furthest edge. She obliged as she was dressed for the cold and preferred being outside anyway. He held the seat out for her before removing his hat and placing it on the table.

'Do I have soot on my nose?'

'Forgive me.' He smiled. It was a crooked gesture, as though his muscles weren't used to operating all the ropes and pulleys that delivered an easy grin. His forehead seemed to dip in sympathetic synchrony as though to him a smile was a creasing of the features, rather than a lifting of them. She was yet to see his teeth and momentarily wondered if they were black, or missing, or false. Is that why he found it hard to smile with ease? 'I was staring, my apologies. Your right eye is helplessly intriguing.'

She shrugged. 'So they say. It's a flaw I've lived with all my life and so these days I neither care about it, nor do I share the fascination.'

'It only adds to your . . .' Katerina decided if he used the word 'beauty' she would make an excuse to leave; she had no time for men trying to charm her. 'Dislocation from the rest of us.'

Her turn to smile. He hadn't disappointed. 'You make me sound like an alien.'

'I'd prefer to say ethereal. It's as though you walk a different plane, mademoiselle, and I do mean that as a compliment. People who are different are far more interesting than the rest of us who appear pressed from a mould.'

'Well, I like symmetry, Mr Horowitz. So in childhood the curiosity of my eye was a burden; I like perfection.'

'There is no perfection in humankind, I'm afraid. War has taught us that.'

'Ah, but there is perfection in the natural world. Take a perfectly round pearl from an oyster, for instance, or a flawless, dazzling white diamond; a conch shell, a lion, an oak, a rainbow, lightning . . .' She watched him nod. 'But worry not, the burden I speak of eased as I matured, and I must admit by the time my little brother came along with an identical mote in his eye, I realised it was not a flaw but an inherited mark. My father said it proved unequivocally who I was and the same went for my brother. We bore our family's signature.' She smiled at the memory. 'He said our job was to carry it forward into new generations. He had a way of viewing problems from their most favourable angle – at the very least, as opportunities.'

'That's a rare quality.' He paused. 'I must admit I'm finding it hard to imagine that the woman I've watched from a distance as my little touchstone of security is taking coffee with me.' At this moment a waiter sidled up. He possessed the typical harried air of all French waiters, she noted, that suggested they couldn't care if you ordered or didn't, but be quick about your decision.

'Mademoiselle? Monsieur?' He had a notebook but didn't bother with it. She could see he'd already sized them up as a couple who would not be ordering food.

'Coffee, short, no sugar. Thank you.'

'Sir?'

'I'll have mine with milk and sugar, please.'

The man reacted with little more than a flare of his nostrils before he turned on his heel to disappear inside the café.

'I think we French are rude,' she remarked. 'Waiters in London are far chattier.'

'That's where you've been recently?'

She nodded. 'A short sabbatical . . . it was work. But then, you would know I've been away, surely?'

He tried his smile again; it worked a little easier this time. 'Yes, I noticed. I'm glad you've returned. My world is ordered again.' This made her grin with genuine warmth; she wondered if he was thinking similar thoughts about how awkward she found the gesture too. 'May I ask what it is you do?' he enquired.

'I work for the Louvre and I was on loan to the British Museum.'

He nodded. 'How exciting.'

'It has its moments but essentially it's quiet, often tedious, highly detailed work. I liken it to being a spy, working in the dark, trying to unlock secrets.'

She watched him hesitate momentarily, as if she'd caught him off guard. He recovered quickly; perhaps she'd imagined it. 'History is exciting, though,' he ventured. 'From fashion to habits, we're forever changing, aren't we?'

'That is true,' she replied.

Their coffees arrived. 'And a black coffee for the lady,' the waiter said, placing down the cups and saucers from his tray. He slipped the bill under the sugar bowl and moved away as briskly as he'd arrived.

She returned her gaze to Daniel. 'I feel history simply repeats. We don't learn from it.'

'The wars?' He nodded, understanding her point. 'Nevertheless, I feel sure most would envy you your place of work and your type of work. What is your specialty, if that's not intrusive?'

He had her measure already, it seemed. 'Jewellery of the antiquities, but I have a particular homegrown expertise in Jewish ritual objects.'

Daniel's giveaway to her was not in a flicker in his eye, not so much as a twitch in his features, but in a stillness that appeared to become absolute.

'Mmm, I thought that might interest you. Jewish, am I correct?'

'You are, although you wouldn't make much of a spy, Mademoiselle Kassel. I think my name alone is a clue.'

She chuckled over her first sip of the hot, tarry coffee. 'How would you know what it takes to become a spy?'

He gusted a self-conscious laugh and sipped his coffee as well. 'You say homegrown. What do you mean by that?'

She hadn't intended to elaborate; she was usually adroit at throwing people off any scent of the secrets of her life that she wasn't interested in sharing. But Horowitz had caught her amidst thinking on the very core of the topic she had learned to avoid. Her mind had become like a Lydian stone against which the Pearls had been dashed to leave their lustrous mark, and at present she could think of nothing else. The visible trace was upon her – had always been – and she had to follow its trail; it was the reason she'd fled from London several days ago, citing family issues.

Her response to the Pearls had been so visceral she couldn't bear to be close to them. She had waved away all offers to study them, handle them, even keep them at her work desk for the afternoon. Mr Partridge, still in shock from her revelation, had acted swiftly. Several hours later she had been summoned to his office and she had been addressed by her correct name, which had felt suddenly awkward. More composed by then, she had tapped at the door, prepared to explain more to him about that morning, or to answer any queries about the Pearls, avoiding discussions about her family with a steady voice.

'Come in.'

What she had not been ready for was the phone call.

'Ah, she's here. Could you hold on for just a moment, please? Thank you.' He'd covered the phone's receiver. 'Mademoiselle Kassowicz, thank you for coming so swiftly. I have a Mr Summerbee on the telephone. He is the solicitor acting for the party that delivered the Pearls – er, your Pearls . . .' He'd frowned, confused, before sending her a reassuring smile. 'The Ottoman Pearls . . . and I've told him the situation we find ourselves in. He would like to speak with you.'

Thoughts had collided. She couldn't be impolite to Mr Partridge, who was clearly trying to help. But she did not wish to speak to anyone formally about the Pearls – not yet, anyway – and she did not dare yet meet with the solicitor who had been engaged to handle the exchange. For all she knew, Ruda Mayek might come along to that meeting as well.

Her boss was holding out the phone. She was trapped. Katerina had no choice but to accept the call.

'Good afternoon?'

'Katerina Kassowicz?' He pronounced her name properly.

'Er, yes, it is.'

'Thank you, mademoiselle. My name is Edward Summerbee and my firm, Summerbee and Associates, has been engaged in London by our client, who is offering the item of a rather dramatic strand of pearls to the British Museum for display. Forgive me, we were of the understanding they might be from the Orient, but Mr Partridge has since corrected me on this.' His voice had a velvety quality to it, the sort that might soothe a child to sleep.

She tried to imagine the man who owned it as a means for remaining calm but her mind came up blank; he was a solicitor and was presumably highly proper . . . old, even. 'How can I help you, Mr Summerbee?'

It was a question that stalled for time and it worked; his pause told her of his surprise, unsure of how best to answer her.

'Er . . . well, this is the only moment in which I can speak to you on this matter but I am acknowledging your claim, which is obviously a surprise to all. It not only adds a fresh complexity to this delicate arrangement I've been charged to broker, but it presumably brings a crime of theft into the midst and —'

'Mr Summerbee, I must apologise, could you just excuse me, please?'

Again the pause. 'Yes, of course. Are you all right, Miss, er, Mademoiselle Kassowicz?'

She liked his voice. She liked that he could wrap his tongue around her name authentically. 'I'm fine, I just . . . I just need a moment, please.' She turned to Mr Partridge. 'Forgive me. I really don't feel very well.'

'Oh, my dear . . .' He took the phone. 'Mr Summerbee, we shall call you back. I'm so sorry but mademoiselle has experienced quite a shock this morning and she really does look rather pale.' He waited, listened. 'Yes, yes, of course. I'll call your secretary soonest.'

Katerina slowed her breathing, inhaling deeply while he finished up the call. She did not wish to disgrace herself in Mr Partridge's office. 'Yes, thank you again. Goodbye, Mr Summerbee.' He replaced the receiver, looking up at her. 'Thinking of you as Katerina doesn't come easily,' he said, apology in his tone. 'I'm sorry for the shock you've had. I'm going to ask Jean to fetch you a taxi. We can't —'

'Oh no, please, Mr Partridge. I only live around the corner, barely a few minutes away. The fresh air is what I need and I shall be fine. I promise you, please don't worry.'

'You're quite sure?'

She nodded and found a smile.

'Then please just take the rest of the afternoon off, and should you need tomorrow as well, let Jean know. I'm truly sorry for today's events.' He shook his head. 'Extraordinary, and no doubt painful for you to see these again; I'm making the presumption that they were taken from your family?'

'Stolen during the war,' she explained. 'Thank you for under-standing, and there's no way that you could know; I have not used my real name since I was a youngster.'

Her superior looked further appalled and before he could start a fresh apology, she continued. 'Good afternoon, Mr Partridge – thank you for your kindness today.' She didn't want to say she'd see him tomorrow because her mind was already racing towards escape and putting as much distance between herself, the Pearls and Ruda Mayek as she could. She had no intention of returning to the British Museum the next day. By then she intended to be disappearing into the vast metropolis of Paris.

And so here she was, contemplating the reawakened horror at the sight of the Pearls. She had hoped running away from them was the best immediate solution, but the shock rode with her on the train and the ferry back to France. It walked alongside her all the way back into her Parisian home. The apartment over the last few days felt too small for her problem, which is why she'd headed outdoors, with cigarettes and in search of coffee because she'd run out. Shock sat now on her shoulder and urged her to use Daniel Horowitz, a stranger who could not hurt her; she needed someone to talk to, to let the poison out with . . . Perhaps talking aloud to this random man, who had no vested interest in her life, might help her unlock the demons she kept incarcerated.

He's Jewish. He will understand, a voice inside her counselled. *He's safe.*

Was she really going to do this? More than twenty years of silence, and she was about to tell her story to this man when five minutes ago she'd not so much as known his name? She waited for that inner voice to answer. *Why not?* It finally said.

Daniel, she noted, waited, patient. He wasn't even looking at her, happy to broaden his gaze to the grass and the sparrows skipping around.

Katerina took a low, silent breath before audibly clearing her throat. His gaze returned, landing on her lightly, anticipation in those warm brown eyes.

'It's hard to know how to answer that question,' she admitted.

'From the beginning, perhaps?' Daniel replied, and signalled to the waiter for a second coffee.

4

Daniel Horowitz's sombre expression was a mask for his turmoil of thoughts. Normally sharp and agile, his mind leapt to conclusions fast; he could make the swiftest of decisions while calculating the odds of a successful outcome quicker than most. Other arithmetic problems he solved in his mind more like sport . . . or, as his sister had once accused, because he was a freak.

Freak? No, he couldn't agree. He was just someone who had developed habits that helped him to keep his mind tidy, as he preferred to think of it. Adding, subtracting, multiplying, dividing – manipulating numbers to come out in a way that pleased him was a pastime; nothing sinister. It was about feeling secure.

Right now, though, his thoughts were chaotic. This was Katerina Kassowicz! She was the link; the only one, as far as he knew . . . his single chance. For fifteen years he'd waited. He'd earned his nickname 'the Crocodile' due to the interminable patience he demonstrated in his work as he waited, watched, pondered, assembled information and all the while convinced himself he was drawing closer to his prey with stealth.

And here she was; not his prey, in truth, but his navigator.

He'd had his eyes cast outwards across greater Europe, looking for the sign of one who could light his path. And all the while the person he was searching for had been here, in Paris.

He was understandably nervous now that he'd found his guide, but years of work and training had taught him how to cover any sign of restiveness. Even so, it was hard to talk to her; words kept trapping themselves and it was helpful that she perhaps imagined him to be another hapless male, hoping to seduce. He would be rightfully called a liar if he didn't admit her looks were anything but striking and her slanted gaze entirely disarming. He liked her laugh too when he heard it moments ago for the first time – genuine but sultry – and he already sensed it was not easily won. That quality alone made it worth toiling for.

The photograph he had of her was grainy and showed a smiling girl of perhaps eleven with plaited hair. She looked like a baby giraffe with lanky legs, slightly knock-kneed, extending from beneath the hem of her summer frock with puffed sleeves. Now look at her. She presented like a movie starlet; she certainly had the poise of a couture model. But that's not why he was finding it hard to contain his excitement. He would have settled for, and felt a thrill at discovering, any one of the children in that photograph. It could have been none of them whose path ever crossed his and an hour ago he could have been convinced that this was to be his fate. He was blessed, though: she was here. And if he'd been able to wish for one, then it would have been Katerina, the eldest of the troupe . . . the one with the most knowledge, the longest memories that he would need.

His daily prayers of nearly a quarter of a century had been answered, so surely with her unannounced arrival into his life that it made his task feel close to holy. Daniel felt no guilt for what was ahead. Katerina was his salvation but now the real journey was beginning.

He needed her to speak so he could lose himself in focused conversation. But she remained silent. Nevertheless, he'd made it this far in one hour with her and so he must keep faith that his reluctant manner would intrigue and reassure her. He could tell she was at some sort of crossroad, as if trying to make the most difficult of decisions. The quip on the park bench about her smoking was a gamble that had delivered to him tenfold. Who'd have thought he could persuade her to sit down with him with such ease, and now, if he was reading her correctly, it looked as though she was going to stay for a while and tell him about herself. Could he be that lucky after years of feeling like he was walking in the wilderness?

The lie about helping her across the icy ground had been confidently spoken. It was true that he had seen her slip once on ice and it was that recollection of a passer-by who had reached for her that he'd borrowed. He'd used that buried memory of hers to create a whiff of truth, like the cunning spy he was. If this wasn't the single most important case in his life, he'd take a moment to appreciate his coercive skills, but time was precious and he needed to be focused on Mademoiselle Kassowicz. He knew he had to show a certain amount of indifference, so as not to frighten her.

Daniel had watched her for a week, coming and going through the gardens; he'd shadowed her once to her home – an apartment fringing the Natural History Museum district on the Left Bank – but he dared not linger or be picked out as a stranger in that neighbourhood. His well-honed instincts were telling him this was a closed person who would not respond to him moving too obviously into her life. And she could shut him out as easily as stepping on an ant; all she had to do was accuse him of harassment or simply speak to the police, and years of patience would be undone.

And so the Crocodile had stood, made to leave and been rewarded by her trust. Daniel heard his companion clear her throat. He returned his gaze and tried his best not to stare at the oval of emotion, particularly those eyes that were startling even without the mote. Their unexpected hesitation between violet and green gave the impression that her maker couldn't decide which suited best. So now, depending on the light and presumably her mood, they shifted from the cobalt of the stained glass of the famed Sainte-Chapelle in Paris to the Egyptian blue of a goblet he'd seen in the Louvre believed to be from Mesopotamia circa 1500 BC. He thought she'd appreciate his comparison, given her career.

She lowered her gaze briefly in final consideration and it meant he could enjoy looking upon her angular features, including a soft cleft at her chin and cheeks that needed no shading to create shape; they were the ideal defined frame to welcome the bow of her lips.

'From the beginning, perhaps?' he'd chanced, and as he'd spoken these words had taken the liberty of raising a hand to catch the attention of the waiter. When the man looked over, Daniel signalled for a second round. Katerina showed no inclination to bolt and his anxiety began to quieten with relief that he had made her comfortable with his silence.

Locking his attention back on his companion, he watched as she dragged long fingers through her tumble of chin-length hair that from a distance could be mistaken for brunette, but close up it had the burnished sheen of treacle. In the old photo she had looked quite fair. Did she now colour her hair as some women did, or had it darkened in her maturity? He shouldn't be this intrigued. He should focus on what she could deliver to him. Her hands caught his attention. Her contemporaries wore their nails long and painted them all colours. But not Katerina. Her nails were natural, deliberately filed to be blunt, but they were nonetheless attractive with perfect nude fingers.

She shivered, replacing her gloves, and knitted her fingers on the table before her.

'I was born in Prague,' she began. Her voice was quiet enough that he had to sit forward. Its timbre leaned towards liquid darkness but it had a fresh rasp in it that he knew came from talking about something he suspected was never discussed. He noted that emotion moistened her eyes, which she kept fixed on her laced fingers. 'Our family was not poor. We had a tall, rambling house in the old quarter, and . . .'

He watched her swallow. This was hard for her, and he experienced a moment's helpless guilt at shattering the fragile enclosure she'd built around her memories. He was hungry for those recollections, though; needed them like a starved man needs a knuckle of bread to survive the next day. Even so, shame entered his heart like a tiny splinter that would burrow deeper to vex as much as hurt.

'. . . and a summer villa about a day's journey away along the river and into the hills.'

There would have been far more, he thought; the Kassowicz family was part of the Jewish aristocracy of the region, but she had only a child's memories. He would not correct her. The coffees arrived, the detritus of the previous serving cleared swiftly, a fresh bill tucked under the sugar bowl, and the surly man was gone again.

She shook her head and seemed to rally her thoughts. 'We were a happy family; I was the eldest of several children although sadly my youngest brother died in 1939. He was under a year and we all loved that little fellow. His name was Petr.'

'What did he die from?' He was being polite, showing he was listening in earnest, but he knew there was so much more death to come.

'They never fully explained.' He watched her sit up straighter and meet his gaze; her serious mouth gave a mirthless twitch. 'Forgive me, I have not shared this with anyone, but I probably need to.'

'Why now?' He couldn't help himself.

'Because something happened a few days ago that has changed everything.'

'Everything?'

Her second coffee steamed untouched next to her red and white packet of Pall Mall Longs and a tiny silver lighter. 'You know how your ritual of watching me pass through the gardens keeps you feeling safe, Daniel?'

He nodded gently, embarrassed by the lie.

She gave a small shrug. 'I have found that it is much better for my health if I keep my memories locked up. Then I too am safe.'

'From the war, do you mean?' Now that she'd begun, the moment was right to push her along.

'From before the war, when my family was alive, and yes, from the war itself because I was chosen to survive.' Her voice sounded bitter to him.

He took a long sip of his sweetened coffee and decided he needed no more. She didn't seem interested in her second cup. 'Would you like to walk, mademoiselle?'

She nodded. 'I would, thank you.'

He rose to pull back her chair and dug in his pockets to find some francs to leave on the table. He overpaid but he didn't care to wait for change. The waiter would get a good tip this cold morning.

'Come, I do believe walking, looking ahead and not at someone, can sometimes make talking easier.'

She cut him a rare soft smile and he matched her step, not risking taking her arm, instead clasping his hands behind his back. 'Apart from Petr, how many siblings were there in your family?' He knew the answer but needed her to resume her story.

'After me came a sister, Lotte, then the twins, Ettel and Hana – before our beloved Petr arrived into our lives. My life changed irrevocably around my twelfth birthday, when Hitler's Nazis stomped across the cobbles of our beautiful city and took it for their own.'

Now he needed to shift her away from the pain; it was too early to go there where the open wound seeped. It was quite the balancing act, but he'd done this many times previously with prisoners and with people who had been detained under no charge but were suspected of having information. The trick was in the dance by the spymaster in obliquely approaching the topic he needed his victim to reach but without realising they had arrived.

'What did your father do?'

'He was mostly involved in glass manufacturing but I knew him principally as a historian and art collector – to me that's what he did. From a child's perspective, his other businesses seemed to run themselves.'

'Ah, I see,' he said. 'So your apprenticeship in artistic appreciation was at your father's coat-tails?'

She nodded and he was pleased the gesture was accompanied by one of her half smiles. 'Yes. I learned so much at his side – that's what I meant about being homegrown.'

He looked up deliberately and her gaze followed. 'My joints tell me it will rain shortly.'

'Perhaps.'

As if by divine order, they felt the first light spatter and raindrops glimmered on their shoulders. He cast silent thanks to the heavens for their aid.

'Your joints seem to have an acute sense, Mr Horowitz.'

'Mademoiselle Kassel,' he said, carefully using her contemporary name, 'I don't want you to take this the wrong way but I live very close by.' He pointed towards one of the grand pairs of gates at the end of a pathway they were approaching. 'I have a large, airy apartment minutes from here that I share with a pair of strange cats. Forgive me, but I don't wish to keep interrupting you or prodding you for information. I am intrigued by what you have to say and would gladly sit down right here on the frozen ground, in the rain, and hear it – every word. But I'd rather hear it from the comfort of an armchair with a merry fire burning and some soup simmering on the stove. I sense pain and I'd rather you expressed it, if you feel inclined, in a secure environment rather than one open to eavesdroppers or the elements.' He avoided swallowing or it would show his tension. This was the moment! 'Would you consider walking back to my apartment – if that does not strike you as too forward or intrusive?' Daniel held his breath. He would soon know if the quarry was going to startle and bolt.

She didn't. She considered his invitation in that still, rather serious way of hers and then fixed him with her sad gaze.

'I do need to tell someone. This story must be shared, especially now. I believe another must hear it so that should anything happen . . .'

'Happen? Mademoiselle, please, you have nothing to fear. I am here. I will protect you.'

'You, Mr Horowitz?'

He had to be careful. 'As I protected you from the ice,' he lied, 'so I can protect you from your memories.'

She gazed at him with pity. 'I'm not sure you can, but you are Jewish and you are a survivor, so I anticipate you too have a story to share. I will hear yours if you will hear mine?'

'Yours will be far more intriguing than mine. I survived because we got out early.'

Waves of her hair shifted and shone their golden darkness as Paris blew a chilling, moisture-laden wind over them and the raindrops became heavier.

'Come, let's get into the warmth before we both catch a chill.' He undid the large umbrella he carried and leaned the black dome over her.

She fell in step and he led her towards his private place where no other guest had ever been invited. He found her silence unnerving as they walked. He hadn't fibbed about the distance – it really wasn't that far; a few minutes – but he would struggle if she were to keep her own counsel for the duration.

'Did you know these gardens were inspired by the Boboli Gardens in Florence?' he offered.

'I did.' She cut him an amused look. 'I too am a student of history, Monsieur Horowitz.'

'Daniel, please,' he reminded her. 'Forgive me, of course you are.' The deliberate slip, adroitly delivered, opened a safe path for them to move onto.

'Marie de' Medici recreated a palace in the likeness of the Pitti Palace and she had hundreds upon hundreds of elms planted,' she said, and he watched her arm unfold from that angular shoulder like a mathematician's compass being extended to inscribe an arc. As they passed, leather-clad fingers gestured towards a familiar avenue of those elms in splendorous growth, preparing for their fluttering bright green mantle of summer. 'She began with eight hectares but kept acquiring land and expanding her formal gardens until they sprawled across thirty hectares.'

He enjoyed listening to her and joined in, happy on this assured, easy path for now. 'Which turned to forty hectares when she confiscated neighbouring land owned by the Carthusian monks.'

'A woman to admire,' Katerina quipped, cutting him a sideways glance of amusement, and he felt a thrill of delight to discover that she did possess a wit after all.

Daniel politely guided her through the tall, gilded iron gates first and sensed, perhaps even before she did, her mood shift back to where they'd begun this conversation.

'So, I'm listening, Daniel,' she said. 'You were going to tell me about your family?'

'I shall. There are my parents, both hale, and my sister, who is married to a giant of a fellow with a ruddy complexion and a heart as big as the potato farms he owns in Wales. They have three children, so I'm a proud uncle to a nephew and two nieces who call me Uncle Danny, while my sister and her husband call me Desperate Dan behind my back.'

'Because you're not married?'

'You have a quick mind, Mademoiselle Kassel.'

'Oh, I think I share a similar fate,' she replied. 'Your sister sounds happy.'

'She is. And her children have grown up in a world that knows peace in Europe.' He watched her nod thoughtfully as he steered her around the main boulevards of the 6th neighbourhood, heading to a tiny enclave sandwiched between it and the 5th arrondissement of Paris, both highly prized.

'Are you?'

'Happy?' He knew very well what she'd asked but was stalling for time.

'Yes. Are you?'

'I'm not sure how to answer that.'

'Really? Do you wake up in the morning feeling optimistic?'

'Let's say I hold out hope for the world.'

She gave one of her half smiles. 'That doesn't answer my question, but I like the sentiment. Where is home for you?'

'My father was born in Germany, he moved to Sudetenland and I was born in Klatovy.'

'So we are both Czech?' She sounded astonished.

'It seems so.' He knew he should feel ashamed at the deception of innocence but to him his war would not end until he ended it. 'My father owned breweries and conducted much of his business in Germany, and he became anxious that we should leave Europe after that first election following the enactment of the Nuremberg Laws.

None of us wanted to sail for America – that felt so far away. With friends in England it was the easier choice and it kept us closer to our homeland.'

'Do your parents enjoy England?'

'They do; they adjusted quickly for our benefit, I'm sure. They missed our life in Bohemia but now I don't think they can imagine being anywhere but Marlow, alongside the river. They're a little more fragile each time I see them but nevertheless they are in good spirits.'

'I wish I could say the same of mine. I envy you your happy family. The reason I have none of my siblings or parents is because of one person.'

In that moment Daniel understood that years of watchful patience might be about to deliver to him his single way to catch a monster.

5

'This is it,' he said, pointing to an entrance with a varnished timber door. 'The former owner assured me Picasso stayed here, although why I can't say because his Montparnasse studio is within the same complex.'

'All of this is yours?' she said, frowning at the tall townhouse that she could see backed onto a leafy courtyard.

'No. I live in the studio at the top. If you don't mind stairs, it will give you a lovely view across Paris.' He took out a key and opened the door, stepping aside for her to enter. He noted her hesitation. 'This is unusual, Mademoiselle Kassel, I agree. Why don't we knock on my neighbour's apartment door and let her know you're coming upstairs with me? She's the eyes and ears of the building so she probably already has her antennae switched on.'

As if she'd heard, the door to the bottom-floor flat opened. 'Good day to you, Monsieur Horowitz,' spoke a voice attached to a short woman in an apron. 'I was just making some tarts,' she explained as they took in her floured hands and she let her gaze linger on Katerina. 'Good afternoon, *madame*?'

'Er, Mademoiselle Kassel is joining me for a bowl of soup. I can't believe we ran into each other in the gardens – her parents and mine go back. Severine, this is Madame Bouchard. She's a fine baker; I keep telling her to open a shop.'

'Oh, go on with you, Monsieur Horowitz.' She turned a fresh and appraising gaze on Katerina, who nodded politely.

'Good afternoon. I can smell how wonderful the tarts are,' she admitted.

'That's the first of them. I shall be baking a few more. Maybe I could bring a slice up for you both?'

'That would be splendid,' Daniel said. 'Severine?'

'How can I resist?'

'Your figure tells me you resist plenty,' Madame Bouchard remarked, grabbing her own belly.

They obliged with a grin.

'You shall have a warm slice of tart to follow your soup.'

'Excellent,' Daniel agreed. 'Thank you so much.' He gestured to the steps. 'It's three flights,' he warned.

They began the ascent, their footsteps sounding gritty against the stone steps.

Katerina glanced at the wrought-iron balustrade curling ahead and above them. 'I don't usually eat much but I suspect I'll have an appetite after this trek.'

At the door, he sounded slightly out of breath. 'Welcome.' He led the way in.

Two cats stared with baleful, cross-eyed indifference at them from the end of the corridor for a moment or two before disappearing into the room at its end.

He sighed. 'Brother and sister. I don't even like cats. They're seal-point Siamese, whatever that means. More relevantly, they're a pair of bullies.'

'Why do you have them?'

'A neighbour asked me to look after them and then callously left the neighbourhood and his cats with me.'

So he has a kind heart, she deduced, allowing him to help her off with her coat, into which she tucked her gloves and scarf. He hung up both their coats before leading her down the passage into a vast room where the pair of Siamese awaited them.

Katerina gave a sigh of pleasure as she emerged into the large space, with windows that claimed an entire wall and tall ceilings that raked to an apex. 'Oh, this is wonderful.' The piano towards one end of the room captured her attention but she resisted it for now, even though she wanted – no, needed – to lift the lid and touch ivory keys once again.

'If I were an artist, yes. The light that floods in from those windows, I'll admit, is extraordinary and sort of magical, because it seems to occur no matter what time of day.'

He waited, giving her a moment to feel comfy, and she sensed him watching her move across the parquet flooring to the window to look down.

'I hope you use that glorious courtyard.'

'It's a sun trap for sure, but no, I don't. I keep myself to myself.'

She understood him better than he could know; a kindred spirit. And while hers was no match for his apartment, the ambience felt much the same: lonely, quiet, surrounded by shelves of books and essentially still. It was only the twitch of a pair of cats' tails that moved in this moment. They had taken up positions flanking a door that she presumed led into the private rooms.

She turned from the oriental glare of the Siamese. 'I'm filled with admiration that you have made room for a piano,' she said, unable to hold off mentioning it a moment longer and with a tone in her voice that suggested genuine pleasure. It was an unguarded moment and she registered the surprise that lit in his face.

'I'm no pianist, although I bought this one from the previous owner of the apartment who couldn't take it with him. I liked how it looked in the room, but more than that, it made me feel comforted. Do you play?'

She wanted to say no but out it came. 'As a child I did. But the war . . .' Katerina let a sad smile leak into her expression. 'I haven't had access to piano as an adult.'

'Play. I won't watch. I'd love to hear some sound come out of it. Let me get the fire lit and that soup on to warm.'

She could hear him igniting the gas on the stove as she strolled over to lift the lid of the instrument, its timber casing so highly varnished she could see the room reflected in its polish. It smelled newly waxed and she added another aspect to the character she was building in her mind about her host. Private, tidy, kind, can cook, watchful . . . that last one was the complex one. She didn't know whether to feel worried or impressed by the fact that he had observed her in the past.

'It's a Steinway,' he remarked, returning to the room. 'A 1925 Model K vertegrand upright.'

'Impressive.' She moved across an octave, not ready for the delight that trilled through her at the sound of the notes.

'It certainly impressed Gustav Mahler,' he said over his shoulder as he stirred the embers of the fire, coaxing life back into them. 'Apparently he is said to have remarked that he couldn't have imagined an upright piano that could satisfy a pianist's requirements in every aspect . . . or words to that effect.'

'Well, if it's good enough for Mahler,' she remarked, blowing on her fingers to warm them. 'Let's see what I can remember.'

She was surprised at how easily the notes came back and how her slender fingers reached for the right keys from memory, blueprinted over hours of practice at her family's Steinway grand. The music carried her, lifting her on its sad notes all the way to Prague, back to the drawing room where she would play for her parents.

They would sit in silence, appreciating the earnest notes her hands coaxed into life, her father normally with eyes closed, nodding in time with the rhythm. Through the music she could see such detail, down to the contented smile of her mother as she listened.

'Severine?' She opened her eyes, realising her cheeks were wet. Daniel was holding out a handkerchief.

'Forgive me,' she whispered. 'It's painful to remember.'

'Nothing to forgive. Your memories are vital – not even war can steal those from you.' She noted his gaze shifted away from where it had been lingering on her gently.

She nodded, presuming her tears had touched him or more likely embarrassed him. 'Sometimes I wish it had,' she admitted, taking the cotton square with gratitude to dab her cheeks. He still cut his gaze away to where her hands rested on the keys. 'It doesn't help to recall a happy childhood when you have nothing left of it.'

Daniel cleared his throat. 'Come and sit by the fire. You're trembling.' He didn't reach for her to offer a hand, nor did he touch her, she noted. He simply gestured, guiding her to a comfortable armchair near the happily crackling flames. 'That was a melancholy piece.'

'It's how I played it. I'm rusty. When I used to play it, it wasn't sad so much as quiet and pretty.'

'Let me fetch you that soup. Just sit here and get warm.'

She kept her mind deliberately blank, allowing herself to be momentarily mesmerised by the fire. She could hear Daniel in his kitchen, his sounds of domesticity a comfort as she felt the warmth begin to cloak the chill and still her tremor that she wasn't convinced was from the cold. The vault was open and the demon was out, dancing with the flames, swirling around the room, poking and prodding at her with glee.

He returned this time with a tray, upon which was a neatly rolled, starched napkin of white linen held in a silver ring that had his initials engraved in a looping scrawl to form an emblem.

'DJH,' she read aloud.

'They're my grandfather's. I was named for him. Daniel Joseph Horowitz.'

'So you were saying, you got out?'

He nodded. 'At the first sign of anti-Semitism, even before the riots began to occur, my father packed us up and took us first to Switzerland in 1934 and then to England in 1936.'

'Did he fight?'

'My father was a professor of mathematics so his skills were better used at Bletchley Park. My mother and us two children were sent north. We lived in Yorkshire for a while.'

'Yorkshire! I love the region and its city. That explains the intriguing lilt to your accent.'

He shrugged. 'After the war our family moved to Buckinghamshire; my father returned to a quiet teaching post and as I mentioned my parents still live there.'

'And you came to France. Why?'

She sensed he was reluctant to discuss this, something in the sudden tautness of how he held his body. It was subtle, but there.

'Eat up,' he urged. 'I wanted to travel but I especially wanted to improve my skills in French and I love Paris. I wanted to witness it emerging from its Nazi overlords. I was too late to see flags being torn down and street names being changed back into French but I got here in time to enjoy the people of France collectively breathing again. Using their own money once more, speaking French with joy and not in defiance.'

She nodded, could hear the passion; there was no doubting his sincerity but she couldn't fathom what he wasn't saying. Years of living a life of suspicion had taught her to pay attention to what wasn't being told, what the body language was fighting to conceal.

'What do you do, Daniel – for work, I mean?'

'I'm a businessman.'

She gave a soft smirk. 'That's vague.'

'I'm in shipping, essentially. Import and export of anything that anyone needs to move around Europe and the Eastern Mediterranean. I have done some longer haul between Europe and the Americas too. I prefer to work out of Paris, but the main office is in Calais. I travel a lot for my work.'

She sipped at her soup with care, swallowing silently, thinking about how casually confident he was in delivering that response, and beneath his seemingly relaxed answer she heard a rehearsed explanation.

He gestured towards his own bowl of soup. 'As you can tell, I'm not very good at socialising. I work alone – prefer it that way.'

'Well, you're a fine cook, Daniel,' she said, knowing their conversation needed something gracious added to it at this awkward point. 'Your soup is most delicious, thank you.'

'You are so welcome. It's strange but wonderful to be sharing my food.'

'You never have guests?'

He shook his head. 'It never occurs to me to ask anyone over.'

'Yet you didn't hesitate in asking me.' She watched him blink; she had tripped him slightly.

'It's true, I surprised myself by talking suddenly on that bench – it slipped out, really. And then when you did begin to speak, I wanted to help. I felt you needed to keep talking and sometimes . . . well, talking to a stranger is easier, don't you think?'

'I do. So, you told me your immediate family were saved. What about your greater family?' she said.

'Lost to the round-ups, ghettos, detention centres, trains.' He shrugged in past sorrow. 'There were friends too. One in particular – my best friend, who was ultimately sent to one of the death camps in Poland for a more brutal end.'

'I'm sorry.' Empty words. She hated that phrase being offered up to her because it brought no comfort when it came from people who had no part in the shame. But she forgave herself, for what else was there to say?

'Tell me about your father's art collecting . . .' He stood to poke at the fire, which she knew was a deliberate act to give her time to gather up her thoughts. They needed no shepherd; they were ready to start trotting themselves out for the first time in at least a decade.

She had finished her soup; she dabbed at her lips with the napkin and set the tray aside. Daniel was right: the light streaming into the apartment was glorious enough to please any painter. 'And you suggested I start at the beginning.'

'I did,' he said, returning to his seat, not so far away that she felt isolated but not so close that she felt scrutinised.

'So, I shall start by telling you my real name is Katerina Kassowicz.'

He sat back in feigned surprise. 'Katerina.'

She smiled. 'I haven't heard my name spoken aloud and in the Czech way, with the trilled "r" and soft "j" sound in so long,' she said, explaining why her eyes must appear misty. 'It feels powerful to speak it . . . with no shame, no fear.'

'It's such a beautiful name and sits on you well. Kassowicz. I know of your father's firm. I'm sure our family had glass made by his factory. Jablonec, right?'

She nodded. 'Because of the hard sand of the region it was perfect to have the factory based there in northern Bohemia. My mother wouldn't move there, though. Prague was her home. As I say, we wanted for little as a family. As a result, it was a charmed life for me. I learned languages, music – both piano and violin – I learned to cook at my mother's side and attended concerts with my family at the Municipal Hall, a glorious Art Nouveau building.' Katerina gave an expression of soft regret. 'My mother loved music, encouraged me to learn to read it, play it . . . I remember my life as wonderful until the start of my teens. My father taught me from my earliest childhood everything he could about art and the antiques he enjoyed and collected. I grew up sharing his interest. And then, when Hitler arrived in Prague and sent down his edict from the castle that Czechoslovakia was now a protectorate of Germany, together we began a new sort of collection.'

Daniel gestured to the light blanket slung over the arm of the sofa. She gave a brief smile of thanks, wondering how he knew that despite the fire and the sunlight, she was feeling chilled. It was as though her temperature was dropping as she re-entered that frozen day in mid-March 1939. She wasn't aware of kicking off her shoes, wasn't conscious of tucking long legs back onto the sofa and beneath the blanket; she didn't register that she looked away from Daniel and into the fire because she was back in Prague now and it was finally time to relive what she had avoided for so long.

6

● ● ●

March 1939

Baron Konstantin von Neurath arrived by train into celebrations that lasted all day. He was the Reichsprotektor and my father deduced that the German strategy was to take everything it wanted from Czechoslovakia without provoking out-and-out rebellion. I was old enough to understand talk of politics, although if I'm honest I was more interested in whether Alexandr Clementis would be allowed to meet me unaccompanied for a hot chocolate at the weekend. My parents were still to give me an answer. I listened to the men talk. I always paid attention to my father because growing up around him I'd decided that he rarely wasted words. If there was nothing to say, he did not fill a silence, but when he spoke there was a point, even if he was just being playful.

Even so, there was nothing amusing about the Czech late winter of 1939, or so I gathered from the conversation he was having with one of his oldest friends in our sitting room, as I served the small cakes I'd baked with my mother that morning. We'd filled the surface I had dented with a well-aimed thumb with a sweet-ened paste of poppy seeds. Her recipe was legend in our circles.

'No, Rudolf,' my father warned, taking one of the proffered

cakes. 'Thank you, dear. Ah, still warm, perfect,' he said, smiling his appreciation at me before returning his attention to his guest. 'They've sent in a diplomat: silver-haired and silver-tongued so they can steal our freedom while making us believe that we retain a sense of power in governing our nation.'

'You don't trust the delegation from Bavaria that's out there feeding the city's starving?' Rudolf asked, surprised.

I was replacing the cake plate on the table but I was watching my father as he bit into the small koláče, nodding his appreciation as its sweetness hit. 'I am not fooled, Rudolf. Who do you see starving around our city? Do you see children begging on the streets?'

Rudolf shrugged and shook his head.

'Exactly. There are refugees from Sudeten who could use a feed but that's it. We have no proliferation of beggars and certainly no Jewish homeless. This is all propaganda. I'm also hearing that all our political parties will be dissolved.'

'When?' came the reply, full of disbelief and challenge.

My father sighed. 'Any moment, I suspect.'

'And us Jews?'

He glanced my way then. 'Does your mother need you in the kitchen, Katerina?'

I shook my head. 'No, Papa.' The look I gave him urged him to let me remain.

'I think I will have that second cup of coffee, please. Tell your dear mother to put the pot on again.'

As I closed the door, I heard my father's low response. 'I suggest you all follow my lead and make a meeting soon with your solicitors to update your wills; get your affairs in order and then instruct them to hide those wills or send a copy to a neutral party, well away from Czechoslovakia.'

Katerina suddenly looked up from the soup bowl still cradled in her lap. 'That's the last normal day I remember in our household, in which we hosted a guest with the good china. It's also the day I felt the first clamp of genuine fear. Until then everything seemed to be either exciting, dare I say, or just plain inconvenient. To me it was politics and the government would sort things out. I was still too young, my mind filled with an awakening to boys. But I knew my father too well and he was frightened, that much I could sense, and so I did leave the room that day, realising it was an escape and not banishment. I decided I didn't want to know about inevitable war, the overrun of Poland or Neville Chamberlain's miscalculation that Hitler would see reason. I didn't want our family under threat.'

Daniel watched her shake her head and a dark wave of hair fell across her cat's eye. To him it was one of the most erotic moments he had experienced in the company of a woman. All he had to do was cross the floor and offer an arm of comfort. Even if she denied him, she'd know he cared enough to risk rejection. But it was as though he were glued to his seat.

'It was bad enough that we were all still mourning the loss of Petr.'

He cleared his throat of the charge of lust that had made its way there.

She flicked at her hair and pointed briefly in the direction of her eye. 'The one who shared this mark with me,' she reminded him.

'How do you think Petr died?'

'From a fever is all we were told.' She made it sound matter-of-fact but he could hear the soft undertow of choked emotion. It was still raw for her. 'His end was the beginning of our troubles.'

Troubles. She was fast becoming his favourite wielder of the understatement. 'What do you mean?'

'Everything from that moment in our lives went bad. Petr's death was like the siren that set off our spiral into the abyss of despair – or, should I say, pit – that none of us would clamber out from.'

He sensed the query was rhetorical because she was smirking to herself in what looked to be a private but bitter jest.

Katerina rallied. 'Look, I know how dramatic that sounds but it is precisely how I felt in 1942 – I could trace back all the unhappiness to the day Petr died in 1939 . . . and it summarises how I was feeling when you sat down next to me on the park bench this morning.'

Daniel suspected there was no point in offering placations. This woman was a survivor. She didn't need his hollow words. 'What *did* your parents explain about Petr? It seems odd that they didn't say more.' He needed her to keep talking so he could ease her towards what he wanted her to talk about in depth, but it took a light touch to guide someone towards a subject that they most likely wished to avoid.

She lifted a shoulder, with an expression of helplessness. 'Us children, full of our excitement of a happy weekend with our friends, walked back into a house that had been drained of colour, sound, movement and, above all, spirit. Our home was still. Even the hall clock's pendulum had been tied so it no longer ticked away the minutes. The atmosphere was thick with dread.' She sighed. 'And then we heard the wailing. What wouldn't we have given for the silence to have continued once that began.'

'Your mother?'

She nodded. 'She couldn't be consoled. She wept without pause for days. In the end my father had to call in our physician to have her sedated, but even then she moaned while unconscious. I kept a vigil, for my father was physically drained as well, and I had to continuously remind myself that it wasn't just my mother's grief – he too had lost a son. And us . . . we had lost our only brother, our family favourite because he was so tiny, often sick. However, if you could get Petr to deliver his rare smile, it was as though he reflected the sun. He was one of the chosen – an angel, I'm sure of it. That's why he was taken from us.'

'Why?'

She shook her head, taking her time thinking about her response. 'Because I think he needed to be spared the horror. Petr was still pure; nothing about life had tarnished him yet and so nothing did. He escaped to a better place. We buried him a few days later in a private ceremony just for the immediate family. My parents wanted no other mourners, not even my father's closest friend, the man honoured with holding Petr at his circumcision.'

'Why not?'

'Well, Levi was living in England then, so it would have been impossible, but my father simply didn't want any other mourners. He was damaged and was only just holding himself together for us children while my mother was lost to her grief. She had to be held by us just to stand, and in the end we borrowed a wheelchair, she was so infirm.'

'I'm truly sorry.'

'Her heart was broken and I think everything else about her began to fail. She rarely smiled again. We never heard her pretty voice singing lullabies. The woman I knew as the mother I adored and who loved every bit of me – all of us – began to disappear. Little by little we lost her, a fraction more each day, until within a couple of years she was a skeleton, clothed in living flesh that resembled my mother but nothing of that person was left. Her spirit had fled, perhaps to join Petr.'

'I'm trying to imagine the sad household you lived in.'

'We were never in doubt about our parents' love for one another, but I was old enough to sense that from 1939 we were living in a house run by people who had become strangers.'

'She blamed him?'

'Yes. I believe she laid Petr's departure from our family at my father's feet and I never understood why. It was never discussed, or if it was, then not openly; I wish it had been. I wish I could listen to her rage and understand her pain but she gave us nothing – only her despair and her bitterness. Perhaps she knew Petr's death was only the first . . .'

It was an opening but he didn't want to leap through it. He needed Katerina to give up her story in her own time. He finally shifted. 'May I take that from you?'

'Thank you. It was delicious.'

'You are most welcome. You don't eat much.' He risked the jest.

She seemed lightly amused. 'I eat all meals but breakfast.'

'They must be tiny servings.'

'Perhaps. But I've just always been gangly. My three sisters were not. I think they would have grown up to resemble our mother and her line; we can see from photos that her female relatives were petite with big busts, but I was all my father. Always taller than my peers as we moved through childhood, knock-kneed for a while, flat-chested until I was well past my fourteenth birthday. I think Petr may well have turned out the same gangly way; he was long for a newborn, my mother used to remark, and he seemed to grow like a weed, despite being colicky. I still can't fathom how ill he became in such a short time and sick enough to die . . .'

He took their bowls into the kitchen, talking over his shoulder. 'I'll put some coffee on. If you need the bathroom, it's through there.' He pointed.

'Thank you, I might.'

When Daniel returned, he could hear water running and Katerina was absent. He set down coffee cups and saucers on the low table, adding a jug of milk and a small bowl of sugar. She reappeared, moving in that familiar glide of hers across the parquet floor. He noticed she felt comfy enough to walk around in stockinged feet. Even without the heels she stood tall, and it was not just her stature but the way she held her body straight and to its fullest height.

She withdrew her limbs in neat formation, tucking her legs beneath her again on the sofa.

To Daniel she was like a fascinating piece of origami that could be folded into an impossibly exquisite form. He wished he could stop staring and cleared his throat. 'You were thinking through something difficult today. Would it help to go back to that topic?'

Katerina glanced at the window. The softer afternoon light had changed the colour of the room, picking out the floors and panelling with a burnished warmth. Daniel threw another log on the fire and it spat and hissed as fresh flames erupted.

'You really need to learn why you and I happened to meet this morning. It's relevant or I wouldn't mention it.'

'All right.' He felt a trill of guilt. 'Tell me.'

'I was in London on loan to the British Museum and I was called in to see if I could help with a fascinating and historic piece of jewellery that had been offered to the museum as an exhibit.'

'Didn't the museum know its history from its owner?'

She gave a sad attempt at a smile. 'Honestly, I don't know what they had learned from the person offering it. The offer was being made through London solicitors.'

He nodded, frowning. 'For privacy purposes?'

'Privacy, and also creating some distance, no doubt.'

'So, they called you in. Why?'

'Because of my expertise in antiquarian jewellery. All museums around the world and particularly those in London and Paris are sensitive about acquiring pieces that may have belonged to Jewish families.'

'Yes, of course.'

She shrugged. 'As it turned out, I was able to tell them a great deal about that piece. I knew its provenance and its series of owners from its incarnation to the day and moment of its theft from the Kassowicz family in Prague in 1941.'

He stared at her, open-mouthed. Katerina stared back at him, fresh fire in the cat's eye as she remembered.

'Who stole them?' But he could guess. His voice was thin, as though his vocal cords were stretched in fear.

And she finally spoke his name. 'A man called Ruda Mayek. Although he stole a great deal more than just the Pearls . . .'

By October 1941 I no longer recognised our lives. The synagogues had been shut down, considered subversive. Jewish children no longer went to school, universities were closed to us, we were regis-tered as 'Juden', we were not permitted to use parks or take any entertainment, and my father could only buy food between the hours of four and five in the evening. Our wealth was the buffer but even us children could see it wouldn't last. There was a place north-west of the city called Terezín; Jews were being rounded up and sent there under the guise of being protected in a place especially built for us. It was originally a medieval fortress but to us it was a walled ghetto. Too many whispers were coming back that it was merely a transit camp for transports east to the concentration camps. We were sure it would be our turn soon.

With my mother's withdrawal from life, I had to step into that gap and become mother to my sisters. And I think in some ways I became Papa's closest companion; we would talk late into the night and this made me privy to not only his thoughts but his knowledge of what was happening to us and our country.

'We're doing our bit, Papa.' I was referring to the small museum he had set up. I'd been learning by doing volunteer work

at the Ceremonial Hall, with its links to Vienna and various cities in Germany, so I was a genuine help. I say small, but it was garnering much attention and so many items that it had become a full-time occupation: I was no longer attending school and instead curating the articles. Even the Occupiers were comfortable with our endeavour, one Nazi official even quipping to me that when the Jews were wiped out of Europe, it would be good to have a history resource for the German people.

As a result of our careful curation over the last two years, I had acquired skills in Jewish reliquary in particular, but we were also permitted to catalogue a lot of the jewellery, art, gold and silver, precious porcelains, sculptures, books . . . We had a fine collection of porcelain, including my mother's Dresden dinner sets that were envied in Czech aristocratic circles. Of course, none of that was in our possession any longer. Almost everything we owned – save a few belongings we'd secreted – had been confiscated. Our mansion home behind the city's centre was now housing a senior Nazi, while our apartment on Parizska Street near the old synagogue was the residence of one of the German officials.

Synagogues were being destroyed all around us. We were sharing a run-down apartment with three other families. It was only a matter of time before they collected us in one of the round-ups, which is why late one spring evening, huddled around a tiny fire, my father told me his plan.

'Tomorrow I want you to gather up your sisters. Don't pack anything. I don't want to draw attention. Put together a few items for your mother – photographs, mainly. They help keep her lucid.'

I didn't agree with him on this but I no longer cared that my father was fooling himself on the matter of our mother. If that gave him courage, so be it.

'What about jewellery?' We'd managed to hide small pieces in the youngsters' toys.

'Only that which we can carry.'

'The Pearls?'

'I had those moved to the summer villa by a friend.' He put a finger to his lips. 'No one is to know.'

They were our most important item, not just because of the history attached to the Pearls but because of how precious they were to my mother's family. Their value was incalculable but they were also a liability. I held my tongue as I frowned.

'What are we doing?'

'We're leaving the city.'

'Papa!'

'Listen to me. Ever since Hitler appointed Reinhard Heydrich as the Acting Reich Protector for Bohemia and Moravia I've felt our days are numbered. His rise through the Nazi Party has been meteoric and he has supporters in Himmler and Göring – these are fearful men, my darling, with no conscience about us Jews and our plight. Terezín is next for us and I think we will be separated, sent to different work camp. Your mother . . .' He couldn't finish. I chilled at him saying aloud what most adults discussed only out of the hearing of their children. But I was not a child to my father any more; more his conspirator.

I barely recognised him. He had always been lean but now he was haggard; he had developed a stoop and his cheeks were hollow, his eyes sunken, haunted as if holding a dreaded secret. By comparison to others I believed we were still eating reasonably well but he was either choosing not to consume his fair share, or he was not benefiting from the nourishment. I was convinced he was heartbroken in a way I was not privy to.

'I do understand about our mother,' I assured him.

He continued as if I hadn't spoken. 'It is said that Hitler believed Protektor von Neurath was mollycoddling us in Prague.' I opened my mouth in astonishment but no sound came. My father pulled a ghastly smile – more of a smirk. 'Yes, can you imagine it? He thinks we need better management and a stronger man is required for the job. And so we now have someone whose great claim to fame is being amongst the first to be awarded the coveted Death's Head Ring of the SS.'

Czechoslovakia was now in a state of martial law as Heydrich began to hunt every resister. We watched police cars move through our streets taking prisoners to be shot, to be tortured, or both. As I walked across our cobbled roads, my yellow star clearly on show, I noted neatly typed-up notices attached to street lamps and shopfronts proclaiming the names and dates of birth of the latest victims or those the Germans hunted.

'You do realise the Gestapo charges the families of the executed for the cost of the shooting and the public placards, don't you?' my father said. I knew it was a rhetorical question and did not reply. His voice had a tone of terror in it. 'They're abominable! Heydrich is demonstrating he will not be nearly as tolerant as von Neurath.'

While the thought was petrifying, I suppose I wasn't surprised. As young as I was, I'd lost the dreaminess of youth; I'd become cynical and I feared I was fast becoming resigned to hearing the knock at the door and seeing German police with their hated swastika badges arriving for us. Imprisonment, being worked to death in some place like Terezín, felt inevitable. Dare I admit that death sounded not exactly welcome but perhaps the best outcome? My life until 1939 had been full of possibility and promise; now it felt like my world had reduced itself to blocks of twenty-four hours, each of them filled with the angst of survival. This was no time for ambition or dreaming . . . but I allowed myself a tiny streak of hope, like the first slash of dawn as morning cuts through night. Thin but luminous hope sustained me that I might live to see the world at peace again, that I would make it through whatever fresh trauma came our way in order to bear witness to a Nazi humiliation.

I recall the day that a triumphant Adolf Hitler arrived in our city. We Jews were banished, not to be seen on our own streets while the leader of the Third Reich was driven up to the castle accompanied by what I presumed to be enforced fake cheers from a stunned crowd. We learned he enjoyed an honour guard in the first courtyard, which sickened all of us, I'm sure, before he appeared at one of our proud castle's windows. Third floor, third from the left. I always hated that window from then on.

One tiny moment of joy was learning that Hitler had ordered the destruction of the statue of Mendelssohn, the revered composer and pianist, who was Jewish, from the top of our former concert hall – now our parliament building. Its rooftop boasted lifelike sculptures of all the famous composers. To our amusement, the soldiers given the task couldn't make out Tchaikovsky from Handel, so one wit suggested they look for the one with the biggest nose as he was bound to be the Jew. The statue of Wagner, arguably Germany's most beloved and lauded composer, was torn down and smashed. Mendelssohn looked on stoically and he survived. He too was part of my defiance.

If my father's summary was right, then Heydrich was a man banged out from the same mould as his leader – emotionally, any-way. Physically they couldn't have been less alike. I spotted Heydrich once; my fairer hair and lighter eyes allowed me some scope to roam, especially if I took the risk and didn't wear my yellow star – it was worth it sometimes to get better food for the children. He liked to hurtle around in an open-topped Mercedes-Benz made especially for him. It was said he refused an armed escort because he doubted any pathetic Czech would dare to take aim at him. I watched with loathing as the blond, hawk-nosed, milky-faced brute with a receding hairline revved his engine with frustration as he had to slow for a group of schoolchildren crossing the street not far from the old royal palace where he spent his *working days. According to the gossips, the man who planned to humble the Czechs and rid the country of its Jews liked to drive home to his family in the country. He preferred his children to grow up in the bracing air, well away from our beautiful but tense and traumatised city.*

I think if I could have lifted a gun from my pocket that day I spied him, arrogantly leaning on his car horn to speed the teachers and their charges on and out of his important way, I would have gladly given my life to make an attempt on his. I recall wondering in that moment as he roared off again, not even noticing me or any other passer-by, if I could be capable of such violence. But then I remembered my shattered family and all the families crowding into what had become a Jewish ghetto and I decided I might indeed be capable if the circumstances presented themselves. It was October 1941: he'd only been in Prague a month, and I can't imagine a Czech man, woman or child, Jewish or otherwise, who didn't fear him.

It soon came to pass that he was planning medical exams for the entire population as he strived to work out who in the region could be saved for 'Aryanisation', as they called it, and which of us should be destroyed for having unwelcome racial traits.

'Your honey-coloured hair might yet save you, Katerina,' my father lamented. 'Your sisters, though . . .'

'Stop, Papa!' I told him. 'We don't need saving. Tell me about your plan to leave. How are we going to make our escape?'

7

It was the shrill sound of a doorbell that forced Katerina Kassowicz back from her recollections to see that early evening had stolen across Paris and the light was failing in Daniel's studio.

She watched the smudge opposite stir.

'Are you all right?' he asked gently as he stood.

She nodded. 'It's painful. This is why I try not to look back.'

'I'm sorry if —'

'Don't be. I make my own choices. I didn't know it had become so late. I should go.'

'No, wait!' He tempered his tone. 'That will be Madame Bouchard with our pie. Let me refresh the coffee and share a piece with you. Don't hurry off . . . please?' He didn't wait for her response, leaving the room as if scurrying away could force her to remain seated. She did. He returned with the bustling neighbour from downstairs, bringing with them the aroma of baked pastry and the oozing caramel of roasted fruit that brought a fresh and different sort of brightness into the room, as though sunshine had been trapped in the food.

Madame Bouchard arrived mid-conversation with Daniel but

immediately smiled broadly. 'Hello, dear. Monsieur Horowitz tells me you have a headache.'

Katerina threw a look at Daniel hovering in the doorway behind his neighbour, wearing a look of apology.

Or she'll stay, he silently mouthed in plea.

'It's not bad – one of those low, annoying ones.'

'It's because you don't eat enough! Get a slice of this down you.' She beamed. 'Shall I serve it up for you?'

'Er, I will have a slice a little later, if I may?' Katerina replied graciously. 'I've just swallowed a couple of aspirin and they tend to make me feel a little queasy.' She tapped her belly and made a small grimace. 'I can't wait to try it, though,' she promised.

'Of course, of course. It has cooled to perfection and I've glazed it with a fresh fruit syrup, so make sure you eat it while it's still just warm. I've brought rich cream to go with it.'

'You do spoil me, Madame Bouchard,' Daniel joined in. 'It smells magnificent.'

She made a happy clucking sound, like a hen. 'So, should I leave it in the kitchen?' She was holding the tart but didn't look prepared to give it up just yet.

'If that's all right?' he offered, and as she turned her back he whispered to Katerina, 'If she could, she'd check my bedroom for rumpled sheets as well!'

She put a hand to her mouth in amusement.

Madame Bouchard was back. 'I've left it on the counter and the cream in the chiller but don't leave it to get too cold,' she impressed upon them.

'We won't.' They said it together like teenagers being left alone in the house for the first time. They shared a secret amused glance.

'Enjoy it, my dears, and I hope you feel better soon, mademoiselle. I'll say goodnight on your way out.'

'Yes, thank you again,' Katerina replied.

When Daniel returned from seeing his neighbour off the premises, his look of dismay prompted another grin from her. 'Did you catch the artful way in which my overseer was ensuring that you didn't have any designs on staying longer than she considers appropriate?' He gave a sound of despair.

'Perhaps we should tease her.'

'Yes. Oh, please stay all night,' he groaned, hardly hearing the audacity of the invitation, intent on his frustration instead. 'She makes me feel like a child. Heaven help me if I did want to have a woman spend the night with me.'

Katerina laughed and again there was the smoky authenticity of genuine amusement. 'It happens because you allow her to push you around.'

'Does anyone push you around, Katerina?'

'Not any more,' she said, her expression becoming sober. 'Not for a long time,' she added, and recalled when that turning point was.

8

It was October of 1941. We had made it to the country house, but not without a lot of help and clandestine arrangements. We were moved in two transports: my father, mother and my younger sister Lotte, followed by me with the twins. I know my fairer looks made it possible for me to sit up in the car without nearly as much fear as the others might have had, and we tied the children's hair back and put on bonnets to hide as much as we could. Our clothes were high quality, which no doubt helped too. I sat in the front of a large vehicle owned by a Czech industrialist who ran a sugar factory, a long-time friend of my father who was determined to see us to the relative safety of the hills. I was inwardly frightened but not to the point of trembling or looking guilty; I was able to muster a laugh, even sing a song with my sisters at the checkpoint. Either our companion was already familiar with the men or he'd paid them off handsomely. I can't bring to mind the details but they seemed more relaxed about people leaving the city than entering it, so I don't recall any awkward questions. I think the fact we were in an expensive car, wearing borrowed furs and looking every inch the wealthy Czech family, meant we were waved through.

I do, however, remember feeling a lurch of sadness to be leaving behind the gymnasium where I had been planning to ace my exams in readiness for my senior school years before attending university. I would miss walking the youngsters to their school before hopping onto the rumbling tram for the journey to mine. I used to stare out of the window as we clanged and clattered along the way from our posh neighbourhood, passing avenues of pines and maple.

I especially liked the linden trees that clustered around our expansive family home which looked a bit like a grand doll's house with its symmetrical facade and neoclassical lines. It sat raised on a mound a couple of miles behind the castle in which Hitler and his henchmen now roamed, like emperors of old, while my father who had helped build Prague's industry was now only permitted to carry limited currency at any time. Everything else that we couldn't successfully hide was taken.

I can remember the roses used to grow wild around our home and I could chase my baby sisters through sweet-scented arbours – at least half a dozen of them. In winter we'd play under the central staircase and sometimes, if our mother would permit it, we'd step out onto the upstairs balcony, which had a grand balustrade and soaring Ionic columns that overlooked the stairs and the iron fencing that ringed the house.

It was from this balcony that we tearfully let our canaries fly free. Each of us children had two that we kept in huge cages at the bottom of the garden. The gardens were like a small private park and we could step into the aviary, it was so large and airy for our birds. But before we were forced from the house we'd heard that Jews would not be permitted pets and so rather than have the canaries killed, we gave them freedom. As we made our charge to the country house I felt like those canaries now, fleeing for our lives.

On reflection I suppose the German soldiers policing that checkpoint knew if we were running, there really was nowhere to run to. We were headed west, after all, towards Germany – back into the old Saxony region – so I doubt they were terribly worried that we'd be Jewish escapees, nor would they care. My burnished golden hair that I made sure I had brushed to shiny and had deliberately kept loose I tossed back and forth as I feigned my laughter and sang my songs. It played its role. The sun was out, it was a dry autumn day and the checkpoint soldiers were enjoying what they no doubt presumed was the last of the mild weather. I assumed this was hardly a busy gate, or an important one, so it looked to me as though they'd given the job to the youngest of their men. One winked at my glance and I couldn't help but be flattered. His grin brought a warmth to my cheeks and I gave him a surreptitious and perhaps even flirtatious smile in return. I could hate myself now for it, given what was to come, but at the time I was still much of a child that was having to behave as an experienced adult.

Our family villa was in Hvozdy, always a beautiful drive out of Prague towards Slapy where the dam and reservoir had been recently begun. Czechoslovakia had plans for a hydro power station too and while I didn't enjoy all the heavy works around the peaceful countryside, I knew my father applauded its arrival.

'Think of the electricity to our homes, our businesses . . . think of the jobs for so many men and women as a result. So many families can now look forward to giving their children an education, those children going on to university to become our new doctors, dentists, engineers, bright thinkers and doers.' He was always so optimistic, my father.

As soon as I saw the Vltava River on my left, its serpentine laziness snaking alongside, I began to feel the fear of our escape dissipating. I knew this Bohemian countryside well; we'd been coming to the villa each summer since my birth, and while we'd not spent many winters here, the thought of an autumn holiday in a favourite place after the blight on Prague felt like all my birthdays were being celebrated at once. My shoulders lost their tightness, the frown I hoped I'd hidden with a fake expression of pleasure I could now feel easing, and the tightness in my belly relaxed.

'We could call in at the bakery?' my companion suggested, nodding over his shoulder towards the girls. 'Try and keep it normal, eh?' He didn't look scared but I recognised the taut tone that he couldn't hide.

'That's a lovely idea, thank you, sir.'

'Call me Tomas, please. You're old enough,' he said. 'I feel so badly for the family, Katerina; none of you deserve this.'

'No Jewish family deserves persecution but my history studies assure me this probably won't be the last time.'

'Heavens! Your father told me you leaned towards seriousness but now you're speaking like an old lady. Try to keep your youth burning brightly within. We need the young to keep their hopes alive.'

I nodded, even though I didn't feel especially hopeful. My father had been surely referring to his eldest daughter of now rather than his eldest of years gone; I didn't remember being a sober infant. In fact, I remember my mother laughing at me and wondering how they would ever keep my personality under control because I was so precocious. Maybe that quality had dissipated, but not through choice. My teenage years ahead were meant to be about discovery, empowerment and romantic ideals but looking towards them I could only see bleakness. Everything optimistic had been chipped away and yet I felt guilty for my dark thoughts, knowing we were still faring better than most of our poorer counterparts.

We pulled into a tiny bakery, famed for its bread made with caraway, a place familiar enough to be part of the tapestry of my life. The smell of its pastries still rising to their full burnished height in the oven and steam escaping through the chimney to perfume the immediate surrounds reminded me of every good memory that I'd managed to trap and keep safe. Every party, every family picnic, every birthday, new frock, well-played piece of music, each highly graded essay or exam, each laughing kiss from my parents felt as though it was wrapped up today in those familiar sugar-scented pastries.

'Wait here,' Tomas advised. 'We can't be too careful. The reason this place can keep going is because it's a favourite of the Germans who take a drive out. They make sure it gets far more than its fair share of ingredients, but sugar especially, as you can smell, is here in abundance.'

'Are soldiers here?' I asked, hearing the fresh fear in my voice as I craned to scan the surrounds. The bakery was nestled into the valley, nothing else around it but a few scattered houses and the river to its front, the hillside to its rear. It hunched in a hollow like a fairytale cottage with its merrily smoking chimney.

Tomas cut me a look of sympathy. 'I'm being especially cautious, that's all. I see no other vehicles and we're here a bit early in the day for picnickers. Just be still; act normal. I won't be more than a couple of minutes.'

He was as good as his word, but during his absence I decided it must be how a mouse feels when it is forced to move out in the open, knowing agile and cruel predators are all around.

Tomas arrived back at the car, all smiles. 'Not another customer in sight,' he reassured us, handing me a box of sweetened cheese pastries to share in the car. He put the loaves he'd also purchased onto the back seat between the girls and I felt more at ease once we were on our way again, with the car smelling of the spicy anise aroma of warm caraway.

Licking sugar from our lips made the world feel happy for a few seconds. My sisters perked up in the back and began to plan their unexpected sabbatical from school. It was uplifting to hear their happy chatter.

'What about you, Tomas?' I said, testing the grown-up taste of using his name. 'I mean, this is surely not safe for you?'

He lifted a shoulder. 'I offered, Katerina. Your father once gave me money when I needed new equipment to keep the factory going. He did not ever discuss the return of it.' Tomas gave a gust of sadness. 'He said one day he may need a favour and knew I would give it without hesitation. That was nearly a decade ago and his investment, if I could call it that – although we both know it was a gift – has helped to make me an extremely wealthy man. Without his help at that moment I might well be poverty-stricken now. So, risk or not, your father is one of the best men I know, and I could not live with myself if I didn't help when he asked.'

'And my father wouldn't ask unless he was desperate,' I added.

Tomas nodded to let me know he was only too aware of that.

'Did you make the first run with my parents?'

'No, my manager did, in his van with a pile of deliveries. Your mother was in front, travelling as his sick mother. Your father and sister were hiding in the back.'

I felt nervous enough that I was sure I was trembling like the leaves in our autumn wind and, like them, clinging precariously to their parent . . . in my case, parents. 'But they're safe?' I needed his reassurance.

'Sitting around the fire at the villa, I promise you, and probably more worried about us getting through.'

The bright morning had given way to grey overcast with moments of a murky blue overhead like a freshly gathered puddle. Marshmallow clouds that threatened rain but without much ferocity hung like tall floating palaces that drifted, slow and deliberate. It was as though they needed the time to admire their reflection in the river that was equally languid that day so that barely a ripple shivered across its surface to create a near-perfect mirror. Trees had thickened around us to become woodland that I knew would soon become forest, and all of this familiarity closing around me was building fragile – but oh such welcome – security. Autumn always struck me emotionally as a time for healing, curiously enough. I am a creature of winter; I am someone who likes the cooler months and the threat of snow and freeze to force me indoors, to go within myself. I was born in February amidst a frozen winter and my spirit likes to believe various natural outside forces played their role in who I might become. My father tutted but I did like the idea that the stars, the tides, the seasons show up in me somewhere. And autumn – because it is cold but still relatively mild by the standards of a Czech winter – I feel it's a contented time of withdrawal, for the mind and body to find some peace from the industry of spring, the busyness of summer.

I think I smiled out of the window at my fanciful thoughts at that moment; the beloved countryside had wrapped its reassuring colours and landscape around to cocoon me in a thin but welcome peace. I looked up to my right, knowing I would see the famous spa that my mother used to favour.

Tomas noted the direction of my gaze. 'It's entirely overrun by soldiers now. The Germans love it.'

'It's awfully close to the villa,' I murmured.

He gave a dismissive sound. 'Katerina, the villa is yet forty miles from here. You must stop fretting.'

I trusted the adult's perspective. I couldn't let go of the fear but I let go of the immediate worry. Once we began to climb into the hills, a tentative sense of wellbeing began to layer a new shield, and within ten minutes of leaving the main road and the forest closing around what had now become a track, I started to convince myself the Kassowiczs who had survived in the protectorate these last couple of years might, by winter 1941, become invisible.

'Will you stay overnight?'

'No, my dear. I might head back straight away because I don't *want the checkpoint soldiers to change shift. I need the same men to see me return.'*

'But what if they notice we aren't in the car?'

'They won't recall you were in it, Katerina. They don't remember so much detail. They're young men with little more than an evening drinking fine Czech beer concerning them. They'll simply recall Mr Vavroch of Prague passed through with some family and yes, he returned to the city within hours.'

I thought of the young soldier who had winked at me, and feared that he would remember.

Katerina stopped talking and Daniel was lifted rudely from the languor he'd found comfort in. The combination of her smoky voice, watching her body move, how her lips formed their words or her head shook hair that fired golden when the dancing flames caught its natural shades had put him into a state of inertia. He wondered what it might feel like to watch her toss her hair free . . . it would surely reach her shoulders, but just like Katerina was tightly wound within, her hair whenever he'd seen her was kept slick and neat in a bun or a ponytail.

She waited, and he cleared his throat.

'Are you all right?' he asked, feeling lame for being repetitive. His voice sounded gritty from not being used while hers sounded parched. 'Another drink, perhaps?'

'Some water, please.'

He fetched it and returned, concerned. 'I'm sensing we're at the most difficult part of your story,' he offered, tiptoeing with care around her emotions.

'Not the most difficult so much as the most terrifying. When you confront evil in its purest form, it's actually only the sense of horror that makes you realise you are breathing. If not for the atrocity you face, you might float away, swoon, die of fright, disappear into madness . . . It's the abomination that sadly makes you alive, makes you cling to life, survive at all costs.'

He suspected that she realised she was becoming agitated, her voice heightened by the emotion, and he watched her reel it back in. The anxiety gave her a helpless quality that only made her more attractive, in his opinion. Her vulnerability in this moment touched his heart and he decided he would live to hate himself if he forced her to confront the monster now.

'Why don't you rest?'

'Rest? No, I must go.'

'You can't! I —' As she snapped him a fierce look of enquiry, he diluted his order, turning it into an appeal. 'I really must hear the end of your story. And maybe . . . well, perhaps it will feel like a relief to release it, share the load?' He didn't want her to see him holding his breath so he stood, moved to close the curtains, worry the fire, give her the space she needed to make a decision.

'It is not your burden to bear, Daniel. You are a stranger.'

'Stranger? We've broken bread together. I would like to hear what happened next. I would like to hear your whole story of how you survived the war and made it out of Czechoslovakia to live in Paris, work in London, and drink soup with a friend who watches you walk through the Luxembourg Gardens most mornings.'

'. . . and afternoons,' she added in a voice that had a slight arch of admonishment within it.

He put his hand across his heart. 'Guilty.'

'And what will Madame Bouchard think if I linger much longer?'

'I'd love her to think it!' he responded.

Katerina sighed and checked her wristwatch. 'It's nearing six.'

'The night is thus young.' He waited, tense for her answer but effecting a soft shrug that gave the opposite impression, he hoped.

Her gaze narrowed. 'You know, Daniel, my father always saw the good in people. I now realise that was his downfall. And this special quality of his gave me my flaw.'

'Flaw?'

'You see, I trust no one. I am suspicious of every person I meet. I figure they either want something or they're lying. I'm not proud of this trait but it has helped me to survive.'

'And you think I'm not being honest . . . that I want something from you?'

'I suspect we'll find out,' she said, diplomatically evasive but hardly putting him at ease. 'But not tonight. Now I must go home.'

'The tart?'

She sighed. 'Tomorrow. If it's not raining, we can picnic.'

'And if it is raining?'

'We'll decide then.'

'When?'

Katerina took in an audible breath as she considered her options. 'Do you mean your day is free?'

'It is. I was having a few days to myself, which is why I was able to read the newspaper on a garden bench mid-morning.'

'All right, then. I shall be calling into the museum tomorrow mid-morning to meet with my colleagues. I need to let them know I'm fine, and . . . well, anyway, how about you meet me at the Tuileries?'

'The pond?'

'Perfect. Shall we say noon?'

'We shall. Let me fetch your things and we can hail a taxi.' He returned with her coat and held it for her.

'Thank you.' As she put on her hat and wrapped her scarf with practised ease, he watched her carefully pull on her slim leather gloves. 'It's been lovely to meet you, Daniel. You've been most generous.'

'Will you be all right?' At her look of enquiry, he shrugged. 'I feel I've helped you to open a long-hidden wound.'

She nodded. 'You could say that. But it's the inevitable lancing of a wound that hasn't healed. I had to face this conversation after what occurred in London.'

He frowned.

'You'll have to wait until tomorrow to learn about that.'

'I shan't be able to sleep!'

'Take a pill. It's what I intend to do, because now the thoughts are free to roam, I need sleep of the entirely unconscious type. Don't come down – I'll get a taxi at the end of this street easily enough and I can avoid your neighbour if I tiptoe down alone. Will you explain to her?'

He nodded.

'Goodnight, Daniel.' She leaned in and kissed him on each cheek, turning swiftly on her heel, and was gone. She never saw him reach to touch his skin where her lips had pecked gently, nor did she look back to where he watched her glide down the darkening street away from him.

9

HAMPSTEAD, LONDON

April 1963

He glanced out of the window into the late afternoon, hopes rising; this was his favourite time of year. Spring had arrived and the days, though still chilled, brought him the happier mood that came with the season of new life. Buds were bursting into colour, the sun was no longer thin and gave genuine warmth to the day, while the birds and animals of the surrounding heath were busy at their parenting. But most of all Hersh Adler – as he would prefer to be known – loved this moment because he knew it was only perhaps only a fortnight away before the swimmers, anglers and picnic parties began to return in numbers to enjoy the famous Hampstead Ponds of his neighbourhood. By May, he would be back into the swing of his role as a pool attendant and working long into the delicious English twilight.

It wasn't a slight to his parents; he had done his best to explain this longing to his mother. Yes, he led a good life, knew that he was loved, was fully aware that as their only child he had a secure future to take over the grocery store when his father retired. He was grateful that in the meantime he earned a generous wage working alongside his parents in the shop. He had repeatedly reassured his mother that his need to volunteer at the swimming ponds was not him turning away from the family he loved but simply an attempt to learn about his past, from where he came and to whom he originally belonged.

'You belong here, Henry.' His mother had never felt comfortable calling him by his real name. 'Why do you need to be Jewish when you've been raised in an Anglican family? You've never known any other life but this one.' It was an old argument that had been debated since he'd turned sixteen. This was simply last night's version.

'Because, Mum, I *am* Jewish. Somewhere in Czechoslovakia is a Jewish family that once had a son called Hersh Adler.' He remembered how he'd held up his hand to stop her inevitable rush of words. 'I understand they are likely dead. But what if one of them survived? What if I have a brother or sister?'

His mother didn't answer. He wondered if she cared about his lost family, whether she wanted to mutter '*So what?*' to his question. He couldn't blame her for feeling threatened and she'd been the most loving and dedicated of mothers, so he had no doubt that from her perspective this was a treachery . . . and it hurt.

'Son,' his father had said quietly from his armchair in the corner – he liked to read his newspaper from this spot while gently puffing on his pipe when the shop closed early – 'what your mother is trying to do is save you pain. We've never hidden from you the truth that your family sent you to safety in England and we were chosen as the lucky recipients of a bonny ten-month-old from Prague and that you are Jewish. But over two decades have gone by and the world knows you as Henry Evans, son of Helen and John – is that so bad?' Hersh had hung his head, hearing the unsaid accusation. 'We only want the best for you. We want to give you everything we can for a good life ahead.'

'I know, Dad. I'm not ungrateful. But both of you obviously think that my looking out for information on the Adler family is somehow a threat to what I feel for you. And it isn't. I don't know anyone else as my mother and father – so how I feel about you both is never going to change.'

'Good,' his mother said, pursing her lips to stop them wobbling.

He took a breath, not wishing to hurt the people he loved most. 'But what else is never going to change is that England might refer to me as Henry Evans, but I was born Hersh Adler in Prague, I am Jewish and I have Czech in my soul. If there's any chance of at least knowing the people or even people who knew the family I came from, that would set me at ease.' He nearly felt out of breath but he didn't want to be interrupted. He inhaled now. 'I'm not looking to do anything with the information other than to understand myself. I feel —' He stopped, shaking his head.

'What, son?'

He gave his father a smile. 'I suppose, Dad, that I feel incomplete . . . restless to know my past, who I really am. And what I'm doing by volunteering at the Ponds – apart from keeping people safe – is keeping up with the latest news. Someone might know someone . . . don't you see?'

'Of course we do!' his mother said. 'But what good will it do you, Henry, to learn your whole family was killed in one of those terrible camps? How will that help?'

His gaze softened as her eyes became glassy with the tears she'd been fighting. 'Then I'll know they're dead, and . . .' He shook his head. 'It would be like closing a book. The wondering will end.'

Older, wiser, different words, different moods, different seasons, but it was essentially the same conversation with the same outcome of an upset mother and a disappointed father.

'I won't be long,' Henry said a little later after sharing a more convivial conversation over a pot of tea with his parents.

'No one will be swimming now, surely?' his mother quizzed.

'I'm just going for a walk – stretch my legs and get some air. Tomorrow's a big day. Dad and I are putting through the monthly order.'

She touched his cheek as he kissed her.

'See you a bit later, Dad.'

His father glanced at the clock on the mantelpiece. 'Are you going to listen to the next instalment of *The Archers* with us?'

Hersh looked at his wristwatch. 'Thirty-one minutes? I'll be back in half an hour.' He grinned. 'Promise.'

He left their terraced home in Pilgrim's Lane at a trot and headed towards Willow Road and the sprawling woodland and gardens of the Heath, towards the swimming ponds. He'd read about its history at the local library. Fed by the River Fleet, they were originally dug into impervious clay as reservoirs in the seventeenth and eighteenth centuries. Today the three ponds closest to his home served as outdoor men's, women's and mixed-bathing pools. Many of London's Jewish community lived in and around the Hampstead region and so it was natural that they would gather in the warmer months to picnic, for walks, to push their children in prams, to play and to swim in this place. That latter pastime required supervision, and as a powerful swimmer who'd chosen not to take his prowess further than his regular exercise, he was warmly welcomed into the group of volunteer attendants.

It was here, though, where so many of the Jewish community gathered, that he could share news of 'home'. He'd found a small cohort of Czech Jews, refugees, all mothers who gathered for a gossip, usually after the children had been dropped at school. Now, after years of seeing him around the pools, they were no longer wary of him stopping to chat.

They called him Hersh, which was pleasing but somehow – he couldn't entirely explain why – the name had never sat easily on him. This was why being referred to as Henry by his family, their friends, his friends at the neighbourhood school and now at work, felt easy. His mother had even begun muttering about changing his name officially to Evans . . . and perhaps one day soon he would agree to that. Hersh still clung to the hope that he might find his way back to his family, which had been the intention of the parents of *Kindertransport* children, though that had been impossible for most since the atrocities of the war on Jewish folk had been revealed. In the meantime, he probed for any information that could lead him to the Adlers of Prague who gave up their infant son to the safety of strangers in a faraway country rather than risk him to the Nazi occupiers.

He tracked away from the main road and the ripe whiff rising up through a manhole from the sewer below to his favourite path that took him between tall hedgerows of woodland hawthorn and oaks behind them. Sycamores prospered like weeds in the grassy areas and ivy clambered around anything it could find purchase upon. The early evening light was dappled through the trees and landed on him as soft as a mother's kiss.

He thought about his real mother, the one who had given birth to him. She would have been dark-haired, he imagined, but did he get his height from her or from the man she married? His father . . . he wanted to know him! He only allowed himself to think about the Jewish family when he was here, on the Heath, where he felt more like Hersh and rarely like Henry. He'd taken to wearing a *kippah* now and then when he was on these pathways; had hidden one in the crook of an oak branch. He didn't consider himself religious. *I just want to know what it's like*, he'd thought. He didn't wear it often – just when he was feeling angry at not knowing the truth of his life. The anger came in unannounced waves; he didn't raise his voice or lose his calm. Instead he felt his mood dip for no reason and he'd try and explain again to his parents and inadvertently bring his mother to tears and watch disappointment in his father's gaze . . . in eyes of grey-blue. Both his parents were fair and blue-eyed.

So, did he look like his true father, then? The strangeness of his eye; was that the mark of his line? Did anyone else have the mote? Did they survive the war? If not, where did they perish? So many questions, the main one being: was it hard to give him up? Did they send other children away? Was he missed? Did she sing him a final lullaby? Why did they choose Hersh as his name? Why didn't it feel comfortable on him?

'Hello, Hersh.' An oval-faced girl with luxuriantly springy hair, the colour of the oak bark in winter, was smiling at him. Eyes darkened green, with a hint of copper warming them, regarded him and he felt the heat of the message they sent.

'Oh, hello, Nissa. I didn't see you coming around that bend.' They hadn't known each other long, only meeting at the end of last autumn.

Her smiled widened with invitation. 'We're taking little Michael out for some air.'

Hersh crouched to tickle the infant's chin.

'He cries and the only thing that soothes him sometimes is tucking him into his pram and walking around for an hour. Does us all good.' She grinned.

'Where's his mum?'

'Ruth's back up the path with my parents.'

He stood up. 'It's mild enough that everyone should be out and about.'

'It is.' They stared at each other awkwardly while the baby gurgled beneath them. Too late, he heard voices of imminent arrival. 'Oh, here they come,' she warned, making it sound casual.

Hersh regretted his hesitation but smiled in greeting at the new arrivals. 'Good evening, Mr and Mrs Gellner. Hello, Ruth.'

'Enjoying this lovely evening, Hersh?' Mr Gellner asked.

'I am, sir. Did you see anyone swimming?'

'None. They'd be fools if they were. It has to be freezing in that water.'

Hersh laughed. 'And still they do.'

'How are Mr and Mrs Evans?' Mrs Gellner asked. 'I must pay a visit to your mother. I promised to make some poppyseed cake for her. She wants the recipe too.'

'I don't blame her. Yours is the best.'

She flicked away his praise but clearly enjoyed it all the same.

'They're both very well, thank you,' he continued, 'and waiting for me to return so we can listen to *The Archers*.' He grinned.

Both women checked their watches with sudden alarm, while their youngest daughter, Nissa, didn't take her gaze from Hersh.

'Come on, Ruth. We'll miss it,' Mrs Gellner urged, all of the other Gellners sufficiently distracted not to notice Nissa's shy smile at the young man in their midst. *Ask me,* it said, *and I'll say yes.*

He felt himself colouring as a result. Soon he'd find the courage to take her out . . . perhaps even kiss her. He'd have to steal it, though, for her parents may not approve of the Jewish boy with the blond Anglican parents with their Welsh surname. Nevertheless, if he didn't change his name and remained Hersh Adler, they wouldn't disapprove, especially of a potential husband with a flourishing business he would inherit.

'Our best to your parents, Hersh,' Mrs Gellner said, squeezing his wrist.

He nodded with a smile, robbed another glance from Nissa and realised he still had his hand on the pram handle. He let go as if slapped for his impertinence.

'Oh, Hersh, before I forget,' Mr Gellner said, 'there was a most interesting program last night on the wireless. It was about the *Kindertransports* from Prague. They were interviewing its hero, Nicholas Winton. Did you listen in?'

Hersh frowned, shaking his head.

'Pity. It was very moving, particularly when he spoke about how brave and trusting the parents were to hand over their children to strangers on a train platform. It made me think of your precious family in Prague that went through this trauma.'

Hersh felt like Mr Gellner was tapping into his thoughts. 'I often think about that time too,' he said, careful with his choice of words.

'Yes, I don't doubt. Until I listened to him I'd only considered the *Kindertransports* as a generous opportunity to help a desperate situation. I hadn't fully contemplated the emotional struggle for the mothers giving up babes in arms, infants on their hips . . . little ones they adored. Mr Winton spoke of the despair and how some mothers panicked and struggled to let go of their children in the final moments – there were a couple he mentioned whose mothers in the moment simply refused.'

'How sad for them all.'

'Exactly. "Damned either way" is essentially how Winton described it. He felt only deep sorrow for those women who did walk back into the city of Prague with their children who had been destined for the safety of Britain and from thereon faced an unknown future.'

'What a waste of a seat to freedom.'

'Oh, well, I gather there were any number of willing parents, certainly by the final two trains, so terrified of what was happening in Prague that they offered up their children on the spot. No luggage, no paperwork, no guidance . . . I've been trying to imagine making the snap decision to kiss tiny Michael here goodbye, knowing it was almost certainly the last time I'd see him.'

'Papa, stop!' Ruth chided gently.

Mr Gellner shrugged. 'I'm just saying, we are one of the most fortunate families that escaped. Hersh's mother, who presumably wasn't so fortunate, did something more brave than we can imagine to protect him.' He cut a look at Hersh. 'Forgive me, I hope you don't mind me mentioning that?'

'No, sir, and I've never thought of it that way,' Hersh admitted, and it felt like a door had opened in his mind.

'God cannot be everywhere at once. That is why He created mothers,' Gellner said in a gentle tone. 'That's Rudyard Kipling, although I'm sure I haven't quoted it correctly.' He grinned. 'But you catch my drift. Goodnight, Hersh.'

They parted and Hersh began a slow loop past the mixed bathing pond and back to the main road. It should get him home in time to share the country's favourite radio program with his parents.

His mind was not on the fictional English village of Ambridge, though. It was in Prague – not that he knew what Prague looked or felt like, but he'd read much about it in his local library and the British Library and had come to the conclusion that he had been born in one of the world's most beautiful capitals. But where was the family who had lived there with him? He would keep hunting, listening out for news, and maybe he should try and learn more about the *Kindertransports* themselves.

10

They had arranged to meet at the Grand Basin in the Tuileries Gardens.

'Be prepared to fight for a chair,' Daniel had quipped.

Katerina arrived first, or so she thought. And she arrived earlier than noon so that seats were freely available. She paid her sixty centimes for two and chose a pair at the southern end that put her back to the Louvre to give her the view that never got old for her. She could gaze directly through the Grande Allée of the gardens all the way to the Place de la Concorde and on to L'Arc de Triomphe at the top of the Champs-Élysées. Tourists often remarked on and travel writers wrote of the straight line through these gardens. It might appear that way, she thought, knowing the truth that it was far from a perfect line; the unsuspecting eye could be tricked.

It was a typically clear spring morning in Paris: sparkly, as though viewing the day through a crystal, but the chill of its air hit the back of her throat like the sharp end of an icicle. It was definitely milder in London, but Paris would catch up and soon these gardens would be teeming with families, couples, friends and lovers strolling through their beauty.

'Good morning, Katerina,' Daniel said, moving into view from her right. She'd been looking for him and yet hadn't seen him steal up on her. She only knew it was him from his voice because despite her dark glasses, she still had to shield her gaze from the sharp sun slanting across her vision that turned Daniel into a dark shape. She could tell he was lifting his hat politely from that thatch of dark hair. 'May I join you?'

'Of course. I even saved you a seat . . . and didn't have to claw anyone's face to hang onto it.'

He shrugged. 'You know how it can be in summer. We could have had a free bench seat near the bush.'

'We could have,' she said, rewrapping her thick scarf to cover her neck and shoulders. She was well rugged up in fur-lined boots and gloves too. Katerina reached into her bag for cigarettes; her first of the day. 'But I chose these individual chairs that feel recklessly decadent at thirty cents each.' She threw him a grin as she made to light up.

He surprised her by reaching for her wrist to stop her progress. 'Did you have breakfast?'

She cut him a playful glare.

'Good,' he said, 'because I brought it, even though it's near midday.' From the bag she hadn't noticed him carrying he pulled out a thermos. 'Tar-black Colombian coffee, unsweetened,' he said, holding it up with a flourish. 'Put those things away,' he said, feigning disgust at her Pall Malls. She'd only smoked a handful since London. 'Happy breakfast.' He had also brought thick slices of his neighbour's glossy tart but her attention was on the caffeine.

'You are civilised.' She grinned.

He poured them each a cup into a plastic beaker. 'Black or red?'

'Both a bit Nazi,' she quipped in a whisper only for his hearing and he shocked himself as he exploded into laughter.

'I wasn't ready for that.'

'Yes, must be careful who overhears. Not an amusing topic. But I'll take black for my mood.'

'Really?'

She shook her head. 'Gallows humour, forgive me. It's just, I know where our conversation is headed and I'm afraid to confront it.'

'No need to yet,' he said. 'Or ever,' he added with a sad smile. She couldn't tell if he meant it. 'Let's enjoy this wonderful space for an unguarded while as friends.'

'All right.' She sipped.

'Is it good?'

'Delicious, thank you. So . . . did you know that we're sitting on the Historical Axis?'

'We are?'

'Yes. More to the point, we are oriented on a precise 26-degree angle that follows the course of the sun from its rising in the east,' she said, pointing her long arm away from the right angle as she squinted again into its brightness, 'to where it sets, west of Paris.' The movement across his sightline shifted his vision to his left. 'This is the identical orientation of Notre-Dame Cathedral, so we can begin to understand that this is not just a series of monuments along a designer's ideal aesthetic. There is symbolism at work.'

'What are you suggesting? A conspiracy?'

She shrugged. 'Not really, but perhaps a secret plan. We don't know . . . Freemasons, Egyptology . . . it's open to interpretation, but it's rather nice to think there might be some obscure mystery in how our grand monuments have evolved.'

'You mean down the generations from architect to engineer, to designer or artist?'

She nodded and he shook his head in wonder. 'You have surprised me.'

'Consider the three arches: the Carrousel, the Arc de Triomphe and the Grande Arche?'

He nodded.

'The Carrousel was first. The Arc de Triomphe doubled its size. And then the third doubles the size of the one before. Coincidence?'

He shrugged. 'You tell me.'

'We don't know.' She laughed. 'But just to keep you awake at night I'm also going to tell you that the distance from the Carrousel to the Obelisk is one kilometre. And from there to the Arc de Triomphe is two kilometres.'

'And to the Grande Arche it's four, right?' he stated, his expression quizzing in disbelief.

'Correct. Still coincidence, you think?'

'And it ends at the Grande Arche?'

'No, I think generations of architects and designers will enjoy playing with the notion that the Historical Axis has its mystery and they will pay attention to what has gone before . . . following the seeming rules and the meander of the Seine.'

'All the way to the forest of Saint-Germain-en-Laye?'

'Perhaps. The Sun King would surely approve.'

Daniel laughed. 'Well, I love what I'm looking at,' he said, and when she turned to regard him and noted he was staring at her, he shifted his gaze and cleared his throat. 'Look how far we can see from here. All the way up that grandest of avenues.'

'It's intentional, let me assure you, that our eyes are led to that wide Champs-Élysées. Fields of Elysian,' she said, translating the true meaning of the boulevard's name into English suddenly. 'Heaven on Earth.'

'And expensive too,' he added to make her smile, and offering to take her beaker. 'Finished?'

'Mmm, yes. I hope you're not going to complain if I smoke and don't eat any tart?'

'I won't. You make smoking look elegant.'

'Helps me to think.' She took her time lighting up the Pall Mall and once again Daniel kept his counsel, spending the time emptying the dregs of the cups and returning the thermos and uneaten tart to the bag. Katerina blew out the smoke from her first short pull on the cigarette, and while the second drag and subsequent release steered her into the calm she needed, she realised she likely wouldn't finish the packet of cigarettes. She'd keep them as a souvenir of London, or perhaps a reminder of the sharp turn her life was taking. 'Shall I continue?'

'Please. I recall you had arrived at your family's country house, reunited with your parents. October 1941, I believe?'

'Very good, Daniel. You are paying attention, aren't you?'

He didn't reply. She took a third puff on the cigarette and began to talk, sitting forward to hug her own body's warmth. She did not remove her sunglasses.

Being intact as a family again, and all of us feeling safer than we had in many months, prompted a small celebration after a few weeks of settling in. Even my mother seemed to climb out of her gloomy shell for a brief time and she was vaguely animated when she cooked for us, with my father's help. I often offered to assist with the preparations but he shooed us all from her kitchen.

'Let her potter in her favourite space.' He shrugged. 'Who knows, the familiarity and all of us in such good moods may help her to find her way back.'

I gave a sound of exasperation, shaking my head at his rationale, but it occurred to me that perhaps it pleased him to see her busy, even if all we ended up with was porridge or eggs. I think I'd forgotten in the scenario of me . . . us . . . losing our mother to her misery at the death of Petr and the arrival of war, that my father had lost the love of his life. So I found a smile for him and nodded. 'What can I do, then?'

He walked back into the parlour and put an arm around our mother. I heard him whisper but couldn't hear the words. She came back with him, much to my surprise.

'Why don't you and the girls pick some mushrooms for us?' It was wonderful to hear her sounding so normal and I hugged her tight. I suspected it wouldn't last but while it did I wanted to enjoy it. 'It rained yesterday so it's perfect mushroom-hunting time. I'll make some kyselo,' she promised and there was the smile I'd grown up being loved by.

The thought of the hearty mushroom and sourdough soup made my mouth dampen with anticipation. I rounded up my sisters and after much back and forth over which hat and mittens belonged to whom, we clambered into boots, scarves and overcoats and proceeded out into the garden, towards the back gate. I looked back to wave at my father, whose eyes were moist with what I took to be both relief and tenderness for us together.

Our garden gate, which led into the forest surrounding the villa, sat within a dry-stone wall that I remember my father building when I was probably not much older than six. Now juvenile ivy leaves reached out on slender creeping shoots, finding every nook and cranny of the stones to cling within, while the larger adult leaves layered themselves individually over those stone pillars to catch whatever sunlight they could. It was effectively a gown of glossy emerald leaves and this threshold we crossed always gave me the impression we were entering a fairyland.

I think I probably needed this vision of leaving behind the sadness of our reality and moving into a magical world where all that resonated was the singing of birds, the vague rustle of small creatures in the undergrowth, the odd flash of a startled rabbit's fluffy tail and the promise of autumn mushrooms. October was the *perfect time to be searching out our quarry and it didn't take long to start filling a basket with fat brown-capped fungi that had pushed their way to the surface over the last few days. My mother hadn't lied; the ground was spongy from the rain and smelled of damp leaf litter while the air was scented with a primitive, earthy aroma that spoke of something meaty and rich. While my mother would gladly accept the pravák mushroom – a simple wild edible fungus, with a small tight cap and a bulbous stem that likes spruce forests – I knew she'd love to see us troop in with a basket of delicate chanterelles, famed in this region.*

'You need to find a smell that reminds you of apricots,' Lotte told us, sniffing a beauty she'd picked. 'And if they're leaning towards orange rather than yellow, ever-so-slightly darker at their centre . . .' She bent down and picked one from the ground. 'This is what we want – only the genuine chanterelle with wrinkles but not gills.' She sounded so like our mother I had to smile.

Hana was grimacing at the basket full of mushrooms the colour of egg yolks. 'Why they can't look entirely different is stupid. What's the point?'

Her twin, Ettel, grinned. 'Well, we're not identical but most people can't tell us apart, can they? And there's surely some point to us.'

'Two delicious ripe mushrooms,' I remarked absently in response as I moved in on a rich clutch of the fungi.

For some reason this tickled the girls and they peeled off in gales of laughter. Lotte and I threw each other a mildly exasperated glance that turned to chuckles, mostly I think from the novelty of hearing laughter coming from our siblings. It was a rare sound.

We wended our way slowly back to the villa and could see the red tiles of its roof glimmering through the tall trees as the ter-racotta caught autumn's thinned sunlight. The rain had coaxed the forest floor into yielding its mushrooms but the sun was warming it and the trees releasing their oils. We walked through a perfumed cathedral that reminded me of citrus peel as much as fresh herbs and newly mown grass.

We arrived back at the house chattering, with steam billowing from our mouths, pinched cold cheeks and much warmer, fuller hearts than a few days before.

Our mother seemed pleased to see our basket; it caused her to smile, which in itself was a balm, but when she touched the cheeks of the twins I teared up and had to leave the kitchen as talk of soup began in earnest. This was to be followed by stuffed goose necks that my father had managed to purchase. And he'd also hunted down enough ingredients – I don't know how he acquired them – for a fruity sweet bread that he'd assured us he was going to bake. Its real name was bublanina but we called it bubble cake. Us girls were banished to go off and read, play – whatever we felt like – and our parents were going to prepare tonight's feast. I decided I would provide music for the preparations and so I lifted the lid on the piano, and after many weeks of not feeling like creating sound from those keys, I closed my eyes and allowed a complex piece – it was Liszt – to emanate from our music room. 'Un Sospiro', it was called. I was aware that I was a gifted and indeed ambitious pianist with a private dream to give concert recitals around the world but this was a solo that I was yet to master, especially its rolling melody that was passionate, searching, desperately romantic . . .

Everyone else in the villa would have only heard its beautiful music but for me it was about all that was lost to me. 'Un Sospiro' means a sigh, and that was precisely my mood. All that could have been: the romances, my career, falling in love, sharing a life, building a family, the fashion I loved, my music, my art, my passion for antique jewellery . . . All of it lost. All of that sadness somehow turned into an uplifting but simple melody that was nonetheless complicated by the need to cross hands constantly across the keys.

My left mostly played the harmony while my right took care of the main melody – like two halves. My life had become that. One half of me allowing myself to dream because in dreams lives hope, but the other half of me that faced daily life knew there was no hope.

I was into the most complex part of the solo when I thought I heard the bell on our door jangling.

Before I could end my piece, my father stepped into the room with a visitor . . . and this was the moment I remember with more clarity than any other, for it was the moment all of our lives changed irrevocably.

———

Katerina realised that Daniel was sitting forward too and he'd lightly covered her gloved hand with his.

'Are you all right?'

She nodded but it was a lie.

'Come on, let's move or we'll seize up.'

'Move to where?'

He shrugged. 'Let's just walk. It will warm us up. How about we make for the Hôtel de Crillon? We can —'

'Are you mad? I'm not dressed for the Crillon.'

'Katerina, you are always dressed for the Crillon! Even going to work you look like you could step right onto a catwalk.'

She gave him a look of soft exasperation.

'Anyway, who cares? All right, we walk and we can double back onto the Left Bank. I know a tiny hotel in St Germain where we can sit by a fire and have another coffee.'

'All right.'

They stood and stretched, and Daniel gestured up the gardens so they could trace a path to the northern end, where Katerina recalled that centuries previous Marie Antoinette, deposed Queen of France, had been driven on a cart pulled by two white horses.

'I thought the guillotine was closer to l'Orangerie?' Daniel queried.

'The guillotine was moved to near the steps we're walking towards,' she confirmed. 'Here she was able to look at her former palace and gardens, above which stood the glinting guillotine on a clear autumn day. King Louis XVI was executed the previous year and shown courtesies that she was not,' Katerina noted. 'She stepped onto the scaffold unassisted. The story goes that she even had the composure to apologise to the executioner for accidentally treading on his toe, although I often wonder if it was the former Queen's final defiance. She lost her head to cheering crowds a fortnight before her thirty-eighth birthday.'

'She had a trial, at least. Not like our people, persecuted and executed because we somehow offended a single man's ideal.'

They were approaching the Octogonal Bassin. More people had gathered here on this fine day; a small troupe of children were floating paper boats.

'We'll go up the steps, trace around Place de la Concorde and move back onto the Left Bank. Look in on some of the booksellers.'

'Sounds good. Talking over the past feels cathartic, although I wonder if we spoke to the girl on the cusp of womanhood, whether she would be more anxious about missing school and her friends than worrying about the loss her future dreams.' She sighed. 'Shall I continue my recollections?'

'Only if you want to,' he lied, trying to keep the desperation from his voice, as they began to ascend the northern stairs and move towards the Left Bank.

It was Ruda Mayek who had entered our home.

'Oh, my darling, don't stop on my account,' he urged, that

familiar unsettling gaze arcing across the room to land upon me: all of me. I'd never fully understood if he despised me or found me attractive, but if we were ever together in a room, his impaling look never strayed far from me.

Ruda had been visiting our villa since before I was born. As a boy he had come with his father to hunt; his father, perhaps two decades older than mine, was full of wisdom about the region that my parents had purchased into as their summer playground and was somewhat of a father figure to them. Before our villa began to fill with the sounds of children and he began to suffer some illnesses, he was a regular dinner guest. I never knew him but his son and only child continued the family friendship as he became a man.

Most of us change in looks as we grow from children into adults; some of us begin chubby and become gangly, while other infants don't show any of the promise of the beauty to come. Ruda Mayek seemed to be in a special class, though. According to my parents he was 'the most beautiful child they had ever laid eyes upon'.

My mother said his hair as a youngster could appear white sometimes, it was so fair, and in his early years his eyes always seemed too large for his face, but the oddity served him well, making him appear angelic and other-worldy. 'His eyes possessed a crystalline quality like the waters of our spring in the mountains but rimmed by a thin, defining circle of navy,' she'd explained once.

'Yes, it gave the impression that he was always looking into you,' my father had commented with a baffled shake of his head. 'It could be disconcerting to be looked at so intimately by a youngster. Even when he was silent you always knew when Rudy was in the room; you could feel his gaze upon you.'

Rudy – his affectionate childhood name had remained with us – was in the middle of the music room now, his secretive smile touching me with the underlying suggestion that was always there

when he looked at me, his curious, pale eyes still ringed with darkness, still looking into me but also through me.

He was into his twenties when I came along, and was often
charged with watching over me as the new gurgling baby while our
parents ate together; his mother died young from influenza, as I
recall. By the time Lotte was born, and I was nearing four, Rudy
was heading back into the military for another few years, having
already done his service. His father mentioned that he may become
a career soldier and essentially he disappeared from our lives, other
than rare visits. When he returned for good we were all closing in
on a decade older and he was past six foot with a muscled frame he
carried surprisingly lightly on his long, lean legs. Now the yellowy-
white hair that had hung in careless waves when he was a youngster
was trimmed short, glistening against his scalp, and his pale skin
took the sun surprisingly easily so he appeared healthy from its
glow. The squarish face that I remembered as a little girl had turned
squarer still and his jaw had lost its youth to become defined,
shaven closely to reveal the neatest of mouths – thin, actually –
behind which I knew sat two equally neat rows of small teeth that
I recall he always took great care with.

'Brush your teeth diligently, Katka' – his friendly name for me
that I privately resented – 'because your smile is what gets noticed
first . . . and then your beautiful hair, of course.' He said this to me
when I was around eight and he was a man approaching thirty.
He'd arrived for supper and had come up to say goodnight. As the
eldest I got a room to myself and the privacy it afforded.

To be fair, I had liked Rudy as a small child. He was as interested in me as he was in the adults; he found time to push me on my
swing, teach me how to climb trees. He seemed to enjoy my childish
conversations, took genuine interest in my musical ability and made
me laugh. But, for the first time, in my quiet room, the other
children asleep, my parents' voices drifting up from the kitchen,

I felt deeply uncomfortable. For the first time in my life I felt cornered . . . hunted.

I was in my nightdress, my hair plaited either side, and he smelled of the forest, bringing a sharp, fresh bouquet of the resin from the pines and spruce. He sat on the bed I was yet to clamber into, his clean smell matching his precise, neat clothes. His family were not wealthy but Rudy took pride in his appearance, and as young as I was I sensed he enjoyed all the attention that his striking appearance won him.

'I came up to give you a kiss goodnight, Katka. Is that all right? I didn't want to miss you.'

He looked huge in my small bedroom, as though his shoulders could touch either wall. What could I do but nod?

'Here, let me help tuck you in?'

I hesitated mainly because it was unusual; Rudy may not have been a stranger to our family but something inside was giving me pause. I was too young to understand what it was warning me against. 'Is my papa coming up? He normally tucks me in,' I said, animal instinct taking over. His hand lay motionless on the turned-back covers in a gesture of welcome.

'Yes, of course. He'll be up shortly. In you go,' he said, his tone light and friendly.

I had no choice, and as I clambered in I felt that same hand running up my calf. At first I just thought it was him assisting, accidentally grazing my skin, but then the pressure changed and I could feel him reaching as high as my naked bottom beneath my nightie. It caressed and squeezed. I froze and it was removed quickly, as though his hand had indeed simply slipped as he'd helped me in. 'There,' he said, tone still light and affectionate. 'Comfy?'

I nodded. I wasn't scared yet so much as confused. I was having bad thoughts about someone who surely didn't deserve it; the doubt made me tense and silent. But then I felt his hand slipping beneath the covers again and I knew it was real and the family friend we were meant to trust was breaching it in the most unimaginable way. I couldn't cry out, I couldn't move; I stiffened in terror like the tiny creature I was beneath the bulk of the huge predator that was stroking my leg, getting closer to the top of my thigh and what sat between my thighs.

'You are so beautiful, Katka. Who will rival your looks in years to come?' he cooed. His voice had lost its lightness and now sounded thick, as though he was fighting to keep it under control. 'You are going to be the most desirable young woman in all of Czechoslovakia, do you know that?'

I didn't answer; I couldn't shake my head, let alone voice anything. I was as chilled as the snow crystals that hung on the branches of the fir trees outside. That smell of the conifers I would thereon always associate with Ruda Mayek.

'Little Katka, such a tease. You used to excite me when you bounced on my knee as a tiny, giggling girl, and I used to love standing at the bottom of the tree watching you climb . . . you had such lean thighs beneath your frock. Pushing you on that swing – it's why I liked to face you, Katka; you'd scream with pleasure when I pushed you hard and you'd open your legs to steady yourself as you rushed back towards me.'

All of this was said in a soft conversational tone as though he were soothing me off to sleep.

'I used to imagine you screaming as a grown woman beneath my touch.'

He seemed to shudder and then his hand touched the most secret part of me. I seem to remember being grateful for the small mercy that his lids closed over his penetrating stare in that moment. He let out a sigh, and while I didn't understand what the frightening bulge in his trousers meant, my instincts told me this was my chance and I finally found the courage to draw back a breath to scream.

Perhaps he heard that intake, or rather he sensed its potential, but while his hand whipped away from me, the other covered the yell and I tasted the pine forest. His stare forbade me and he shook his head slowly with what I felt was menace, although I couldn't articulate that then. I know I felt more frightened by his narrowed gaze, which had turned so cold and forbidding it was like the promise of winter for the rest of my life if I said anything, and I began to tremble.

Then, suddenly, the Rudy my family knew was back and he was smiling, busily tucking me into my sheets, making sure the feather coverlet was plumped around my chin to make me feel safe. My breath was still trapped in my chest but I carefully watched him reach for a book from the nearby shelf to place across his lap and within moments he was reading aloud to me. His voice had lost that tight, throaty quality and his eyes were wide open now. From time to time they glanced at me as if to check I was enjoying the story but no doubt to ensure I was returning from shock. It was a surreal situation: I was tired, the story – 'Rumpelstiltskin', my favourite – was so familiar and comforting it was lulling me into a stupor that kept telling me what had happened was my mistake. I didn't need to be afraid any more, and when I heard the creak of the stairs and knew it to be my father's tread, relief washed through me. The pale gaze that gave me a final glance carried a nuance of warning that I guess all children understand, no matter how young we are.

Yes, I understood – Our secret, it said. I hadn't imagined it and I hadn't misunderstood. I knew I could never speak of it to anyone because he made me feel complicit in what had occurred.

11

● ● ●

She stopped talking. Silence trapped them in front of one of the second-hand booksellers and Daniel had the grace, she noted, to give her a moment to regroup her thoughts, while he no doubt feigned interest in the dusty tome he reached for.

The *bouquiniste* began talking to him about it being a first edition. Daniel glanced back at her as the man spoke and in that moment of heightened awareness Katerina could swear she felt his sorrow reaching out to offer comfort. Then he put halting words to it after smiling at the man and handing back the book.

He touched her elbow lightly and they continued walking. 'I don't know what to say that might help. I'm so sorry to hear this, Katerina. No child should . . .'

No. No child should, she thought as he left his remark unfinished. Katerina lifted a shoulder slightly, trying not to feel pity for herself. 'It was a long time ago,' she dismissed, masking how much it mattered.

'Your parents never knew?'

She shook her head. 'Because I never told them.'

'Why not?'

'How do you put that into words as a young child? Who would believe me that our family friend, so trusted, would do that to me? It's so shocking too that as the victim – especially one so young – you're not sure what it is, or why it happened; sometimes even *if* it happened. He made me feel that I caused it. Even now as I try and make sense of it I do so with an adult's perspective. But I was still a baby, really.'

'Did he . . . I mean how far . . .?' Daniel couldn't even say it.

She helped him out. 'No. But if we'd been alone for any longer . . .' She swallowed. 'I certainly sensed he was losing his inhibitions.'

Daniel murmured a curse of sorts that she couldn't hear but didn't need to in order to understand his revulsion.

'Late twenties, you say?'

'Thereabouts. And privately enraged with unfulfilled ambition.'

'To be what?'

'Rich and powerful; what else? His family came from modest means but their desire for wealth and status was tangible. It's why they befriended us, I'm sure. And looking back I can see how that whole family, including the mother when she was alive, coveted the world my parents lived within, both at Hvozdy and more so in Prague at the big house in its leafy neighbourhood of wealthy Czechs. One occasion when they visited – his father and he – I remember how Rudy's eyes in particular had burnt with something intangible. I think now that it was envy, and also anger that we, silly little children, had so much to look forward to.'

'You say your father saw the best in everyone, but rarely the flaws.'

'He took everyone at their word and believed only the best of each. The Mayeks had a voracious desire for status and wealth. Back then we simply gave and received friendship; we didn't realise they had an agenda.'

'What did his father do?'

'I think he was a councillor, so that gave him some standing in the community, and he ran the local grocery store. But while his son was pressed from a similar mould, it was the newer version.' Her tone had a cynical edge now. 'Rudy lusted for riches, status, but above all, the power and recognition that go with it.'

Daniel nodded and allowed a silence to lengthen between them.

She broke it first. 'Did you know these sellers were known as *bouquinistes*? Antiquarian books and the selling of them along the River Seine date back centuries.'

He smiled. 'I am convinced ancient history makes you feel safe.' She nodded. 'Let's wend our way to the hotel for something warming to drink. How about some cake?' He enjoyed the pleasant smirk of laughter this prompted. 'Katerina, you're so trim – thin, in fact – I don't think you ever have to worry about what you eat.'

'Years of restraint, I suppose. I learned to survive on very little.'

———

Daniel smiled as if he understood but of course he didn't. He hadn't had to survive more than the inconvenience of war. He'd only become involved militarily in the final year of the conflict and by then his clever mind had kept him on British soil, working for the government's war effort rather than as a soldier. Still, it wouldn't do to not empathise by trying to walk in her shoes.

Nevertheless, she'd delivered him. After years in the wilderness of information, this exquisite, damaged woman of Prague had brought Ruda Mayek, the monster he hunted, to his door.

Daniel had needed to restrain himself when she first mentioned the name. He'd known it was coming and still he'd wanted to jump to his feet and yell his excitement, but that would have given the wrong impression of his intention, and of course it would have frightened Katarina back into the shell where she hid. He, Daniel Horowitz, was likely the first person to coax this tale from its owner in more than two decades.

And he needed all of it because Katerina Kassowicz was going to lead him to Ruda Mayek, if the bastard was still alive . . . and if he was, then Daniel would take no small pleasure in delivering him from existence.

So, he didn't want to break the magical spell of this day that had coerced Katerina's memory into giving up its secrets. If she went home now, he might never see her again, least of all hear the rest of her story.

He'd led them to the hotel in St Germain that he'd promised. 'Come on, let's have a meal. Then you won't have to think about dinner,' he urged.

'I never think about dinner,' she quipped and he believed her.

'Yes, but I need feeding and it's past midday.'

As she agreed with a smile and watched him signal to the waiter that they would like a seat in the restaurant, she reminded him about a visitor from the United States who had caused a stir with his remarks about French eating habits. 'Do you remember?'

He shook his head.

'He was a sociologist and made the comment when interviewed that the French stick to a strict regimen of three meals a day and are happy to remain hungry in between.'

'Are we?'

'Oh, our children are given their *goûter* after school because they're famished, but do you eat anything between your meals?'

'I don't.'

'Well, there you are.'

The waiter had seated them and was flicking out napkins across their laps and handing them each a menu.

'And he made the observation that sticking to such strict meal-times was akin to living behind a cage in a zoo.'

Daniel laughed. 'Well, give me the French zoo any day to the American one!'

'*Touché*,' she said. 'Just a niçoise salad for me, please,' she said to the waiter.

'Two,' Daniel added. He was not famished but he liked that they were now anchored into seats and a situation conducive to talking. 'No wine. Perrier.'

'Very good, sir,' the man said and disappeared from their view.

'Happy?'

'That you're eating, yes,' he replied.

Katerina smiled. 'You're killing me.'

'Only with kindness,' he jested. 'Tell me about the Pearls.' It was the right moment to ask this. 'I mean, I want to hear what happened when you saw Ruda in the piano room that day when you were older, wiser to him, but the Pearls have me intrigued.' He'd diverted her to the jewellery because he was worried that she might be frightened to open the door onto what happened next with the monster of Hvozdy.

'Ah, the Pearls, yes,' she sighed. 'That part of my story really belongs to my mother. She first showed them to me when I turned thirteen.'

I laughed at my mother standing on a ladder, while the top half of her had disappeared into the roof. Her voice sounded muffled, captured by the musty yet somehow comforting air of our attic. Each of us had a trunk up there with old toys, curios, various memorabilia that seemed important for us – or our parents – to keep. None of us was allowed up the ladder for fear of falling, although I was nimble enough with all my tree-climbing expertise that I could have ascended at twice the speed and dexterity of either of my parents. Her legs disappeared now as she pulled herself into our attic.

'What are you looking for?' I yelled up. I could hear her creaking around, the timber struts gently protesting their irregular use. The chemical smell of naphthalene drifted down as my mother had clearly stirred something that had mothballs buried within.

'I want to show you something,' she called back and then I heard only murmured sounds. I waited, listening to the timber, knowing roughly whereabouts in the roof she was by those sounds. And finally I heard a yell of triumph. 'Here they are!' I could make out. 'I knew we'd brought them. Your father prefers to carry these with us each summer holiday here at the villa.'

Her legs reappeared, gingerly stepping down, feeling carefully for the next rung of the ladder. Dust motes floated down with her to catch the light and dance around us like tiny sprites.

I frowned. 'What is it?' I'd not seen this velvet bag previously, so now my curiosity was fully piqued.

'He couldn't bring the small chest they were originally in – it's bronze, decorated with ormolu, and very heavy. So that's back at home in the cellar,' she said, 'but we wanted you to see these at long last,' my mother continued, leading me to my parents' bedroom. I couldn't tell if the suspense was deliberately being built or if it was in my imagination. 'You're old enough now and soon eligible for the biannual ball hosted by the Baroness. I think we might work out how you might wear these for that special night.'

So she'd already given the main clue that this was jewellery. I waited as she laid out a velvet bag of rich carmine, the fabric so thick the folds held their shape to look like the ridges of the hills our villa sat amongst. She began to fuss with the golden plaited ties, as thick as my fingers, that bound the bag tightly at its top. *Education about art and antiquities at my father's coat-tails suggested that I was looking at something that may have belonged to the nobility, perhaps even royalty, given its colour.*

My mother lifted the contents halfway from their velvet prison and I gasped – predictably, I suppose – and my mother beamed, holding the Pearls half in, half out of the pouch.

'Darling Katerina, I wore these to my first ball and your grandmother wore them to hers. I hope you will have the opportunity to do the same. Once is enough, as it was for me and for your grandmother.'

I stared at the serpentine curves and drops of glimmering pearls and then my mother pulled what I could only describe as a rope of these lustrous stones free of the bag to reveal a teardrop-shaped gem, in the colour of the ancient ice of a glacier I'd seen in an encyclopaedia. And yet it was more cerulean than blue, now that I tore my gaze from the iridescent pearls to the gem itself.

'It's a sapphire, darling, from Kashmir in India's north, and many centuries ago it was apparently worn in the ceremonial headdress of the maharajah's favourite elephant!' she exclaimed, laughing at the notion. 'It was probably thieved and found its way into what is now Turkey, but back then was part of the Ottoman Empire. You really should get all this history from your father but in short, this piece was constructed at the behest of the king . . .'

'Sultan,' I corrected. I didn't mean to sound in any way haughty, but I was absorbed by the fascinating story and I wanted to be sure I understood it properly.

'Oh, yes, whatever he was called. He had a vast harem of women awaiting his pleasure. They were called his wives but as always there were favourites. The head wife was given a special name, not that I recall it —'

'She was called the sultana.'

Her mother waved the clarification aside. 'The story goes that she remained his favourite and these pearls were strung for her in early medieval times.'

'How were they worn?'

I remember how my mother tittered and then urged me to let her place them on me. I watched, fascinated, as she hung this carefully entwined single rope around me like a garment where it sat heavily sinuous, cold against the parts that touched my skin. I was tall for my age but the gemstone hung low on my belly. My mother smiled again. 'I'll tell you what that stone means and why it hangs where it does, darling, when you're old enough to understand.'

I looked back at her quizzically. 'Tell me now.'

She shook her head and grinned. 'Next year, maybe.'

'How did we come to have these?'

She told me what she could, but I learned they went back through generations. 'Do you like them?'

'They're beautiful.' I frowned. 'Why are you tasting them?' I asked, astonished.

She chuckled. 'Do this,' she explained and I followed her, lifting one of the fat, gleaming pearls to my mouth.

'Not tasting, testing,' my mother assured me. 'You know your father and his almost religious fervour for authenticity. He showed me this when they first came into our possession. What do you feel against your teeth?'

'I feel the grit of sand.'

'Good. I'll teach you what he taught me. I've never forgotten how amusing he made it sound. It's an old jeweller's trick. Your father explained these fabulous pearls were the work of a host of oysters who'd been so irritated by something foreign that had found its way into their shells that they began to coat it with a substance known as nacre, I'm sure he called it. It is this coating of calcium that produces the marvellous luminosity of a natural pearl, grown wild in the depths of waters either fresh or salty by a vexed mollusc, as he described it.'

I was young to be acquiring such sophisticated knowledge in jewellery, so that mental image of the angry oyster stuck with me. 'So many genuine and perfect pearls,' I breathed, testing a few more.

'Yes, my darling girl, and one day these will be yours. I told you they've been in my family for endless decades, handed down from mother to eldest daughter. They've always been known in our family as the Ottoman Pearls.'

I never did get to wear the Ottoman Pearls outside my mother's bedroom.

Katerina gave a fleeting polite smile to the waiter as the salads arrived; their leaves were crammed with tuna and studded with fat, black olives, both gleaming from the heavy drizzle of olive oil. '*Bon appétit*,' the man wished them.

'And now they've turned up at the British Museum,' Katerina concluded.

Daniel nodded his thanks, eager to be rid of the interruption. 'And you want to know who is selling them?'

'Not selling . . . not immediately, anyway,' she corrected, holding up a slender finger. 'They have been offered as an exhibit, although I gather they carry a caveat that should the British Museum wish to have them within its permanent collection, then it could purchase them.'

'I see.' He wasn't ready to push her into the inevitable. So again, with his renowned crocodile-like patience, he backtracked, pulling them both away from where he desperately wanted to lead

Katerina. He diverted her with his skill, making it sound effortlessly casual. 'I didn't know that about testing pearls.'

Masterfully distracted, she gave a soft smirk. 'It's a cursory test – a reliable one – as is the bounce test.'

'Bounce?'

'Fake pearls bounce high when dropped. A true pearl will only make it half the way back.'

He gave a tutting sound of pleasurable dismay. 'Anything else?'

She frowned, and he liked watching the arc of her eyebrows knit briefly. 'Obviously today there are more sophisticated ways. The museum will have the Pearls authenticated via X-ray, no doubt.' She prodded at her salad, very little making it onto her fork and ultimately her mouth. She chewed carefully before continuing. He found all her mannerisms addictive to observe. 'But my father said an old torch and a jeweller's loupe will give you most of what you need to know about whether they're natural or cultured. I should add that the more spherical the pearl, the more precious it is – so, the paler, the rounder, the bigger each sphere, the zeroes will just keep being added to their value. And each one of the pearls in that rope is near perfection in its roundness. And their colour . . .' she shook her head and he sensed sadness.

'Tell me.'

'I was simply recalling that if a pearl is creamy, that's one thing – it's what you'd expect. But the paler and silvered pink the pearl, the more iridescent it is, the more precious it becomes.'

He could guess. 'And I'm going to assume that each pearl in yours is not only perfectly round but perfectly pink?'

'Pinkish,' she qualified. 'You don't want *pink*, but you want the suggestion of it. The perfect pearl and thus the perfect set of pearls gives off a blush when in motion around its wearer, but there's a silvery quality like mercury to the very best.'

'They sound amazing, even without the sapphire.'

'They are unique. Priceless. Irreplaceable, dating back to the thirteenth century.'

He blew a soft whistle, genuinely impressed. 'I think you need to eat.'

'I think you need to stop mothering me,' she cautioned but with the softest smile he'd seen from her since their conversation had begun.

'It feels good to look after someone.'

'Is there no one in your life?'

'No one I choose to spend my life with, other than family.'

'But you live in France. Why?'

'Anonymity.' It was only a half lie.

She shook her head, looking back at him slightly perplexed. He sensed Katerina knew when a person needed their privacy; she'd presumably spent a lifetime guarding hers.

'Well, you're a good listener, Daniel.'

He liked to hear her say his name.

'You know more about me than any other living person,' she admitted. 'And I'm not sure how it's happened.' She waggled her finger. 'You have cast a spell on me.'

No, just a particular and well-honed set of skills, he thought.

'I can't remember the last time I allowed the memories such free rein.'

He waited.

'It's out now and I have no experience of how to pull it back into its box. I shall share it with you now and then perhaps I shall feel unburdened and able to walk away from it. Is it possible, I wonder?' she said now almost to herself, fork held in long fingers. 'That in getting it out, releasing all the pain, I can let it go? Perhaps not fully, but maybe I can live a life that doesn't taste so constantly bitter.' She gave him an unexpected and genuinely warm smile. 'I'm rambling to myself.'

'And the Ottoman Pearls?'

Her damaged gaze cut back from the window and across the table to him, sharp as cat claws. 'I don't know.'

He heard only the truth in her uncertainty.

'Apart from your family, who knows of their existence?'

'My parents didn't make a habit of discussing them and certainly not of revealing them to people. They were a showpiece and hardly something you'd pull on for an evening. They were an heirloom to be passed down, worn maybe once, perhaps twice on special occasions by the fortunate woman of the line.'

'You care about them, surely? I mean, they're yours.'

'They were meant for me. I've never taken ownership of them. I've never put them on since the day my mother placed them around me to demonstrate how they should be worn.'

'You want to claim them, though, right?'

'Do I?' She lifted a shoulder. 'I'm not convinced I need them in my life. They would only reinforce what I've lost and potentially become a fresh curse on a life that needs no more pain. I wouldn't have occasion to wear them, I wouldn't ever sell them, I wouldn't even want to look upon them, so there's no point.'

'But . . .'

'You can't walk in my shoes,' she said, her tone sad.

'I want to try. Finish your salad and your life story for me. I need to know it . . . all of it.'

'I can't eat any more.'

He looked at her plate of food, rummaged with but still nearly as full as when it had arrived.

'I insist you nibble on some more tuna and eat the boiled egg.'

'You're such a bully, Daniel.'

'I'll take that as a compliment. Right, eat while I order some coffee and then I want you to take us back to the moment Ruda walked in on you playing the piano.'

Soon enough coffee began bubbling on the small stove behind the bar and the smell of roasted beans gave up their parched smokiness into a fruited, spicy aroma that wafted across to envelop them. Katerina had swallowed two more mouthfuls from her salad and then pushed her plate forward. She began to speak as the plates were removed and fresh black coffee arrived before them.

12

● ● ●

'Oh, my darling, don't stop on my account,' Ruda Mayek said, but Liszt was lost to me.

I stood, shocked to see him. He glowed with health, as though some sort of new light that empowered him burnt within. He'd reached his late thirties and I could see his hair had darkened beneath but still had that overall whitish quality. It had receded at either side of his forehead but somehow that hadn't detracted from his strong Germanic looks. If anything, it added maturity.

'We have to call our old friend Mayor now,' my father told me, sounding amused. 'He did it.'

Rudy hadn't taken his gaze from me. I felt as though he was undressing me from afar.

'Congratulations,' I pushed out, smoothing my skirt, fingers suddenly clammy.

'Well, it's been a while, hasn't it?' he said and I glimpsed the small teeth. 'Must be half a dozen years, maybe longer, since we've all been together.' I nodded. 'And look at you, Katka, so grown-up, every bit as beautiful as we all knew you would be. You'll be breaking hearts by the time you turn sixteen.'

My father shrugged as if he had nothing to do with how I'd turned out, and when he reached for the door handle, his back to us, Rudy licked his lips, making sure I saw the gesture.

Memories I'd buried resurfaced and I felt like a frightened child again.

'Come on,' my father said. 'Let's be seated for our evening meal. Your mother has made her delicious kyselo.'

It was a rowdily happy supper, with the youngsters being more talkative than I could recall. Their cheeks were still pinched pink from their walk and the warmth of the house made the tops of their ears look dusted with rouge. For just a moment or two, I had a brief sense of security that the villa had closed its familiar and welcoming walls around us to keep us safe. But then I glanced at our guest and wished he were not present to spoil this interlude. My mother, sadly, did not emerge from the kitchen. I tried to persuade her to join us and share the food, but she'd withdrawn into herself again and preferred to eat quietly in the parlour.

Our guest barely noticed her absence and lacked the grace to enquire after her, which was odd in itself and should have told us that this wasn't the social visit he was making a pretence at. When my father mentioned that his wife had not been the same since the loss of our brother, Rudy gave a careless nod. 'I don't think I'll ever understand women,' he replied. I could see my father was cut by the lack of consideration in the remark, but he was too generous to show it.

'Well, it's best we let her be. Her soup speaks her love for all of us.'

I was required to serve and did my utmost not to tremble as I ladled the soup into Rudy's bowl.

'Why isn't this being served in a cob?' Lotte enquired. Perhaps she'd already forgotten rationing and who could blame her? Life at the villa felt almost normal.

'We couldn't get so much bread,' I cut in quickly.

'I can get as many loaves as you need, Katka. You just have to ask me nicely.' His tone was oily, his words slippery to match. The thought of owing Rudy anything terrified me suddenly.

'Do you have a uniform as mayor?' one of the twins enquired.

'Yes, I have rather a grand outfit I must wear on formal occasions,' he said. 'It's like dressing up for a pantomime.'

The girls giggled and Rudy spent the next few minutes entertaining them as we drank our soup and shared the single loaf we did have. I realised they were now around the age I had been when he violated me and I hated to watch him oozing his charm over two more innocents. Fortunately for me, I suppose, he had been away and hadn't had the opportunity to see me again. That would explain his surprise, for I had changed from child to teen – a mature one at that – in the intervening six years. I'd listened quietly to his conversation with my father about spending some time across the border in Germany, where much of his extended family lived. He'd worked alongside his uncle and cousins in manufacturing, and learned a lot about business, it seemed, and about being opportunistic.

'We helped equip the army,' he bragged. 'Our engineering firm became a munitions factory . . . I hope it's our weapons bombing London.' He laughed but no one else did.

His presence chilled me and the feeling was not just born from the early broken trust but the uneasiness that his discussion prompted. My father, I noted, was not speaking, just nodding – not agreeing but paying attention. I knew my father all too well, and I suspected he was listening more closely to what Ruda Mayek was not saying.

'Do you consider yourself German now?' It was a careful question but a pointed one from my father.

I don't think I wanted to hear his answer. 'Girls, help me clear the table,' I said, standing abruptly. 'I'll bring some coffee.'

My father frowned at my urgency but caught my mood. 'I'm sorry our offering is so humble tonight, Rudy. Next time, if we know you're coming, we will put on a spread more befitting a mayor,' he said, smiling generously.

Rudy put his palms in the air. 'I eat modestly, Samuel. To answer your question, our family always was Volksdeutsche.'

I winced at the Nazi term.

'We were ethnic Germans living outside of Germany. That said, I haven't forgotten where I was born; I was raised as a Czech and I love this land even though the German officials are courting favour.'

The mention of the enemy was contrived; he'd planned to make the point that he was on more than just friendly terms with our overlords. The remark, as I'm sure he'd intended, seemed to take the temperature down in our warm, wood-panelled dining room. Suddenly I was aware that the winter was creeping across the hillsides. Actually, I would have welcomed being frozen out. I'd rather eat nuts and make do with porridge than be accessible to the Germans if they were moving around the village.

My father shared a similar thought, I'm sure, because he nodded at me and I knew it really was time to remove the children. They gave the usual complaints but I bustled them out with instructions to Lotte to take the girls upstairs and ready them for bed.

'Why can't you?' my sister bleated.

'I have to help Papa. Our mother is not going to be serving anyone coffee, as you well know.'

'I thought she was returning to us.'

'Well, she's not!' I snapped and then I felt immediately guilty and hugged Lotte. 'I'm sorry, Lotte, I am so, so sorry. You must know I am sad too but we're safe here and if our mama can have bright days like today, who is to say they won't happen more regularly? We just have to keep being patient. I may be able to find some cake . . . you can take it upstairs and enjoy it, but remember to brush your teeth after.'

Lotte grimaced. 'You sound like the mayor now.'

I flashed her my astonishment. 'What do you mean?'

'When you were out of the room, fetching the bread knife, he started talking about children brushing teeth before bedtime and not ignoring its importance.'

A fresh chill shuddered through me. I remembered a similar conversation with him when I was younger. It was darkly humorous that I thought of myself an adult when I was still essentially a child.

'I don't really like the mayor,' she continued. 'I know he's supposed to be our friend —'

'You don't have to explain, Lotte. I don't care much for him either these days.' I was surprised I sounded so composed. If only Lotte knew my real fear. 'Now, lock the door behind you, will you?'

'Why?' I wasn't surprised by her shock. We had a family policy of doors open.

'Just do it. I'll be up soon.'

I busied myself making up the coffee tray, reluctantly putting a couple of slices of our precious cake onto a plate. I didn't think Rudy went without, whereas for us this cake was the most special of treats. I kept one ear cocked for footsteps up the stairs, but there was no telltale creak on the fifth step and I returned to the dining room to see our mayor touching a flame to a cigarette using a gold lighter. The cigarettes were not a brand I recognised in their orange packet and I could see the packaging had German wording. The lighter was ostentatious, used deliberately to impress. He was making a point that wasn't lost on us. Rudy was a man on the ascent with strong connections to where true power sat.

My father was in earnest conversation but Rudy wore a smirk, one I recognised from the evening in my bedroom. He was a cat toying with a mouse. My father didn't know it or chose to look past it, but I felt miserably sickened for him.

'. . . anything you can do for them would mean everything to me and my wife,' my father finished. He had surely been speaking of us.

I watched Rudy blow out the smoke he'd held in his lungs, angling the bluish cloud to billow above my father's head. It was another arrogant message of power. He shook his head extravagantly as though deeply pondering the dilemma but it was obvious that he was ready with his answer. 'I don't know what I can do, Samuel. You and Olga have always been kind to our family so I would like to help where I can, but the news is grim for the Jews of Czechoslovakia.'

They both turned to regard me, realising I was in the room.

'It's no good trying to protect me from this, Papa. I'm here, I'm in it . . . and I'm Jewish. None of this can be helped. Our mother is not well enough to support you or look after the girls. It's down to me, so you might as well accept that I have to hear what is going on.'

Rudy didn't wait for my father to respond and took longer than he should have to remove his lascivious gaze from me. 'You've heard of Theresienstadt, or Terezín, as we Czechs call it?' he asked my father.

He nodded morosely while I was feeling freshly nauseous at its mention. Originally a fortress from one hundred and fifty years ago that Emperor Joseph II had named after his mother, its town was located near the German border about forty miles north of Prague. We all knew the Germans were gradually taking some Jews there, forcibly, to create a ghetto.

'I heard yesterday that it is now the destination for all the Jews of Prague.' Rudy's emphasis did not fall on deaf ears. He inhaled, letting the smoke escape slowly through the side of his neat mouth.

'"*Every last one*" *was the phrase I overheard. Of course, I'm sure that's exaggerated . . .*' He trailed off and in that pause was a deliberate bait.

Not so long ago my father had expressed a certain amount of relief that such a place existed within the protectorate because other news spoke of transports into Poland to frozen camps that worked their inhabitants to death on behalf of the German war effort. It was the lesser of both evils, in his opinion.

I couldn't say which was worse; I was young, I didn't want to be incarcerated anywhere, and stupidly I believed that my father's status, his importance as a manufacturer, even our former wealth, would give us some sort of defence against being forced to move there.

Listening to Rudy, though, I felt we had been deluding ourselves and it had only been a matter of time. Rich or poor, everyone's turn would come and we'd just had the benefit of the buffer of wealth to hold off the scrutiny a little longer. He wasn't coming outright and saying we would be imprisoned, but there was a clear undercurrent to his conversation that I think my father was trying to distance himself from. Perhaps that was for my benefit.

To help I excused myself briefly to check on my sisters so the men would know I'd left the room. The girls were fine, not ready to sleep, and I didn't force them to turn the lights out. I told them I'd return in fifteen minutes but really I wanted to tiptoe back into the dining room to hear the rest of the dreaded conversation.

Drawing on all my skills to sit in the shadows, I slipped back into the room, hardly noticed by either, and remained soundlessly on its fringe to listen with rapidly growing unease at how quickly their discussion had disintegrated and the power in the room had ruthlessly shifted.

My father now had only pleading in his voice. 'At least the girls could be spared this, surely? Rudy, they're family to you.'

Rudy didn't acknowledge that fact . . . and I was now convinced he'd never held such a sentiment. Sitting here in the lowest light of the room, I think I found fresh clarity. He'd never considered us family; I don't think he even regarded us as friends. I'd now go so far as to believe that Ruda Mayek loathed us and was enjoying the balance of power changing. My father was no longer the rich businessman, us no longer his spoiled, indulged children who'd never known anything but full bellies, warm beds, fine education – a life of plenty. Rudy, however, had endured a tougher, rougher upbringing; his father, I gathered from mine, was not an affectionate man, and without a mother in his life he had been raised in that sombre masculine environment where a box around the ears was likely the closest he got to being touched. Papa had always said our mama had mothered Rudy as best she could but she was regularly admonished by Mayek the elder for indulging his son, who needed to accept his lot and get on with making the best of his life.

So this was Rudy's best: throwing in his lot with the Nazis, not standing up for his true friends, not even attempting to help, and worse, not even trying to console my father. He seemed to be taking pleasure in the escalating discomfort and fear he was cleverly creating through his slow baiting.

'I'm not sure how I can help the children, Samuel.' I remembered a time not so long ago when he addressed my father as "sir". Now he was shaking his head with what I took to be feigned melancholy. 'They are registered. They wear the yellow star.' Rudy spoke to my father as if he were discussing the winter weather rather than the future of our family.

'Then use your influence, Rudy. You owe me this much.' And there it was: my father's first show of emotion, the first time his even tone had faltered.

Rudy leaned forward and I sensed it was with relish. 'Do I? Why is that, Samuel?'

I watched my father swallow. 'Ruda Mayek, what is happening here? We've been family to you since you were a child. Your father was a cruel man to you at times but my wife treated you as her own and I always made you welcome, regarded you as a son who shared in everything we had to share. And now you come to our house as a guest, you eat our food, break our meagre bread, you jest with my children, drink the last of our coffee and yet I hear only threat.'

I wanted to cheer for my papa but deep down I knew his accusation was pointless, for Rudy was playing with him.

'I'm mayor now, Samuel. As someone who must get on with our German protectors, I cannot show favour.'

'Cannot or will not? This is a conscious choice, Rudy. You have sway now . . . surely we can work out how to get the girls to safety?'

'To where exactly? Into Poland? Russia? The German steamroller is crushing all Jews to the east, and the west is no friend to your kind. You should have sent them on the rescue trains to poor old Britain when you had your chance. You might have got the three youngest away.' He glanced my way. 'The beautiful Katka – I wish she didn't have to wear the yellow star.'

So he'd known I was there all along.

'Then help Katerina at least! She speaks fluent German, and you well know she could pass as one. Get her some forged papers!'

'Papa! Stop!' I gasped, risking overstepping a line. 'I would never leave you, never walk away from the girls or our mother. I'm proud to be Jewish.'

'You shouldn't be, Katka,' Rudy lazily oozed, unmoved by the rising emotion.

My father's features slackened with shock at Rudy's words but he rallied as he cut his desperate gaze my way. 'This is about survival,' Papa growled at me. 'I'd never seen my father's emotions stirred to anger. He turned back to our hateful guest. 'If one of my daughters could —'

'Please stop. It is a redundant conversation, my dear Samuel.' The condescension quietened us both. 'Katerina, as charming and beautiful as she is – and as Aryan as she may seem – is still Jewish; she's registered. There are rules . . . law. I am charged to enforce that —'

'I want you to leave!' My father suddenly said, standing.

I was appalled. Not about how rude it was – to hell with Ruda Mayek and any manners being shown to him – but I feared the repercussions of this moment of rage.

'I mean it, Mayor,' my father said, his voice filled with naked fury. 'Get out of my villa, and you should know that you are never welcome back as its guest.'

'Samuel, you really don't want to take that attitude with —'

'Get out!' He was yelling now and I rushed to his side.

Rudy put his hands up in mock defence and stood suddenly. His full height and breadth were dismayingly powerful as he loomed over both of us. With deliberation he picked up his German cigarettes and his flashy lighter and slipped both into his pocket. 'I believe I came with a coat?' He made it a question in a conversational tone.

'I'll fetch it,' I offered, glancing at my father.

'No, he can fetch it himself on the way out. I don't believe I want to share the same air with you, Mayor, for a moment longer.'

I glared at my father; this was only going to turn bad for us.

'You have your head in the sand, Kassowicz. There is no way out. I came here tonight to offer help of a different nature – perhaps not what you had in mind, but it would save you much, er, heartache.'

'Mayor, please,' I offered, gesturing towards the door.

He didn't say anything more but stared at my father for what

I thought was longer than necessary and I could only imagine how Papa was able to hold that terrible gaze as firmly as he did. It was Rudy who looked away first, although my father's shoulders slumped as the mayor turned and walked through the door before I did.

Despite my father's order, I helped Rudy on with his huge and heavy overcoat and watched him pull on his gloves. 'Katka, speak with your father. He cannot hide up here for much longer.' A leathered finger traced the shape of my face from my ear to the tip of my chin. I worked hard at remaining expressionless. 'You really are quite divine; do you know that? All that simmering beauty to stir a man's passions. In a year or two . . .'

I shifted my head away from his revolting touch before he could finish but I did so gently, showing none of the defiance I was feeling. 'Rudy, please, can you help us? I . . . I don't know what my father had in mind, but —'

'No, darling Katka. Your family's fate is sealed. I shall be back, but next time in a uniform.'

A mayor's uniform? It sounded ridiculous but there was no time to ponder that. 'How much time do we have?' My voice was shaking, pleading.

He smiled sadly at me in the dim light of the hallway. 'Don't run, my darling, there are soldiers throughout these hills now and all through the village and the roads leading in and out of it. You would be shot on sight like vermin. Better to wait for me. I shall be able to make it all go easier.'

I didn't know what that meant – I presumed he was referring to transport to Terezín – but I was shaking now and I let him walk away, not pressing him for further explanation.

'I'll see myself out,' he threw over his shoulder.

He didn't return the next day or the next. We were sitting in our drawing room around the fire in the glorious late afternoon light that glowed through windows I'd cleaned only that morning in an effort to keep myself and the girls occupied. They were all playing quietly upstairs and my mother was resting. I had made a pot of tea for my father to enjoy around the flames. I think Ruda Mayek was taking his time in order to keep building our fear of what might lie ahead. And it worked. My father must have discussed a dozen scenarios with me but all were academic; we both knew none of them would work for they all meant splitting up the family and how would we do that? Who would go with whom? What if we ended up in separate ghettos, or some of us were sent to Poland, or worse? No, separation was never going to be the choice. It was when my father suggested we make for the neutral territory of Switzerland that I heard his desperation and it was time for me, at least, to be realistic.

'Papa! How do you propose to get three small girls under ten and our mother, who shuffles around in her own world most of the time, across occupied and hostile territory to Switzerland?'

He ignored me. 'Or south, maybe we head south . . . I hear there are options via Rome. There are parts of the Mediterranean that —'

'Just stop it now! There's nothing and no one who can help us.'

'Money talks, Katerina. Have I taught you nothing?'

'They'll take your money and laugh at you, Papa.'

'They'll take it anyway, my darling child, but I'll feel happier trying to make it buy our freedom.'

'There is no freedom. We are Jewish. We are doomed to this fate but perhaps Terezín isn't such a bad idea. We can stay together. Papa, if we try to flee, they're going to have the excuse they need to kill us. Do you want your children to be hunted down like foxes, shot in the back while trying to outrun the pursuers?' His eyes

glistened wet. It was cruel to speak to him in this way. 'So let's pack and ready ourselves. It's been two days since he was here and I doubt we'll get more than another day, so let's prepare properly – I'll get the girls organised, you worry about Mama.'

'She's the lucky one.'

'Because she's lost her mind?'

He nodded. 'Katerina, she's lost because of Petr. I need to tell you —'

'Papa, forgive her. Remember her as the woman you fell in love with, not who she's become through her sorrows.'

He gave me a sad smile and touched my face with love, genuine affection, and mostly grief at how life was turning out. 'When did you get to be so wise, my beautiful girl? I see myself in you each day but I also see the young Olga who caught and trapped my heart the first time I met her.'

I swallowed; this was heartbreaking and we needed to avoid weakness. 'Come on, Papa. We have to be strong for the girls. There's a journey to be made and who knows what we face at its end.'

The sudden banging at our door startled us and I spilled the tea. I was just handing my father his second cup and in fright I let some of it topple onto my mother's beloved Persian rug. My regret in that moment was so intense I wanted to howl my rage at the world; the yell of anguish came as far as my throat but I was not someone prone to histrionics and my father would not have appreciated a display right then. I wanted to be fourteen, I wanted to still be a child, but as my father stood to answer the incessant rapping at our door, I righted the toppled cup, glanced with sadness at the stain and realised in a horrible moment of understanding that the rug no longer mattered . . . in fact, we no longer mattered.

Katerina looked up from where she'd been drawing invisible circles on the white tablecloth. 'I can't go on today.'

Daniel swallowed his disappointment. 'I understand. You've been talking for a while. All the other diners have gone.'

She looked around in surprise. 'We must go. They're readying for dinner,' she said, embarrassed. Katerina peered out of the window across the restaurant. 'The afternoon is already darkening.' She glanced at her watch. 'No, it can't be so late?' She reached for her handbag.

He gave a sad grin. 'I didn't dare interrupt. I am holding my breath as it is.' He signalled to a relieved waiter for the bill.

'Let me,' she began, opening the clip of the bag.

'Don't be ridiculous. I'm old-fashioned. And it was my idea, anyway, to come here.'

'It was kind of you, thank you. Er, will you excuse me?'

'Of course.' He took out his wallet to pay while she visited the powder room.

On her return Daniel helped her on with her coat and they left the warmth of the hotel to feel the pinch of a chilly spring evening against their cheeks.

'Would you like to take a taxi home?'

'No, I think I'd prefer to walk,' she admitted.

'May I walk you?'

She paused, found a smile and shook her head. 'Please don't be offended. I think I need some time alone.'

'Then, tomorrow? I mean, only if you're up to it.'

'It's the ugliest part of my story.'

'Then tell me while we're surrounded by beauty. How about we stroll through the Musée de l'Orangerie and view Monet's *Water Lilies*?'

She smiled at him. 'I haven't seen them for a long time.'

'All the more reason to visit. I find them restorative to my soul.'

'You go often?'

He nodded. 'Three or four times a year.'

'You continue to surprise me. All right. How about two o'clock?'

'Perfect.'

'I want to say good afternoon but it feels like the evening is closing in. And rain, I fear. I must hurry. *Bonsoir*, Daniel.'

'*Bonsoir*, Katerina. Dream sweetly.' He meant it, but he doubted she could dream anything but darkly that night.

13

* * *

It was a drizzly afternoon when Katerina arrived beneath a striped umbrella to tap Daniel on the shoulder. He had been facing the other way, no doubt expecting her to arrive from the Tuileries, but she had walked the Champs-Élysées to stare mindlessly into shopfronts as a treat as she gathered her thoughts for the rest of her story.

It was still a surprise to her that she was sharing it. That morning in her small apartment as she looked out at the view, made crooked by the heavy rain against the long window panes, she wondered why she was letting all of this poison out. Would it do her any good? Well, if it did anything, it would make her angrier, and in rekindling her fury she might find that old strength that had ensured her survival. In talking with Daniel, she was indeed feeling stronger about what she was sure was coming – a new confrontation with an old foe.

'Right on time,' he said, beaming. 'You've been shopping.'

'An errand.'

'An expensive one.' He grinned, noting the bag from an exclusive store. 'For a man?'

It was none of his business but still she noted how observant he was. 'I like to wear men's sweaters at the weekend,' she said drily.

He shifted the topic adroitly. 'Well, kiss goodbye to that neighbourhood. The new rapid transit system will change its clientele irrevocably.'

She shrugged, not minding that the exclusive avenue would now be more accessible to the general public. 'The wealthy will grumble but it's a good thing for all of Paris and new tourism.'

Daniel gave a careless lift of a shoulder at the remark. 'You look rested,' he said.

'Curiously, I slept well and dreamlessly.'

'Well, we're getting damp chatting here. Mercifully, hardly more than a handful have gone in and at least two have come out again.'

They lowered their umbrellas, shaking them at the entrance and leaving them in the basket provided. Daniel was quick to pay for their tickets. 'You must stop that,' she admonished him. 'I can pay my way.'

'I know you can, but I wasn't brought up to let a lady pay. It's not an insult to accept such a small gift from a friend.'

She nodded. 'So long as I buy the coffee afterwards.'

'Certainly,' he said, looking delighted that there was to be coffee later.

They strolled around the exhibition of fabulous works by the Impressionists: Renoir, Cézanne, Gauguin . . . holding off on the beautiful Monet lilies for later, moving instead to gaze at works by Picasso and Matisse, Modigliani and their companions.

'Not a fan of cubism? At least I think that's cubism.' Daniel observed her dismayed expression as they stood before the portrait *Red-Haired Girl*.

'No.'

'Explain why to me.'

'Well, do you like it?'

'Not in the slightest, but I'm interested to hear why you don't.'

'Hmm, well, to me there's beauty in everyone. Even a plain woman might have lovely hands, pretty eyes, a sweet smile, a slim neck . . . He hasn't looked for the beauty in this girl at all. Look at how he's accentuated her jaw and chin, one eye larger than the other and her mouth so high and pinched on her face.'

'That's what he saw.'

'I'm not keen on portraits, anyway. I prefer landscapes or still life.'

'Because they're lonely?'

'They don't have to be; I prefer beauty in paintings. By that I mean what I personally find pleasing, such as symmetry, clean lines, colours that soothe . . . or just helpless prettiness.'

'Fair enough. So Renoir and Monet for you.'

She smiled. 'I suppose.'

'Let's go see Claude Monet, then.'

They entered the space that was covered by nearly one hundred linear metres of the painter's famous *Water Lilies*.

They sighed in unison. 'Seeing them never fails to make me feel safe,' she admitted.

'Because they're a symbol of peace,' he remarked softly, almost a whisper. 'He donated them on the day of the Armistice —'

'The day after,' she corrected, as she did a slow tour of the pieces that made little sense close up. Nevertheless, she liked looking at Monet's splodges of paint, which only took their real form when the viewer gazed at them from a distance. 'The *Water Lilies* cycle took him three decades.'

'Extraordinary,' he breathed. 'He's managed to give us water, flowers, trees, clouds in the most random manner and provide the illusion of a limitless whole.'

'Beautifully said,' she complimented him. 'It's what he intended . . . "a wave with no horizon, no shore" . . . his words.'

'I read somewhere there are three hundred or so paintings in this series.'

'It's true, and around forty of them in a large format.'

'Let's sit,' he offered, gesturing to a bench seat.

She joined him and they sat in silence for close on five minutes; her back was turned slightly to him and that made it easier to pick up where she'd left her sad tale the previous day.

Katerina could hear the rain drumming gently against the roof. It was soothing rather than distracting and they were still alone; perhaps the rain might keep others away for long enough that she could finish this difficult part of her tale. She began talking softly; sensed him settle back behind her, relaxing into her voice and the hardest part of her story.

––––––––

It was a German soldier wearing his greatcoat and helmet who stood on the threshold. I could see the burly outline of a second man from the porch light but then they both stepped aside and I caught my breath.

Strolling into our villa wearing his trademark smirk was Ruda Mayek and he was in uniform; it was not, however, the dress of a mayor of a small town in Czechoslovakia. It was not even the uniform of a German soldier. No, Rudy had surpassed our estimation of his ambition, and his evil. He looked resplendent in the grey field tunic of the feared SS but as I watched him move confidently across our doorway I noted the boards on his wide shoulders did not signify the German Secret Police. As young as I was I knew what they signified. It was worse – far worse, in fact.

'Forgive me for the dramatic entrance, Samuel. Frankly,

*I prefer my civilian clothes but I'm afraid when I'm on official busi-
ness I am required to wear my Gestapo uniform.'*

*I think we could all tell he was lying about his preference for
civvies.*

*Gestapo. I watched, with dread, as he pointed at the same
shoulder boards that had caught my notice – I was always one for
small details – and as he indicated the poison-green piping that
signified his tribe I had to swallow bile that tasted acid in my throat.
Halfway down his left sleeve was the black diamond patch of the
security forces, bearing the letters 'SD' embroidered in white.*

*'Good evening, Katka,' he said, pretending only now to notice
me, but I think I understood finally that Rudy was always aware
of me, although I was still unsure whether he hated or desired me.
'This is what I'd hoped to avoid a few days ago. But . . .' he said,
returning his attention to my stunned father, still shocked at seeing
the little boy he'd treated like a son arriving at our house with intent
to bring harm. That much was clear. 'I'm sorry that it's come to an
armed escort.'*

*The girls had wandered down the stairs too and were sitting
like a flock of sparrows watching.*

*'Hello, Rudy,' Lotte said. 'So that's your mayor's uniform?
It matches your eyes. They look grey today, like a storm cloud.'*

I couldn't have described him more accurately myself.

*His smile was so fake it hurt me to watch it spread across his
thin, neatly drawn mouth. 'I'm glad you like it,' he replied, even
though that's not what her remark had intimated. He gave an impatient tut. 'Samuel, we must speak.' He glanced my way. 'Alone this
time. Just the men.'*

*My father looked beaten and nodded, gesturing to the warm,
sun-drenched room.*

*Rudy had been carrying his black leather coat and without a
word handed it to me. I wondered where the hat was, but what did*

it matter? His coat was so heavy I had to bend my knees to hang it for him. 'We shan't be long,' he said now. 'I suggest you wake your mother if she's asleep and get her dressed.'

I had no choice but to obey. My mother dithered and bleated like a helpless lamb. This was the worst she'd been in a while, muttering about Petr and how there was no body to visit. I didn't understand; I'd been at the funeral but we were so young, we didn't question why there was no guarding of Petr's body in the process of 'watching the dead'. I remembered the torn black ribbons we all wore to signify our loss and I recall my father taking his off during the brief service but no one remarked on it. I knew my father was hiding something, but my question was lost to my grief of that period.

'Where are we going?' she asked me earnestly.

'Another journey,' I murmured.

'Where's your father?'

'He's speaking with Rudy Mayek, making the arrangements.'

Clarity waned. 'Little Rudy. Always so fond of you, darling . . .'

My eyes were damp with tears that I refused to allow to fall. My poor mother. She was confused and these moments of lucidity didn't ease my heartache. They were like lightning cracks that illuminated the earth for just a second and then it was all darkness again. Right then, I think I wished my mother the blessed darkness of ignorance and confusion. She really didn't need the pain of knowledge that we were all about to be imprisoned.

I led her and my sisters, who were all uncharacteristically subdued, down the stairs to the hallway. I'd packed a small suitcase for each, keeping it light so they could carry it themselves if necessary. The presence of uniformed men in boots with pistols at their hips was not encouraging even Lotte to be talkative.

'Do we have guests?' my mother wondered, and she then

began walking from room to room, as if trying to recall where we were. I was happy to leave her in that happy ignorance and cut a look of warning at Lotte, who seemed to be readying an explanation for her.

The door to the sitting room opened and the image of my father is one I shall never forget. Here was a broken man. He'd shrunk over the last few minutes and in that moment it was as though I was watching my father's corpse, briefly animated. He had no life within and the light that normally danced in his darkish green-brown eyes had been extinguished. Behind him loomed Rudy, who looked to be flicking some lint from his proud uniform.

'Everyone ready? Good.'

I refused to be so compliant in our own imprisonment. 'Where are we going now? It will be dusk in a couple of hours.'

'Your father will explain, Katka. We will need your help with the children.'

I opened my mouth to protest.

'No, Katka, you will listen to me now. What I have arranged is for the best and for your sake. The alternative is unpleasant. I have organised for your father's carriage to be brought out.'

'The barouche?' Lotte said. 'We haven't ridden in that for years. We have no horse!' The little ones giggled at her words.

'We've brought one. It's being harnessed now.'

I blinked at Rudy in astonishment. 'So we're not going down the hill?'

My father squeezed my arm. 'Hush now, child. Do as you're bid.' He whispered to me urgently. 'Please let's not frighten the little ones.'

'The children can ride in our car if you wish, Samuel?' A look was exchanged between Rudy and my father. I watched my father nod and Lotte gave a brief cheer, as if she'd just been told of a great treat, but I felt only talons of fear claw at my belly.

It was time to leave; we had no choice so there was no point in protesting further. I began urging the girls to pick up their suitcases but Rudy put a gloved hand on my arm. He made a small tutting sound. 'Leave it, Katka.'

'But —'

He tsk-tsked again and I tried not to show my vexation. 'The men will carry these for you.' He waved a hand carelessly as though used to giving orders. 'Off you go, help your father to get your mother into the coach.'

'We need to lock up the villa, surely? And the fire is —'

He laid his leathered finger against my lips and it took all my willpower not to recoil. 'Sssh . . .' He held up a bunch of keys. I recognised them immediately as my father's. 'Samuel has asked me to take care of it all for him. Don't worry, I'll be diligent with your valuables.' As naive of the world as perhaps I was, his smirk told me all I needed to know and I didn't want to give him another moment of my precious time. I hurried away to my father and the driver, who were struggling to help my mother into the coach.

'Why the barouche?' I persisted with my father once my mother was finally settled.

His sunken expression hadn't changed. 'So we can travel without being seen. We can pull down the blinds on the windows. He says it is a special consideration he's showing so no one has to see us leave under armed guard.'

'I don't suppose that big car is any sort of hint, though?'

My sarcasm was the last thing my father needed, of course. His look was full of pain when it landed on me.

'I am so sorry, Katerina.'

'This is not your fault.'

'I should have got all of you children away. I shouldn't have listened to your mother.'

I thought he was going to weep and leapt in with a hand to his shoulder and a kiss to his cheek. 'Papa, hush now. What's the use in regret? We can't turn back the pages.'

He held me tight. 'Oh, my darling girl. Regret is all I have to chew on now in this bitterest of journeys. You are my joy – know that. You have made me proud to be a father.'

He was crying. I was crying too. This wasn't forever! I needed him to be reassured, to be my strong father. 'Terezín's a camp, Papa. We'll stay as close as they'll permit and we'll draw no attention to ourselves. We'll survive.'

My father shook his head slowly and a deep sob erupted. 'I wanted to tell you about Petr.'

'Hush, Papa. He's gone. But we're together. I'm at your side and I fear nothing.' It was brave talk to somehow lift him back to the pedestal. I needed him calm and strong for me because I wanted to drop to my haunches, put my hands over my head and keen. It wasn't the cold making me shiver, it was raw fear. No child should watch their father weep or their mother disappear into madness. No child should be forcibly herded into transport with armed men around them. No child should be thinking what I was thinking in that moment as I looked at my father's haunted face. The truth waggled a finger of glee at me. So rather than accept it, I lied to myself and to him.

'Maybe it's easier. It's also more dignified. We don't have to live in hiding, scratching for food. We can join others and together we can help each other at Terezín.'

He nodded, sniffing. 'You're right, Katerina. This is more dignified for our family. It's going to take courage but Ruda Mayek has convinced me that all round it's a better course than what we face.'

What I didn't know then is that he'd decided to state the truth, although at the time I thought he was simply joining me in the lie.

The journey was far shorter than I was anticipating. I'd clung to the vague notion that we were still intending to go down the hill, perhaps taking a back road that only Rudy knew of. But my father *had hushed me and I suppose, deep down in my breaking heart, I knew we were not going anywhere but deeper into the woods.*

Katerina stirred as an enamoured couple, arms linked, walked in laughing quietly to each other.

'I've changed my mind, Daniel,' she said. 'This room of beauty is no place for my ugly tale. Shall we go?'

He didn't argue, picking up his hat and overcoat to follow her to where they'd left their umbrellas.

'Still drizzling but lighter. We can make a run for it and find the closest café.' For the first time, he took her properly by the elbow and they hurried, beneath his larger umbrella, back onto the Left Bank and toppled through the doors of the first café they spotted.

'Something stronger, perhaps?'

She nodded. 'All right, but the bill is mine.'

He held up both palms. They found a booth and sat opposite each other, sliding along the red leather so they were close to the rain-spattered window.

The waiter arrived. 'Er . . .?' Daniel looked at her. 'Pastis, perhaps?'

She nodded.

'*Deux Jaunes*,' he said, 'no ice.'

The two yellow slugs of aniseed liquor arrived with the customary jug of chilled water, drips beading on its glass exterior. 'May I?' Daniel asked, and she nodded.

He poured the cold water into the yellow liquor that historically came perhaps from the Chinese star anise or more likely from the seeds of the Mediterranean aniseed plant, which was part of the parsley family. He wondered absently whether it had been given an extra lift with licorice or sage. He noted that Katerina was looking pale, distracted.

'To you, Katerina, and happier times,' he said, lost for whatever else to drink to.

'To happier times,' she echoed and they tipped their chins back to sip from the narrow, squat glasses.

She pulled a face. 'Never enjoyed this stuff.' At his laugh, threatening to spill the pastis from his mouth, she stared surprised at him. 'What?'

'Why drink it?'

She shrugged. 'Something to do, keep my hands busy, give us a reason to sit here.'

'Would you prefer something else?'

She shook her head.

'What do you normally like to drink – alcohol, I mean?'

'Champagne would be my first choice but I'm not one for anything sugary.'

'I'd never have guessed,' he said with light sarcasm.

'But I do enjoy a small fortified wine on a winter evening. That's my secret pleasure that only you know.' Before he could respond, she added: 'But I prefer the sherries using the Spanish Pedro Ximénez grapes.'

At last he could enlighten her about something historical. 'Originally from Arabic table grapes.'

'Is that right?' She chuckled and the sound was deep and genuine . . . almost like a thankyou for breaking her mood.

'You don't have to tell me more,' he offered, hating that he was even letting those words out.

'I do, though, Daniel. I've got no one else to share this with . . . I'm too far into the nightmare to pull out now.'

He took a slow breath. 'You were in the barouche . . .'

'We were,' she recalled.

The afternoon light was soft and it had warmed the chilly interior of the barouche, which had not been harnessed to a horse in many years. One of Rudy's men was driving it. We were supposed to regard being transported in our own carriage as some sort of special consideration by Rudy. I think it only made it more poignant, more painful. I didn't recognise the driver but he was likely another Nazi convert from the village. The smell of the leather instantly transported me to a time in my childhood when life was uncomplicated and full of happiness. The twins hadn't arrived then; it was just me and baby Lotte. I thought of her in the car ahead, being driven with 'Uncle Rudy' to . . . where?

'Papa. He said you'd explain. Tell me the truth now, are we going to Terezín?'

I watched my father glance at our mother, who was staring blankly out of the window at the thickening forest as the road turned to track and our ride became slower, bumpier. I also noticed he had begun to wring his hands. He wasn't wearing gloves . . . why?

'Papa?'

'Terezín is not a happy gathering place for Jews,' he began. 'The mayor tells me it is essentially a clearing house to other places. The Jews are being sent to camps to be systematically killed.'

I frowned at the ridiculous notion.

'The infirm, the aged, invalids, children, anyone weakened, are murdered immediately. Those old enough to do manual labour and any healthy adults are put to work until they are no longer of use.'

'But —'

'"The Nazis are exterminating the Jews"; those were his exact words, Katerina.' Before I could take a breath to respond, my father continued. 'No child should be hearing this but I only have you, my girl, to explain this to. The mayor assured me that your mother, each of your sisters and I would almost certainly be put to death *immediately on arrival at one of the camps. You alone would likely be kept for working purposes until you could no longer be of use and then you too would perish. However, he gave me a glimpse into all the despair before we would even arrive to be killed. The journey itself, crowded like a tin of anchovies and in train carriages designed for cattle, means a lot of the weak die horribly before they arrive in the frozen wilderness of Poland.'*

He was right, I shouldn't have been hearing this, but I too had aged these last few days, well beyond my years. 'Papa,' I reasoned, 'how can he know this? He's —'

'He knows this because he's been there. He agrees with the killing of Jews. He is entirely enamoured by the ideology of Hitler's Nazi Party and has joined it, hence the borrowed uniform and his new status. He is impressed by the new Protektor Heydrich; is keen to be noticed by him. He will be moving to live and work at Terezín shortly and after that . . .' – he gave a sad groan – 'he said he would relish the opportunity to be transferred to one of those death camps in the east.'

My father wasn't speaking to deaf ears or a mind that hadn't already suspected something traumatic was gathering us into its bleak hold, but even my imagination couldn't have conjured the death camps he spoke of. 'And so, if we are to be spared Terezín, what is this journey about?' I was torn between wanting to know and wishing I could stop the words spilling from my father's lips, but they'd begun their journey and neither of us could prevent them filling the space between his anguished face and my stunned one.

'We cannot be spared. We are registered, so we would be hunted down, separated and treated who dares wonder how for trying to escape. The mayor claims that because of our long family connection, he can make it quick and painless. This is the least suffering he can offer us. What could I do but accept?'

I swallowed but my throat was so dry I felt choked. I tried again and gave a gasp instead. 'What is he going to do?'

'Katerina, I have asked a lot of you but I have to ask more because I can't do this alone. You have to stay strong for the babies. We have to turn this into some sort of game, or . . .' He shook his head.

'They're taking us into the woods to kill us?' I said, my words coming out as more of a hiss than my recognisable voice.

He nodded.

I couldn't even scream, I was so horrified. It couldn't be possible, could it? This couldn't really be happening, and yet here we were, rumbling into the loneliest of landscapes, just our young family of six, with a trio of armed bullies.

'It will be quick, he has promised,' my father repeated, as if that made it any less bitter.

There was nothing to say. I couldn't think of a single response that would offer either of us an easier mindset as we moved towards our death. Death. My life hadn't yet begun and it was about to end, staring at the barrel of a German gun. I would curse Ruda Mayek as it happened. His would be the name on my lips, in my mind as I died, so that in a different life I would remember him and I would hunt him.

The coach lurched to a stop just moments after I'd made this promise to myself. Nothing more was to be said between my father and I as a soldier was suddenly at the door, urging us out.

I could hear Rudy insisting we be treated gently but nothing he could say or do would change this moment, or convince me he meant it, for whatever breath I had left in me I would breathe it cursing him. And if I was to be granted any form of spiritual life after death, then I would commit that life to Ruda Mayek; I would not let him leave my soul and one day, if there ever was to be an hour of reckoning, I would be there to watch him pay for this sin.

All of this was tumbling chaotically through my mind as I took the hands of the twins on either side of me and urged Lotte to walk between our parents and hold their hands.

'What's happening, Papa?' I heard her ask. 'I didn't enjoy that ride.'

'Lotte, it's a special game,' I ground out. I was past fear now. I was at a new threshold; it wasn't yet resignation, it was more like a fury. It burned sharp and bright, sucking the air from my lungs. I was breathing so shallowly I could hear the struggle above all other sounds, which had become sharpened. There was the crunch of our footsteps on the leaf litter beneath; I could hear the creak of Rudy's leather coat, and the birds – far too happy in their early evening song as they watched us pass beneath them. My mother muttered to herself, my father said nothing . . . dead eyes stared ahead. I think I must have worn a similar mask. I was aware of Lotte glancing my way, trying to catch my attention; she was normally so talkative, it often felt like a full-time task answering her endless questions from why a human baby takes nine months in the womb and is still more helpless than most other young of the mammals, to how the sky can be so many colours in a single day. But she had been silenced, old enough to pick up on the mood of the adults.

Ettel was the sporty one amongst us, usually jumping, skipping or turning cartwheels, but she walked now with subdued, shuffling steps next to me, not a hint of bounce in her ordinarily jolly gait. Her hand clutched mine tightly enough that I was sure her fingers must be in pain. Darling, sweet Hana was the opposite of her twin; she would give a smiling sigh at her sister's boundless energy and put her passion into creativity instead. She sketched with a confident accuracy, tried her hand at sewing, knitting, cross-stitch, even baking with a rare fearlessness. Her attention, though, was lost mostly to books with an already precocious talent for literature in one so young; she kept a diary and I wondered how she might be *composing this evening's terrifying entry in her mind. I knew she would never write in her diary again. Above all my panic for my family, I was acutely aware of my shallow breath fuelled by hate and rage.*

I kept repeating in my mind that these were my final moments of life but it was having no effect on me; I don't know what I expected of myself . . . should I scream, weep, beg? I suspect I already knew doing so would have little effect on the preordained outcome. If I was honest, I didn't know how to show that sort of dramatic emotion. Lotte was the dramatic one in our family. I once overheard a friend of my mother's calling me cold; I'm convinced she didn't mean it as an insult but more as an observation, wishing apparently that she too possessed such glacial calm. I never agreed with her accusation; I believe what she was seeing was simply some-one who had learned early how to control their expression and emotion. Control gave me power over myself and situations. It gave me discipline. It projected strength and that made people trust me. It showed me how to be quiet, how to listen, how to learn from what others were not saying because it allowed me to observe. But yes, I suppose I came across as dislocated. And while I didn't feel calm or strong in that moment, my demeanour gave the impression of stoicism. My father was clearly counting on it and so in my last act of devotion to him, I gave it all. I would remain silent, harness the power within and keep my chin high. I would angle my dam-aged gaze at Ruda Mayek until I was dead and I hope he never forgot my accusing stare . . . I wanted it to haunt him.

We'd entered a denser part of the woods, where overhanging branches and bushes had intertwined to form a tunnel of sorts.

'Stop here, please,' Rudy said, uttering his first words since we'd left the vehicles behind. It was politely asked and we obeyed, shocked by the suddenness of the order. 'Katka, would you come with me?'

I blinked. 'Why?'

He didn't answer me, looking instead to my father. 'Samuel, I wish to say something private to Katerina. Please stay here with your family. It shouldn't take long.'

'Rudy,' my father began but our captor held up his hand, making that awful tsking sound again.

'Quiet now, man. Do as I bid. It goes easier if you do.'

Oh, the threat in those words! If the children weren't there I think I would have launched myself at Rudy – at least tried to take an eye out with bare fingers if I could. Tears were leaking onto my father's cheeks and forming rivulets of sorrow into his beard. That image was unbearable. I had to look away.

'It's all right, Papa,' I soothed. I couldn't imagine there was anything worse to come than being led like animals to be slaughtered. I don't think I cared any more because I realised to fight would only make it go harder, as we'd been warned.

I took a step closer to Rudy and he gestured the way forward.

He murmured something in German to his henchmen, but while I was fluent I couldn't hear it properly; it was something to do with clothes. I didn't hear enough to know what he meant and then we were walking on alone. I didn't look back at my family for fear of watching my father break down. I heard Lotte call my name but I dared not respond; besides, Hana had begun to openly sob. There was nothing to say that might console any of us.

We passed a tarpaulin of sorts on the ground – I barely glanced at it, because my gaze was helplessly drawn to the old woodcutter's hut in the near distance. Clearly that was our destination and I began to understand that yes, it was going to get worse before the final release. Panic flared but was immediately quenched by that same wintry sensitivity that told me no amount of panic would serve me. Rudy even held the door open for me and I walked in like the helpless child I was. The door was closed and then it was locked.

'Ah, Katka, alone at last,' he sighed, slipping off his coat with an ominous creak of leather and taking the time to hang it on a hook behind the door.

I breathed, low now and silent, making sure they were deep breaths to find some calm.

Rudy began pulling off his gloves with care. I planned to disappoint him by my lack of interest in him or what he was about to do. I suppose that natural ability to dislocate helped me now as I forced myself to – how can I describe this? – step away from my body in a way. When my mother had descended into her madness accompanied by incessant wailing, threats and accusations at my father, I'd begun teaching myself how not to hear or feel any of the hostility in the household by disappearing within . . . or perhaps it was 'without'. I had learned how to withdraw so I didn't have to hear, feel or think until it was safe to return again. I used that skill now and began to gather myself up and away from the edges of myself so I could no longer feel my fingers or toes; I couldn't tell you where the tip of my nose was. It was a trick of the mind, I knew, but it was my only haven now as I watched my captor unbelting his tunic and removing his pistol, which he held up to me with a smirk. 'I think you'd like to use this on me, yes?'

'I wouldn't hesitate,' I admitted, backing away into the edge of a rough wooden table. It wasn't fully steady on the ground and had a tilt that annoyed me somewhere on the rim of my mind.

He laughed low, genuinely amused. 'I like your spirit,' and he put the pistol on the highest ledge of a crudely made stack of shelves that held everything from old pots to a Bible. 'I have to tell you this, Katka, anything you might do that brings harm to me will be reflected out there with the family I know you love so much. I have no feelings for them so it would not bother me in the slightest to take little Hana and smash her skull against a tree.'

I gasped at his promise of violence, imagining Hana's brilliant brain tumbling out of her cracked head in a pitiful waste.

He nodded, closing his eyes briefly in a gesture of sympathy. 'I know. My aunt once accused me of being sadistic. I was too young to know what that meant but I found out its meaning in due course and perhaps it does describe me.' He shrugged and moved on in a conversational tone. 'Did your father mention that I met Protektor Heydrich?'

I shook my head, still too shocked to speak.

'I think I've impressed Heydrich because I've been appointed to Terezín. I'll be one of the most senior people in that establishment within a fortnight.'

'Why aren't we being taken there?'

'Now, that's a good question, Katka. And I'm pleased to be able to tell you that this is the one kindness I am offering. Your family was always ridiculously generous to me and a debt needs to be paid. Your mother, poor silly fool, used to kiss my cheeks as if I were her own child, and before his own son came along, I think your deluded father regarded me as one.'

'And you repay their generosity like this?' My voice was stretched, as though it were about to snap.

'Yes. Because this is my time now. And I have to prove myself to my superiors. I have done you the most enormous of favours because the army don't know you are up here in the foothills. They thought they'd cleared this region of Jews but your family slipped in with the help of others. Anyway, while you might have got through the winter unhampered, the soldiers would have caught up with you. That's no lie. I am saving your family much despair, I promise you this. It is the single way I am repaying any debt owed to your family, and believe me it is true charity. I know what's out there, Katka, and it's the death camps that beckon to the Kassowicz family. Have you heard about them?'

I didn't flinch. I really didn't know what to say.

'Of course you have.' He smiled; he could surely see the knowledge in my expression. 'The rumours are already reaching back from Poland, aren't they? Certainly to the well connected like your father. But status, reputation and riches won't save you; you must understand that every Jew is to be exterminated – this is Hitler's single desire. Now, I don't make these rules, my dear. Our Führer does. And I am a good and patriotic Nazi.'

He struck a match and lit a candle. I was suddenly so acutely sensitive to my surroundings but particularly to Rudy that I could smell the sulphur of the dead match still in his fingers. Light was fading and I'd have preferred him to let it remain dark so I didn't have to see him.

'I thought you were a proud Czech?' I accused him.

'I am a proud citizen of Czechoslovakia, Katka. This is true. But my family is Volksdeutsche and it's that German blood in my veins that's pounding hard now. I am not hurting my place of birth in what I'm doing . . . I'm making Czechoslovakia better.'

'You truly believe that?'

He put his hand over his heart. 'Truly.'

'Then you are cursed.'

Rudy laughed at me and it was a dismissal. 'It is why your father's little museum in Prague is so touching; together your diligence has built us a resource about a people who will be extinct in a few years and we can show our children – I will enjoy showing my sons – your history and why you had to be eradicated.'

'I pity any son of yours. What an unfortunate child it will be to bear your name, carry your blood. Your bigotry turns my stomach.' I sounded like an old woman. I don't know where I was finding this maturity to stand up to him.

'That's a big word for a youngster. You are too bright for your own good, Katya.'

It was true. I'd heard my father use it only the previous day but it fitted Rudy and I knew I was using it properly.

He shrugged, untroubled, as he unbuttoned his fly. 'You asked, Katka, I'm answering, that's all. I don't mind if it offends you. Besides, you're only fourteen so who cares what you think, anyway? And you're Jewish – that means no one cares about you at all. Do you see the Czech people coming to your aid? No. Do you see your so-called Allies rushing to save the Jews? No. Perhaps they don't mind the Führer's ideals.'

My strength was depleted. I had nothing more to draw on and I'd learned that no amount of defiance was going to help me. Terror of what was ahead froze me against the rickety table. And just as it had seemed in my bedroom half a dozen years earlier, the hut now felt like a room in a doll's house. Rudy looked like a giant again and I had become a miniature version of myself.

'Oh, this won't take long. Just satisfying an itch that's been irritating me for years now.'

'Rudy, don't.'

'I've warned you what I shall do if you resist, Katka. Think quickly now.'

'Rudy, please, I don't know how . . . I'm a virgin —'

'Soon you'll be a dead one, Katka, so does it matter?' He stepped forward and tutted sharply as I took a breath . . . it was instinctive to scream. But his warning finger held in the air stopped me letting it go.

'So I should order the beating of your mother by my men?'

I thought of his henchmen outside, who weren't the boyish, smiling German soldiers of the checkpoint. These were older, bigoted Czechs, collaborating with Hitler's Nazis. They were not soldiers but certainly hardened, going by their grubbied overcoats and stubbly faces. No doubt Rudy had made them promises for their future once he'd achieved his promotion.

'Or perhaps we can break your twin sisters' arms, hmm?'

As traumatised as I was, the understanding that he was baiting me wormed its way through to the remaining area of my mind that still could make sense of life. Yes, he was taunting but that didn't mean he couldn't torture one of us first and enjoy watching me die inside before he killed the shell. And his earlier response struck a chord: did it matter that he raped me before he put a bullet in each of our heads? No. Not to him, and it would not save us if I resisted or went down fighting. I would make it worse for those I loved and I believed that. Perhaps allowing him this fury – and I could see it rising beneath his trousers – meant our deaths would follow swiftly rather than becoming sport. It was incredible in that moment that I was rationalising my own imminent murder and that of my family.

'Do what you must,' I said in a hard voice; I don't know where it came from. A different place, a part of me that I didn't know existed until this moment but perhaps had always been there wanting to show itself. This sense of resignation didn't weaken me, though. In that moment of deep fear it seemed to give me power, delivering back to me a measure of control. I was allowing this. He was not taking it.

No . . . I understood him now. I was not his victim. I was his weakness.

I would take that notion to my grave . . . I weakened Ruda Mayek by my presence and the memory of his weakness would haunt him for the rest of his days, I hoped. I prayed, as he began rummaging to loosen himself from his clothes, that every day from this one forward, my name and what he was about to do to me – to my family – would make him feel the need to look over his shoulder.

'That's the spirit, Katka. I can see your resilience rising – it's reflected in that devil's eye of yours.' He swung me around without warning and shoved me forward, bending me over the table. 'I don't want to look into that eye while I take you.' He ripped the dress at my shoulders so the bodice flopped past my waist and he reached under it to savagely tear at my underwear. I turned limp. I was not going to help him, and all the while he struggled to rip off my garments I could feel his lust pressing against my flesh. Hard and hot. I wildly looked around with my devil's eye for a cleaver – what a stupid thought – but I wanted to hack that pulsing flesh away from me.

Teenage daydreams had let me imagine what it would be like to lie with a man . . . someone I loved, someone I desired with my body as much as my heart. I admit to often trying to imagine what it would be like to have a man inside me. But Rudy was using his body as a weapon; one designed to humiliate, to make me his vessel, his slave. He was showing me my true worth to him through this degradation. But I also knew – and reminded myself – he couldn't resist me. He'd let me see that, know it . . . which is why I was the one with the power, no matter what he did to me.

Searing pain split me. I sucked back a breath suddenly as I felt flesh tear and Rudy forced his way into me. His hand covered my mouth. I tasted metal – was it from his pistol? No, I'd bitten my tongue or broken my lip in that panicked agony that no girl should feel. I could no longer be defiantly limp. I was now as rigid as Rudy was – every muscle in my body felt clenched, and as twilight chased away the lateness of afternoon and dusk rode hard on its heels to banish the last light of this day, so too did my faith in other people flee. I was now a lonely soul. Trust was gone – I was glad I would die that day after this.

The pain was harsh: so intense that it created a vacuum within me, into which I toppled. The table edge banged rhythmically against my pelvis, bruising my hips, as Rudy shoved and bashed his rage into me. With each thrust I think he became angrier. He momentarily pinched one breast so hard I sucked a fresh breath of horror through my nose but I refused to shriek in agony for fear of my family hearing. He lost interest in my body and no longer bothered with trying to suppress my screams. He trusted now that I wouldn't. Instead he pushed my forehead to the table, to improve his angle, I suppose, and I felt the sharp prick of a splinter angle into my skin; strange that I felt that tiny wound above the monstrous injury Rudy had inflicted. Meanwhile I begged in my mind for this to be over and to bring the bullet closer. His breathing became more ragged and he began to grunt. Pain was no longer my enemy. I couldn't feel much other than burning pressure. He would be done soon; I knew that much. I just wanted to get to my family one last time. Look upon them once more.

Rudy gave a final shudder and a sigh that sounded more of disgust than relief. He shoved me roughly forward once again as he wrenched himself out of me. I clutched the table's edge for support or I would have slipped to the floor.

Fluid slid down the inside of my thighs and a new sort of throbbing pain flashed to reach deep inside but also around into the crevice of my buttocks. I was torn and blood was joining what Rudy had contributed. Even so, it was obvious more blood was surely going to run tonight, so I pathetically reached down to pull up my underwear. My violation didn't matter. It really didn't in the larger scheme of what was happening to me, to my family, to the Jews – to the people of Europe. I returned my ripped bodice up and over my shoulders in an effort to hang onto a final thread of dignity. It wouldn't hold but I had to cover as much of my flesh as I could. I did not want my father or sisters seeing the worst of it.

'Very nice, Katka . . . tight and oh so satisfying to take that from you.'

I turned to fix him with a baleful stare. I hoped all he could see was the evil eye that was damning him to an eternal life of hell when his soul was finally claimed.

'Look over your shoulder, because one day we will meet again for your death.'

'Bravo, Katka, you're so defiant. And brave. Look at you holding that exquisite chin of yours so high. You didn't let me down.'

I said nothing. I looked back at him as vacantly as I could. The immediate pain was easing but I think it was more that it was being pushed aside by the shocking reality of what now was coming.

'You know, in a different life,' he continued as he did up his trousers and reached for his belt and pistol, 'you and I . . . well, we might have been true friends, perhaps even lovers.'

No, Rudy, only in your warped and twisted mind could that reality exist, I thought. My stare continued in silence.

He didn't seem to mind; he was only interested in his voice, his notions. 'We might even have considered marriage, despite our considerable age difference. I feel sure you would have given me the son I crave. I have daughters already, did you know?'

I didn't. That was a surprise but I refused to show it.

'There, I've rewarded you for your obedience. I've let you into my life, allowed you to glimpse my closest secret that with every beat of my heart I particularly want to have a son so that my name does not end with this war, should I die through it.'

How did you ever find a woman to love you enough to curse her life and her children's lives with you? I thought, wishing I could say it and carry it off in the same sarcastic, careless way it sounded in my mind.

'Ah, the whims of life, eh? Your father begat a son, then lost him. Is he blessed or cursed by a host of daughters? He seems to love you well enough, though I suspect it's his son he grieves for daily – and now I'm going to take his daughters from him too. I've already ruined his favourite, but shhh . . .' He held a finger to his lips and then touched it to mine in a sort of hideous kiss. 'That's our *secret. We can both take it to our graves – yours a little earlier, I fear.' He smiled his neat smile. 'Still feeling courageous, Katka? One more trial to get through and then you can rest in winter's embrace, you and your family frozen together in time. I'll ensure you're buried deep enough so the forest animals don't dig you up and cart you all off in pieces. Oh, they do that, you know,' he said, in case I wasn't showing enough fear in my expression. I couldn't. My features held the mask I needed, mostly in shock, but partly to deny him what he wanted.*

'So now it's time, Katka. I enjoyed this special, private time of ours. Follow me.'

He pulled on his coat and once again I looked wildly around in the light of the faint single flame but there was nothing to hurt him with – unless I had the fleeting satisfaction of burning him with hot wax. He picked up the saucer with the stub of candle stuck to it and gestured for me to go first through the door.

Along with my virginity, I left my innocence, my trust in people, my delight in life as I stepped back into the forest clearing. I felt ready to die, because I understood now the German remark I'd missed earlier. Rudy had told them to strip my family. Their garments lay in an untidy heap and my family stood naked, shivering uncontrollably; my father tried to cover himself for modesty around the girls. My mother stood there, unsure of why her body was out for all to see. The girls hugged each other. They appeared terrified in the ghastly glow of the candle as Rudy approached. I realised the tarpaulin had been taken away and my family stood on the edge of a pit. This was to be our mass grave.

'Ah, all ready. Good. Let's get on, then, shall we?'

I ran to them, raggedly dressed, and was embraced; I pulled my mother into our circle of tears and fear. The sound of my father's relentless despair and apology cut through the weeping of my sisters and my soothing words. I could smell my mother's talcum powder.

The scent of lavender and violets danced around us as we prepared to die. I'm sure Lotte had grasped what was going on but my little sisters were confused in their fear, wondering when we would be going home.

'Close your eyes, darlings,' I pleaded, 'and the game will end. You have to keep them closed, no matter what you hear.'

They obediently obliged and fell quiet.

I realised the two henchmen with guns had taken position. Rudy was staring at us all and even in the lowest of lights I could see he was smiling benignly at our touching scene. He noted I watched him and a thought seemed to strike him.

'Katka, just step back here, would you?'

I shook my head.

'Remember my warning.' He spoke so softly, even tenderly, that it only made his intimidation greater. I obeyed as dutifully as the girls had obeyed me. What else could I do?

On a signal the men took aim and I don't even know what Rudy said. I was staring at my father. My father was staring back at me – his expression a ruin of apology. I heard gunfire – it seemed to last forever but it was likely not more than three seconds of repeated blasting and I watched my family collapse beneath the ripping of bullets that tore through their fragile flesh. It was my mother who toppled last and I hoped in that horrible vision of blood exploding from her torso that she went to her death without even the vaguest clue of what was occurring. I couldn't say the same for the rest of my family. One of the men strolled over and, turning on a torch, checked the bodies and chose to fire another single bullet from a pistol into one of my beloveds. I couldn't know which.

Fresh fluid ran down my legs; the vague waft of ammonia erupted as I let out a single sob that seemed to come up from my toes where the steaming liquid gathered.

'Oh, Katka, it's done now. No more fear,' the monster said as though genuinely pitying me as my bladder emptied without my permission. 'I want to give you a chance.'

I looked at him in fresh despair but he didn't give me an opportunity for discussion.

'Run,' he said.

I couldn't move, frowning with incomprehension. I watched him unlock his pistol from its holster and I heard the click of what I presumed was him arming it to fire.

'I said run!'

I ran. I didn't want to, I wanted to join my family, but there was fear and indecision and in that terror I couldn't trust that Rudy wouldn't rape me again or make me a plaything – a reward for the men who did his dirty work. Instinct drove me. I was fleet and couldn't imagine where my strength to move so fast had come from. I could hear his laughter through the trees; it carried his derision through the canopy that formed a perfect tunnel. 'I'm a deadeye shot, Katka,' he called from well behind me. 'And quite good in the dark.'

The sound of the gunshot seemed to come after I was felled. It was as though something unseen tripped me. I heard distant laughter from all of them and then I was drowning, being sucked into a place of no light or sound.

Katerina let go of the memory of the smell of the forest and returned to the present and the pungent flavour of aniseed. She'd barely touched her pastis but the strong taste of her first sip remained. Daniel was not meeting her broken gaze and she could understand.

'I'm sorry' was all she could think of to say.

'For what?' He finally looked up from the depths of his drink.

'For making my hideous memories part of yours now. I have

come to accept that my story is merely one sad tale amongst a sea of sorrow. And I'm not just talking about the Jews.'

They stared at each other.

'Katerina, I don't have the right words to express how deeply affected and horrified I am.'

'I don't expect anyone to, which is why I haven't spoken about it to others.'

He covered her hand lightly with his. 'Whilst the loss may not be comparable, I do understand the impotent rage of feeling powerless against him.'

Katerina nodded. 'And why I have, until now, locked him away in my mind. I have to carry on in this world and I can't let the memories send me insane.'

'They won't. The next part to tell is how you defied the monster and survived. You will share that, won't you?'

'I will.'

'Just give me a moment,' he said.

He left her to her thoughts as the rain intensified, battering against the chilly window. There was no point in heading outside yet. She figured she should finish her story and then make a decision about returning to London.

Daniel was back with a hesitant smile, a small array of tarts and a three-inch square of opera cake. 'I've had them placed on one plate because I know you would leave yours untouched, but this way you can pretend it's only me eating.' He handed her the second pastry fork and looked surprised but pleased when she accepted it.

'You should know my other weakness, other than a syrupy sherry, is opera cake.'

'You are playing with me!'

'No.' She dredged up a smile. 'Distracting myself.' She sighed and cut off a neat corner of the small square of cake. 'There is debate about who invented this squat tower of deliciousness.'

She was relieved Daniel was smart enough to let her have this break, happy to let her discuss something mindless. 'I thought it was a Parisian patisserie that was located near the Opera House.'

'And you could be forgiven for thinking that,' she said, cutting off a small triangle of the treat with its several thin layers of almond cake, coffee buttercream and chocolate ganache. 'But the Dalloyau brothers, who served Louis XIV and were ennobled through their gastronomic delights that so pleased His Majesty, would argue that it was their work that inspired its invention many generations later by one of their clever and creative staff. Monsieur Cyriaque Gavillon first trialled his layer cake at the Dalloyau salon on rue de Faubourg Saint-Honoré about eight years ago. It is said his wife named it "Opéra" to celebrate the Palais Garnier. The idea behind it was that just one bite gives you the entire range of flavours for the whole cake.' She put the morsel balanced on her fork into her mouth and gave a sound of genuine pleasure. 'This is a good version of it.'

'Eat up, then. It will cheer you in this moment but what will cheer me is learning how you escaped the forest.'

She nodded as she chewed.

14

● ● ●

I blinked into consciousness but again my animal survival skills warned me to take stock of my situation first. I was alive; that didn't make sense to me, but it was the truth and I needed to accept that I wasn't dreaming. I was prone and cold down my back plus I was aching in many places but none I could pinpoint. I tried to make sense of where I was and realised I was lying on something uneven but my underside felt warmed. I could taste dirt, and grit was in my eyes . . . no, grit was all around. I was buried but with a small air pocket to breathe and I fought the immediate panic.

Stay still, be silent! *I repeated in my mind. The horror flooded back, not gradually but in one terrible blitz of images of bullets and blood . . . and of death, including mine, I thought. Rudy's bullet had found me, I was sure of it, so it must have only wounded me even though I fell. Perhaps I had hit my head or blacked out. What I did decide in this ghastly heartbeat of understanding is that I was lying atop the cooling body of one of my family members. As that dawning ripped through my blurry thoughts like a lightning arc across a night sky, I had to use all of my will to stop myself screaming. I could taste hair now. My mouth was over the head of one of my sisters, I didn't know which. It didn't matter . . . my family were a pile of corpses now beneath me in the pit I'd seen and I was amongst them. And as I was flung here so carelessly it surely meant that Rudy and his death squad had believed me dead as well. They'd obviously found my lifeless body and hurled it atop the rest and covered us with earth, presuming the forest would keep us hidden until the ground froze us and dealt with us in its own way.*

Was it then in that moment that I decided to fight . . . to survive? It's hard to counter instinct; my mind told me to accept it and lie there and wait for death. The freezing temperature of night would immobilise me soon enough but the animal in me overrode my inclination. And with the stealth of a cat I moved in the smallest of increments, using just my fingertips to scrabble through the still-loose soil and reach towards the surface. He had promised a deep grave but he hadn't kept that promise; I felt the breath of surface air within moments. Rudy had been sloppy, cocksure that no one would know we were there. He was likely right.

I created a makeshift breathing hole and despite swallowing soil and insects I was able to take a clear, shallow, silent breath of the night air. And then I remained still. I don't know for how long. I felt like I aged in that time span but the whole of it I spent listening. I strained every muscle, gave every ounce of my remaining energy and alertness to my ears. I knew the sounds of the forest – I knew the call of night birds, the rustle of small animals – but I was listening for the heavier, two-legged animals with guns. Not a cough, not a murmur, not a sigh, not a snore. There was no movement that I could pinpoint as being made by men.

And that's when I allowed the pain to arrive properly. I didn't want to unleash the scream that was gathering so I kept my eyes closed and allowed it to come, but instead of the terrified shriek I'd anticipated, it found its way out as a long, injured growl of pain. I let it rage. I tipped back my head and I howled into the night. I was like a lone wolf but I was not calling for help or friendship . . . or a mate. I was mourning; my pack was dead. I wished I was dead with them. When no more sound would come, I lay there and wept: deep sobs that shuddered through me, shaking my body atop the others, reminding me of physical pain elsewhere.

And then, when even that anguish had subsided, came the silent despair. How long I lay still, buried there with a numb mind to match my cooling limbs, I don't know. At some point rationality crept up on me and I felt like it was speaking in my father's voice. 'Move!' it urged. 'Get away from here!'

I didn't want to leave but I knew I had to. I had been spared for a reason, the voice pressed in my mind.

As far as I could tell, we were still deep into the night and I didn't imagine the grave had any light pointed its way. I went back through the hours of torment and recalled there had been no bright moonlight when Rudy took me into that hut and when I'd emerged we'd relied on the single lumen of a candle. The men hadn't even taken the cigarettes from their mouths in the span of time it took to kill my family.

I shifted the earth until I could feel a soft gust of air upon my face. With the patience of a hunter advancing on nervous prey, I began to shift my position. Every movement was calculated, performed, held still for another long minute until I managed to raise myself onto an elbow, the point of it digging into the flesh of one of my baby girls. I had to fight hard to prevent a fresh sob escaping, reminding myself she couldn't feel it; her spirit had flown and was safe now. She no longer feared life. I was breathing noisily with the effort of simply caging my emotions and perhaps it was in that second of carefully lifting my head to look over the edge of the grave that I decided I would live for her; I would live for all of them. I would defy the Nazi regime and I would survive it.

I scanned the surrounding forest. There was no sign that a slaughter had taken place – nothing to suggest that anyone had been here except this pit where a mother, a father and their daughters lay. It took me another half an hour, perhaps – I couldn't judge – to finally move sufficiently to lift myself out of the grave and stand at its edge. I felt broken, like a wooden puppet cast aside. I didn't know what to do or how to make the next step – in what direction, to whom . . . and why to even bother. All I knew was that I was alone.

I sat on the edge of the grave, glad that it was too dark to make out any shapes below. Time passed in a blankness where none of the subtle sounds of the night forest had any impact on me. It was a void of indecision and blind despair.

Once again the voice of my father broke through, or whichever angel it was that impersonated him. It urged me to stand, to mark the grave where those I loved cooled and then to leave them . . . to find safety for the night. It forced me to move my numb limbs and to come back to the present, to accept my situation and think for myself.

'What other choice do you have?' the voice asked. It was a reasonable question and the alternative was too heinous to contemplate. I wouldn't even know how to kill myself in that moment.

And so I moved. Arms and legs obeyed me. I found a stick, tore off some of my already ripped frock and tied the fabric around that stick. It would be too obvious to ram it into the ground as a marker, in case Rudy came back. So I took more time, scraping my knees and arms using the skills he'd taught me to climb a nearby tree. I slithered along a sturdy branch, begging it to hold, and then with the help of leaves and some creeping ivy I tied that marker overhead, pointing directly at the pit.

I knew roughly where we were in the woodland surrounding our villa and one day I would come back and claim my family.

I couldn't even keep a vigil for them so their spirits could leave safely. But I would make it right one day. There was the temptation to take cover in the nearby hut but nothing could make me crawl back into that place of torture; besides, all I could think of was getting to the villa – reaching home, a safe place to think.

Not risking the path but skirting it, using trees for cover, I picked my way back over the journey we had taken. It wasn't hard to follow as it was mostly in a straightish line that took me from forest onto a track that became a path and ultimately a road. It took me an hour in my estimation, moving slowly but steadily, pushing the physical pain aside to somewhere else. I registered it but I refused to capitulate by using only willpower, I'm sure, plus the charge of vengeance through my body. Finally, I could pick out the shape of our villa, and while there was fleeting relief, it was chased away by a fresh thrill of fear. There were lights on and momentarily I panicked and froze. Rationality returned; who else could it be but the one person I knew it had to be? It was that surety that gave me new courage because suddenly I no longer felt afraid. I had already faced death; believed I'd died. Now I felt only a need to survive and fight him another day. I climbed another tree – one I knew so well it was like an old friend – and from my vantage I watched Rudy moving around upstairs. He had used the key my father had meekly handed over so he could ransack the house. I imagined I could hear him through the silent night, opening drawers and cupboards, looking for money he knew would be there, as well as any valuables. He could have it all, but once again I hoped it would be a curse upon him and bring him no joy.

In the light of my parents' bedroom I saw him suddenly stand from where he'd presumably been crouching, looking under the bed and I saw him place a box on the chest of drawers. I knew from its shape what he'd discovered, and soon I saw the sinuous outline being lifted from their resting place to be admired. To my knowledge no one outside of our circle knew of the Ottoman Pearls, as my mother called them. She told me she'd worn them only once in her married life and warned I'd likely not find many occasions to wear them myself.

'Perhaps on your wedding night, like the chosen odalisques of old,' she had jested with a conspiratorial wink. 'Remember, naked except for the Pearls,' and then she'd laughed at my thunderstruck expression at hearing my mother make a sexual reference. I must have blushed too because she pinched my cheek. 'Oh, my darling, when you're first married and so in love, your clothes will be more off than on, anyway.'

It was obvious he was entranced by his discovery. Rudy stared at them long enough for me to realise there was no point in me waiting there; I would likely die of cold or my wounds, whatever they were, if I didn't get to somewhere warm and dry, with a chance to take stock. I had hoped to steal back into the villa to find clothes, perhaps rest for the night, hidden in the cellar, but I could see now that was a hopeless thought. Rudy was still admiring the Pearls that were now mine, I realised, as I carefully lowered myself to the near-frozen ground. Once I stood upon it, I refused to look back at the villa. This was my new life: heartbroken, damaged, bleeding and on the run.

I couldn't go back the way I'd come. There were only dead people I loved waiting for me there. I couldn't go down the hill into the village, which was swarming with soldiers, and I couldn't remain here. So I headed higher into the foothills. There were a few tiny hamlets I knew of. Perhaps I could steal into someone's barn and at least have this night in safety to think everything through. Short of killing myself and ending it all, which I'd already decided was pointless, there was no option but to attempt to survive the night.

And that's what I think the angels wanted for me. Survival.

I can't imagine any other reason that Dr Otto Schäfer, a German, was pushed across my path that terrible night. I had been picking my way along the tree line, breathing hard in the frigid dark as I struggled uphill, my face whipped by thin stray branches. My mind was still blanked out with shock but instinct forced me to put one foot in front of the other. At one point I realised the hillside was becoming dense with trees and I was going to hurt myself further so I risked crossing onto the road and being exposed. It wasn't really more than a dirt track but I knew it from childhood. It led into the hamlets of scattered villas of wealthy folk, as we had once been. All around me it looked deserted and I became wearied, lost in my need to put distance between me and the slaughter of my family. I didn't hear the purr of the car and it was only when the headlights picked me out in the black night that I startled like an animal and just as helplessly collapsed in the illumination. I was blinded by their eerie glow, like two huge eyes watching me, and resigned to the tall, smudgy shape that appeared from behind them to loom over me . . .

'What on earth!' said a voice in German.

It was not Ruda Mayek. The last vestiges of instinct served me. 'Help me, please?' I said in his language.

He let out a curse of despair and I was picked up, cradled in his arms. 'I could have killed you!' he admonished me.

I didn't reply but lay limp, staring into an oblong face.

'What is your name?'

I thought about lying but I didn't have the strength. 'Katka,' I said, at least making a go at withholding the truth.

'Katka, what has happened?'

I shook my head and now the resilience fled and I wept.

'Right,' he said with a sigh. 'We can work out the past later. For now, let's worry about this moment. My name is Otto Schäfer. I am a physician and I am taking you to my villa. You have nothing

to fear from me, Katka. Do you understand? I will not hurt you but you have wounds. There's . . . there's blood all over you, and now over me,' he tutted. 'I must see to your injuries and we'll concern ourselves with everything else later. All right?'

My silence was my answer. He placed me gently in his vehicle and I remember leaning back against the plush seat and smelling the comforting leather that reminded me of my father's car and happier times.

'You can't sleep yet, promise me.'

I don't think I responded.

'Katka!'

I must have groaned.

'Don't sleep. Do you understand? You have a head wound and I need to look at it properly before I can let you sleep. Are you hearing me? Say yes!'

'Yes.'

'Good, stay awake. It's only up the road a little bit.'

He hadn't lied. We were at his villa before I could drift fully into sleep and then I was being picked up again and carried into a warm house. I heard a woman's voice gasping and clucking and Otto's voice joined it and it became background noise to me. I wanted to sleep. I wanted to forget for a while. But they were rousing me, wanting me awake, if not alert. I tasted brandy, began to splutter, to cough a little, and my head cleared as heat traced its warm path down into my belly.

'Sip more, Katerina.'

I snapped my eyes awake and stared into the compassionate expression of Mrs Biskup, a widow from the village. I panicked but she shook her head kindly as if to say all would be well. 'Let Dr Schäfer examine you.'

There was no fight left in me anyway, not since the brandy hit the pit of my stomach. I just wanted to disappear into oblivion but

I became compliant instead because I caught sight of my reflection in a mirror and couldn't recognise myself, even though Mrs Biskup had. It was as though someone had tipped a bucket of blood over the top of me.

'Head wounds,' the doctor muttered. 'Always a lot of blood,' he continued. 'Why did you lie about your name?'

Mrs Biskup answered. 'Wouldn't you, in her shoes, if you were found by a German?'

I watched his face twist into an expression of disappointment, as if he accepted her excuse but didn't have to like it. 'So there are two injuries here, Katerina. One looks like a trauma created by blunt force.' He peered through rimless glasses using a magnifying glass and I could see the oblong was a handsome face, unpitted with neat, thickish eyebrows over darkly lashed eyes of a sad blue. I say sad because they looked like the colour of the sky on a wet and windy day . . . the sort of day that imprisons a child indoors when all they want to do is run wild and free. His hair was cut short but slightly longer on top, while his exposed ears sat neatly against the sides of his head. He was older than Mayek, younger than my father. In my state I couldn't guess and I would get it wrong any-way; at fourteen most adults seem centuries older. His voice was as gentle as Mrs Biskup's and I had to trust they meant me no immedi-ate harm. She had known me since I was a baby in my mother's arms. Surely she wouldn't help to entrap me, send me back to that grave to lie on top of my sisters and parents?

'Mmm,' he grunted. 'There's grit in here. Did you hit your head? On a stone, a rock, a tree perhaps?'

'Perhaps,' I murmured. 'I was unconscious for a while,' I man-aged to mumble, sticking cautiously to German.

'Yes, that's what troubles me. I'm just going to run some simple vision tests. Do your best.' It took a few minutes while he made me follow his finger, peering into my eyes, shining a small torch into

my pupils. I smelled liquor on his breath but not so much that I imagined him intoxicated. He'd obviously been on his way home from being out for dinner or with friends. 'Good,' he finally said, more to himself than to me. 'That's a relief. You'll have a small scar, I suspect, but it will heal on its own once we clean it properly. Now, this other one,' he continued, moving to peer over the top of my head. 'This is still bleeding heavily, and I think I shall have to stitch it.' He knelt before me so he could look me in the eye. 'What occurred this evening, Katerina?'

The brandy had woken me sufficiently that I could think and I hesitated as I considered my options; I flicked a glance to Mrs Biskup as I wasn't sure of my best course. Would honesty get me flung into Terezín? I thought in a heartbeat that I'd rather die now by an overdose of the doctor's drugs than face Ruda Mayek again in his new role.

'Katerina is from Prague,' she said into the awkward silence. 'Her family – a very good one – has a villa not too far from here.'

'I see. Well, that's good news, then. We should contact them; they'll be worried, surely? But I'm trying to understand how this injury was achieved.' He looked between us both, neither of us offering more. His puzzlement at our silence became a frown. 'Am I missing something?'

Mrs Biskup couldn't know for sure but she was a villager and I imagined she could likely guess at who might be behind this. I suppose in the frame of mind I was in I no longer cared what happened other than not wanting to be handed back over to Rudy. I would take any measure to avoid that. 'I am Jewish,' I said, trying to sound defiant again.

His hands dropped away from holding my head but his confused expression within that sympathetic face didn't change. 'I didn't ask your religion. I asked what happened. How did you get this odd wound?'

I wanted to trust him. 'From a bullet aimed at me as I tried to run away from some terrible men,' I admitted.

Mrs Biskup sucked back a breath of dismay for all of us.

He blinked and I watched him swallow as he took this in. After another protracted pause, the doctor stood. 'Mrs Biskup, please take our guest to the bathroom and allow her to bathe and help her to clean her hair, please. Be extremely gentle and use tepid, not warm, water on her head. Then I shall stitch when I can see the wound properly. Use a soft flannel to soak off the dried blood.'

I reached for his hand, and the hair at his wrist felt downy, tender like his gaze that looked upon me. 'Doctor, if you are going to contact the soldiers, I'd rather you ask Mrs Biskup to drown me in the bath. I won't fight it. Perhaps give me something to make me sleep – permanently, I mean, and make it easier on all of us.'

I could swear his eyes glistened with moisture but the lamp had been turned to highlight my head, so he was now in shadow. 'Katerina, not all Germans are Nazi or even share its ideology. And most of us doctors, certainly the ones who were originally called to medicine as a vocation, don't make a distinction between patients based on anything other than need. Go with Mrs Biskup. I am not about to tell anyone you're here . . . not yet, anyway.'

As she led me away, she whispered to me. 'Is Ruda Mayek behind this?'

I hated that I began to cry but it was answer enough.

'He's trying to make a name for himself, you know, catch the attention of the Nazis. Well, there's no love lost with him, my dear, whereas both of my sons and their families owe their livelihood to your generous father. You can count on my silence.'

I squeezed her hand, not ready to explain that my father was dead.

'Now, you be still. Let me help you so the doctor can take proper care of you. He's a good man, not like the others.'

Guilt erupted at feeling soothed by the warmth of soapy water against my skin while visions of the twisted limbs of my sisters cooling pale in the grave were companions to that guilt. I sat in sullen silence while Mrs Biskup sponged away the obvious evidence of my trauma and I stood silent, like a child, while she dried me. I couldn't climb into my shredded clothes so she brought a pair of the doctor's pyjamas that engulfed me in soft brushed cotton, before I was led back out before him, cheeks glowing from the flannelling.

I had already surmised that the doctor seemed to blink whenever he was disconcerted; I don't know what troubled him in this moment but his sad gaze watched my every step towards him intensely.

He cleared his throat. 'Most young women would probably have to roll the cuffs up on my pyjamas.'

'I used to hate being the tallest girl at school,' I offered in a lame excuse.

'And now?' He briefly smiled.

'Now I don't go to school,' I replied.

He scratched his nose after blinking, looking embarrassed. 'Right, well, come and sit down,' he gestured.

Mrs Biskup gave me a small push in the back to follow his instructions.

'Do you feel a little better?'

'On the outside,' I admitted.

'I couldn't stop it bleeding,' Mrs Biskup said.

'Yes, let's get that stopped with some sutures. Mrs Biskup, perhaps some coffee?' He looked at me expectantly. 'Are you hungry?' I was but I shook my head. 'I think some warmed milk for Katerina, please.'

She left us to prepare a tray.

'So, I'm going to stitch. It won't be too painful because the scalp is forgiving. Will you permit me to do this without a fuss?'

'Yes.'

He moved behind me and tilted my head down slightly before shifting the lamp so he could see the wound clearly and I heard him make a clicking sound in his mouth. 'Just a few millimetres deeper and you wouldn't be here. You say you were running away?'

'Yes.'

'This is like pulling teeth, Katerina. Will you please tell me what occurred?'

'I don't know that I want to recall it.'

'Oh, I think you do. The fury of it is threatening to explode out of you. Tell me. Say it aloud; it might make you feel easier.'

'No, I don't believe I shall ever ease the memory of watching my family murdered, Dr Schäfer, but I shall tell you because Mrs Biskup has asked me to trust you and I have no one else that I can.'

I could feel the prick of the needle pressing into my flesh and the tug of the thread a moment later but, as he'd warned, while it wasn't exactly comfortable, it didn't hurt, certainly not enough to squawk over. I began to talk as he stitched. Mrs Biskup walked in and put down a tray as I was telling Otto Schäfer about our old family friend closing the door of the hut and locking me in with him. I watched her lips purse at the mention of Ruda Mayek undoing his belt. She put a hand to her mouth in a gesture to prevent a sound of dismay.

But I no longer cared about how inappropriate my words were. I had nothing left to respect in my life, and my virginity, though I mourned how it had been stolen, had become the least of my concerns. Rudy was back in my mind, horribly real. 'He bent me forwards over the table so he wouldn't have to look me in the eye – my devil's eye, he called it.'

The doctor took my hand and I flinched. 'Katerina —'

'No, that's only the start,' I said, gulping back fresh tears.

I couldn't control the surge of memory now. It all came out; a detailed recount was relived and I could see the full horror of my story reflected in Otto Schäfer's eyes and fallen expression when he had finished his ministrations and came around the chair to look at me.

Mrs Biskup couldn't watch me. She sat on the edge of a nearby armchair, seated sideways, wringing her hands in her lap, her eyes downcast.

'He made me run but I think he always intended to kill me. This was a final bit of . . .' I couldn't find the right word.

'Sport,' Otto finished for me and his mouth twisted as though the word tasted ugly.

'Yes, that's exactly how it was. It was a game. I was his toy. He could do whatever he liked. I think I knew even as I ran for my life that he didn't intend to give me that chance. I wanted to stay, I really did. I wanted to lie down with my family and have a bullet in my head so my spirit could join theirs. But still I ran.'

Otto was now crouched in front of me looking so wounded by the story unfolding for him that I curiously felt more pity for him than I did for myself. 'So he took aim and the bullet he fired, I presume, created the wound I've just stitched?'

I agreed. 'I heard the laughter and the gunshot. I didn't feel it but I suppose I must have hit my head as I fell,' I said, touching the second wound, 'because I remember nothing after that. I woke up in the grave, lying on the cooling bodies of my naked sisters, my parents beneath them, I suppose. The men must have thought I was dead.'

Schäfer nodded. 'The drama of the head wound would have saved you.' He looked away in disgust. 'Mrs Biskup, I'll need you to take a look at Katerina in case there are wounds . . . er, elsewhere.' He nodded at her. She nodded once back as the couched message was received but I didn't follow their line of thought because I could hardly believe how matter-of-fact I had sounded in my retelling, but there was a hardening inside me. I might compare it to the withering of a rose: all those joyous petals, full of perfume and sunshine, falling away. What was left was the impervious hip with its hard, shiny case that enclosed all the goodness and the secrets of the rose within. In that moment I didn't think anything could hurt me again and I was no longer scared of death in whichever manner it might come.

'This is horrifying.' Mrs Biskup stood; she looked traumatised and wouldn't make eye contact. It was as though she were the victim. 'This is happening all over.'

Schäfer, in contrast, was able to look at me with a direct gaze. 'I have no words that could possibly console you, other than to say you have my protection from here on. I want you to trust Mrs Biskup and let her check for any further wounds. Are you hurting elsewhere?'

'Everywhere,' I replied but I sounded vague.

'I understand.'

Mrs Biskup gave the thanks that I couldn't. 'Her father was one of the finest men you could hope to meet, Dr Schäfer. He had factories, he employed so many people and he was good to them – good to all of us in this village too. When the family was in residence during holidays they would often hold a summer picnic and invite all the village to come up to the gardens. We didn't have to bring anything – although we enjoyed baking for it – and Mrs Kassowicz would put on a feast . . . do you remember that, Katerina?'

I nodded. I really didn't want to remember happy times.

'I don't need convincing, Mrs Biskup,' he replied evenly. 'What has happened to this young lady today is heinous. There are rules to war. My father was a proud German army officer, as was my grandfather, and I grew up understanding they both showed enormous respect for the protection of prisoners. The man who now leads

Germany may have fought in the previous war but he doesn't hold the same regard for the protocol of the military. Katerina, I want you to know that I'm ashamed tonight to be German.' He reached to tilt my chin up so I was forced to meet his stare. 'I give you my word, then, as a man . . . as a doctor . . . that I will let no further harm come to you while you're under my protection. Will you trust me?'

The sorrowful eyes that spoke of wintry days landed softly upon me in what I believed was genuine remorse. It was not his fault but it's true I wanted to blame everyone who called themselves German. 'Yes, but I do not want you going after Rudy Mayek.'

'Rudy? You speak as though you know him.'

'Since the day I was born. He is – was – a family friend. My parents regarded him with much affection.' I forced down a sob. 'My father probably thanked him for his compassion in killing us privately and not making us suffer the indignity and potential torture of one of the work camps.'

'And you do not want me to officially report him? Why not?' He sounded understandably shocked.

'Because he boasted of having the ear of Reinhard Heydrich.'

Otto's brow furrowed with fresh concern and a dawning of understanding.

'Rudy is going to Terezín shortly, or so he brags. He will have a senior position there and I think he'd love to know I'm still alive and potentially within his grasp again. I'm imagining that at Terezín he won't even have to cover up his shame.'

Mrs Biskup tutted as she poured the coffee.

'Put another nip of cognac into Katerina's milk. She needs a long, deep sleep tonight.' He could see in my alarm that sleep frightened me. 'No one is coming here. No one knows you are here and by tomorrow morning I promise I shall have a plan for you. Mrs Biskup?'

'Yes, Doctor?'

'This is our secret. Can I count on you?'

She put a hand over her heart with an expression of dismay that he'd have to ask such a question. 'No one will ever hear a word of Katerina's presence in this house or that I even sighted her . . . not from these lips.'

'There, Katerina. Now you have two friends to trust. Take your milk and go to bed. I'll see you when you wake. You're going to have an aching head tomorrow.'

Mrs Biskup tipped another slug of liquor into my milk, disturbing the wrinkled skin that had formed on its surface while we were speaking. I tasted its fumes as they rose on the steam and the smell of cognac would forever remind me of Otto Schäfer . . . the first and only German I would ever count on since the start of the war.

———————

Daniel could see he had worn her out.

'Enough, Katerina. You must be exhausted.'

'Not particularly; just relieved to have brought that all out into the open.'

He looked out onto the streets, busy again because the rain had subsided. 'I'm going to put you in a taxi. No arguing. Will you meet me again?'

She looked at him. 'Not tomorrow. Perhaps the day after.'

'Then how about joining me for lunch next time we meet?'

'All right. Where?'

'Will you let me cook for you?'

'Your apartment?'

'With Madame Bouchard nearby, of course.'

She gave her smoky laugh.

'Friday? Shall we say noon?'

She nodded. 'That would be lovely. You go call a taxi. I'm going to pay the bill.'

15

. . .

He'd been staring out of his kitchen window since eleven-thirty. He knew her to be prompt but not early; his watchfulness was redundant. She would likely step out of a taxi or move into view at minutes before twelve . . . there was at least another eight or nine minutes before that time. He returned to his stove to stir the stew that had been on a gentle simmer since the morning. He'd cooked it the evening he'd last seen her, knowing it would only improve with age. This meal he'd prepared with much affection felt important; he wanted to impress, wanted to see her close her eyes and smile for him when she tasted it.

He poked the potatoes with the tip of a sharp knife. They were coming along perfectly, boiling gently in their salted water, and should be ready to military timing. He flung the tea towel over his shoulder and returned to the window. The kitchen clock told him she should arrive any moment.

He waited and watched the street corner. He was guessing she would have walked. The day was milder and mercifully dry; he was sure most able Parisians would be stretching their legs after a long winter and the two wet days that had kept people inside.

He caught a flash of colour. How could anyone miss her? She looked heart-stopping in her mint-green jacket with its low neckline. She wore a narrow, knee-length skirt the colour of faded parchment, and her longline navy gloves, matching bag and shoes were daring and yet elegant. Her hair was hidden behind a low-slung woven cloche hat that was the colour of rich milk. He missed looking at her thick, bouncy hair as much as he had missed her company these last couple of days.

He hoped she might look up so he could wave. And then he stepped away from the window in case she did; what was wrong with him, appearing so boyishly lovelorn? He chided himself for losing sight of what this mission was about. His buzzer predictably sounded and his two feline companions immediately left their comfy, sun-drenched spots in the main room to tag team at the hallway entrance with matching glares.

Daniel pressed the button that opened the main door downstairs. 'Good morning, Katerina,' he said through the speaker. 'Ready to run the gauntlet?'

'Ready,' her voice came up, sounding tinny through the speaker. 'Wish me luck.'

He stepped outside to look down the flights of stairs and right enough could hear her indistinctly conversing with his landlady. She extricated herself and he heard the faint click of her heels intensifying as she ascended.

Katerina finally glided up, not looking out of breath this time. She'd paced herself. 'Good morning . . . er, good afternoon,' she corrected, glancing at her watch.

'You look stunning.' He couldn't help himself. 'What a colour that is – so fresh, so spring.'

'Thank you for noticing. I have a weakness for clothes.'

'Along with sherry and opera cake. I learn more each time we meet.'

She smiled as she reached the top step and surprised him with a friendly welcome kiss on each cheek. 'I've brought wine and a treat for that sweet tooth of yours.'

He glanced at the box from the famous confectionery house of Fouquet, one of the oldest sweetshops of Paris. 'Tell me they're fruit gels.'

'Only the best.' She grinned. 'But don't expect me to share them. They're yours. I was torn between those or the spiced *croquants*.'

'You chose well,' he assured her. He guided her inside and took the bottle of wine, admiring it and thanking her again. 'You know I'll eat the whole box.'

'My intention. Enjoy,' she said, slipping off her pale wool jacket to reveal a simple low-necked cardigan of a similar milky colour to her cloche. Hat and gloves were peeled off to leave her unadorned. Again, no gold or sparkling gems for Katerina. 'Ooh, Daniel, something smells unbelievably good and if I'm not mistaken —'

'You're not,' he cut in, delighted, hanging up her jacket.

'*Gulás*?'

'My mother's Czech goulash recipe. I hope I've remembered it correctly; I haven't made it in an age but today it felt right for us to be sharing a traditional Czech meal.'

'Oh, you spoil me. How wonderful,' she said, making for the kitchen. He liked that she seemed relaxed and comfortable in his home.

He followed her to the pot whose lid she lifted with anticipation. 'Thank you,' she said, admiring the bubbling casserole. She inhaled. 'I can smell the marjoram and bay.'

'Two types of paprika, my mother always insists – sweet and the spicier version. Now, don't be disappointed but I didn't have a chance to make dumplings, but my potatoes should be ready.'

He leaned over her to press the point of a nearby knife into the vegetables. 'Perfect. I must tip them into a colander now and let them steam.'

She let him do what he had to and wandered back into the main room. He could hear her addressing the cats and then laughing at their stern expressions.

He stood at the doorway between the rooms. 'Glass of wine?'

'Mmm, why not?'

Daniel returned with glasses of chilled rosé. 'Goes well with our meal and yours needs cooling.'

'*À la vôtre*,' she said, lifting her glass to him.

'*Santé*,' he replied. 'I don't want to spoil this lovely mood with talk of your past.'

She shrugged. 'It's all about escape now from occupied Prague. Exciting, dangerous, the stuff of movies,' she said, widening her eyes with feigned intrigue.

'Come, sit down. I hope you're hungry, although that's probably a redundant hope.'

She laughed. 'I'm hungry, I promise.'

He wished deeply he didn't have his private agenda. Falling in love with Katerina Kassowicz seemed inevitable and he'd never thought love would visit him again; never thought it possible to want to love a woman once more. He swallowed and banished his tumbling thoughts. They ate while Katerina encouraged Daniel to talk about his family and his life growing up in England, and he was happy to do so, carefully curating all that he spoke about, especially when she shifted to his work. He'd had enough practice over the years as a spy so the lies came out effortlessly, he hoped.

With full bellies and coffee a distant thought, a natural silence descended and he felt the time was right.

'Finish your story?'

She nodded.

'I can't imagine what it felt like to wake up in a German stranger's spare bedroom.'

———————

My eyes slitted open and then I was wide awake in alarm. I didn't know where I was and I looked around, wildly trying to make sense of the simple but comfortable bedroom I was in. Daylight seeped through damask curtains the colour of a pink rose at dusk and through the net curtain beneath I could see familiar woodland and hear birds singing their glorious chorus. Visions of lying on my dead family returned to sicken me. I began to cry uselessly and allowed myself a few minutes of pity as I relived their deaths again, but I'd survived and there had to be reason for that. I had to force these crippling memories to a safe but different place in my mind in the same way my father had explained his grief when Petr had left us.

'I only allow myself to think of your brother when I feel particularly strong. Most of the time I deliberately won't let him into my thoughts. It will take years before I can conjure up Petr and smile, remember him the way we enjoyed him.'

And that's what I had to do: avoid allowing them to surface from the grave for a while. I had to get strong, get on with surviving so I could live for them . . . avenge them.

Pain throbbed at the back of my head as the doctor had warned and I reached for my forehead where a soft gauze was protecting my wound. As I had been helped into bed last night I had wondered if I would have no memory by morning – if the blow to my head would blur and lose everything – but no, my recollections were intact. This was day one, I told myself, of learning how to compartmentalise yesterday's events.

As young as I was, I knew I had to put the events of the previous day into a special space in my mind and lock them away tightly.

If I was going to survive, I had to set the trauma aside and focus on hiding. By the time I was fully awake, I had made the decision that I was going defy Hitler by living, but I knew I would need help.

I tentatively stepped out of the bedroom and tiptoed down the hall barefoot. I found Dr Schäfer sitting by a fire, reading. He looked up immediately and smiled. I can't forget how safe I felt in that moment; instinct urged me to trust him.

'How do you feel?'

'Sore. Is Mrs Biskup . . .?'

'She'll be here shortly. Usually arrives at ten. It's . . .' He glanced up at the clock whose grave tick I could hear from above the fireplace. 'Not quite a quarter to nine.'

'Oh,' I said, nodding, unsure.

'Come and sit by the fire. You must be cold. Let me fetch you something to drink. Do you like coffee?'

'You don't have to —'

'It's fresh.'

'Yes, please,' I said. 'My parents allowed me . . . used to allow me to have coffee.'

'Do you take milk?' he called from the kitchen.

'Er . . . yes, yes, please.'

He returned quickly, handing me a tall cup and saucer. 'I've put in some sugar too. You need energy.'

Not just fresh milk but sugar! What a treat. I thanked him for the third time.

'I needed to see that smile,' he said kindly.

I told him of my decision, not only to force the vivid memory of the slaughter in the woods to a corner in my mind I couldn't easily access, but to be strong in order to punish their killer.

'That's very brave of you. You'll find a way to avenge them but for now it's important that we protect your life. I've been giving it some thought and the first thing we have to do is bury Katerina

Kassowicz.' At the way I started, his expression softened further. 'Forgive me, that was a poor choice of words, but this Mayek fellow has to believe you're still there where he left you.'

In that moment I felt I could forgive the good doctor anything. 'What if he's checked or sent someone back?'

'Then he will be scared but he's certainly not going to look for you in the house of a German doctor. Nevertheless, I know someone who owes me a deep debt and they can help me in changing your identity.'

I looked back at him aghast. 'What do you mean?'

'You have to become someone else. You speak German very well but you're not registered anywhere as German so let's not risk that because our records are reliable. Do you speak French, by any chance?'

I nodded. 'I'm fluent.'

He shook his head in gentle admiration. 'You do impress me. All right, so let's make you French, but you were in Czechoslovakia visiting Jewish friends and they've been . . . removed.'

I noticed him struggle to say that final word.

'You can't return to France because of the wartime restrictions so you contacted me in Prague . . . I'm an old family friend and I've brought you here while I was taking a short break in the country.'

I nodded.

'Good. So, is there a name you like that you might respond to easily?'

'I used to have a pen friend in France called Severine. I always thought her name very beautiful.'

'Severine it is. Can you live with the surname of Kassel? It's German enough to please, but Norman enough to be French.'

I actually smiled properly, hard though it was to believe, but there was much to like about this man and I needed to show him I trusted him.

'Originally from the word "castle", and given your bravery, I think it suits you.'

'It's also close enough to my own,' I said.

'I'm glad you approve. You need to leave Katerina Kassowicz behind from today – from this moment. Can you do that? I'm going to call you Severine from here on and so will everyone else. We're going to change your hair, get you some clothes that belie your age so we can reinvent you as a late teenage French national trapped in Czechoslovakia, but under the protection of a German. You're also training as a nurse.'

'I am?' I said with surprise.

'You'll have to be a quick study. We'll say your training was interrupted, but I promise you this will not be a problem, not if I keep you close.'

'And will you?' I sipped my coffee. It was strong, sweet and uplifting.

'I will keep you close, Severine – and safe. I give you my word, and this is my apology to you on behalf of the German people who don't think like Hitler; there are plenty of us.' He stood and moved over to where his case was kept; he retrieved something from it and returned to where I sat. 'Take these. It will ease the pain but it won't ease the itch, and you are not to touch that wound.'

I obediently swallowed the tablets with the remains of my coffee. 'How long before the stitches come out?'

'We'll leave them in for a week. Then we need the wound to fully heal. It will be a fortnight or more before we can put our plan into action but we can practise your nursing skills in the meantime and we can plan. We have the whole winter. Once you get snowed in, few people will be coming up here, so we can keep you safe.' He chanced a crooked grin at sounding so conspiratorial; it was what I needed, though – more than anything, a friend to trust. 'I can hear Mrs Biskup arriving. She's early! We're going to need her help as

I have to return to work in a week or so, but you will remain here, hidden, under her care. Is that all right?'

'Yes.'

'You can't be seen by anyone,' he reinforced. 'Not even an old friend. Only the three of us will know. We must keep it that way all winter, do you understand? No returning to the woods to lay flowers, or prayers over your family. I'm sorry to be so harsh but we're trying to save your life and we have to be suspicious and desperately careful of every move now.' He sounded so earnest. He waited, eyeing me gravely. 'Tell me you understand.'

'I will not break the rules. I do understand, Dr Schäfer.'

'I want you to call me Otto.'

'Then you must call me Katerina if you ever utter my real name. I never want to be referred to as Katka again; it's what he called me.'

Otto nodded with tender comprehension.

So began my strange new life. Otto returned to work at the Bulovka hospital in Prague, where he worked exclusively with German citizens, and I stayed in the villa for the next month without setting a foot outside and spent the time learning to be a nurse. The most I was allowed to do was open my window and breathe the fresh air. I kept my promise to remain hidden. How could I not – I was as terrified of discovery as my two conspirators.

Otto had left a raft of information for me to learn and I proved I was the quick study he had hoped. I couldn't convince a professional if I was under scrutiny but I could get by and was sure that if I wore a nursing uniform I could likely fool patients. My external wounds healed. Mrs Biskup's Christmas came and went. Neither she nor I felt like celebrating the arrival of 1942; Heydrich had already closed every synagogue and had now ordered the state police to intervene against any Czech nationals befriending or helping Jews.

I feared constantly for Mrs Biskup but she was adamant that if we never broke the rules of the house, no one would ever know. There was nothing in my room to suggest a woman slept there and we hid the few clothes we'd gathered for me in the cellar – they were always crispy cold when I brought a change of blouse or skirt up from beneath the floor. Plus, we had a plan that I would climb into the loft space should anyone arrive unexpectedly. Although we felt safe that there was no reason for anyone to visit, we practised me being able to get into the loft smoothly, missing the creaky floor-board and moving so quietly no one could hear so much a sigh of timber, and fast. Mrs Biskup timed me from all corners of the house should that fateful knock ever come. I could be secreted in around fifty seconds. There was a telephone at the villa and Otto rang each evening at the same time. He'd give two rings, then hang up and then ring another three times and put the phone down. That was my signal that I could safely pick up the phone on the next ring – it would be him. We spoke briefly, always in French or German; never about his work, always about my health and how I was feeling and about my studies. He would test me over the phone too. I looked forward to hearing his voice but hadn't realised how much I yearned for his company.

'I shall be at the villa this Friday.'

I wasn't surprised by how I thrilled at the news.

'How long for?'

'Just the weekend.'

'Stay longer,' I groaned.

I liked hearing his low, albeit brief, chuckle, coming from Prague.

And so we continued our strange existence. Through the harsher snowy months of February and March I lived alone with visits from Mrs Biskup only every third or fourth day, depending on the weather. Otto would come perhaps twice a month now as he *didn't want to draw suspicion of returning to his holiday villa too often through the winter. My more reserved nature lent itself to this hermit-like existence and I barely noticed I hadn't spoken a word for sometimes more than twenty-four hours until I lifted the phone to answer and realised my voice was gritty from lack of use. I snatched at the phone.*

'Hello, Otto.'

'Not too lonely?'

'I'm fine,' I said. What else was there to say? 'I'm enjoying reading some of the books you have here. I did use your gramophone a couple of times . . . on very low volume, of course.' I didn't tell him that I'd caught myself dancing and immediately stopped swaying to the music; it didn't seem right to enjoy it quite so much.

'Stay distracted, Katerina.' He still preferred that name, it seemed, despite his promise. 'Whatever it takes, just keep your mind occupied and your body healthy. I'm worried about you being left alone after . . .' He didn't want to say it.

'My mother always said I was a secretive child. This trait got me into hot water a few times because I didn't offer up information but it meant I was a "reliable vault", as she called me.'

He didn't say anything and I presumed he was waiting for me to explain why I'd mentioned this.

'I . . . I guess what I'm doing now is keeping a secret from myself. I've put the horror in —'

'A box within a box within a box,' he said, sounding the identical words over mine.

He couldn't tell I was smiling.

'Your advice helped.'

'I'm not a doctor of psychiatry but it seems the only wise way to proceed – for now, anyway. Not forgotten but put away so you can survive without it undoing you every moment of the day.'

'Despite the constant reminder I'm living with.'

'Yes.'

I nodded. My voice remained steady and even I could understand how rapid my toughening up had been since the night of my family's death. 'I want to live so that I can punish Ruda Mayek.'

'You stagger me, Katerina. It's easy to forget you're still just fifteen. It will be good to see you and remind myself that you are still a child, despite . . .' He trailed off but there was an undertone of something meaningful in that final remark. I realised only much later that Otto had made this comment as a reference for himself – a piece of advice he should observe, because his fondness was evident to me. He cleared his throat. 'See you Friday night for dinner.'

'I'm already looking forward to it,' I admitted. 'I shall cook for you.'

He laughed gently but not mockingly. 'What a treat.'

'I'll make the traditional Czech meal we were going to share on the evening my family was separated.' That was my new way of referring to that terrible night. I hadn't broken down into sobs since early winter and spring was around the corner now.

'Mrs Biskup will bring you everything you need,' he said.

'She'll interfere,' I said affectionately.

'Cook up a storm, the two of you. I'll bring wine. You're old enough to sip with me.'

I gave a grin of brief pleasure. It seemed heinous to do so but I couldn't help the glimmer of teenage happiness that rushed through me as a fresh sense of hope . . . like stepping out of cool shadows to feel the sun's warmth.

My scalp wound was well healed and any scarring could be disguised by my thick hair, which was the topic of our conversation now. Dinner was finished and the three of us were seated in armchairs around the fire. It was still fiercely cold.

'If we make it dark brown, it could do the opposite of what we want,' Otto admitted.

I heard what he didn't want to say aloud: that it would make me look more obviously Jewish.

Mrs Biskup frowned. 'Let's lighten it, then, and cut it shorter.'

I tried not to baulk. My mother had always loved my long hair but my attachment was purely an emotional response; whatever it took, I would agree to.

'And I think some make-up will make Katerina look a lot older.'

'Call her Severine. We really must,' he said, as much for his own benefit as hers.

She gave him a look of apology. 'Leave her looks to me. I can do it. You will just have to trust us women.'

'You can do it now?'

She couldn't help a smug smile. 'Come with me, Severine.'

I stood to follow, watching Otto stoking the fire and settling down to read a book that I recalled being a favourite in our family's library. He noted my interest.

'Have you read this?' he asked.

'No, but I know the story. My father told me about Manderley and the way Rebecca haunted the second Mrs de Winter.'

He nodded. 'The house is as important a character as the people who lived in it.'

I could never tire of Otto's smile and enjoyed watching it break. 'You can rely on your father's judgement. Without Manderley's brooding presence, the story wouldn't be nearly as sinister, or as powerful.'

'Sounds like you know it well.'

'I've read this several times. It reminds me of my favourite book, Jane Eyre by Charlotte Brontë, but that was written a century ago.'

'And like a special piece of art, it never loses its lustre. Papa taught me that any sort of art should prompt an emotional response.'

'Indeed it does. I read Jane Eyre each year for how it makes me feel. I think you'd enjoy it for its variety of themes, from spirituality to a young woman trying to establish her independence within a patriarchal society.'

It intrigued me that his favourite book was about a woman. 'Perhaps I could read yours while I'm here?'

'Alas, it is in Germany but I shall acquire a copy for you.'

Mrs Biskup returned looking vaguely exasperated. 'Come on, Severine. This is going to take hours.'

We disappeared, to re-emerge past midnight when we found Otto dozing in the armchair, the fire down to embers and Rebecca leaning on his chest, which just for a silly, childish moment I imagined was a soft spot that I might like to rest. He stirred at our murmuring and blinked several times before his mouth gaped.

'Well, say something, Doctor,' Mrs Biskup admonished him. 'Isn't she beautiful?'

'I . . . I hardly recognise you, Katerina,' he stammered.

'Her name is Severine,' she reminded him with a tutting sound. 'And that's good!' she added, clapping with excitement. 'Isn't that just what we want?'

'It is,' he breathed, staring at me. He looked unnerved, as though he might be noticing me as an adult for the first time, although I had always sensed he liked me just as I was . . . and perhaps constantly fought the attraction.

I enjoyed the sense of power. My blush intensified. 'Are you both sure?' I wondered aloud, hesitantly reaching for my hair, which had lost at least six inches and was now falling in gentle curled waves on one side, pinned at the top of my ear with a tortoiseshell comb. The other side was swept up into a soft roll and clipped to hold it in position. Its colour, with the aid of a bottle of magic, had turned several shades lighter to a hue like baled hay. Mrs Biskup had taken to my face with a bag of cosmetics. It felt like she'd been painting my skin for an hour, yet when I looked in the mirror I saw only dewy, pale colouring around my eyes. She'd plucked, shaped and darkened my brows into a neat bow. She'd blackened my top lashes but left my bottom lashes untouched.

'Don't want you looking like a harlot,' she'd muttered beneath her breath.

We lightened the foundation with some vanishing cream, not that I needed much on my young complexion, but we were trying to make me look older. We used lipstick to make do as a barely blushing rouge for my cheeks and to tint my lips.

When I'd looked in the mirror I'd felt I'd aged a decade and I think Otto was feeling the same way now.

'Now we have a new problem, Mrs Biskup,' he finally said.

'What's that, Doctor?'

'There isn't a person who wouldn't look twice at Severine now!'

There was a moment's horrified pause before we all shared a sad laugh. I was going to have to get used to the feeling of weight on my face and the gooiness of my lips. I had to tell myself not to pout. Every other woman seemed to get used to it; so would I.

'But don't let this worry you,' he assured me. 'Hiding in plain sight is sometimes the best ploy. People may look but they won't recognise you and I doubt very much where we're headed that anyone would be in a position to recognise you anyway. Mrs Biskup, are you expected home tonight?'

She shook her head.

'Then please, both of you, join me. Let me tell you about my plan.'

After about ten minutes of explanation he stopped speaking

and waited for us to respond, but I remained silent, half in shock, the other part of me excited at the notion of returning to Prague by the end of summer.

Mrs Biskup filled the silence. 'Dr Schäfer! You can't expect this girl to walk around real hospital corridors pretending to be a nurse.'

'She'll be under my protection. She can be my administration assistant so she doesn't have to work on the wards, and she knows enough now to get by.'

'You know exactly what they'll think she is.'

'Well, let them! We know it isn't true.'

I let the debate fly around me. The truth was that I was reeling from the realisation that I was returning to Prague to work in the main hospital alongside Otto – where the patients were German. There was plenty to be achieved before I could go, of course. We all understood that.

Mrs Biskup finally sat back unhappily and clasped her hands in her lap. 'What if she is found?'

'Found? She'll be seen daily. No one has to "find" her because no one will be looking. Besides, it is far more dangerous if she is discovered here, alone, and we already know what will happen if she is. I'm at a loss too. None of us invited this problem but it's ours and I think my plan has merit. I can keep my eye on Severine constantly. She won't be alone as she is now and if I sense anyone prodding around with an unhealthy interest, I'll take steps to get her away to somewhere else.'

'Where?'

'I don't know!' he snapped, the closest he'd come to showing his despair. 'I don't have all the answers. I have thought this through, though – two sets of forged papers are ready – and I've told the hospital I've found the right helper and she'll be joining me in August, which should be around the right time . . .' He trailed off. We both understood.

I looked at Mrs Biskup. 'Will you be all right?'

'Yes, of course. You know I'd do anything for you, child.'

'The hospital administration knows I've been needing some-one to scribe notes for me. It will keep Severine away from patients and behind a desk.'

'I can do that,' I assured them. 'I really don't think I can hide out here indefinitely. Each day makes it more dangerous and we've still got the whole of spring and most of the summer to get through when people return to these parts.'

'Agreed,' he said. 'I do think you should take your chances with me in Prague.'

'But what about —'

He hushed me with a hand. 'We will trust Mrs Biskup. Once we have the first stage working, I will devise the next part of this plan, which is to find a way to get you both out of Czechoslovakia – somewhere neutral.'

'Where is neutral?' his housekeeper demanded.

'Switzerland, but if not there, then we'll find a lifeline, perhaps via Holland to Britain, or we may have to look at a longer, southern route into Italy and . . . perhaps onto one of her islands, and . . .' As he ran out of ideas, he dragged a hand across his face to show his frustration. 'I will find a way. I promise.'

16

Lost in Katerina's storytelling, Daniel sensed Otto Schäfer falling in love with his charge and felt a trill of jealousy trace through him of a man he didn't know. He felt envious of the stranger for knowing the young Katerina, as Daniel found himself increasingly powerless in the presence of the older, wiser version.

In her company for less than an accumulated twenty-four hours, the hunter had somehow been stripped of his armour; her tears didn't enfeeble her. No, they weakened him instead. Now there were two women he knew who had been ruined by Ruda Mayek. What had begun as a personal mission had, over the course of Katerina's tale, become a crusade on behalf of all the lives lost or broken by him.

Her voice trailed to silence and she stared at him as the weight of the stillness that had formed around their quiet conversation pressed in. The torment wreaked on the youngster of 1941 was evident in the woman she'd become. He understood that it explained so much about her distant air, the cool attitude, the seemingly impenetrable frostiness of her expression in repose. This was not a prickly or difficult woman, even though she might appear that way at first. This, he now grasped, was a damaged soul, a locked-up replica of the person she might have been had she been allowed to take the train to safety in 1939.

If he'd been captivated by her while he'd studied her these past weeks, he was now certainly her prisoner.

'Does every man who meets you fall in love with you?' It slipped out before he could censure himself.

She looked up, perhaps startled by the bluntness of his enquiry. 'Why would you ask such an oddity?'

He lifted a shoulder that felt heavy from being still for too long. 'Mayek, Schäfer . . .' He was reluctant to speak his own name aloud but it was on the list in his mind. He shrugged again as if to say, *Isn't that enough?*

Her gaze speared across the room. 'Hardly a crowd worth mentioning.' He felt embarrassed for revealing the truth of his thoughts. 'Besides, what Mayek did was not about love. It was about power and it rose out of impotent rage. As for Dr Schäfer, his care for me came from a response to horror. On that first night he was not a German and I was not a Jew; he was a man more than twenty years my senior and I was still in my youth. He felt the normal reaction to protect the young. I see him as a humanitarian. If it turned to admiration of a different sort, he never acted upon his feelings – other than to be so true to me that he risked his reputation and his life for mine over and again.'

Daniel tried to regain some ground. 'Love of the most generous kind,' he offered.

'Indeed.' She frowned. 'I loved *him*, though.'

He was surprised by this admission.

'I loved him like a substitute father. I loved him as the brother that was taken from me. I believe, now I look back at that teenager, that I probably thought I loved him as a man too but I was too inexperienced to recognise it as anything but a crush, riding high on depthless gratitude.' She looked around, as though for the first time feeling aware of how long she'd been talking. 'Madame Bouchard must be getting suspicious.'

'Such a notion thrills me,' he said, bringing some amusement back to their conversation. 'I want her to accuse me of having a beautiful woman share my bed.'

'And you don't mind lying?'

'Not in the least.' He widened his eyes comically as if enjoying the notion and it prompted her to laugh.

'I doubt hers and my paths will cross again after today, anyway.' She reached for her bag.

'Do you have to run away immediately?'

She nodded. 'It's turned late.'

'Coffee, then. Let me walk you back and we can drop in to a café.'

'All right, but you may only walk me part of the way,' she compromised.

He dared not push too hard. 'Then you can tell me what happened in Prague.'

They managed to dodge Madame Bouchard and Daniel pretended this was a blow to his self-esteem and won another half smile as they walked in a much more companionable way. Each time his arm brushed hers he felt a fresh flash of pleasure, and when she allowed him to gently cup her elbow to guide her across the road, Daniel felt the awakening of romance. It was a wraith through his body, electric and dangerous, bringing the ghost of the past to lodge itself in his throat and remind him of a near lifetime given deliberately to loneliness and regret. He had felt he needed both companions to stoke the flames that kept the glow of anger bright but now he glimpsed what his life had missed; what he had turned away from all these years.

He cleared his throat. 'Shall we walk around the park, take the longer route?'

'Longer route to where?' she said, entrapping him. He had nearly spilled a truth of knowing where she lived.

'To however far you'll permit me to accompany you,' he replied, glad they were not facing one another or she might have seen the fear flicker across his expression at the potential revelation.

'Les Deux Magots,' she said. 'Do you know it?'

He gave a snort. 'Yes, of course I know the famous café. I frequent it often.'

'Why?'

'That's a good question,' he acknowledged as they skirted the familiar gardens once again and turned left to join the grand Boulevard Raspail. 'I told you my father was not sent to fight with the Allies because his skills were better suited to the essential service of espionage.'

She cut him a side glance. 'He was a spy?' She sounded impressed. He hadn't anticipated this.

'Yes, of sorts. He worked at Bletchley Park. Have you heard of it?'

'I don't think so,' she said, tightening the scarf at the neck he was working hard not to imagine kissing softly.

'Why should you?' he admitted. 'Anyway, he never spoke about his work, not even when the war ended. He described himself as being in administration, to be as vague as possible. I only learned a couple of years ago that he was part of the team that ran the Allied spy networks in France. He helped with their training. There was one he spoke of fondly. He was impressed by her. They used her to set a honey trap to ensnare a ranking German.'

'And?' she said, sounding intrigued.

'She got her man. But the twist to the tale is that no one counted on a French Resistance fighter falling in love with her too. He was a lavender farmer, turned *maquisard*.' He frowned. 'I can't fully remember the story but what I do remember from my father's tale is that it was incredibly dangerous.' He spotted the spire of Église Saint-Germain-des-Prés. 'Did you know the tomb of René Descartes is located in the church near the café?'

'You are a well of trivial historical information this afternoon,' she accused him with some affection.

He shrugged. 'Tell me when I'm boring you.' He steered them towards the square and to the café. 'Too cold for outside?' He didn't really want to sit in one of the red moleskin booths before a mahogany table, preferring the café furniture along its shopfront.

While the café itself was filling with chilled patrons and becoming noisy, the clutter of small tables and chairs outside were still empty. It didn't seem to matter to either of them that the crowding tables meant one could tap one's cigarette ash into either neighbour's ashtray. He was relieved to see in her expression that their loneliness appealed before she replied.

'I don't mind being outside.'

They found a spot as far from the doorway as they could, and while they were still settling themselves the waiter arrived. Daniel glanced at Katerina in question; he already knew what she'd likely request but didn't want to presume publicly. He sensed she would not enjoy such familiarity.

'A black coffee, please,' she said.

'Hot chocolate for me,' Daniel answered the man's silent enquiry. At Katerina's raised eyebrow he felt the need to explain. 'Too much coffee gives me reflux.'

'Your weakness for sweet things, more like,' she said. The waiter disappeared with a simple '*Merci*'.

They were interrupted by a street seller offering tiny brooches of rosemary, its slightly antiseptic fragrance reaching him. Daniel didn't want any but the thin, round-eyed child standing next to the seller, holding the lead of a puppy with its ribs outlined, prompted him to reach into his pocket and hand over some centimes. He waved away the rosemary. 'Sell it over again,' he said with a smile. The trio moved on, shooed away by the waiter arriving with their drinks and the bill.

'That was kind,' she remarked.

'The child is probably trained to steal my wallet but how can we not give a few coins?'

She nodded as if mentally tucking away his gesture. Did she see it as a weakness, he wondered? 'You haven't told me why this café is such a regular for you,' she reminded.

He sipped the chocolate; it was dark and thick, heavy enough to settle in his belly to warm it and stop any stray rumbles. 'Oh, that's good,' he admitted, watching her remove her gloves so long fingers could clasp her cup and be warmed.

'This was the café where the lady spy first met her colonel.'

It was perhaps the first time since they'd introduced themselves that he'd genuinely surprised her. A look of pleasure skipped across her features; there was a sparkling in her eyes and her mouth began to crinkle towards a full, broad grin but was held back by a caution of disbelief. 'Are you fibbing, Daniel?'

He reacted with a look of injury, putting his hot chocolate down and raising palms to his chest in a show of surprise. 'No! Why would I?'

'Oh, I don't know. You're secretive. You share but it's often about trivia so you can hold back what you don't wish to share.' He watched her and she shrugged. 'An observation. I think you're a clever charmer.'

'I don't understand.' He frowned.

'It could be taken as a compliment, of course.'

'And yet you don't mean it in that way.'

'Daniel, I've mentioned I'm suspicious of everyone – I've

taught myself to never take someone at face value. That includes you.'

'Have I given cause to doubt?'

She didn't reply immediately. 'I do recall slipping on the ice now in the park but it wasn't you who assisted me. It was an older gentleman.'

He forced himself not to swallow; not to lower his gaze with guilt, or to so much as blink at what was clearly an accusation. But his silence damned him. He should have made some sound of vexation.

She took a second drink from her cup and drained it. 'It doesn't matter; I've enjoyed your generous company. But I should be going,' she sighed.

She deserved the truth. He'd never thought himself capable of giving it to anyone but the accusation felt like a blow to the belly, even though she was avoiding using the harsh word of 'liar'. It winded him to think this was the notion she would take away from their time together.

She made a move to stand but he leapt in, hardly daring to believe what was rushing to his lips. 'I'll tell you the truth if you won't leave me yet.'

Her gaze had a razor's edge when it cut back to him. Gone was all humour. The days of progress were now dormant while the fortress quickly rebuilt itself around her.

'Please, sit,' he urged.

She didn't waste words protesting, or energy remaining standing. Her angular frame folded neatly back into the small café chair and the waiter was back.

'Again, please,' Daniel said, simply to be rid of the fellow.

'Have you been lying to me since we met?'

He wanted to look away from that searching gaze with its strange eye that surely haunted anyone who made contact with it.

'I haven't given you all the truth,' he sidestepped. He saw the low, long intake of breath in the swell of her chest beneath the coat as she tamed her disgust. 'You and I are not so different.'

'Is that so?' she jabbed. 'Except I gave you my hardest truths.'

'And you deserve mine. I just don't know where to begin.'

'How about the beginning?' she said, echoing his urging of their first meeting, but there was no smile.

17

● ● ●

Daniel had never felt as confronted as he did in this moment; it was akin to being made naked in public without warning and everyone turning to stare. He was about to speak what had never been uttered previously and all the physiological symptoms of shock were evident in his body, from the instantly dry mouth to the fluttering sensation in his belly.

'Hard, isn't it?' she said, but not unkindly. 'Let me help you. Us meeting wasn't entirely a coincidence, was it?'

How could this situation have gone so wrong so quickly? Just half an hour earlier they had been smiling together over goulash; they had become friends. Now she looked at him as though he were the enemy.

'How long have you suspected?'

She gave a customary lift of her angular shoulder. 'Perhaps from the moment we met. I wanted to believe you. It's not that I don't trust your good intentions; you've been generous and found me in the most vulnerable moment when I think I needed to be listened to. But you didn't find me in that moment, did you?'

He shook his head.

'I think you contrived to meet me on that garden bench and what I obviously want to know is why. It's not for romantic reasons because I might have seen a sign of that by now. But let me continue to be honest, even though you haven't been. It was the memory of slipping that made me realise you hadn't been truthful because I do pride myself on being observant.'

He was surprised by how embarrassed the admission of guilt made him feel. He dropped his gaze. 'Our meeting in the gardens was orchestrated.'

Katerina looked disappointed to hear it, as though she'd genuinely hoped her presumption was wrong.

'I'm sorry to let you down,' he admitted. 'I didn't know you a few days ago. Now I think of you as a friend.'

'Is that supposed to make it feel easier being lied to?'

Daniel shook his head. 'No, I'm just giving you the truth you want.'

'How treacherous of you. I fought against instinct and decided I should trust you.'

'You *can* trust me.' He could hear the bleat in his voice.

Katerina took time to light a cigarette. He watched in growing shame each graceful move of her hands until he heard the soft inhalation and waited for the funnel of pale smoke to escape from her mouth. He wanted to kiss that mouth in apology. He wanted to kiss her for his salvation. It sounded overwrought and yet no one but he could appreciate the epiphany of this moment; not only was he allowing someone else into his heart again but he was considering making bare his inner self, now that his exterior had been stripped away. She regarded him as if allowing him the time to wrestle with his thoughts and reach this conclusion.

She took time for another two silent drags on her Pall Mall and then she bent the cigarette in the ashtray, crushing its embers as their second round of drinks arrived, the debris of the first removed. The waiter's arrival and departure broke the tense spell.

'All of it, then, or I walk away from you now, and if I do, we shall not speak again. I will no longer consider you a friend.' He opened his mouth to assure her but she held up a slender finger like a schoolteacher. 'If I sense a lie, Daniel, and I usually have a well-attuned radar for anyone who prevaricates, I shall get up and leave anyway and the terms remain the same. I don't know what you're up to, but you had better be honest with me now.'

That single finger felt more terrifying than a blade aimed at his throat; not only did he need what she could give him but he needed her in his life now. He felt as though he could compare himself to a wandering man, lost, parched, who'd finally found the stream, the one that would slake his thirst and lead him out of the wilderness . . . As dramatic as he knew that image was, he couldn't let her go.

Without second-guessing it, he tumbled straight into his story, keeping it simple, unemotional, as his training had taught him.

'Everything I told you about my family is true.' He found his courage and looked at her intently.

She gave a little nod that told him she accepted this and so he moved on with fresh confidence.

'I started school at four, earlier than most, and there I met a frighteningly intelligent and mature girl. She was also starting early, so we felt like kindred spirits.'

'What is her name?'

He hesitated momentarily. 'It was Ayla,' he said in a voice that spoke her name aloud softly for the first time in two decades. It weakened him, but Katerina's gaze urged him on.

'Ayla and I became inseparable. I remember our parents joking that they might as well plan for our marriage now . . . we were probably seven by then.'

Katerina's expression lightened to share a sad smile with him.

'My father urged hers to leave Czechoslovakia with us. Ayla and her brother were both enormously talented students; we could tell from as young as primary school that these two had so much academic potential. Her true gift, though, was music. She composed from eight but she was my equal in mathematics and barely tried.' He gave a sigh. 'She wasn't enamoured by numbers as I am, though. As for her older brother, his ability with science was scary. He was destined to do something extraordinary in the field of physics, I feel sure. Because of Ezra – that's her brother – their parents finally decided America was the best place to head to continue his education and explore his talents. Our application to Britain, in the meantime, came through swiftly. They began their application for emigration but the process took far longer than ours – longer than anyone could have anticipated.'

He cleared his throat. 'The borders were closed in 1941 before their visas were granted and then it became illegal; all were banned from leaving the country.'

Katerina remained still and silent, forcing him to speak on.

'The family was sent to Terezín in December 1941.' He could all but hear the cogs of her mind turning in ghastly realisation and he nodded. 'As you were escaping his clutch, my darling Ayla was entering it.' He watched now as Katerina blanched. The anger that had sat like a barrier between them dissipated and he felt her sympathy reach across the table like an invisible hand and stroke his cheek.

Her gaze was now all pity. 'Daniel, I don't know what to say.' She sounded breathless.

He shook his head. 'Ruda Mayek was there, as you know, and he took a special interest in Ayla. She was not yet eighteen.'

Now she did reach across the table and he felt the cool of those long fingers wrap around his hand and he trembled. 'Excuse me,' he murmured, and pretended to sneeze but they both knew he was catching tears before they fell. He had never cried for Ayla. His sadness had built like a poisonous boil beneath the surface and speaking about her had lanced it. He was glad they'd chosen the lonely seats outside.

She didn't seem discomfited by his emotion. 'How do you know what occurred?' She had taken his hand again.

'Ezra survived Terezín. He never met Mayek, only saw him from a distance, and can't remember him to describe him. He was sent to Auschwitz, and don't ask me how, because I can't imagine, but he survived that place of horror as well. I mean, he's not the same – how can he be? He never did fulfil his potential. He eventually returned to academia, where I imagine it felt safe, and he lectures in physics these days at an American university to promising bright students who no doubt remind him of himself at that age.' Daniel met her gaze. 'He spoke only once of what occurred to his family and has refused to talk about them since. It seems your nemesis found many novel and brutal ways to humiliate a young woman on the cusp of life.'

'He's a psychopath.'

'He's the devil,' Daniel added. 'A monster that walks this earth in plain sight.'

'Will you tell me the rest? I mean, how I fit into this story, apart from the obvious link.'

'It's the obvious link that binds us, Katerina. But I want to tell you all the truth so you cannot accuse me of holding back or lying to you. It won't take long; there's not much more other than to know that when I learned of Ayla's death after the war, I couldn't recover easily from the loss. We had been the closest of friends until the moment my family left Czechoslovakia. It was no longer our parents who plotted; it was she and I who spoke of marriage and we had made a promise that as soon as she turned sixteen we would be betrothed, and on the day following her seventeenth celebration we would be married. I, of course, left before those ages ticked around but we wrote to each other twice a week as long as our correspondence was getting through, and I think it was through those letters that our deep love for each other matured. It wasn't just youthful admiration, or a crush, or even habit. No one understood me better than Ayla; no one laughed with me as she did or made me feel as invincible as she could. And I couldn't save her. When I discovered how she suffered, something darkened within me and when I learned his name, nothing was ever going to stop me hunting him down and bringing him to justice.'

'Do you mean justice as the world understands it?'

He shook his head. 'My justice.'

'And would you be capable of that, Daniel – in the moment, staring at your victim? Could you end his life?'

'That's the other part I have yet to explain about myself.' He paused; she waited with a parted mouth as though wanting to say more but not daring to. Again he felt the urge to kiss those neatly sculpted lips. 'I am Mossad. It's the national intelligence agency of Israel —'

'I know what it is,' she cut in.

He nodded. 'Former Mossad, I should say. I retired several years ago.'

He watched dawning loosen her brow and slacken that tightly held pose. He had surprised her. That was the only positive.

'You've been spying on me?' The accusation cut through him like a hot blade. He had a fleeting memory of her curled up on his sofa, weeping, considering him a sort of safe island as she emptied her sorrows in front of him. She'd trusted him these past days but he sensed the inward snarl of an injured animal, cornered and turning on its hunter. 'This has all been a lie?' she continued. It was as though she was testing the notion, saying it aloud, trying to come to terms with his duplicity. 'Why didn't you just ask? Why the duplicity?'

'You say that now, but you are the first to admit that you're suspicious of all; that you keep yourself to yourself. I couldn't risk frightening you off. So I had to tiptoe into your life.'

She shocked him by standing. 'Manners demand that I thank you for . . .' She shook her head. 'For what, I'm unsure. I don't know how to give a name to what we've shared, but I regret it now. Not sharing anything with anyone has kept me strong and safe for years. I betrayed old instincts with you – I blame seeing the Pearls again.'

'Katerina, I can be relied upon,' he assured her.

'Really? To tell more lies, do you mean?' She looked around for observers. They were giving the customers inside some afternoon entertainment, as it would take only a dullard not to realise they were arguing.

He stood, tense. 'I'll walk you home.'

'And you'd know where that is?'

Suddenly it mattered to him to be trustworthy in her eyes . . . to be important to her, like Dr Schäfer. He still needed to find out what had happened to the good doctor but for now he felt he had a hill to climb in terms of re-establishing his credibility. Only the truth would work from here on – and what did it matter? They were both chasing an identical and elusive shadow but he'd never been closer and he'd never had her power to fuel his hunt.

'I do.' He reeled off the address off rue Buffon that housed the original Natural History Museum of France. He might as well come clean. 'I've followed you home only once and I know you like to arrive at the Louvre via the botanical gardens, skirting the labyrinth that is in your neighbourhood, and then you avoid the main humdrum of the streets by cutting across to the Luxembourg

Gardens. I think you enjoy being in gardens even if they do take you a slightly, how can I say, zigzag route.'

He felt obliged to forgive her the look of pain reflected in her astonishment.

'How long has this been going on?'

'Only since you returned from London,' he admitted, anticipating the question and almost drowning her words, hoping the short timeframe might help his cause.

'So all that talk of being in the gardens with a sense of well-being when you saw me, your daily ritual of waiting for me . . . all a fabrication?' She didn't wait for his answer. 'Well, you're good, Mr Spy, I have to admit it. For someone who prides herself on suspecting every new person she meets of having a negative agenda, you hoodwinked me. Your skills are exemplary.'

Nothing in her bitter-sounding compliment made him think she would take another step by his side. And still he tried.

'Katerina, I do believe you're suddenly one aspect of my world that gives me hope.' In spite of her anger he watched the frown trace across her forehead. 'You know how it feels to be young and lose the people you most love and rely upon in the world. I don't compare myself to your situation other than to say I lost the love of my life. And I have never recovered. For the first decade of that score of years Ayla and I were parted, I didn't know her fate. For the past ten years I've lived with a poison inside that has blackened my view of the world. I haven't opened myself up to companions, to romance, to friendship . . .'

She dropped her gaze and he knew she likely felt a moment of sympathy for him.

'Until now,' he added, baring himself as though opening his chest for the blade to be plunged in. He fully expected it but he needed her to know that her arrival into it had changed his bleak world of the last twenty years.

The observers watched on while Daniel noted her struggle to make her decision on his fate.

———————

Katerina finally looked up, ignoring the audience, and shivered as though only now realising how cold it was. The revelation about Daniel had clearly caught her normally reliable radar napping. He'd tricked her and she could recognise that it was a mix of annoyance and embarrassment that had prompted her brisk response. No damage had been done. The release of the toxic tale meant she had walked out of her apartment this morning feeling lighter of heart than she could recall. Yes, he had lied but not in order to romance her or to steal from her; he'd been respectful, kind, a very good listener, but she was still unaware of why he had pursued her and she couldn't help but feel a prick of intrigue to know what he was up to. It was curiosity that provided room in her heart to give him another chance to impress her. Daniel had a big job ahead in convincing her he could be trusted, and he had no more than fifteen minutes walking back to her apartment in which to achieve that.

'You can walk me home, Daniel – I'm guessing you may know a shortcut?'

He smiled sadly, not showing his relief. He said nothing but fell in step with her, sensibly waiting for her cue.

'What do you want from me?' she said.

'I'm surprised you'd ask that,' he replied, sounding glad to have the recriminations behind him and eager to get on with why he'd set up this masquerade to trap her. 'I don't know what Ruda Mayek looks like. To tell the truth' – he frowned and caught her look of irony slanted at him across a square shoulder – 'only truth now,' he assured her, 'I only found out about Mayek a few years ago. Until then I believed Ayla died at the hands of the guards of Terezín. I spent years researching the name of every soldier I could hunt down who did time at that place. My role at Mossad gave me authority and access that is denied to most and I diligently checked and cross-referenced every name until I had a file of men, most with photos, some without. Germany, as you would know from your own work, was an exemplary record keeper and the Nazis were the finest exponents of keeping detailed records. The lack of photos would have been Czech sloppiness at a very local level and of course one of the photos I didn't have was of Ruda Mayek, who arrived at Terezín during December 1941. He was there for fifteen months and then I have him bobbing up at two Polish death camps – one of them Auschwitz, although Ezra does not recall hearing his name there and doesn't believe he ever saw him.'

They were entering the vicinity of the Natural History Museum, making for the gates that would lead them through the gardens; these would take them to rue Buffon and her tiny street. In her mind she joined the dots of what he'd said, arriving at the only conclusion she could.

'You want me to recognise him for you.'

'Yes.' He didn't embellish.

'How did you know me?'

'Ah, I have been looking for anyone who could recognise him since the war ended. I am a spy but I am also a diehard analyst. I like to look at a puzzle and solve it. I knew that this man called Ruda Mayek came from a hamlet just outside Prague, so I focused my efforts there to find everyone I could who might have intersected with his life. There was a small window of chance for me. During 1948 and into the following year, the Soviet Bloc, which has taken over Czechoslovakia, supported the newly created State of Israel. I was part of the framework that helped remaining Jews who wished to emigrate to Israel to do so out of Czechoslovakia. It meant I could get into the country in an official capacity and I managed to hunt down Mayek's home.'

She gasped.

'It was deserted at that stage – most of the village's houses were empty by that time, or accommodating squatters of sorts, a few people starting again. There were a couple who recalled Ruda Mayek but their descriptions made him sound like every other German. The town hall had been burnt down so all of its records were gone. I was looking for photos of him, you see – perhaps as mayor. He wasn't mayor long enough for there to be many. Can you imagine none were to be found in his home? All removed from albums or frames in a deliberate attempt to cover his tracks. He might even have burnt the municipal building or arranged to have it torched, for all we know. But I did find a number of other photos carelessly cast aside at his home and amongst them were a few that featured a family called Kassowicz. And on the back of one was the inscription: *Taken by Rudy*. You were a child in that photo but there were enough snapshots of this family that I realised he must have spent time with them. It didn't take much digging to discover who you all were, your father's standing, and that the family Kassowicz disappeared sometime in late 1941. There are no records, no matter how I searched, of any of your family turning up in any of the concentration camps. As I say, the German records are reliable. So where were you all? I had no one else to count on and my single hope was that just one of you children had survived, wherever you were.'

'You pinned all of this on the hope a Jewish child of Prague from a photo with Mayek's name on the back had survived the Holocaust?' She was past sounding incredulous.

He shrugged. 'There were five of you, and to the best of my knowledge none entered a camp. I had to hold out hope that all or some of you had got away, and so I remained patient, waiting for a sign. Don't think I haven't chased down every lead, though, for anyone, not just a Kassowicz, who might have known Ruda Mayek.

I've been looking for years. But it was you who answered my prayers when the Pearls appeared and I got word through my London office that a war criminal *might* have surfaced through a potentially stolen piece of jewellery that one of the museum's experts knew intimately – was in fact claiming to be the owner. It was a breakthrough but I didn't realise how important until your Mr Partridge was interviewed by one of our people and he told us about you. Once I heard the name Kassowicz I couldn't contain my excitement. I learned you'd been living and working in Paris for all these years but of course you had a new name . . . I would never have found you without the emergence of the Pearls.' He shrugged. 'So I waited for your inevitable return from London, watching the Louvre for your arrival.'

'I didn't see you,' she said.

'You never would – unless I wanted you to. Katerina, all I need is for you to recognise him for me. We have some photos taken at Terezín and Auschwitz featuring groups of the garrisons. You might be able to pick him out from one of those; you can certainly give me the best description I'll have of him, even if it is of a man from twenty years ago.'

'In order to do what?'

'To end his miserable life.'

'You don't even know he's alive.'

'I know you believe he is.' And before she could respond, he continued. 'The re-emergence of the Ottoman Pearls alone has so profoundly affected you that I am guessing you won't sit still and would never forgive yourself if you didn't find out who is behind them. You've pieced together the story of Ruda Mayek for me. It has to be him —'

'Or his family, or someone he sold them to, or a collector whose lap they've fallen into, or someone who has dug them up from where he buried them during the war, or —'

'Yes,' he interjected. 'There are all of those potential scenarios but still you want to know, don't you, Katerina? You want to confirm whether it's him behind the piece arriving at the British Museum.'

They angled into her narrow street and she could see her building already. His time to convince her was ticking down.

'How old was he in 1941?' he asked.

'Oh, I don't know . . . perhaps mid-thirties.'

'So he is at least mid-fifties now – he still has years ahead to enjoy his life, while our lives grind along in misery from our past. Would his death bring you peace of mind?'

'Yes.'

'Do you believe he's out there, living an easy life on what he stole from your family, from others? Do you think he believes he got away with his monstrous acts?'

'I do now. And while I've convinced myself otherwise, perhaps I always have believed it.'

They arrived at her apartment building's short flight of three shallow steps.

He paused and surprised her by taking her hand. 'Then . . . for Ayla, for Lotte, for the twins, for your dear mother and father but especially for you, the woman who defied him by surviving his brutality, I am going to kill him.'

She regarded his face, which had known few laughter creases, and saw herself reflected in it. To others like him she must appear serious, aloof, guarded . . . damaged by life. Standing outside her doorway, digging and finding her keys in the bottom of her crocodile-skin handbag and hearing Daniel's strong words, she finally made sense of the cauldron of feelings that had been simmering since she'd laid eyes on the lambent Pearls again. Her response tumbled from her as though a second person within was framing and speaking her deepest-kept thought.

'No, my pain is not yours to share – and that's not me being noble, Daniel; it's me selfishly protecting what belongs to me. My hurt, my memories, my physical injuries at his hands, my mental torment from his actions. I understand your heartache and I sympathise but Ruda Mayek does not belong to you. You cannot bring Ayla back or heal me by confronting him, for within me are the ghosts of all the dead, including Ayla. I have known him; I have suffered directly beneath him – you have a much lesser claim.'

Through what was beginning to sound like a mission statement, she'd watched Daniel's features slacken with confusion before tightening with alarm. His thick eyebrows met. 'And?'

'And you are not going to kill him on my behalf.'

'But why, Katerina?'

She slipped the key into the lock and twisted it until the door opened. Stepping over the threshold, she turned and fixed him with a stare, like pressing a drawing pin into a cork noticeboard. She needed him still, fully concentrating, while she took a heartbeat to consider the shocking decision she had reached and was now about to air. It had taken twenty years of silent suffering to know this other person within had the right to say it. She gave permission and her darker self spoke.

'Why? Because *I* am going to kill him.'

She closed the door on her words and the look of horror that swept across Daniel's face. She ignored the banging behind her and the calling of her name. She scorned the day by closing curtains and creeping beneath her bedcovers. Finally, Katerina allowed the terror of her promise to carry her trembling into the depth of unconsciousness to sleep on the thought of how she would actually end Ruda Mayek's life.

18

* * *

Hersh stood at the doorway of the dining room, not wishing to intrude across the threshold as a ritual was taking place. He watched with growing admiration as Nissa moved around the table lighting holy candles that would usher in Shabbat and begin the day of rest that the Jewish community observed. Growing up in an English household Hersh had had little choice but to follow the ways of his foster parents. The Evans family were not without their piety, eating only fish on Fridays, not working on Sundays – not even playing cards, which they all enjoyed, because playing snap or rummy somehow constituted blasphemy – and while he had not attended Sunday school, he had certainly walked beneath the vaulted ceiling of the parish church each weekend alongside them. His father had proudly told him that a church had been on that site for one thousand years.

As Henry he had listened conscientiously to the prayers and the service, had stood when his parents stood, had knelt when they did and had shaken the hand of the vicar most Sundays, but he had struggled to feel as one with the congregation. It was only when he'd first tiptoed into a synagogue at fifteen, taking a *kippah* from the basket at the door to cover his head, had been welcomed by other worshippers and shown how to proceed that he'd begun to feel his faith finding him.

He'd lived a double life as Henry and Hersh these last years, which included giving his attention and care to two faiths, believing both essentially asked the same thing of him – a generous spirit.

His family had objected at first but they were grocers to so many in the Jewish community that they couldn't prevent him attending the synagogue, as countless shoppers remarked on how happy they had been to see their son at prayer. He'd had the conversation with them when he was in his mid-teens that they must not disallow his heritage and his only link to his 'dead family'. The effect had been immediate, and presumably because he attended Sunday morning services with them, his mother and father no longer frowned on his interest in Judaism.

And now he'd found the courage to let them know that from here on he would be spending Shabbat with Nissa's folks.

'It's the most important time of the week for a Jewish family and I simply want to be part of it.'

'Why?'

'Well, I like what it stands for. Everyone essentially stops work and gathers around a table for wonderful food, good company, singing . . .'

'And?' His mother had sensed there was more.

'And I like Nissa. I want to spend time with her.'

He'd watched the glance pass between his parents.

'You're fond of her, we've noticed,' she'd replied and he'd nodded with a shrug.

'If they don't mind,' his father had mumbled around his pipe, flapping his newspaper.

'Mind? They'd enjoy it if you both came and shared their supper as well.'

'Well, we'll think on that,' his mother had said, looking suddenly embarrassed.

He knew he should have been at prayer with the other men this evening but his father had required help with an unexpected early delivery of goods that needed to be unloaded, stored neatly and some of it unpacked and stacked onto shelves. He'd watched the clock, knowing it was vital that he arrive at Nissa's in the hour before sundown.

Hersh had only just made it with cringing apologies, grateful for the lighter evenings that had saved him. Now he smiled to regard Nissa's dainty movements as she prepared to touch the lit taper to one of the wicks.

'I'm single, Hersh. I only get to light one,' she said and he wasn't sure if there was a special message being passed to him in her innocent explanation. 'My elder sister and my mother may light two each.'

'One for each of the family – is that right?'

'In our household that's how we do it. We're lighting an extra one this evening, though.'

'Why?'

She grinned and her coquettish glance made his pulse speed. 'For you, of course.'

Hersh smiled. 'I gave some money to a person who was begging on the corner before I arrived. That's right, isn't it?'

Her expression had straightened out of respect – they both knew it would be frowned upon if they flirted in the presence of the holy candles. 'Yes, before we kindle the Shabbat candles we have been taught to give charity to others. Now, hush, I must do this properly and say my prayer.'

He watched her light the wick and then drop the taper onto a metal tray for that purpose; she'd already taught him that she must not extinguish a match or taper used for a Shabbat candle. 'It must go out itself, Hersh, or be extinguished by someone who has not yet accepted Shabbat because the moment I light this wick, Shabbat has begun for me.'

Hersh enjoyed the elegant movements of her slim arms and long fingers as Nissa stretched out her hands towards her candle and moved them inwards in a circular motion. He knew she was ushering in a special holy guest. She did this three times before she murmured a prayer of blessing. He noted she didn't open her eyes immediately but let them remain closed in private prayer. He couldn't help but wonder what she prayed for and allowed himself a moment of indulgence that her prayer was about him and that they might be allowed to discuss marriage very soon.

Daniel was waiting for Katerina the following morning, standing on the other side of the street watching for her to emerge. She wasn't surprised to see him and noted a change of clothes so he'd been home and returned, but for how long he had been observing her entrance she couldn't judge. Overnight her decision had cemented and she stepped out confident in that plan. He caught up with her, falling in step with a long, floating stride. She smelled baked yeast scenting the air.

'Morning, Daniel. That must have been an awkward wait, with people wondering what you were up to.'

He paid no attention to her jibe. 'We have to talk.' Direct, this time; he was no longer being cunning, she noted, and despite his fresh set of clothes and neatly combed hair, the darkness surrounding the spy's eyes told her that unlike her he had not slept. She'd not woken for nearly ten hours. When she had, she'd realised it was in the same position she'd curled into and fallen asleep. This surprised her; whatever her dreams had been, they had not troubled her. And if she was honest, today she felt strong. It may not last – she was a realist at heart – but even so, it felt powerful to have this new purpose against Rudy's silhouette that had shadowed her all these years. She'd pretended he was dead, had allowed herself to entertain it as a defence, but confronting him – now that she suspected more than ever that he lived – was the only way forward.

'I shall not change my mind.'

'Katerina, you don't —'

'I'm known as Severine Kassel in this neighbourhood.'

He put up a hand in acknowledgement of his slip, hurrying to keep up with her. 'You have no experience of what you're proposing.'

'So what? There's a first time for everything.' She dropped her voice. 'Even killing.'

He paused in what appeared to her to be fresh dread and she moved on; she was halfway across the rue Buffon before he caught up with her. 'Please, can we talk?'

'There's nothing more to discuss.'

He grabbed her arm, but gently. 'Have you had your breakfast coffee? There's a café over there.'

Katerina felt an eddy of pity for him. He was rightly concerned. 'Black coffee,' she confirmed.

He gestured to one of the small tables outside. Only one other person was seated, hunched over a newspaper, smoking. She could see the remnants of his breakfast bread; the tartine crumbs were scattered around the coffee bowl. The street was busy: people had their chins dipped into their scarves against spring's nip as they headed to their offices, while the café was thronging with workers grabbing their morning hit. She watched them toss some coins onto the counter before swallowing their caffeine, still standing, in quick gulps and departing, many of them lighting up immediately from the distinctive Disque Bleu box as they passed her. The smell of the tobacco that the French favoured was in sharp contrast to what the English chose in their smoother, sweeter smokes originating from the Americas. In France, so many preferred the darker leaf of the Arabs and now she understood that it likely still felt senti-mental, even patriotic, to smoke the Gauloises or Gitanes that had protruded from the lips of their infantrymen and the romantic *masquisard* Resistance fighters of the south.

Daniel arrived with two steaming cups. She preferred a shot of espresso in the morning but she wouldn't be churlish.

'Thank you.'

'What is your plan?' He'd obviously decided it was pointless to try and dissuade her.

She sipped the diluted version of the tarriness she wanted. 'At this point I am going to arrange a meeting with the English solicitor who is acting on behalf of the party offering the Pearls for exhibition.'

'You sound as though you've created some emotional distance for yourself.' He looked impressed. 'You're a constant surprise.'

'Daniel, I've had a score of years to teach myself how to be unemotional. There has to be a reason for denying myself the most basic of human traits and maybe this is it; perhaps life was prepar-ing me for this hunt.'

He nodded, eyes narrowing. 'You do believe him to be alive, then?'

She frowned and tapped her blunt nail against the cup. 'In my line of work you assemble facts first. You gather everything that is obvious about a piece: its size, shape, distinguishing marks, all of its aspects on display such as gems if it's jewellery, style of painting if it's an artwork, type of stone if it's a sculpture and so on. You look for any labelling or marks that might reveal its era or maker. Then your knowledge comes into play – what do you know about this sort of piece that might hint at its origins, era, value? Finally, instinct is allowed to roam: what is your expert gut telling you?'

'Instinct is last,' he said, pulling a face of doubt. She watched his gaze dart around; he seemed on edge.

'Perhaps in your line of work it comes first but I make early decisions with what I can see as my platform. And all I can see in my situation is that the Ottoman Pearls that belonged to my family . . . to me . . . that I personally witnessed being thieved by Ruda Mayek have re-emerged. But I know nothing about what's happened to them, or to him – other than your claims – since November 1941 when I climbed down from that tree outside the villa. I'm not sure that answers your question. The point is, he could be alive and if he is, I will find him.'

She sipped her coffee and he waited, perhaps sensing she hadn't finished. 'You've now confirmed he did go to Terezín and that he then went on to use all of his cruel skills in the death camps, but I have no factual evidence of that or his survival of the war. He could have sold the Pearls, or buried them and someone else dug them up; he could have given them to a third party . . . And any of those scenarios could have occurred since 1941. So, I have to rely on facts – what I personally know. And what I know now is that my only link between the Pearls and Mayek in this moment is the English solicitor. Yesterday, if you'd asked me, I couldn't have remembered his name – that's how little attention I paid. But I have his card. Mr Partridge, my superior at the museum, mailed it to me.' She flinched a smile at the memory of poor Mr Partridge's stammering response in the frigid silence while they were all still staring at the fat, creamy pearls. Katerina returned to a frown. 'The solicitor has chambers at Lincoln's Inn Fields,' she continued.

'Do you even know where that is?'

'Does it matter? It's London and it's where I'm now returning.'

'What about work?'

'I'm not due back at the Louvre for a fortnight. This is my time now and I plan to spend it well.'

'Let me come with you.'

She cut him an irritated glance. 'No.'

'Why?'

'Why would I? You're a liar, remember. I don't feel secure.'

Pain smarted in the narrowing of his gaze as if he'd been genuinely wounded by her remark. 'I will never lie to you again.'

She heard the truth in the grittiness of his voice; it hurt him to have to say it, to admit again to his deliberate beguilement. Katerina suspected that Daniel didn't want friendship. He wanted more. And in this she felt a genuine sadness. There had only ever been three men in her life: one she'd witnessed murdered; the second now lived in Switzerland as a respected physician, loved by his family, and his peacetime needed no rekindling of war memories. They would continue to exchange brief letters for the celebration days they marked – his for her Rosh Hashanah, and she remembered him in December for Christmas festivities. The third she rarely spoke openly about.

Each was too important in her mind and there had never been the right mindset for a fourth. Daniel, she could see, was having thoughts that she might be the woman who could save him from himself. He likely saw similarities in their reserved, secretive personalities; he recognised shared pain, and now Ruda Mayek bound them in grief. She could feel his admiration building, crashing against her like waves on a rock, but she had to make him understand that she was an island, isolated, and she planned to remain that way, especially if being imprisoned for murder was to be her final sorrow.

'Daniel, I appreciate that promise of truth but there's another promise that would mean as much to me.'

'Name it.' He sounded confident.

'Don't fall in love with me,' she warned.

He had reached for his cup but put it down again. No, he hadn't expected that caution. He dipped his head to gaze into the black liquid, as though expecting to find answers in its darkness. 'A little late for me to be making that promise, I'm afraid,' he admitted, without looking up. 'I don't have my spy guard up, Katerina. You're sitting in front of a helpless man now. I'm like all the men who have surely loved you and you've dissuaded, and all of those you didn't even know about who have likely been fascinated by you on sight, intrigued by you, demented by you with your chilly self-containment.'

'I don't mean to —'

'I know,' he assured her. 'It's your defence but I don't have that specific armour. I thought I was impenetrable, as you probably think you are.'

'I am, Daniel. Why are you looking around – are you expecting someone?'

He gave her a scowl of disdain.

'Then look at me.'

He offered his pained gaze.

'I have no susceptibility to being romanced, or to falling in love. I'm almost embarrassed to admit it, but . . .' She shook her head. 'He took it all away from me.'

He smiled sadly and looked at her for a long time before nodding gently. 'It's a state of mind, Katerina, and as long as you let him control your mind, he's winning. He might as well have shot you dead all those years ago in the forest. As blinded as I am by the need for revenge, I can assure you that love is a state of mind too . . . and you can find that mindset.'

She gave him a look that conveyed her disagreement but he was not to be deterred.

'Some lucky fellow is going to come along when you're least expecting it and all the while you're convinced you're a fortress, he's going to cross the moat and scale the walls and batter down the stronghold around you.'

She gave a mirthless chuckle at the metaphor. 'Well, we shall see.'

'But it's not me?' He clearly needed her to say it.

Katerina took a slow breath and shook her head. 'No shiny chain mail or white steed,' she observed, hoping the lightness would help.

It did. As sad as he looked to her, she admired that he dredged up a smile.

'It doesn't change that I want to help hunt him. Mayek has been the poison eating away at my life too for a decade.'

'All right. I'll hear your advice, because you've got all the appropriate experience. But Daniel, if and when the time comes, I go to him alone.'

He gave a sigh as if resigning to her. 'Only if I am convinced you're safe.'

Katerina felt a fresh spill of vexation that he was once again staring past her. 'I go alone,' she repeated. Her tone sounded like the stab of an icicle and he flung up his hands in what looked to be defeat.

19

❖ ❖ ❖

LONDON

Lincoln's Inn Fields was a surprise. As a scholar of antiquity, Katerina had read up what she could about their destination but it was nevertheless a delight to lay her gaze upon the more than 300-year-old square that was designed and laid out by none other than Inigo Jones. Once home to noble families in the seventeeth century, it was here that the Royal College of Surgeons found its place and where one of the Inns of Court resided and men of the law had their chambers.

Having told Daniel this fact, she continued, 'Of course it didn't always have such lauded residents. There was a time that it was crowded by day with beggars, vagrants and cripples selling their mendicants and by gamblers, thieves and prostitutes at night.'

They'd emerged from the Underground station, pleased they didn't have to use the lift but could ascend to street level via its escalator. As they arrived onto High Holborn, Katerina mentioned that this tube station had stored various precious artefacts from the British Museum during the Blitz. 'Daniel, are you listening?'

He looked distracted, scanning the street as they emerged from London's depths, frowning with a spy's suspicion.

'I can tell I'm boring you.'

'You could never bore me,' he replied, taking her elbow in a friendly and non-proprietorial manner. 'I am listening to all your interesting stories. I happen to know that it also used to be the interchange between trams and tubes before the London tram network closed a decade or so ago.'

They were walking towards their destination based on directions she had scribbled out. She cut him a wry glance. 'I forget London is familiar to you. I don't need these directions?' She held up the note.

'I know where we're headed,' he said.

'Are you quite sure? Because I'm convinced I could have got us to where we're going faster. You've taken us a very roundabout way, and what was the curious business of getting on and then suddenly dragging me back off the train on the Underground?'

'I told you, I thought taking a different line might be faster.'

'Was it?' She frowned. 'I counted two more stops.'

'My mistake.' He offered no more and seemed to want to change tack. 'I thought you'd enjoy this route that gives you a look at the area.'

She let her interrogation drop away.

'New Oxford Street to our backs,' he continued. He pointed. 'Keep walking that way and we'll reach your British Museum. And we'll approach from Chancery Lane so you can walk beneath the famous Gate House.'

'There were turnstiles here somewhere, I gather,' she said, 'that kept cattle enclosed once upon a time when this was little more than grazing land. And in the Royal College of Surgeons they supposedly had or perhaps still have gruesome exhibits including the skeletons of an Irish giant who was well over eight feet tall at his death and an Italian dwarf who wasn't much taller than two feet.' She grinned at his raised eyebrows. 'Ah, is this it?' she said with

wonder as they entered a grand archway with vast wooden doors at
its end.

'Welcome to Lincoln's Inn Fields. Wait there.'

'Why?'

'I thought I'd take a photo,' he said, pulling out one of the
new-fangled Instamatic cameras she'd seen in shop windows.
'May I?'

She looked puzzled. 'Why?'

'Maybe I'd like to build some happier memories for you. Wait
there. Just one or two – you'll thank me in time.' He skipped a few
steps back, ignoring the exasperated workers who had to flow
around them. He turned to face her, clicked a few times, looking up
in between each shot and urging her to smile but she wouldn't oblige.

'I think of London as enormous,' she admitted, as the camera
was put back in his pocket and she walked on a few steps. She was
delighted to see how the enclave opened up onto an airy square of
mansions around lawns and gardens. 'And yet nothing ever seems
that far away; to think my old flat at Bloomsbury is easy walking
distance, and so is the West End and Covent Garden.'

'The famous Hatton Garden diamond district is over there,' he
said, pointing east. 'Temple Church, spiritual home of the Knights
Templar, not far either.'

'All the beautiful railings were torn down for the war effort.
I wonder if they'll ever replace them?' She didn't need him to
answer. 'Do you know I read that Samuel Pepys used to stroll with
his wife through these gardens and Charles Dickens was a lawyer's
clerk here. Rumour says that during spring he enjoyed spitting
cherry stones onto the heads of the legal fraternity.' She sighed at
his chuckle. 'Sir Thomas More would also roam these streets. Don't
you love touching history, Daniel?'

If he answered, she didn't hear it. She scanned the several-
storeyed buildings, a hotchpotch of architectural styles because of

constant additions and renovations down the centuries. People were moving in all directions although the signs that asked them to remain off the grass were being diligently observed; the British were the most obedient of peoples, she noted. But around them moved a restless stream of bewigged barristers, harried-looking solicitors, she presumed, nervous clients searching for legal advice and a swarm of workers carrying files and briefs to and from various offices, entering and exiting the busy square from various gates. To her there was an atmosphere of brisk tension. Everyone seemed to have somewhere to be quickly, yet no one broke into a run or openly showed impatience to another.

She only noticed now that Daniel had lingered near the entrance and he pointed to a shop window that she hadn't noticed, to their backs as they'd entered the arch. 'This is the bookshop to the legal fraternity. Centuries old, and has been here at Archway since the 1800s, apparently. They lost all their books twice during the war.'

It was an odd nugget of information, him sounding distracted as he spoke, but she smiled and pushed on, walking them down one of the gravel paths. 'So, we're looking for . . . oh, there it is,' she said, pointing to a door that was painted a jolly green and stood out from the narrow and dirty brown-red bricks of its walls and the swoop of iron railings that curved away from it onto the street. 'This is where his offices are.'

They approached and she was suddenly glad Daniel had insisted on accompanying her; this solicitor was her only link to the Pearls and whichever dark hiding place they had emerged from. Perhaps Daniel would see, hear or glean something she may otherwise miss; every nuance now felt important.

He nodded, glancing around self-consciously as she knocked. A young man opened the door, formally attired, clean-shaven and offering an enquiring smile.

'Good morning. May I help you?'

'Er, yes. I would like to see Mr Summerbee, please.'

'Come in, please.'

They followed into what looked to be a warren of offices but he guided them through a door into a hushed reception room. 'I'm one of his clerks. Is he expecting you?'

'I'm afraid not, but I've come from Paris to see him. I'd be happy to make an appointment,' she said, already suspecting her presentation and charming manner would get her a meeting with the solicitor shortly, if not immediately.

'Please have a seat. He's extremely busy but I'll just have a quick word with his secretary. May I have your names, please?'

'Thank you.' She smiled. 'I'm Severine Kassel and this is a colleague, Mr Daniel Horowitz.'

Daniel had clearly noted the warmth she'd shown the man and whispered from the corner of his mouth. 'Well, he's toast.'

'He's sweet,' she remarked, noticing the slight glance of mistrust angled at her by the plain secretary as the clerk was explaining their presence. The woman wore her hair scraped viciously off her face into a high bun. She mused that if the secretary lost the thick-rimmed tortoiseshell glasses, loosened her bun or not make such a prune of her mouth, she'd be attractive. It was clear the secretary was not favouring the cold call but Katerina could tell from his body language that the young clerk had won through. He returned and she looked at him expectantly.

'Miss Bailey is finding some time for you. It may be a few minutes, but he will see you.'

'That's excellent. Thank you so much, er . . .'

'I'm John Honeywill.'

'Lovely name. Thank you.' She smiled broadly and he returned it with a blush.

'I'll, er . . . leave you with Miss Bailey.' He glanced,

embarrassed, and departed to the sound of Miss Bailey tapping an angry rhythm on her typewriter.

'Mr Summerbee won't be long,' she called out.

'Thank you,' they said together, although Daniel could pull a face of feigned terror without being seen and Katerina widened her eyes to caution him not to make her laugh.

Clearing her throat, she began removing her gloves and scarf. She'd packed lightly for this trip but she was wearing her favourite coat of the cleanest A-line, in a mustard yellow with a small collar and an invisible fastening at her shoulder. It only just grazed her knees. She'd daringly paired it with the darkest of sage-green woollen tights and matching gloves, and while she had toyed with the idea of a hat, it may have intimidated the presumably conservative legal man they'd be meeting, so she'd opted for a green, mustard and ruby paisley headscarf.

They heard a phone buzz and Miss Bailey answered, 'Yes, sir.' She looked across at them. 'I can show you in now.'

She stood and they followed down a short, carpeted passageway regarded by the line of sitters in baronial-type portraits on either wall before Miss Bailey's thickly woollened legs stopped before a door and knocked gently.

'Come in,' came the reply.

They entered and a man stood up to walk around his desk. Katerina blinked as he extended a welcoming hand and a broad, bright smile that landed on her with authentic pleasure. Not old, then. Not stuffy either, as she'd imagined judging from his superbly tailored single-breasted suit that hung off his shoulders with dash. Everything about its shape was 'today' but he'd couched his fashionable taste in a sartorial dark fabric to perhaps fool his peers.

'It's not often we have French visitors to Lincoln's Inn. Welcome to you.' His tone was as bright as his name and the daring thin red stripe she noticed in the charcoal worsted fabric; Edward

Summerbee was a surprise. He shook Daniel's hand before gently taking hers and she thought for one moment he was going to kiss it but he politely held it. '*Enchanté*, Mademoiselle Kassel. Mr Horowitz.' He regarded her without any obvious sense of embarrassment at holding her gaze for a heartbeat longer than most men could. There was nothing suggestive in that look but he smiled deeper as though he sensed her taking stock of him. 'Please, do sit but let me take your coat. Miss Bailey, some tea for our visitors, perhaps?' He glanced at Katerina. 'Just got in a lovely Brackenridge First Flush.' He returned his attention to the secretary.

'Of course. Er . . .' As she turned, Katerina got the impression that Miss Bailey would prefer her to decline, and while she had no idea what a Brackenridge First Flush was, she nevertheless did the opposite, out of a sense of mischief and to amuse Daniel.

'Thank you, Miss Bailey. Black, please.' She slipped off her coat to reveal a plain mid-grey dress that hugged her silhouette and was deliberately worn to catch the attention of the man who now cleared his throat and looked away as he took her coat and hung it on a nearby stand.

'Same for me, thank you,' Daniel said.

'Er . . . and some lemon, if possible,' Katerina added, timing it perfectly as the secretary turned, and enjoyed the terse glance Miss Bailey snipped at her.

The secretary left and Edward gave a low chuckle. '*Bravo, mademoiselle*. You've done in minutes what I have dreamed for years of doing.'

'What's that?' she enquired.

'Oh, now, don't be coy. Getting under the skin of Miss Bailey is a feat. You've got her measure. She's a dreadful bully. There are times when I feel like I'm still at school, half expecting her to give me a detention.'

The tone in his voice was helplessly enjoyable. It had a smiling quality; the sort of voice that should be on radio, talking about biscuits or confectionery to make people want to run out and buy the products.

'Mr Horowitz has a landlady just like Miss Bailey, don't you, Daniel?'

'Oh, she's not that bad,' Daniel said with a single amused tut in her direction.

'Brothers in arms,' Edward said, winking his way.

The reference brought her sharply back to why they were there. 'I appreciate you seeing us without an appointment,' she began.

'Don't mention it,' he said in the words of a perfect gentleman. She could imagine he had deadlines dropping on him like bombs but he would likely still act as though she and Daniel were the only reason he'd bothered to come to the office today. 'Anything that interrupts writing advices for barristers is welcome in my day. How was your journey from Paris?'

While they made small talk Miss Bailey arrived back in the office with a tray and laid it down before them.

'Would you like me to wait, Mr Summerbee?' She gestured at the teapot beneath a handsome tartan cosy.

'No, no,' he said, with a small wave of slightly gnarled hands that surprised Katerina now that she focused on them. They were like an aberration in his otherwise impeccable appearance. 'I can be Mother.'

Daniel chuckled. 'An expression my father has adopted.' At the solicitor's look of puzzlement, Daniel explained how his family came to be in England.

'Marlow's so beautiful,' Summerbee agreed as Miss Bailey closed the door. 'But you choose Paris? I can't blame you. The city of love.' He glanced at Katerina. 'Are the two of you . . .?'

'No. Daniel and I are friends; he's helping me with my enquiries.'

'Good,' he said, and she was unsure of his meaning. 'So, tell me what brings you here and how our firm can help?'

'It's not your law practice so much as you, Mr Summerbee, who might help me,' she said.

He nodded as he poured their cups of tea. 'That sounds intriguing.' She half expected him to wink. 'Do go on, please.' He plopped a slice of lemon into her tea.

Katerina took the cup and saucer from his crooked fingers and lifted a shoulder slightly. 'Mr Summerbee, um, I was recently seconded to work at the British Museum from the Louvre.'

'How marvellous,' he said, as he handed Daniel his tea. 'Both favourite haunts of mine. I could envy you,' he admitted.

Katerina explained her role, choosing her words with care as they all sipped and she drew Edward Summerbee into what she hoped was an invisible and helpless bond. He was paying close attention to everything she said while she scrutinised his face for telltale signs of anxiety. She hoped Daniel was watching his body language, which might clue them in to what the solicitor wouldn't want to reveal. She tiptoed closer, knowing he had likely not yet understood that the Katerina Kassowicz he had briefly spoken to weeks earlier was the same person sitting before him, using her pseudonym. She was acutely aware of ambushing him.

'Of course, I had no idea what I was about to be shown. I wasn't ready for what was lifted from the velvet bag.' She thought she was building the story at the right pace so that he wouldn't fail to hear it all but when his objection came, it arrived firmly.

His expression blanched instantly, both hands raised, palms forward in polite submission. 'Please, mademoiselle, I have to stop you. Oh dear, I realise what this is about and I absolutely insist you don't speak another word about those Pearls, or we'll all be in trouble.' He stood.

'Wait, Mr Summerbee —' she tried.

'Please hear her out, sir!' Daniel added.

'Forgive me. No.' He meant it. While his kind demeanour had not changed, she could see in the jut of his chin he would not budge. He breathed audibly. 'I must explain that my reluctance is not through choice. You must understand that legally I am bound and I cannot hear any more. I am a solicitor acting on behalf of a client who possesses that item. It's my client's interests that I am legally bound to protect. I'm sorry.' He offered a sympathetic glance that she could feel was genuine. 'The piece you speak of is known to me, of course, but I am not permitted by law to discuss it any further with you, most especially if you are about to claim a vested interest and . . . I deeply suspect you are.'

She tried to assure him but he looked spooked and she suspected he would unlikely hear what she was saying even if she could get him to pay attention.

She returned her teacup, still steaming, to its saucer and Daniel did the same.

'You're welcome to finish your tea,' the solicitor said, although she could tell there was no point.

Katerina stood. Again Daniel followed suit.

Summerbee moved a step away from his comfortable chair towards the door; his fine English manners at war with his legal obligation to toss them from his office. 'Now, Mademoiselle Kassel . . .' He suddenly frowned. 'Clever. I was told the claim was from a Katerina Kassowicz.' He shook his head. 'We spoke . . .'

She nodded, caught in her ploy. 'Yes, briefly.'

'And Severine Kassel?'

'Is how everyone knows me; has known me for the past twenty —'

He shook a hand as if doing a royal wave to stop her. It wasn't meant to be rude. She suspected if he were a child he'd be calling out *La, la, la, la*. 'I don't need to know.'

'Maybe you should put your fingers in your ears, Mr Summerbee?' she offered.

While he looked taken aback by the remark, she saw amusement flare deep in eyes she'd thought were grey but had changed in the light . . . or maybe it was mood. It didn't matter, she'd caught him off guard. He possessed a sense of humour. She'd store that away because she had no intention of letting Edward Summerbee escape her. Not now.

'Your experience would have taught you any sort of claim must be done via the right procedures.' His voice took on an appeal. 'There are protocols and I think you should observe them and no doubt I will be advised accordingly via the museum but for now I . . . I simply cannot speak with you on this topic.' His gaze flicked between them but Daniel was clearly taking his lead from her, waiting for Katerina to make the decision to retreat behind her line or advance for battle. She chose to give the solicitor some space and themselves a chance to regroup. She opened her handbag and took out her gloves and the scarf that had been neatly folded around them.

The men held the brief silence while she tied the scarf around her neck this time. She knew it looked perfect against her dress, against her complexion too; Summerbee could hardly not watch her and so watch her he did. Maybe she'd just got a little bit beneath his skin.

'My sincere apologies, Mr Summerbee. It was not my intention to put you in an awkward position. It's actually not what you think.'

'Even so,' he said, relief loosening his broadish forehead and flickering in eyes whose colour she now couldn't help but compare to faded denim. She had a pair of bell-bottoms that were almost identical in colour to his worried expression.

She released him and his lovely gaze. 'Again, sincere apologies. Daniel, we should go.'

Daniel gave her a glance of such scorn, she had to look away.

Summerbee guided them across his office floor as she spoke. 'I can talk to Mr Partridge at the museum again and seek some further help through him.'

'That's the way,' Summerbee said, herding them both towards the door. 'Miss Bailey!'

Katerina churlishly let herself believe the secretary likely had her ear pressed to the door, she arrived so fast. 'Er, thank you, would you kindly show Mademoiselle Kassel and Mr Horowitz out and let Miss Farthing know that I have a letter to dictate.'

It was an excuse: a poor one, but he was rattled. Katerina understood and felt some sympathy. It had always been an ambush, which she felt badly for because he was a gentleman and even in the brief time they'd spoken, she'd found him impossible to dislike. She turned now and fixed him with a stare, aware that he was helplessly drawn to the curiosity of her eye. Whatever worked, she would use.

'I realise that as a lawyer you set personal feelings aside and never judge your own clients, Mr Summerbee, but even in the brief time we've been together I can tell you are a good man. Let me warn you that your client is not, and this is the reason I could not risk giving you my real name.' She hoped this caught his interest. 'Be careful that you don't live to regret representing his interests.' She took Summerbee's knobbled hand as if to shake it in farewell but squeezed it instead to impress upon him the emotion she was feeling, even if her careful words could not. And then she turned away and allowed him to watch her tall figure glide behind Daniel and seemingly out of his life.

20

● ● ●

On the gravel path she took Daniel's arm. 'Keep walking,' she warned, remembering which view Summerbee's window gave him. 'He's surely watching us.'

Daniel obliged, patting her hand in a gesture as if to say *Well, you tried*, but his words to her expressed anything but that sentiment. 'What are you playing at?'

'Better to win the war than the battle, Daniel.'

'I realise you deliberately left doubt in his mind but are you hoping he'll make contact? If so, how?'

'No, I plan to make contact again with him.'

'Miss Bailey won't let you through the gate.'

'Miss Bailey is no match for me,' she assured him. 'The next time Mr Summerbee and I speak it will be in a more convivial atmosphere with no Miss Baileys in sight.'

'I'm not sure I like your plan.'

'You don't have to. Edward Summerbee is my only pathway to Ruda Mayek and I am not about to walk away from that trail now I've found it.' They moved beneath Archway again towards Chancery Lane. 'Cheer up, Daniel. I promise you he will meet me again. Come on, let's head back to Bloomsbury.'

The fact that she'd left London in such a hurry meant Katerina still had her keys to the flat at Museum House and the rent was still paid for another few weeks. Daniel had slept on the sofa the previous night but now as they arrived back at the mansion house, she didn't need him to say anything to sense the arrangements were about to change.

'Coffee?' she offered. 'I'm sure there's still some left.'

'Katerina?'

She kept talking, even suggesting they might go to the museum and look at the Pearls. 'It would be unusual, of course, but not unthinkable that we could hold them. It would be good for you to —'

'Katerina, I'm leaving.'

She knew he was unhappy but his plan took her by surprise. 'I thought you wanted —'

'I did. I've changed my mind, though. I think I'll return to Paris on the night ferry if I can get a berth this evening.'

'But . . .'

'You're on that path you spoke of and I realise I can't dissuade you. So, if anything, I figure I'm a burden. I need to go to my office and check in with Tel Aviv anyway.'

She nodded, genuinely disappointed. 'I've overlooked that spies – even retired ones – have masters,' she said, to let him off easily so he didn't feel the need to make excuses for his caution around her . . . or, more likely, for his jealousies. She watched him look at his watch.

'I might leave now for London Victoria, if that's all right?'

He looked on edge as he packed up his few items, glancing out of the window a few times, she noted.

'What's out there?'

'I'm just counting taxis, gauging whether to stand on your

street and hail a cab or head towards St Pancras.' His excuse sounded contrived.

'Walk the few minutes to the museum. There's a taxi rank,' she offered, returning to her kitchenette at the sound of bubbling coffee.

Daniel glanced out again, not disturbing the net curtain.

She re-emerged. 'Did you want coffee, or . . .?'

He shook his head. 'I'll go.'

Katerina frowned at his urgency but didn't feel she had any right to pry into his bruised feelings.

'Care to walk me down?'

She hadn't expected the offer. 'Yes, of course. Let me grab my keys. That door notoriously slams behind us residents.'

As they opened the front door, Katerina saw it. 'Oh, look, there's one!'

Daniel whistled and the cab driver looked out and wagged a finger once to say they'd been noted and drew to a halt. He turned back to her and she felt his soft gaze. In a way she wished she could give him what he wanted but Daniel would have to be happy with what she might be able to give him instead – Ruda Mayek.

'I'm sorry,' she began, feeling an apology was necessary.

'Don't be. I can rejoin you if you need me but you might get further with Summerbee if I'm not around.'

Inwardly, she knew it made sense to operate alone. 'As soon as I know anything more or make any headway, shall I send a telegram?'

'Phone me.' He took out a card and gave it to her.

'That's in England.'

'It's monitored twenty-four hours. They can reach me quickly and then you don't have to worry about going through the international operator. I can fly in if necessary.'

She nodded, clasped the card and wrapped her long fingers

around it. 'Goodbye, Daniel.' He looked like he could use a hug and she didn't hesitate to wrap her arms around him, even though it might appear unseemly in broad daylight on her apartment steps.

He hugged her in return. 'Be careful, Katerina.' He stood back to regard her.

'I promise,' she said, crossing her heart to make him smile.

'There's a jigsaw piece outstanding. Describe the man we're hunting. I might use the time while you're here to once again go through the records if I have a description.'

She shrugged. 'Others have described him for you and it was no help.'

'I feel I understand him more now through you. I know the evil I'm looking for . . . previously I was searching for a ghost. You will draw a mental picture better than anyone and then I'll feel like I'm being productive.'

The taxi purred at the kerb, the driver seemingly unbothered by the wait. He'd begun glancing through a newspaper.

'All right.' She blinked, hating having to recall his appearance. 'Over six feet in his prime, flattish features in a squarish face and always clean-shaven while I knew him. His complexion ran to pink, and the last time I saw him he wore his yellowish hair cropped extremely short in the Germanic way so his scalp was almost exposed. He had a smile that was cunning – rarely any warmth in it. And his eyes were oddly disturbing.'

'More than yours?' he said in surprise.

'Definitely. His gaze was unnerving in a cold, searching way. Unless Rudy has worked out how to swap his eyes, close up you can't mistake his pale irises, whose circumference is encircled by a darker outline.'

'Oh, that's a new fact,' he said in a tone as if tasting a delicacy.

'They're intimidating; the edging is a navy outline to far paler eyes. If you can find a photo in those excellent German records, you won't be left wondering whether it's Ruda Mayek, even if the name is different.' She shivered from thinking about Rudy but also from the cold. 'Your taxi driver will be getting impatient.'

'No, he won't. The meter is all that matters. Well, I want to hear you say that you will not physically chase down your prey without telling me first.'

She met his stern, sad gaze. 'I promise you, Daniel, that you will know first before I go after Mayek . . . if I can even find him.'

He nodded, leaned forward and kissed both of her cheeks softly. 'I'll miss you.'

'Safe travels,' she called to his back and he lifted an arm in farewell before hurrying towards his taxi.

Katerina waved again as he got into the cab and waited until the vehicle had turned out of her street and Daniel was gone. For someone who was used to being alone most of the time, she felt strangely deserted as she turned to go back inside.

She didn't notice the man who'd been watching them step out of the doorway of the pub up the road, lift his collar and walk down the street towards her flat.

Katerina used the time alone to write two letters. One was brief and affectionate, which she dashed off while smiling. The other took nearly two hours to craft. She then changed for the cooler evening. The garment was her usual clean, narrow line with no embellishments other than neat front pockets that sat symmetrically at her hips. The dress was invisibly darted from breast to pocket, with three-quarter-length sleeves. Three aspects made it eye-catching: the first was its provocative scarlet, the next was its daring hemline that grazed mid-knee and when she sat would reveal enough leg to be arresting, and finally its scooped neckline. It didn't dip enough to be considered in any way bold, but it did show off her angles spectacularly and with no jewellery to detract attention, anyone looking at her would first notice her long neck. Her chin-length hair flicked out and bounced with good health rather than hairspray. She paired the dress with dark court shoes, hid her outfit beneath the familiar dark mustard coat and stepped out to find a letterbox where she posted her single-sheeted letter before hailing a cab.

'Lincoln's Inn Fields,' she said, hauling the heavy door closed behind her and sinking into the vast rusty-red leather seats. She would never lose the novelty of riding in a big black London taxi.

As she'd anticipated, the friendly cockney driver couldn't help but glance in the mirror and catch her eye.

'You in trouble, miss?' He winked. 'Need a lawyer? Wouldn't bother, if you ask me; they're all about the money.'

She grinned. 'I'm meeting a friend,' she lied.

'Oh, well, that's different, then. Must be handy having a solicitor for a friend.'

'He's a solicitor advocate, actually. Means he can represent his clients in court.'

'Cor, blimey. Lucky you don't have to pay for one of those. I've carried a few in my time and when I hear them discussing their rates . . . well, makes me eyes water, miss.'

'I can imagine,' she said. 'I'm just going to read something quickly.' She had to cut off the chat or the conversation was going to stretch and she had already lied enough.

'Go right ahead, miss. I'll get you safely to your destination. You want the Chancery end?'

'Archway. Yes, please.'

'Traffic will be murder but that's my problem, miss.' He mercifully stopped talking while she pretended to read over her letter to Edward Summerbee. This had to work. Surely, he wouldn't be able to resist . . .

It was odd that she thought about Otto Schäfer in this moment.

There was a quality to Mr Summerbee that she recognised as belonging to Otto as well. She frowned as London rumbled by, reaching for it, dismissing the obvious similarity of empathy – she hoped that was a given in most people who were old enough to remember the war. No, it was something else, but it eluded her as she noticed they'd entered High Holborn.

'Anywhere here is fine,' she said, and after tipping him well, she returned once again to the green door, took a breath, and rapped using the brass knocker.

John Honeywill opened the door, beaming as he recognised her. 'Mademoiselle Kassel.'

She was impressed he remembered her name but then she remembered his. 'Hello again, Mr Honeywill.'

'Are you expected by . . .?'

'No, I won't disturb Mr Summerbee again. I just wondered if you'd do me a good deed?'

'I'd like to help,' he said.

She removed a thickish envelope from her bag. 'This is a letter that I'd be grateful to have delivered into Mr Summerbee's hands . . . not Miss Bailey's, not just into his office, but handed to him personally with the message that I implore him to read the contents this afternoon and to meet me in the tearooms – the address is there.' She pointed to where she'd scrawled the teashop's details on the back of the envelope. 'I'll wait for him – until it closes, and beyond if necessary.' She watched the clerk lick his lips as though sensing that what he was weighing up doing was perhaps inadvisable. She pressed her case. 'Nothing in here can hurt anyone in the law firm, John. Nothing in here in fact can hurt anyone outside of it except, perhaps, bring attention to a war criminal.'

His gaze snapped away from the envelope to her face.

She nodded. 'Did you lose anyone to the war, John?' She was betting he had – hadn't everyone?

'My sister. She died of a fever – she was just twenty. She was a nurse in one of the military field hospitals. She was braver than I.'

'I think you might have been too young to go to war,' she chanced. He blushed. 'Then for your sister and for all the other sisters now dead – I lost three of them to this war criminal I speak of . . . and not one of them had got past their first decade of life.' She had struck a chord: John looked mortified. 'Would you deliver this for me?'

'And Mr Summerbee can help?'

'I think Mr Summerbee can give me some advice that will help.'

'Well, then, I can do that.'

'Don't let Miss Bailey know,' she warned.

He grinned, took the letter and pushed it into the inside pocket of his suit jacket.

'And the message.'

'I won't forget.'

'John, I don't know how to thank you.'

'It's a simple task, mademoiselle. It requires no more thanks. I'm . . . I'm very sorry about your family.'

She smiled her appreciation. 'I won't forget your kindness,' she said and squeezed his arm before turning and leaving, once again deliberately passing the solicitor's window, hoping he would look up to see her moving through his day again.

Katerina sighed to herself. Now it was a waiting game. Would Summerbee take the bait? She left the attractive square as the afternoon light was failing and the shadows lengthened across the lawns. She shivered beneath her coat, which was not doing a very good job of keeping her warm, designed more for a late Parisian spring than a gloomy early spring in London.

A wispy drizzle began to encourage people to open brollies and step up their pace as peak hour drew closer. Katerina didn't for a moment anticipate that the solicitor would keep strict office hours – he looked like someone who would continue working if the job was important or had a tight deadline. The firm was Summerbee & Associates, so his practice depended on his diligence. She would wait. The invitation was there.

Katerina found the tearooms, ordered a pot that she didn't feel like drinking and toyed with the inevitable cup that ended up steaming in front of her. An hour passed and the clock on the wall told her it was nearing a quarter past six; she ordered a second pot she also had no intention of drinking, apologising for letting the first go cold and only now noticing how crowded the café had become. The drizzle had presumably turned into a shower and as she looked up it became a downpour. People scurried in to escape the rain, steaming up the windows and bringing the smells of the city with them. She'd arrived before the crush and been able to sneak a table for two by the window. She stared out now and hoped for a glimpse of a familiar tall figure.

'May I?' someone said, and didn't wait for the response.

'Oh, I'm waiting for someone,' she declined, fully anticipating the Englishman to apologise and move on. He didn't and instead sighed as he made himself more comfortable. He was a stocky, darkish man; not really English-looking, now she thought about it, but with a fine southern accent that she imagined her friend Catherine would say was 'straight off the Kent Weald' or 'right off the Sussex Downs'. Katerina's ear for language and music gave her an equally well-honed sense for picking out accents.

'Forgive me for barging into your space. I'll leave once your companion arrives, I promise, but as you can see there's nowhere else to sit and . . .' He trailed off apologetically, indicating that there really wasn't space in the busy shop and definitely no more seating.

She tried not to show her exasperation and gave a tight moue of assent.

'Do you come here often?' he said, untucking a damp newspaper from under his arm.

'You're joking me, aren't you?'

He looked offended. 'Actually, no. Just being polite, having gatecrashed your table.'

'No, I have never been here before,' she replied, her tone brisk. She began digging in her bag for something to look at or read. Her fingers landed on a pencil and she clutched at it, searched for a receipt to scribble on and look busy.

'Well, I hear they do a fine brew. How's yours?'

'A fine brew,' she replied, unable to mask the sarcasm.

'Do you work around here?'

She decided he was too dull to catch on to any of the signs, from tone to body language. 'I don't, no. And I might suggest you stand and let that lady behind you sit down instead.'

He glanced behind his shoulder. 'She's busy talking to someone; I think I'd be a nuisance.'

'Do you? I can't imagine why,' she remarked. 'I just want to be quiet, actually.'

He looked surprised. 'Quiet? In a busy café? Why come in here if you want quiet?'

She sighed. 'Please. Either drink your tea in silence or give your seat up. I really don't want to talk to anyone.'

'But you said you were waiting for a friend. I don't see —'

'He's here,' said a new voice. 'I'm her friend.'

Katerina looked up into the earnest face of John Honeywill and although it was not the person she'd hoped would come, she nevertheless wanted to hug him for the rescue. She realised all she was doing was giving him a crooked smile of relief.

'Shall we step outside?' he offered, thumbing to the door.

'Yes, please,' she mouthed. She didn't care if she got soaked. 'I don't have an umbrella but let's go anyway.'

He not only held the door but he managed to also expertly flick open a large black umbrella that she was sure could engulf three people. 'Here,' he offered, 'share mine.'

'Oh, are you sure?'

'Mademoiselle Kassel, Mr Summerbee always says an Englishman never leaves home without his brolly, although I can see a Parisian lady takes her chances,' he said in a mildly admonishing tone.

'Then I am a lucky Parisian.' She waited beneath a dome of black, the rain beating a steady rhythm against it like a thousand heartbeats. Glad to be leaving the chatty stranger behind, she was nevertheless having to come to terms with the fact that Summerbee had refused her invitation. 'Thank you for meeting me,' she said into the awkward pause.

'Mr Summerbee asked me to.'

'And what else did he ask of you?'

'That I apologise to you on his behalf.' At the sneer she couldn't hide, he leapt to his superior's defence. 'He does have another appointment this evening. It's been in his diary since the beginning of the week.'

Poor Honeywill; he thought that might reassure her. Well, it was not this fellow's fault that she was getting damp at her ankles and cold, feeling bereft of ideas. Katerina hadn't realised how uncomfortable her silence was making him. He began to offer information he perhaps shouldn't.

'Of course, it is a social engagement, but all the same, getting to Piccadilly from here at this time of day can be murderous.'

Murderous. The very word seemed to sum up not only her anguish but also her mission and her mood. His uttering galvanised her: if Edward Summerbee was going to avoid her, then she would go to him. 'Oh, yes? Was there any other message he sent, John? He has information that can help me.' She watched him roll his lips with warring thoughts. 'Perhaps I could go to him, as his time is stretched?'

'Oh, mademoiselle, I don't think turning up at the Café Royal is wise.'

The Café Royal? 'I just need to talk with him briefly.'

'Perhaps I might suggest you ring the office tomorrow?'

Hmm, yes, and face the sour response from Miss Bailey? 'Maybe I will do that,' she lied, uncomfortable about tricking Honeywill but knowing her next move. 'You've been very kind to me, John, thank you.'

'May I hail you a taxi, Mademoiselle Kassel?'

'You may.' She smiled.

Her unwitting accomplice let out a piercing whistle to the one taxi that everyone seemed to be hoping to hail. The driver could hardly ignore that sound.

'I wish I could do that!' she admitted as the black car slowed for them.

He grinned, opened the door and helped her in. 'Good evening, mademoiselle. I hope . . .' He looked lost for what he hoped.

She shook his hand. 'I know. Good evening, John.' When the door closed she glanced at the man watching her in the mirror. 'The Café Royal in Piccadilly, please.'

'Righto, miss. It's going to be murder getting there.'

'So I gather.'

21

* * *

'That wasn't so bad,' the taxi driver admitted, nodding towards the familiar semicircular canopy of the famed Café Royal with its spot-lights illuminating people moving past it in the now mercifully light drizzle.

'Thank you, driver.' She handed over the money. 'Keep the change.'

'Obliged, miss, thank you.'

The hotel's doorman was at the taxi awaiting her exit and as she extended a long leg out to the damp thoroughfare, he shifted a voluminous umbrella over her.

'Welcome to the Café Royal.'

A newspaper seller half-heartedly offered her an *Evening Standard* out of habit. Horns blasted and a double-decker bus rumbled by, splashing water from a puddle onto a nearby pedestrian who squealed. Katerina sympathised, noting the woman's stock-ings were now soaked with grimy water.

'Good evening, madam. Let's get you out of this mucky night,' the doorman said, enveloping her in his welcome and his vast umbrella, emblazoned with the emblem of his establishment.

'Thank you.' To her right the neon lights of Piccadilly Circus yelled that Gordon's Gin was doing battle with Martini for her attention, while Max Factor insisted its brand was the only lipstick a girl needed today.

She gasped as she emerged into the reception hall of marble floors and walls, replete with stone fireplaces above which sat huge gilded mirrors. 'I feel like I've stepped back into Paris,' she murmured, pulling off her headscarf.

'That's the point, I think.' The doorman grinned. 'Built by a Frenchman and opened a century ago to bring the sense of a great Parisian salon to an otherwise stoic Victorian London.' He flicked away the droplets from his umbrella before he tapped his nose conspiratorially. 'Between you and I, these days I think it's favoured too strongly by pop stars fuelled with hallucinogenic drugs than it is with its former patronage of royals, society doyennes and literati.'

As she gazed back at the doorway with its vast bank of stained glass she shook her head in small wonder.

'By day it's spectacular, and inside is grander,' he promised. 'Are you meeting someone, madam?'

'I am. A Mr Summerbee.'

'Ah, yes, he arrived about half an hour ago. Through those doors. Enjoy your evening.'

'Thank you.'

Katerina Kassowicz moved in the direction of the doors that she was determined would lead her straight to her planned and, she hoped, final meeting with Ruda Mayek. Whether it ended with his death or her own, she couldn't control, but she was prepared to risk her life in order to end his.

The doorman hadn't lied. Katerina had arrived in a salon that she presumed was the main dining room. It was like entering a world of *la belle époch*, a different era that seemed to fling her back to childhood and the elaborate theatres and music halls of Prague. Gilding on every spare inch of wall glittered and wall lights twinkled their reflections in mirrors that lined the vertical spaces to make the salon seem ten times its true size. Velvet, heavy wood and a painted ceiling depicting naked nymphs and cherubs at play in the clouds tried to trick her into feeling as though all her worries were outside.

She spotted the English solicitor leaning forward across a table from a blonde woman, who was coyly covering her mouth as she giggled helplessly. There was no doubting Summerbee's charm; she'd fallen beneath its spell earlier in the day and had entertained hope that he would open himself up to helping her in any way possible. The negative outcome had felt like a slap. He was stronger than she'd anticipated and immune to both her persuasive skills and her usually reliably disconcerting presence. She watched him blaze a smile at his companion and press his amusing point; the woman's laugh carried across the vast, still relatively empty space. It was early and they were one of two couples having cocktails.

A waiter had approached, offering to take her coat, but Katerina wasn't paying attention, not even as her coat was slipped off her shoulders; it was hard to concentrate amongst all the Second Empire surrounds that were so reminiscent of France, plus the realisation that she had no plan for this confrontation. It was her second ambush of Summerbee and she suspected he was not going to be easy to convince.

'Good evening, madam. Er, can I show you to a table, or . . .?'

'You can, thank you. That one over there.' She gestured towards the laughing couple.

'Mr Summerbee's table?'

'He's an old friend. I'll just stop by and say hello.'

'Yes, of course.' The man looked relieved. He gestured forward and she glided silently on the plush ruby carpet towards her victim.

Katerina breathed deeply, hating to put herself in the situation of making a spectacle; she hoped the solicitor would suffer the usually dependable British trait of politeness in public overriding all other emotion. The waiter nodded at her as they approached and then cut away with her coat, leaving her to make the final few steps alone and the inevitable unhappy greeting. She was close enough now she could hear Edward's conversation.

'. . . and he yelled "Jump!"'

The woman laughed harder.

'What else could I do? I jumped straight in, fully clothed.'

Katerina felt a moment's regret at spoiling their fun as the woman tipped back her chin, entirely entertained with unrestrained amusement. As he sat back, pleased with his efforts, he became aware of Katerina. He looked deeply at her and then away as if momentarily stunned but it turned immediately to a frown . . . a precious moment to gather his thoughts.

'Forgive me, I know I shouldn't be here,' she began.

'You're following me?' He sounded so offended she was momentarily lost for the right words.

She could hardly deny his accusation. Katerina glanced at the woman, suddenly all amusement gone from her expression. 'I'm sorry to intrude,' she said to her. 'I need a few words with Mr Summerbee.'

'No, she doesn't,' he assured her, his voice hardening from the convivial tone it had possessed just a moment or two earlier. 'Mademoiselle, this is most inappropriate —'

'So is murder!' she snapped and looked around, immediately lowering her voice. 'You can see I have no shame, Mr Summerbee, because honestly there's not a lot left for me to lose.'

He blinked, angry and concerned at once. 'This is neither the time nor the place, mademoiselle.'

'I don't care about what's right or polite, Mr Summerbee; surely you can tell that much. Have you read my letter?'

His generous mouth thinned at being interrogated so inappropriately. His companion cleared her throat and stood. 'Alice, don't . . .'

'Edward, it's fine. I'm just going to powder my nose. I shan't be long.' She glanced at Katerina as if permission was being given but not before laying a proprietorial hand on his shoulder for Katerina's benefit. 'Back soon, darling.'

She replaced the attractive woman, seating herself opposite the solicitor.

'This is so wrong of you,' he asserted, glaring at her.

She blinked and he cleared his throat as drinks arrived with a new waiter, who was none the wiser that the women had been swapped. She noticed the salon had begun to fill with other cocktail-hour patrons who would, she presumed, become diners in a while. The atmosphere was turning jollier but she imagined it would never be allowed to crowd. They had their privacy, but she only had minutes.

'A Sidecar for the lady,' the waiter said, putting down a champagne bowl glass that blazed orange and had a sugar crust around its rim and a curl of orange zest floating like a smile on its surface.

She played along to keep the peace. 'Looks delicious, thank you.'

The waiter nodded. 'That's the very finest French cognac with curaçao, triple sec and fresh lemon juice. And for you, Mr Summerbee, I have your Negroni.' Edward thanked him and the man departed with a small nod.

'Right, say what you have to and then I'm going to have to ask you to leave.'

She nodded. 'Did you read my letter?'

'I did not.'

Another surprise. A horrible one. She had felt certain Summerbee would not have resisted the contents of her thick envelope. He was proving to be a conundrum and in spite of how quietly distraught she now felt, her estimation of his integrity had escalated sharply.

'You looked shocked but I cannot imagine why,' he growled, grabbing his cocktail. He drained a slug of it. It looked like an unhappy swallow with the sour look that followed. 'Now you've ruined my favourite drink.'

She gave a mirthless grin. 'A small price. Does your conscience not demand that you —'

'Mademoiselle Kassel, or Kassowicz, or whatever name you're using now, I have a paying client. How can I say this to make you understand that I have a legal obligation and responsibility? I am bound by the law of the land. There are rules, codes of conduct – just sitting here with you is potentially breaching that.'

'Then breach it properly. Help me! Your client is a cold-blooded murderer. He is a Nazi responsible for the torture and deaths of many. I watched him murder my parents and my three sisters. Each of those girls was under ten years old. If you touch my head here,' she said, reaching behind, 'you will feel a scar. That's the track his bullet left when it missed killing me in 1941. It was shot from his pistol and I heard his laughter when it hit me.'

His gaze, burning with anger, felt as though it would scorch her if he didn't look away. She could tell he was moved – genuinely shocked. His companion had re-entered the salon and was approaching. She really should leave.

'Read my letter, Mr Summerbee, and then make a decision. I don't claim to know the law but I suspect there must be occasion that if you feel following client instructions could damage your firm or your reputation, you have an option to refuse.'

He looked back at her as if they were both speaking different languages. He laughed but there was no amusement in it. He raised his glass to her. 'To a well-made Negroni,' he said. 'I'll read your letter, mademoiselle,' and took another swallow of his cocktail.

She noted his large, crooked hands around the fragile stem of the glass and was inwardly horrified to feel a pang of pleasure at the silly flashing image of those hands cupping her face rather than a glass. She coughed slightly and surprised herself by picking up the other woman's drink and sipping. A zing of citrus chased by a heavy warming of powerful French brandy woke her up. 'It's all I ask,' she remarked.

'Oh, I doubt that, mademoiselle.' He stood as his guest arrived. Katerina followed suit. 'Alice, you shall have to forgive me. There's some urgent business I must attend to that Mademoiselle Kassel has brought to my attention.'

'Edward, surely . . .' She frowned.

'It's my fault, something I've overlooked.' He kissed her cheek. 'Come on, I'll get you a taxi and I promise to make it up to you tenfold.'

Alice slanted her a look that felt so cutting, she could imagine a thin ooze of blood across her cheek. 'Thank you for ruining our evening. And there I was trying to be gracious.'

'Alice . . .' he began, a tone of warning.

'No, Alice, you are right. I'm so sorry and you have been most gracious, but this really is urgent and important,' Katerina tried.

It only appeased the woman slightly, and she made sure Edward understood that making it up to her was going to cost him a small fortune.

At the main entrance of the Café Royal they looked out into the murkiness of the night and Edward turned to her with a resigned drop of his shoulders. 'Oh, blast! I think I left my wretched brolly in the taxi,' he grumbled.

'Will the hotel lend us one, perhaps?'

'I'm sure, but look, let's just hail a taxi and work it out from there.' The doorman was not to be seen so they stood in the drizzle at the kerbside.

'Can you try not to hate me for the next hour, perhaps?'

'I don't hate you. I hate being manipulated.'

'Then can you pretend at least?'

He sighed and she watched his body relax. He'd forced the change but she found the shift in tone helplessly attractive. 'I once went through those revolving doors,' he said, pointing back towards the entrance of the Café Royal. 'I was leaving – as Elizabeth Taylor and Richard Burton were arriving.'

Katerina's eyes widened with wonder; all she'd hoped for was for him to stop glaring and grinding his jaw, but conversation she hadn't anticipated. She felt a fresh flutter of admiration for his gallantry.

'I had to go around twice, I was so stunned. She is truly and ridiculously beautiful. I think they were drunk and it was about two o'clock in the afternoon, but they seemed to be very much in love, laughing a lot, both fitting into one compartment of the revolving door. Gosh, I would love to have squeezed in with her and that low-cut dress.'

Katerina let out a gust of amusement at his admission; she hadn't picked Edward Summerbee to go near the topic of sex but he seemed not at all abashed for mentioning it.

Edward suddenly craned his neck and let out a piercing whistle. It must be one of the rules of employment at Summerbee & Associates, she thought, wondering if Miss Bailey could also whistle up a cab as easily. The doorman hurried up alongside to hold a huge umbrella over them while they waited.

'Where did you learn to make that enormous sound?' she asked, desperately wishing she could dab the drop of rain that was running down his long, straight nose.

He sniffed, dug inside his coat to his jacket pockets, fished out a large handkerchief and dried his face. 'Ooh, sorry. Er . . . On the family farm. I learned from my father how to train dogs.'

'Really? Farm boy turned lawyer.' She sounded impressed.

'Oh, well, my brother was the better farmer . . . better with all things physical, whereas I suppose I took advantage of a good education.'

'I think you're being modest.'

He shrugged.

'Do you miss the farm?'

'Every day,' he said, and she felt touched by the soft pain in his words.

She watched him glance to the doorman in thanks as the taxi purred up glistening in the rain.

Edward gave the driver his address at Lancaster Gate and sat back. The vehicle rumbled past the great Georgian sweep of Regent Street, out of Piccadilly proper and towards Hyde Park Corner.

'Now I just have to explain to Violet and Pansy why I have a beautiful multilingual foreigner with me.'

She stiffened at the thought of disapproving women at the other end. 'I'm sorry, I made a presumption,' she said, colouring as she thought of Alice. 'I didn't realise you were married.'

'I'm not. Violet's an old friend and Pansy is her daughter. They live with me.'

This struck her as odd but there was never any accounting for the eccentricities of the British.

'They retire early, especially Violet. Pansy will likely do the polite thing and introduce herself but I doubt she'll stay.'

'I see.'

'It's rare I have visitors.'

'It's rare I accept invitations.'

'I didn't invite you.'

'And still you are taking me to your home.'

He held up a blunt finger. 'My home office.'

She gave a shrug as if to say it was much the same to her but Katerina knew this was more than she could have hoped for and needed to curb her pointed remarks.

He began humming a song – it sounded nervous, as though he was already regretting them being together like this.

'Do you like the Beatles?' she asked.

'Very much. I went to see them earlier this month at the Royal Albert Hall.'

'I wouldn't have picked you as a popular music man . . . but it's not fair to judge, is it?'

'Especially should you get it wrong,' he replied.

'I have a . . . friend . . . who would cut off an arm, I'm sure, to see the Beatles perform.'

He gave an easier smile. 'You should take her to the Majestic later this month – they're performing in London again.'

'It's a he, actually.'

'Oh, well, take him.'

The rain began to subside and by the time they'd stepped out of the taxi, no umbrella was required.

They stood outside a row of elegant wrought-iron railings that belonged to a wide terrace of identical cream buildings that screamed, *Important and wealthy people live here.* 'So here we are.' He appeared more comfortable now they were at his home. He made an expansive gesture across Bayswater Road. 'That's Kensington Park, and if we keep walking through, you'd come to Kensington Palace.'

'Ah,' she said, getting her bearings.

'If it's dry, I usually walk to my offices. It takes me a full hour but it's a straight line from here so I get to stare into the windows of places like Selfridges on my way. And sometimes I angle through the great park on a different route.' He gave a brief grin. 'Means I always arrive with a clear head.'

'I wondered how you managed to cut such a lean figure if you dine out at grand places like the Café Royal.'

'So you've been pondering my physique, have you?' he teased, and Katerina was glad the spill of the street lamp couldn't show the warmth that erupted across her complexion. Nevertheless, she was grateful for his graciousness at setting his understandable snarls aside for the time being.

Edward found his keys and opened the door to the house embedded within a grand stuccoed terrace of English baroque. She could swear there was French detailing but she couldn't linger in the cold and so stepped into a quiet world of soaring ceilings, ornate decoration and marble fireplaces.

'I'm afraid this is my housekeeper's day off, so we shall have to look after ourselves. Ah . . . and here comes Pansy. Miss Violet won't be far away.'

A small terrier arrived from upstairs to clatter across the black and white tiles of the reception, followed by an elderly version, and Katerina watched a happy reunion.

'They're dogs!' she said, and knew the remark revealed more of her thoughts than she wanted.

'I can't imagine what else you thought they may be,' he said with a wink that also took her by surprise. The dogs sniffed around her ankles, tails wagging. 'They're my best friends, these two,' he added. 'Shall I take your coat?'

She allowed him to help her slip the garment off.

'Let me just hang this up,' he said, opening a cloakroom door and taking out a coat hanger. 'Right, follow me into the parlour briefly. It will be warm there.'

She obeyed, not allowing herself to ponder the notion of how strangely comfortable she felt around Edward Summerbee. She liked how he could hover between the charming entertainer and the cool professional. Allowing her into his private space was no little generosity, she was sure, which perhaps meant she – or at least her plight – had worked her way beneath his defences. It was entirely unfair what she had done to him; he was now essentially breaking the very laws his status as solicitor advocate needed him to always uphold. But then the murder of her family was unfair too, and that trumped all.

'Mademoiselle, I was planning on eating out tonight as perhaps you'd have guessed, so you'll forgive me if I poke around in the fridge for something to eat.'

'So long as you read my letter, I don't mind what you do.'

He nodded. 'I have it right here,' he said, tapping his jacket pocket over his heart. 'A man must eat, though. And so must a woman. Can I offer you something?'

'No, thank you.'

'It makes it awkward for me to chew if someone is watching me.'

'I'll look away.'

'No, you won't. You'll share what I have or I won't read.'

She nodded. 'All right, I'll eat.'

'Well, let's see what we have,' he said, pushing through the door and into a kitchen-cum-parlour that was warmed by a range. It was homely, painted soft sage green and cream with lots of domestic clutter. He noted her taking stock. 'I don't cook. This is all Mrs Lawson and her acquisitions.'

She nodded. 'I think it's cosy, although I reckon I could fit my apartment in Paris into this area alone.'

He grinned. 'It's a big house for one person and two small dogs to rattle around, I'll grant you. But it belonged to our family – my mother was not a typical farmer's wife and she liked her city dwelling. I couldn't bear to part with it.' He dragged open the heavy door of the refrigerator. 'Aha, soup. How about I warm up some delicious . . .' He paused while he checked what sort of soup he was offering. 'Looks like pea and ham hock . . . sound good?'

'Thank you. Can I help?'

'Bowls over there. Spoons in there. Napkins . . . oh, look around. You'll find what you need,' he said, reaching for a saucepan.

'Why don't I warm the soup and you grab the rest because you know where to look?'

'Good plan, Dr Watson.'

She frowned.

'Sherlock Holmes?' he tried again.

She frowned deeper.

'Oh well. Ladle in that drawer and matches to light the gas over here.'

She watched him pull off his jacket and drape it around a chair; it had a flamboyant red lining he could keep mostly hidden from his colleagues. She liked his secret life of fashion. Her letter was visible in the inside pocket and she looked away as he pulled off his monogrammed cufflinks – the conservative did battle with the liberal inside him – and began rolling up his shirtsleeves to get busy laying the table. 'I think some wine . . . yes?'

'All right.'

He poured them both a small glass of white wine he found in the fridge. 'It's a lovely Chablis.' He handed her a glass. '*Santé.*'

She raised her glass to him before turning back to stir the soup. Katerina leaned against the warm range, sipping Chablis – which was delicious – and stirring gently and absently at the soup.

'How did your hands become so oddly shaped?' This had troubled her when they'd first met and now it nagged harder; she hadn't meant to blurt it out but at least it kept the conversation going.

He put his glass down after his first sip and glanced at them. 'These really are farmer's hands, although I blame endless matches of rugby, which I still play a little today, plus a lot of happy gardening, carpentry for a hobby . . . and increasingly a bit of arthritis coming on.'

He sounded so homely, she wished she could enter his life just for a day and know what it felt like to be someone who, outwardly, seemed so content and at ease with the world.

'I do like the law, though,' he continued. 'I know it can often feel unfair but the law is about fairness. It's about living by rules that treat everyone the same no matter your creed, your colour, your social standing.'

'Now, you know that's not how life works, of course,' she said, feeling the wine hitting her empty belly.

'I do. I know there are people who spend every waking hour trying to out-manoeuvre the law. Nonetheless, my role is to negotiate between parties to get the best outcome for my client while ensuring we observe the law.'

'Is that why you're here with me?' There was no point in tiptoeing around the subject that had clambered into the taxi with them, dodged the rain with them, now sat drinking wine with them. 'I want you to know my letter contains only the truth . . . and the truth is what the law is surely all about?'

'Do you know something, mademoiselle? Everyone believes theirs is the truth.'

'Let me say it another way that might appeal to the man of law: everything in my letter contains only fact.'

'Good. So . . .' he sighed. 'Let me read.'

He sat down at his scrubbed pine kitchen table and opened her letter while Katerina tried not to hold her breath for too long, or to watch him too intently.

She watched him run the tip of his tongue around the outline of his generous lips, which turned up slightly at each edge, giving the impression that Edward Summerbee had a permanent slight smile. It was echoed by the lines that flanked his eyes; they too flicked gently upwards so the overall look was one of someone on the brink of laughter, who seemed to know no sorrows. It had to be the liquor on an empty stomach that was prompting her irresponsible thoughts – the new one wondering what it might be like to taste those lips as he had just tasted them. This flippancy irritated her but it was also such a novel feeling that she didn't want to let it go fully . . . just to push it away for now.

He read on, turning the pages with crooked fingers, and she watched his expression darken and continue to fall as the gravity of her story began to press his shoulders down.

She placed two bowls of soup down between them.

'Only you can help me,' she said as he looked up from the final page to draw a slow breath.

Edward sighed. 'Mademoiselle Kassowicz —'

'It's Katerina,' she corrected. 'I would enjoy hearing you call me by my true name.'

'Then you must call me Edward.'

Light from the candle that he'd lit between them caught the spark that flashed in his gaze. She sensed the helpless connection between them that was nothing to do with her manipulation of the situation. She'd felt it at the first hello and she'd been trying to touch what it was ever since and now she knew. What she had been reaching for today on her journey to Lincoln's Inn Fields to deliver her letter arrived like a bomb exploding in her mind. And it was as foreign a feeling as it was helplessly alluring . . . like a narcotic she'd discovered that might ease the pain of years of suffering.

It was, she now understood, the unbridled, unfamiliar, delicious attraction to another person. It was the feeling of being fourteen and hoping Alexandr Clementis might try to kiss her; it was the impossible hope that Dr Otto Schäfer would know how much she desired to fall into his arms and spend the rest of her life in his safety . . . and now it was, hard though it was to believe, Edward Summerbee and his tough yet kind, amusing yet professional manner that had got under her guard. More than two decades of building a fortress around her feelings and he'd unwittingly found a way through with his self-effacing style, those sympathetic eyes and a pea and ham soup that he insisted she share.

Daniel's words arrived in her mind to haunt her: someone unexpected would arrive into her life and she might learn how to find the mindset to discover romance and love. Perhaps she would let a fourth man into her world . . . perhaps.

'Katerina . . .?' He tested the name. She enjoyed it spoken in his voice. 'Are you all right?'

'I am. Sorry. The alcohol probably,' she fibbed. 'I forget to eat sometimes.'

'I hope you will not consider it impertinent if I tell you that in spite of you forgetting to eat, you look exquisite. That shade of red is most dashing on you. Miss Bailey would need to take a couple of aspirin and have a lie-down, I suspect, if she looked at you tonight.'

She gave a low laugh, genuinely amused at their running joke about the poor secretary.

'Nice to hear you amused.'

'It's not a habit of mine,' she admitted.

'Not laughing?' He looked at her as if he barely understood the meaning of the words. 'Well, that's just a sin,' he said. 'We must rectify that and teach you how to throw back your head at least . . .' He feigned concentration, pulling at a pretend beard, which encouraged a broad smile from her. 'Oh, at least three times a week. I'll give you some pills.'

'Thank you, Doctor.'

His countenance grew serious as he began to spoon soup to his mouth. 'I could hardly not be moved by your letter.'

She followed his directness. 'Aside from rape, after watching him murder all in my family, I told you he shot me and this was done after urging me to take my chances for freedom. He enjoyed watching me trying to escape. I was flung onto their corpses, presumed dead by the time he'd had his fun at my expense.'

Edward looked ashen in the low light of the parlour. 'There aren't sufficient words to convey my horror, Katerina. And you're so blunt about it.'

'I wanted you to have the raw facts. He stole the Pearls and now I suspect he's either trying to absolve himself of his sins – of his connection to us through those Pearls – or he's using immense patience to find a way of making his profit from that theft.'

'Or both,' Edward murmured, frowning.

'Most likely,' she said.

'You can't be sure it's him, of course.'

'No, but you can,' she said, nailing him with a stare.

'How does Mr Horowitz fit into all of this?'

'Daniel is Mossad.'

At this his eyebrows lifted, crinkling the wide forehead, which swooped to a slightly receding hairline that was not unattractive in the way it framed his symmetrical features. Edward kept his hair trimmed short, and though it looked dark in this light, she imagined as a child he must have had fluffy golden hair that settled into a nutty colour in adulthood.

'He's hunting the same man,' she continued. 'That's how we came to be associated.'

'You indicated your friendship was platonic?'

It was rhetorical and she remained impassive.

'You could have fooled me.'

'What makes you say that?'

'Oh, I don't know. Perhaps the waves of hostility that were directed at me as you were giving me your undivided attention.'

'I think Daniel may have developed feelings,' she said, deliberately playing down what she knew. 'But it's likely because he sees us as kindred spirits. I've set him straight. We barely know each other but he has shared my story and I have shared his.' She gave him the abridged version of Daniel's loss.

He listened in silence but his expression grew grave as his soup cooled.

'So he has an understandable grudge. Katerina, I want to help you but I'm not really sure how. You see, I don't know this man, Ruda Mayek, of whom you speak.'

'But – your client, he . . .?'

'My client is a European legal firm. Now, who *their* client is I am not privy to. They are representing his or her interests but I am not; I am representing theirs. That's it. I will never learn the name of their client, especially if you believe it is this brute; I suspect he would have moved with immense care to protect his identity.'

'Could you ask, perhaps?'

'I could not,' he said. It was gently spoken but she recalled from earlier in the day how adroitly final he could be in the softest of tones. He had done it again: stilled her. 'That would be breaking every rule that I am bound by. It would embarrass my firm, it would compromise my professional name, and I have to tell you it would be in vain, Katerina. The lawyer at the other end of this contract will no sooner reveal his client's name than tell you that you can keep the Pearls.'

'No, you see, I think that's where there's a misunderstanding, and perhaps I should have stated this from the outset.' She paused, giving herself a heartbeat to be sure she wasn't lying. 'I have no intention of making a claim on the Pearls.'

He showed his surprise by pushing his soup bowl forward as though he'd lost interest in his food. 'Good grief. Why ever not? You say they're yours.'

'They are. But they represent only pain. And they're hardly a simple item of jewellery that one clasps around the neck for a night out.' She smiled, hoping to lighten the mood that had turned suddenly heavy around them.

He gave a sad twist of his lovely mouth; it didn't quite make it, but it approximated a smile for her.

'I am comfortable that they go on display in a museum, whether it's the British Museum, the Louvre, or one in Prague – Russia, even – all the way back to the palace in Istanbul, if need be . . . so long as it is stated that they were donated by the Kassowicz family. Let them be admired by all. I don't particularly want to see them again, let alone wear them, but I will not allow him to profit from the Pearls, or to wash himself of the theft or my family's murders.'

He'd been watching her closely as she spoke; she knew she was showing more emotion than she normally would but it was important to convey, emphatically, that her motivation was not the Pearls. They were simply the proof.

He sighed. 'You're so intense. Have you always been like this?'

'I've become like this,' she admitted.

'It's not unattractive but it's certainly single-minded.'

'I've been looking over my shoulder for most of my life. I'm not sure you can imagine what that feels like. I've feared but also hoped that one day there would be a reckoning with Ruda Mayek; I wanted to convince myself that the war claimed him and yet I never truly believed it did. And so I've been cautious to the point of . . .' She lifted a shoulder. 'Well, to becoming so introspective that

I find it hard to let anyone in now. But no, as a youngster I was social; I loved life and I looked forward to it.'

'I think you're perfect as you are. Well, apart from that tiny mark in your eye that is so intriguing.'

Katerina had thought herself immune to the raft of regular compliments that were lauded upon her. 'My brother had it too but not my sisters; all three girls had lovely but unremarkable eyes.'

'Brother?'

She nodded and explained, including her father's repeated attempts to get the children away on the *Kindertransports*. 'Petr would be twenty-four if he'd been put on the train but he died of a sudden illness. Even if he had survived, Mayek wouldn't have let him live anyway, so I shouldn't let my thoughts stray like this.'

He helped her by moving her thoughts on. 'You didn't explain in your letter what happened to the kind doctor.'

She disturbed the neat shape of her hair with a self-conscious rake of her fingers. 'Otto? He was my hero. Still is.'

He smiled, encouraging her. She'd never told anyone the detail but it felt easy to talk to Edward – even easier than Daniel. 'Otto was my saviour. He saved my life twice – first on the night of the murders and keeping me hidden in his holiday villa, and then hidden in plain sight in Prague, as he put it. I lived briefly in the servants' quarters of his apartment. He'd coached me in nursing skills in case we needed that as a full-time cover but I was regarded as the housekeeper and no one scrutinised, to my knowledge.'

'Oh, tongues must have wagged,' Edward scoffed gently.

'They may have, because I know he was troubled. He was married, you see. His wife is Austrian; they lived on the border at Salzburg and he wrote and told her about me. It was the measure of the man he was. He was not a liar or a cheat.'

'Tell me he wasn't in love with you.'

'He wasn't in love with me,' she said, warmth creeping up her neck. 'But that didn't mean I wasn't in love with him.' *There it was!* She'd openly admitted her heart's secret.

'That's understandable,' Edward assured her. 'You were still a child and vulnerable. I'd consider it odd if you hadn't fallen in love with him.'

'He was extremely handsome . . . that helped,' she said as she cleared their bowls.

'How old was he?'

She shrugged, turning back to the sink. 'Around the age I am today, I suppose. He would be in his late fifties now. If he knew how I felt about him – and I suspect he did – he went to pains to protect me from any temptation and didn't allow me to make a fool of myself. He never overstepped his role as protector and I have no idea if that required his energies.'

'As a man I can take a good guess that it did,' he suggested.

'I don't know what repercussions my presence in his life had on his marriage. We only lived like that for a short while because circumstances pushed us to take action. When we parted in Czechoslovakia he asked me not to try to reach him and he admitted that his wife struggled with the notion that he had a platonic relationship with a young Jewess. She was a good woman . . . a loyal one. She obviously never mentioned it to anyone else and I presume destroyed his letter that spoke of me. And so, out of respect for her, especially for not turning me in, I have never seen him again since the war. We exchange polite cards once a year that I think simply reassure each other that we're still alive, but beyond that I wouldn't know anything more about him today.'

'That's sad.' He frowned at her.

'It is. But it's also right. He loved his wife.'

'But he lied to her because he loved you too, I'm convinced.'

She pretended not to set any store by his remark, waving it away. 'Otto is someone I put on a pedestal. He kept me safe.

Sometimes I'd file for him, closeted in his office. I kept fearing I'd be tapped on the shoulder by Gestapo but it never happened, although I was never off my guard.'

He gave another twist of his mouth in private amusement.

'What?' she said.

'Are you ever off your guard?' He grinned. 'I'll make some coffee. Tell me the rest.' He busied himself as she spoke.

'I'm presuming you know about Heydrich? He was the most powerful man in Prague.'

'I know about the assassination attempt by the Allies. Who doesn't?'

She nodded. 'But did you know that he didn't die immediately? He was injured and brought to the Bulovka Hospital.'

'Oh my . . .' He trailed off, looking stunned.

'The Reichsprotektor of Bohemia and Moravia was lying on a ward not far from where I hid in plain sight and Otto was on the team of doctors caring for him. They'd sealed off the hospital just about and no one could get into or off that ward of Heydrich's unless they had full German clearance. It was a moment of high panic for us. The threat of discovery felt horribly real – imminent, in fact; they kept doing spot searches and each evening they'd sweep through the wards, the offices, checking IDs, et cetera. I had brilliantly forged paperwork but it took every ounce of courage to remain calm and friendly each time they asked to see it.'

The coffee bubbled on the stove. He removed it to pour two cups. He handed her a small black shot in a short cup and couldn't know how impressed she was. 'I can't even imagine how terrifying that must have been,' he said.

'Otto knew Heydrich was dying. His wound drainage was copious from damage to his spleen. They did everything of course to save him but Otto didn't trust everyone else's optimism.

You have to understand we were both living on a cliff edge of daily panic.'

Edward nodded as he stared at his coffee. His face didn't suit such a grave countenance, she decided; his surname alone defied such misery. 'I don't feel like reliving this, Edward, so I'm going to give you the short version.'

'Please,' he said, as if he too were suffering. It didn't even feel odd that he hadn't asked her if she took her coffee with milk; it just felt right that they both drank it short and black.

She sipped. Surprisingly rich and strong. 'We had several burns victims on the ward following an explosion at a munitions factory. There were women too and Otto told me he only expected one to survive and if she did she would be so horribly scarred she would be unrecognisable as human.' She cleared her throat. 'I don't know if he helped that woman to her death and disposed of her corpse in the hospital crematorium, but I became her. My face was covered in bandages and he wheeled me out of that hospital on 26 May 1942, the day after Heydrich's operation to repair a wound to the vertebrae. They removed metal that had shattered his rib, punctured his stomach and lodged in his spleen. It was serious but everyone was cautiously hopeful despite the discovery of horsehair in the wound, which I later learned was from the upholstery of his roadster following the bombing. But Otto wasn't going to wait for a recovery or a death; either way he felt the situation far too dangerous, especially if Heydrich didn't survive, as I imagine every doctor in the hospital would suffer recriminations. Himmler, his boss, as you likely know, was not a reasonable man. So, using every contact he had, Otto got us out with his superbly forged paperwork and I arrived in the next country as a German-speaking Frenchwoman called Severine Kassel.'

'So he smuggled you out of the hospital but under what pretence?'

'Something about removing me to a spa in the mountains where the brisker air would help the wounds "cool".'

Edward scoffed at the thin excuse.

'You have to appreciate, no one cared about the woman with the burns. The hospital was on the highest security alert for whoever might be entering – not exiting it – while Heydrich was in recovery and word had it he was brightening, speaking to his medical team. The mood was buoyant that he'd make a recovery as we made our run for it. You know the rest of his story, but Otto pulled in all of his favours and got Mrs Biskup into Switzerland too. We felt she might be in danger and she couldn't bear not to be with me – I'd become the daughter she didn't have. She wasn't close to her soldier son and he was married to a woman she didn't especially like.

'Anyway, it was touch and go for a long time, as I was at the mercy of strangers who were being paid or owed Otto as opposed to wanting to help us. It was a fraught journey full of tensions and possible discovery at any moment . . . and yet we made it and started life in Lausanne. Switzerland was in an awkward situation, surrounded by fascist nations, pressed upon by the Nazis but determined to resist that ideology even though it supported the notion of conservatism and strong leadership. I leaned on my French language, keen not to be seen as a German. The family who looked after us were bankers, friends of Otto's. They were generous and we remained safe until the war's end; I did part-time work at the bank and at a library. They never knew I was Jewish and I am not sure if that would have made a difference . . . it may have.' She shrugged. 'Otto, of course, couldn't let suspicions be raised about his absence. Once he knew we were safely on our journey, he returned to Prague and his work at the hospital.'

'So he told anyone who asked that the burns woman was now in the mountains?'

'No, that she'd died. And the news was lost amidst all the drama of Heydrich's death and the horrific repercussions for the village of Lidice, where the Gestapo supposedly had intercepted a letter belonging to a local family who had a son in the Czech army in Britain. All adult males were executed as a result, along with more than fifty women, and the rest sent to concentration camps, as I understand. The village was burnt to the ground as a final reprisal. But rumour has it that Hitler wanted thirty thousand Czechs to be slaughtered as a price for Heydrich's assassination, which makes one hundred and seventy-three lives taken sound trivial . . . and yet . . .'

'I know. Don't upset yourself.' He handed her his handkerchief and she sniffed gratefully into it.

'I'm sorry,' she said, muffled into the linen, before squaring her shoulders. 'I learned they sent Jewish slaves from Terezín to dig the graves for the slaughtered. Rudy probably offered them up for the ghoulish work,' she snarled.

'And your friend?'

'Mrs Biskup?' She smiled. 'Lives happily in England now, up north. I visit often – I know the top half of this country, particularly Yorkshire, quite well but not the south. I can walk the moors but I get lost in London.' She gave him a rare soft smile. 'Of course, Mrs Biskup loves Paris and has stayed with me many times, although age is now catching up with her. She hasn't visited for a long time.'

'Katerina, I don't want to trivialise anything of what you've told me, but the main aspect – for the purposes of our conversation – is that you survived.'

'Now you really do sound like a lawyer,' she admitted.

'I find myself trapped in the midst of a curly and, frankly, dangerous matter.' He sighed. 'Dangerous to my firm, is what I mean. On a personal note, I would like to help; of course I would.'

She felt her spirits lift.

'But my hands are bound. If I transgress, I'm opening the firm up to prosecution.' He dragged his misshapen fingers through his hair and it occurred to her that despite his fashionable appearance, he didn't set much store by it and was likely happier out of his sharp tailoring from a Savile Row specialist. Perhaps he far preferred corduroy and gumboots.

'I don't want you to get into any trouble on my account.' She meant it.

'I like to live on the edge, can't you tell?' He smiled and she felt that gesture land on her and go deeper, searching for a response that was more than a surface one. She wasn't imagining the strengthening bond between them; he was feeling it too. She was unprepared to be experiencing the sensation of attraction but helpless within it.

'I can see from your sartorial taste that you don't mind taking risks.'

Now he laughed. 'Miss Bailey didn't approve of my red pin-stripe either.'

'Oh, I approve. Very much so. I like a man who dresses to please himself.'

'Do you?'

She lifted a shoulder. 'You could be boring in a charcoal pin-stripe. But I would say you are right out there at the forefront . . . I have no doubt we'll see you in florals and sweeping lapels by next year.'

'Slow down – let's respect my profession. They'll have me dis-barred if I allow my lapels to get any wider than I've already pushed it,' he admitted, with a sly grin at her sharp observation. 'All right, Mademoiselle Kassowicz,' he began, as though switch-ing back to his formal role, and yet the pressure from his gaze, filled with amusement, suggested he enjoyed the playfulness and would like to extend it. 'While we've been here sipping coffee, I've had a thought.'

She waited.

'Did your father leave a will?'

She blinked; she had not expected this unlikely query. 'What would be the point? The Germans —'

'But did he?' he said, leaning forward and unexpectedly squeezing her hand warmly.

'To my best knowledge, yes. Both my parents made wills together.'

His gaze widened and he let go – she missed the touch immediately. 'Tell me more.'

She explained all that she had told Daniel just days earlier about her closeness to her father and how he had begun to use her as a sounding board and indeed a vault for his thoughts and actions. 'When he and my mother made what he said were their final wills in 1939, he gave them to his closest friend in the world, a man called Levi Körbel, who handled all of my father's business affairs of a legal nature.' She shrugged. 'No doubt my mother was still capable then. Father instructed Levi to make copies and send them to one of his international affiliates – I remember that now! I've only in this moment recalled my father impressing that I now shared the knowledge that their final wills existed.'

Edward gazed at her and she could see she was saying all the right words because his expression seemed to brighten immeasurably. 'What is the name of the legal firm – I'm presuming your Mr Körbel worked out of Prague?'

'Er, yes, I've been to his offices but I think he and his family were taken to Terezín too, so I doubt . . .' She shook her head, not wanting to say it.

'I understand. Do you recall the name of his legal practice?'

'Körbel and Associates. What are you thinking?'

He gave a shrug. 'It's slim. Leave it with me for now. It breaks no rules in terms of my client confidentiality or . . .' He nodded to himself. 'Oh, are you all right?'

She lifted a hand, embarrassed. 'This is the first time since the shock of seeing the Pearls again that it feels as though I can take some heart . . . I've felt lost, entirely out of control, and that's not my preferred state of mind.'

'No, I can gather that. I can't imagine you ever going . . . well, wild,' he admitted, but it was said with such tenderness she couldn't take offence.

'I wish I could, believe me. I'd love to have just a single day of feeling entirely free: no concerns, a sense of abandon . . . a day of . . .'

'Debauchery?' he offered, sounding helpful, and won her unexpected gust of amusement.

'You are a surprise, Edward.'

'Good. Why?'

'Because you're kinder than I hoped, more amusing than I thought you capable, and definitely someone I can say I'm glad to know.'

He sat back and considered her words as if testing them in his mind. 'Do you know, I think that's one of the nicest compliments that has ever come my way. Thank you. I'm glad I haven't disappointed, although I continue to stress that I must tiptoe through this minefield. I can't be seen to be assisting your case and I must remain within the confines of my legal responsibility to my client.'

'You can't tell me where the law firm you're representing is based in Europe, can you?'

'No, I'm afraid I can't,' he said, standing, and she looked away with disappointment. Summerbee removed his jacket from around the parlour chair. 'Of course,' he continued, not looking at her but in a tone that had a sighing quality. 'What the unwittingly loose-lipped museum staff might accidentally spill is not something I can control,' he said.

Their gazes met and she twitched him a smile.

22

● ● ●

As he had helped to slip the coat from Katerina's shoulders earlier, Edward had felt dangerous stirrings of affection for a stranger he knew better than to be fraternising with. This meeting contravened his code and yet how could he not be moved by her story? The personal test of not opening her letter had made him feel like a dog left alone in a room with a freshly roasted chicken and being asked not to touch it. It was why he'd called Alice and hastily arranged an evening out.

It couldn't have been easy for the proud, contained woman he'd met in his office that morning to lower herself to stalking him to the Café Royal tonight. He found himself respecting her determination, despite wanting to be angrier with her for forcing him to blow off his date for the evening. Offending Alice was the least of his problems; she was pleasant enough company and they both enjoyed each other infrequently. Nevertheless, he had begun to feel uneasy that she wanted so much more from him. Her patience troubled him; he presumed she was waiting for him to offer something he had no intention of giving. Most women he met fell into the Alice category.

Severine Kassel – or was it Katerina Kassowicz? – was a rare creature; he'd felt an immediate electricity between them and yet she had an aloofness that made her more attractive than simply the package she came in. This was a woman who, in any other circumstances he would helplessly chase. Professional constraints required him to run in the other direction so he'd carried the letter with him that evening, fully intending to dispose of it at home in the fireplace – he wanted no trace of it in the office. That's what he had told himself. He refused to admit he'd kept it close because he couldn't fully let it or her go yet.

And now reading her tale had sickened him. All of his training and experience as a solicitor had taught him to be measured in his approach. Everyone has a story, everyone can skew an argument their way . . . that's what his favourite tutor had reinforced. *And from their perspective, right is always on their side.*

Nevertheless, he had toppled into her shocking tale and burned with hidden fury on her behalf. It was rare for him to feel the arrival of rage. So now he had to know more. If it was true that he *was* now indirectly working on behalf of a Nazi collaborator, then he wanted no professional part in these dealings.

It would be hard to deny the beauty of Katerina Kassowicz; it struck him that she wouldn't be able to hide her natural presence wherever she went. It was like going to Brighton Beach and amongst all the unremarkable pebbles finding one dazzling seashell of mother of pearl. The thought reminded him of what had brought them together. Pearls that had once belonged to a sultan and been worn by his naked bride. What could he say? He wanted to get to the bottom of the enigmatic piece and help the authorities catch a murderer if it turned out that the man she called Ruda Mayek was the same person behind the offering of the Pearls to the British Museum.

More worryingly was that what he had thought were the

strong walls of his life were now feeling suddenly vulnerable. Just the length of her slim neck, which he'd gazed upon as she'd dropped her coat, weakened him, and any remaining resolve he might have possessed had been washed aside by her hard-won laugh, which caught his attention more than her sorrows. It felt like a prize to be earned.

'Why aren't you married?' she suddenly asked over her shoulder as he followed her back into the reception hall of his home.

It felt like the 64-thousand-dollar question. 'I love women,' he began. 'The problem, however, is they love me back.' He said it with such a sense of dismay that Katerina's body shook with amusement. 'It's not funny. It's just a bit scary: they latch on or they make me feel so guilty I want to hide myself in the bathroom and never come out. Their phone calls make me tremble because they're persistent and some will sort of stalk me . . . turning up at places they know I frequent.' He cleared his throat but she didn't take offence at his remark; no doubt she understood that they weren't directed at her on this occasion.

'Edward, there are lots of lonely women. It's cruel to charm them and then expect them to feel content at being shut out.'

'I don't understand why we can't solve each other's loneliness . . . just for a single night.'

She dissolved into a low laugh, unable to protect his feelings. 'That's because you're a horrid man, incapable of understanding how the minds and emotions of the majority of women work.'

He nodded. 'This is true. I don't understand women. Being upfront with them, telling the truth, ends up hurting their feelings, while if you fib, gild the truth to protect those feelings, you're accused of being a vicious fraud.' He paused. 'I'm going to admit something to you now that I haven't admitted to anyone before.'

Katerina waited, amused, for his next admission.

'It's caddish, but it's far easier to have a brief fling with a married woman, especially if you can ascertain that she just wants some affection she can't get at home, while having no intention of disrupting her otherwise happy home life.'

'That's very convenient.'

'It can be,' he said, nodding with a grave expression. 'I will not risk my heart again.'

'Again? What happened?'

He tutted, as if annoyed at having to recall it. 'It was broken once and I can't face the repair again. Rejection hurts for so long, I swear it can change one's personality.'

He gestured across the hall but she didn't move.

'Who rejected you?'

'That's rather curious of you,' he admonished.

'Well, I'm hardly going to know her, and it's your past, I'm presuming, so it's academic, surely?'

Her logic was hard to argue with.

'She was the only woman I've ever said the words "I love you" to. I met her in my first year of university and I never wanted to be with anyone but her. I was so in love I was pathetic and that was likely the problem; I wanted to give her the world. I said yes to everything. I was like marshmallow and probably enormously irritating to be around by the end of it.'

She turned and frowned in sympathy.

'She married my brother.'

Katerina opened her mouth in surprise.

'That was nineteen years ago. They have a beautiful family and they are very close and wonderful together, but I have found it extremely difficult to be around Sarah without feeling pitiful.'

'Nineteen years on?' She looked at him, incredulous.

He shrugged. 'I'm sincere, what can I say?' He stood to change the subject and the atmosphere. 'Shall we go to my study . . . I think clearer there?'

They were followed by two dogs now whose nails gave an account of their passage across the parquet floors. He opened the door and let her step through first.

'My goodness, this is unexpected,' she said, looking around with an expression of wonder.

'What did you anticipate?' he asked.

'I expected Edwardian . . . at the very least, Art Deco furnishings, but not this clean, sparse design.'

'Well, before you panic, the rest of the house is still very much a mishmash of late Victorian confusing into Edwardian, like the parlour.' He sighed. 'I got the London house, my brother got the farm and its properties. Our parents were traditional, as you might have guessed and I haven't yet had the heart to take a big stick to this place that holds so many fond memories. I'm testing the waters in my study.'

'Well, it's modern and I can't fault your taste.'

'Thank you. Can I offer you a nightcap? Sherry, perhaps?'

'A whisky, please.'

He nodded with obvious pleasure at her choice. 'We'll make that two. Ice? I can fetch —'

She shook her head and took out the comb that had held her hair in a pleat to let the soft waves drop to the sweep of flawless skin below her throat.

He could see the pulse of her heartbeat tap gently where he stared and he wanted to kiss it. 'Er . . . right,' he said, blinking as he turned. Was she doing this to him on purpose? 'Just neat, then. I have a malt so smooth you'd think you were sipping liquid silk.' He didn't dare turn back yet, taking the minute of splashing whisky from his decanter into two squat glasses to compose himself and his ranging thoughts.

'I like this room very much,' her smoky voice continued behind him. 'It's not quite clinical but the lines are sparse . . . beautiful and calm. Is this Hans Wegner, the Danish designer?'

He was forced to turn and note where the long finger pointed to a matching pair of chairs. Edward nodded, genuinely surprised. 'It is. I bought those wishbone chairs about three years ago. Everyone else was watching the debate between Kennedy and Nixon; meanwhile I was admiring the chairs in which they sat.'

She laughed at his remark and he couldn't help but feel like a child being awarded a gold star. He admonished himself for the notion.

'Wishbones? Is that what they're called?' she said.

He handed her a glass and tried to pretend he didn't feel the skin of her fingertips against his as she took it, looking back at the chairs. 'I made a special trip to Denmark to Carl Hansen and Son to acquire this pair.'

'They're stark. Gorgeous lines.'

'I'm impressed you'd recognise him.'

'I've seen them in galleries from time to time; never knew their name. Tell me why you like them?' She gestured at one. 'May I?'

He nodded and watched her fold her frame neatly into the wishbone chair. Her exquisite lines were a match for Wegner's design.

'Well, firstly, you would know why already, now that you've sat in one.'

'Superb,' she admitted. 'How can timber be this comfortable?'

'It's Danish hardwood and the seat is a hand-woven unbleached paper cord.'

'And secondly?' she enquired, lifting her glass to him.

He clinked his with hers. 'Er, secondly, it's the love of carpentry, I think. Look at the exquisite arc of the chair's top.' He touched the edge, barely inches from touching her. 'It's steam-bent maple and rounded in a way to allow freedom for the person seated.' He sipped his whisky, felt its vapours rise at his throat and fume in his head while the liquor slipped down his gullet, like a warming blanket for the inside. Everything was beginning to warm to a sizzle. This fire was moving beyond simply dangerous to the law firm. It was threatening to thaw his heart.

'Freedom to do what?' she asked, and he saw it: when she looked up there it was . . . invitation. It was tentative, unrehearsed and not even flirtatious – but it was there.

With the sound of Miss Bailey screaming *NO!* in his normally sensible mind, Edward Summerbee shocked himself by following his threatened heart instead. 'To do this,' he replied, cupping her oval face with his free hand, turning her towards him. Without further hesitation he bent to kiss her, helplessly closing his eyes when his softened lips met hers. He'd been watching them move most of this evening, longing to know them. He tasted the honeyed flavour of the malt she'd sipped and much as he wanted to, he didn't remain, pulling away gently to give her a chance to slap him and leave.

He watched in wonder as she refrained, instead touching a hand to her lips as if sealing his kiss with her fingertips. In silence she turned, placed her glass onto the nearby desk and in a fluid movement stood to look eye to eye with him with her imperfect stare.

'I have never been kissed like that before.'

He realised he was holding his breath and was now uncertain of her meaning. 'It wasn't more than a lingering peck,' he declared, needing her to make the next move.

'And still no boy in my youth, no man in my adult life, has ever kissed me romantically. It was fleeting but it was as beautiful as your wishbones,' she admitted, sounding awed.

He knew his expression fell. 'Surely you've kissed . . .'

She shrugged sadly and shook her head.

'Never?' He knew he sounded appalled and should drop it.

'Kisses in greeting, kisses of affection with friends and . . .' She stopped. 'No kisses of romance.'

'We must address this immediately,' he said in his doctor's voice of earlier. 'May I kiss you again?'

'Yes, I think I must insist; we shall make your kiss the benchmark by which all other kisses are judged.'

He half laughed; was she teasing him or being truthful? 'Katerina, is this genuine?'

She understood immediately but took a moment to reply. 'I need your help; we both know that, but what you don't know and should is that I wouldn't set aside my integrity to win it this way. Believe me when I say I would give no man so much as a second glance unless I chose to. If I'm honest, I feel a bit out of control in your company.'

He grinned, their lips so close he could, if he wanted to, trace the outline of hers with the tip of his tongue. 'You have my permission to go wild.'

Her laughter filled the room and also his heart as she tightened her long arms around him and he remembered little of the next few minutes. He kissed Katerina Kassowicz in a way that could only be reminiscent of his first real kiss, with Daisy Langford behind his father's tractor on a chilly Guy Fawkes Night, both of them smelling of the bonfire smoke and sulphur. That kiss had fractured his ability to think straight. He had lost his sense of time and was sure they'd kissed for hours, when it was probably only moments. But that's how it felt now: like he was discovering the joy of kissing for the first time with all its trembling awakening.

And yet it troubled him, as he sank deeper into their embrace and Katerina held him tighter still, that it was a flashing thought of Miss Bailey's dismay at threatening his career, his fine reputation, for a woman. Edward snapped his hungry thoughts back from the bedroom, where this kiss was taking them, and away from toppling in love with the Czech beauty.

He was still holding his whisky glass when he broke the spell and pulled himself away from her. Edward placed the glass down deliberately and his voice was tight with fear as much as loathing for treating her so carelessly. 'Katerina, I don't know what's in my head.' He took a low breath of courage, knowing his rejection was rude and could only give affront, especially after her admission. 'I've already breached professional distance. Forgive me, I . . .'

She stood apart, clearly embarrassed. That expression lasted only a few heartbeats before she gathered herself. 'Please, don't apologise,' she said in a voice like a winter's wind. Katerina held a hand up. Her expression was blanched, tight with controlled emotion. She'd admitted something so personal and this surely felt like he was throwing it back in her face. 'I'm certainly not going to mention it to anyone and I feel sure we can rely on your discretion.'

He could feel her building the fortress around herself. The gaze he now feared, one filled with icy disappointment, perhaps mostly at herself for leaving herself open to this pain, landed on him now and he found it hard to hold the searching look of that cat's eye.

'Apart from me contacting the museum about the party behind the Pearls, is there any other advice you can give me without compromising your position?' Her voice was hard, like a hammer against the nails of her words.

He was still remembering the kiss and was angry with himself for lacking the mettle to resist her, her letter, her powerful story. Edward Summerbee shook his head. 'I want to but I cannot help you . . . not like this and certainly not from this perspective. It's compromising and will only become more awkward.'

He watched her nod with resignation. 'May I use your telephone, please?'

'I can call you a taxi, if that's —'

'It's not. I must make a couple of urgent calls. One will be to Europe. I shall pay you for it.'

'Don't insult me,' he said, deeply cut. 'Here,' he twisted the telephone around on his desk. 'Please feel free to make whatever calls you need. I'll leave you alone. Violet and Pansy would enjoy being fed this evening.' He turned and left the room, burning with his internal shame; the transgression was his, not hers, and he was glad he had managed to keep his tone even.

Edward took his time feeding the two dogs, essentially using it to find his equilibrium once more. They'd gone into the study to hatch a plan; he was the one who had hijacked it. He wanted to repair the damage but didn't know how. It was the noise of her footsteps in the hallway that had him moving swiftly out of the parlour again.

'Let me help with you that,' he said, but she had already fetched her coat, pulling it on quickly. A light waft of her perfume reached towards him to sadden him. He'd lost her.

'I'm fine, thank you.' She opened her handbag and her purse.

'What are you doing?'

She offered three crisp five-pound notes. It was far too much. Their dark shade of blue matched the mood in the hallway and the young Queen of England, unlike previous denominations where she looked ahead, stared directly at him with accusation from Katerina's hand. 'Please,' she insisted.

He refused to move. 'I told you —'

'I am indebted to you. I'll leave the money here,' she said, placing the notes on the sideboard near some wilted flowers that his housekeeper would surely refresh tomorrow. Even they spoke of the atmosphere between them.

'Katerina, could we —'

'No. I'm sorry, but I think I've taken too much already of your time. I was wrong to ambush you this morning and even more ridiculous to hope that I could persuade you to offer some insight into my situation. I've behaved badly and I want to apologise for all transgressions today, particularly . . . well, let's not mention our intimacy. If we could leave it at that, you would save me some heartache.'

She wasn't looking at him. Edward reckoned few people had disappointed her more than he had this evening. He hated himself.

'I don't want your money.'

'Well, I don't want you . . . er, thinking that I came here this evening to . . . to —'

'I don't think that!'

'That's a relief. I can find my own taxi. Thank you.' She walked ahead. Violet whined from the stairs.

Edward glared at his dog and returned an awkward gaze to the woman now reaching for his front door.

'Katerina, where will you go?'

She blazed an angry look towards him. 'That's none of your concern. Goodnight, Mr Summerbee. Our paths will not cross again.' She yanked the door open and left to walk down his path without looking back. He wanted to run after her, apologise, find some common ground for them both to retreat to, but he knew she would punish him.

A taxi, like a treacherous dark beast, moved down his street. He watched her lift a long arm in hope and the taxi driver slowed the vehicle. She got into the back, slanting him one final disappointed gaze before the taxi shifted into a higher gear and took her away into the shadows of Kensington.

Katerina Kassowicz was gone and Edward had never felt more hollow at abiding by the rules of his profession and the oath he'd taken at the bar.

23

Across town in the neighbourhood of Bloomsbury a man waited in the shadow of an unlit doorway, his gaze fixed upon the threshold of a mansion block called Museum Chambers. He glanced from time to time to the flat in the gods where he knew there lived a woman called Katerina Kassowicz, but who went by the name of Severine Kassel. Time was ebbing; he had anticipated she might be home by now. He'd watched her climb into a taxi with the solicitor; he'd not been able to follow quickly enough in the rain and so he'd come to where he knew she must return. He flicked his lighter to briefly glance at his watch, extinguishing the flame a second or so after ignition. It was nearing ten. Couldn't be long now.

Further down the same road, seated in the dark of a London taxi, Daniel observed the man in the doorway he had nicknamed the Watcher. The taxi driver – after a brisk price negotiation – had obliged him by switching off his light and leaving the vehicle to go for a cup of tea and a smoke and to relieve himself. An hour, he'd said. It wouldn't be cheap. It didn't matter. Daniel paid up-front.

This left him alone in the back, entirely hidden in the shadows and able to keep the Watcher in view. He saw the flare of a single flame that was put out almost as soon as it caught and he trapped the image in his mind of a tall man in a long raincoat, wearing an old-fashioned felt trilby that couldn't fully hide his square, flattish face. Daniel was patient but it was another twenty minutes before the figure emerged from the doorway, clearly resigned to the fact that Katerina Kassowicz would not be returning to her flat this night. The man of the Mossad took in every movement of the Watcher as he tucked his scarf tighter, raised an umbrella and ambled towards the taxi in which the spy hid, but Daniel felt confident in the dark, having already taken the precaution of having the street lamp smashed the previous evening by a couple of teenagers. It was worth the pound spent so no light could spill into the spot where the taxi was deliberately parked.

The Watcher had an odd gait. There was an obvious limp and Daniel gathered that pain was involved simply by the cast of the man's features from that snapshot he held in his mind. It was old pain, though, because the Watcher shuffled along in a rhythm that revealed the gait was now habitual: part of him. He passed beneath a street lamp and Daniel got his first clear glimpse of his prey. The height that would have held him beyond six feet had become stooped, and beneath his overcoat that he was buttoning up against the cold he carried a big belly. He adjusted his hat, sweeping back a few wisps of golden hair against an otherwise bald pate. Fluffs of that golden hair sat around his ears, he noted, as the trilby was pulled down firmly now to cover them. As he passed, Daniel turned and saw the taxi driver walking back to the vehicle.

He experienced a moment's sharp alarm when the limping man paused directly alongside the vehicle to light another cigarette. A cough that came immediately on the back of his first draw from it seemed to arrive from the depths of his chest, rattling up to explode wetly; he gave a groan of pain but again it sounded rote, as though he was expecting it.

'You should give up the fags, mate,' the driver said, arriving at the vehicle.

'Is this your taxi?' the Watcher asked. Daniel heard the European inflection even though it was well couched in a British accent.

'It is. Just returning from a break.'

'Can I hire you?' He coughed long and loud again; it was the hack of a bronchitis sufferer and he was observed from the vehicle wiping his mouth with a large handkerchief to clear it from whatever had ridden up on that cough.

Daniel felt a clench of fresh anxiety. Would the taxi driver take the fare? He could be forgiven for agreeing, given that they'd only negotiated for him to sit in the taxi, alone, for one hour. If the driver opened the door now and the light came on, Daniel would have to barrel-roll out of the opposite door and run for it. He'd be seen, of course, but could not risk being identified; he hoped the fake beard would hold up its end of the bargain in the dark. He slowed his breath as he'd been taught, his hand already gripping the door handle, ready for flight.

'I'm sorry, mate,' the taxi driver said. 'My shift's done. I'm turning in for the night. But listen, you keep going, take a left and not far from this corner is a rank. There's two cars there right now.'

'Oh, that's helpful, thank you. Goodnight.'

'Night, mate.'

Daniel made sure the Watcher had turned and begun his distinctive limp down the street. The driver's door opened, the light he'd feared switched itself on and he ducked.

'Yeah, I thought so,' the driver said, his cockney accent sounding suddenly broader. 'Wot you up to then, mate? Watching 'im? I did you a solid just now.'

'You did. Could you turn the light off, please?'

The driver obliged, closing his door and physically switching off the light so they were plunged into darkness.

'I shall double the fee.'

'You'd want to. I don't like peeping Toms.'

Daniel rummaged for his money and peeled off five ten-pound notes. 'That man?' The driver nodded. 'Is a war criminal. And that mansion house he's watching – he's looking for a woman . . . and he means her harm. She's an innocent.'

'Are you a plain-clothed "D"?'

'Sort of.' He nodded, trying to skirt the truth of whether he was a policeman.

'Why didn't you say so? Keep the money.'

'I insist. You could have been earning this past hour . . . and you should know you've helped the woman.'

The driver took the money. 'I'll sleep straighter for knowing that. All right, then, I'll drop you somewhere on my way back to Pimlico. Victoria Station all right for you?'

'Perfect,' Daniel murmured.

A different taxi lurched towards another of London's great railway stations. Inside, its passenger was glad of the cabbie's cheerful conversation or she feared she may just weep. How could she have laid herself so open to hurt again? She wouldn't allow herself to ponder this now – it was too painful. She needed distance and her plans were set; people were already in motion on her behalf.

'You've missed the last train, miss,' the man continued after she'd mentioned she was headed to Yorkshire. Her spirits plunged at this news. 'So I think it will have to be a hotel for tonight.'

She considered heading back to the flat but she wanted to be within walking distance of the first train out in the morning and not to have to negotiate London traffic. The idea of backtracking to Bloomsbury now would feel like she was treading water. And still smarting from rejection, she needed to be in motion with her new plan. Besides, she was in such an unhappy frame of mind, the loneliness that the Bloomsbury flat offered might undo her. No, the dislocation that a hotel room could achieve would help her mood.

'Where's the closest hotel?'

'The Great Northern, of course, but you might prefer a guest house, or . . .'

'No, that will be fine. I have no luggage and I think landladies might frown on a single woman arriving this late at night with no overnight bag.'

He grinned into the rear-view mirror. 'I think you're right, miss. Righto, it's not far now. You know when the Great Northern Railway corporation built King's Cross Station, the Victorians hated it. They were used to lots of ornamentation and the new station back in the late nineteenth century was offensive in its simplicity.'

It was a rare feeling but she welcomed the conversation. 'Northerners are known for being no-nonsense, right?' she said, deliberately encouraging him and drawing on what she'd learned over her years of visiting Yorkshire.

'Exactly! They couldn't care a whit; they wanted straight-forward and functional. It was built by being squeezed beneath Regent's Canal. It was enough of a feat of engineering to achieve that without worrying about making it fancy.'

She smiled in the darkness, pleased by his historical knowledge. Enviously, she watched him take a final drag on his cigarette and flick the fag end out of his side window, blowing the smoke out with it. 'Are you French?'

'I am,' she lied.

'Just visiting?'

'Bit of work, bit of sightseeing.' She distracted him from her story. 'St Pancras must have looked like a palace by comparison when it was built.'

'Oh my word, yes. Caused quite the storm and probably cost ten times as much. They say Euston's Great Hall and portico cost more than the entire build of King's Cross. Cubitt also built the hotel I'm taking you to. It's a little more glamorous but was still simple and stark for its time. Here we go.'

The hotel's curving sweep of tall architecture came into view. 'Oh, I don't know,' she admitted. 'I'd pick this as instantly Victorian with those gabled windows and chimney stacks.'

'I've always liked it.' He winked as he turned to switch off the meter.

She thanked him, paid, told the young man who raced out to open her door that she had nothing to carry in and was through the main doors in moments to register for an overnight.

'No luggage, madam?' the desk clerk enquired.

'None.' She sighed inwardly; best to lie. 'I was supposed to be here just for the day but I became delayed. I'll take the first train to York tomorrow morning.'

'Ah, of course, it is very early too. Sign here, please. I'm not sure we'll be open for breakfast by the time you'd need to leave, madam. I recall the first train is at ten to six, so you'd need to check out by around twenty past five.' She was impressed by his knowledge. 'Can we pack something for you?'

'Thank you, but that won't be necessary. Five-fifty, you say?'

He nodded. 'A strange talent to know the train schedule, I agree.' They shared a smile. 'But so many of our guests are either travelling to or from Yorkshire that it feels necessary to the job to know one's way around the timetable.' He turned away to fetch her room key. 'Is there anything else we can help you with this evening?'

'Nothing, thank you.'

'Room 89. Good evening, madam.'

She knew he didn't entirely trust her tale but she didn't care and frankly it was clear nor did he.

Katerina could still taste the tender kiss against her lips and hoped the novelty of the hotel room would create the distance she now needed. She took a shower after taking care to hang up her dress, which she'd have to wear again for the trip north, and rinsed out her underwear. She was fortunate that she'd left some travelling clothes on her last visit with Mrs Biskup.

Katerina fell into an uneasy, irritated sleep where Edward roamed, muttering about needing to learn how to laugh and whether she would mind if he kissed her again.

She checked the alarm clock at her bedside every hour, it seemed, and finally at nearing 4 a.m. gave up on her slumber and got dressed. She checked out and went in search of a chemist that opened by five for travellers and bought some make-up and toiletries, including a toothbrush that she used in the station bathroom.

She would call Mr Partridge when she got into York in the hope she could ease from him the detail that might give her a different pathway to Ruda Mayek's present whereabouts.

Katerina purchased her ticket for the first train leaving for the northern capital. She made her way to the station tearooms for a cup of coffee she didn't especially feel like, with her mouth still minty from the cheap toothpaste. She had twenty minutes before her train left. She reached for yesterday's newspaper that was strewn on a nearby table; anything to blank her mind and not think of Edward Summerbee.

The man she was trying not to think of could think of little else but Katerina.

Although the bed looked carelessly rumpled, he had barely dozed. From before midnight, Edward had instead sat rugged up in his dressing-gown in an armchair near the window, counting through the hours, some of them with a brandy-laced malted milk, while he stared at the empty street that Katerina had exited from. It was not much past four-thirty when an eager blackbird began his first call out; Edward had noted over the years that the morning after rain prompted the sweetest song of these most favourite of English birds and in a few months this fellow would be singing for a mate.

In the lonely hours of the night he had gone over the previous evening repeatedly. It was the letter – the brutal, factual, unelaborated explanation of her story in all of its tragedy – that had trapped him in the emotion of the Kassowiczs. His normally well-disguised vulnerability had caught him without much warning. His father had been right all those years ago when he'd suggested to Edward that he practise in the area of human rights.

'Your empathy will get you into hot water otherwise,' he'd counselled.

Normally the civil cases he dealt with didn't force him to confront the wetter side of people's lives – mostly he worked within the confines of their business dealings. It had not occurred to him that the dry brief from the overseas law firm to be its conduit to the British Museum would embroil him in potentially criminal scandal by walking his firm backwards into the darkest period of Europe's history. Edward had attempted to imagine but failed to touch what it must have been like to be that child and to undergo such torture. Given the composed woman he knew, it only added a fresh feeling of admiration but it brought with it a new layer of personal torment for him. Herein lay his dilemma. To help Katerina would be to ignore everything demanded by his role as a solicitor working on behalf of a client. To not help her contravened everything his role as a compassionate human being demanded. He'd wrestled with this and after finally stirring from his armchair to Mr Blackbird's singsong, he was no closer to a decision.

What he had come to realise was that at no point during his recriminations did he regret the impulse to kiss her. It was hard to believe that his was her first romantic kiss. Edward stood and stretched, half shaking his head in wonder; he should have worked harder at it! But what kept him unable to sleep was that on the one occasion she'd handed over trust and allowed a man to become intimate, he'd treated her carelessly.

'No,' he said to the wardrobe mirror he found himself standing dishevelled before. 'That's not how it was. It was about being careful, not careless,' he assured his reflection.

Semantics, the inner Edward sneered. *You let her down.*

'I'm not her solicitor,' Edward reminded himself.

Yes, but you regard yourself as a gentleman. You let her down as a man.

'Heaven help me, now I'm arguing with myself,' Edward admonished himself, turning away and heading for the bathroom.

His conscience had the last word: *Otto Schäfer was German and he didn't let the young Jewish girl down.*

'Fuck Otto Schäfer,' he growled through the needles of hot water that washed away the soap and, he hoped, his vacillation. Swearing made him feel better momentarily, yet in the next moment he knew he was lying to himself. Otto Schäfer was Katerina's hero and rightfully so. Edward Summerbee, whom she'd hoped might be her shiny knight, had turned out to be a coward, hiding behind a code of practice instead of favouring one of chivalry.

The thought of cowardice arriving in his mind shocked his angry towelling to stillness; water ran from his head to form bigger droplets and ultimately rivulets that made their path down to his ankles to create soggy patches on the bathmat. Damp and dark of mind, Edward tested the notion and felt he couldn't tolerate living with it.

'Right!'

It was said with finality but it felt like a new beginning.

24

● ● ●

As the woman he couldn't shake from his thoughts was waiting for a train to Yorkshire at King's Cross Station, Edward Summerbee was asking the international operator to put him through to a number in Switzerland. He hadn't fully completed his path of thought last night and they'd become distracted. However, he was now of the belief that if Katerina could establish that the Ottoman Pearls were recorded in her parents' wills, copies of which might still be held by Levi Körbel's affiliate, then a case might be built for proof of ownership. That could be all that would be required to bring criminal charges and hunt the bastard down if he was still alive. It would also release his firm of any further obligation to the negotiation of those wretched Pearls and perhaps allow him to help her more fully. That idea felt heartening.

He couldn't remember feeling this galvanised in years; Katerina Kassowicz brought problems to his life, there was no doubt, but she also brought something fresh and invigorating . . . she brought hope to an otherwise hollow existence that was not unhappy but mostly lonely.

'I have the Geneva number,' came a voice out of the void.

'Thank you, operator,' he replied and waited for the beeps and pops of the operator at her work and heard the phone ring nearly five hundred miles away. It wasn't answered and the operator came back to him.

'Try again, please,' he instructed.

This time the call was answered almost immediately.

'Marco?'

'Yes?' said a familiar but vexed voice.

'It's Edward Summerbee.' He heard the curse in French and laughed. It didn't need translation.

'Edward, it's . . .' He imagined his friend squinting at the clock. 'It's not even six!'

'Sorry, old chap. I've got a question that could save a friend a lot of time and expense if you could answer it. It's a bit urgent, or I wouldn't . . .'

He heard Marco unsuccessfully stifle a yawn. 'All right, I have to be at the office early today anyway. How can I help?'

Edward explained, keeping it short and simple and his tone light so he didn't sound as anxious as he was feeling.

'Körbel and Associates, you say?'

'Yes, contact was lost during the German occupation but my friend is trying to settle an estate, actually, and she believes that company to be holding the most recent documents.'

'Contesting a will?'

'Yes, the usual mess.'

He heard his friend sigh. 'How are you, Edward, anyway?'

'Old . . . cold. Business goes well, though.'

'I'm happy for you. And before you forget to ask, Helena misses you and so do the children. You were meant to visit last year. Come soon.'

'I promise to make amends.'

'Good. Give me until nine-thirty – I'll ring you when I get into the office and have done the digging you need.'

'Thanks, old friend. Talk shortly.' When he replaced the receiver, his heart felt lighter because now at least he'd done something positive behind the scenes for Katerina. If it turned out that the interests of Körbel & Associates were still with its affiliates in Europe, then he would hand over the information to Katerina or her representative and it would be up to her and her supporters to take the next logical step. He could do no more.

Or could he? He stood. There was one more thought that had snagged in his mind last evening when she'd spoken. The mention of the *Kindertransports* had taken purchase and only because he'd met the stockbroker and humanitarian Nicholas Winton, who had saved so many young lives through his efforts. Winton had visited Edward's university just as his final exams were completed. He was one of the lucky ones to get his finals finished while he was juggling his military cadet training. He hadn't been old enough to vote but he'd leapt at the chance of joining the RAF for fear of being considered 'essential services' because of his family's extensive farming expertise. The fear was unfounded; his brother had been called up and joined the army, distinguishing himself, while his father had been drafted into the Home Guard. Edward had been keen to train as a pilot but whomever the decision-makers were, his seniors had seen fit to preserve him as ground crew. It was during this time he'd offered his services, as immature as they were, to the evacuation of children, whether it was out of London to the safer countryside, or from places like Czechoslovakia into Britain. While he did not have a hand in the *Kindertransport* effort, he'd been on the rim of it, aware of those making the rescue trains happen, and after meeting Winton, he'd offered to help with any legal paperwork.

Edward set off for his office while it was still dark, well aware of Violet and Pansy's disapproval of the early start, but barely noticing the morning's chill as he walked briskly to Lincoln's Inn. By the time he arrived his thoughts were burning with the idea that just maybe he could leverage some of those old rescue train contacts and, if nothing else, he might be able to put Katerina in touch with other Jewish people her own age who had survived the occupation of Czechoslovakia. It was a small gesture but it was something to ease his consternation at not being able to give her what she really wanted.

'Good grief, Mr Summerbee. I didn't expect you yet,' his secretary remarked as she blew the fresh steam off her cuppa.

'I could say the same to you, Miss Bailey.'

'No, sir, I'm always here before eight,' she said.

He cleared his throat at the error. Obviously he was the one who was uncharacteristically early. She was really quite pretty, in a schoolmarmish way. 'Couldn't sleep,' he admitted.

'Tea's still hot in the pot. Can I fetch you a cup?'

'You can, thank you. Oh, by the way, I'm expecting an urgent call from Geneva. Interrupt me if you must. It's important I speak with the caller.'

'Very good. You go in, sir. Fire's on.'

He shook his head as he entered the warm cocoon of his quiet offices, which overlooked the main square of Lincoln's Inn. Life had been neat and ordered and really quite pleasant. Now Katerina Kassowicz had arrived into his orbit to stir it up. *Damn her*, he thought, not meaning it for a second.

He shed his coat and took a few moments to warm himself in front of the fire. Miss Bailey knocked and didn't wait for his answer before pushing through with his steaming cup. 'Here we are, sir. Is there anything else?'

'Not right now, thank you. I've got some files to read, so if you could keep the wolves at bay, I'd appreciate it.'

'No one's getting past me, Mr Summerbee,' she assured him,

and he believed her. 'I'll buzz through that Swiss call as soon as he rings.'

She left behind a trail of rose and other exotic notes that he didn't particularly like. He'd smelled it rising off the cardigans of other female staff and in the streets when people oozed out of the tube stations. It was obviously popular. He blinked as he sipped, trying to capture the name. Ah, that's it . . .

'Chantilly,' he murmured, unimpressed. He'd seen it on the counters in department stores. It made him think of how Katerina smelled. He didn't know the perfume she wore. There was something dark and peppery about the fragrance that lifted from her skin and as they had talked and she waved those long hands around to accentuate her explanations, the pepper sweetened to spicy petals as though he were walking across a mossy pathway littered with geraniums as brightly scarlet as that dress she wore.

He put the cup down noisily to clear his mind of her image; this really would not do. Edward flicked through his address book; he could ask Miss Bailey but her inquisitive nature would prod around and work out why he was making the call. Then her disapproval would arise because it was connected to 'the French woman'. No, better he did his own sleuthing. He found the number he needed and placed the call, going through the process of small talk before he arrived at his topic.

'Oh, well, you're testing me now. We've only got the original old files in archives.'

'Perhaps a couple of names from 1941 of Prague-based children who may have been around the same age as my friend – perhaps thirteen to fifteen – when they left. This woman is all alone with her traumas and I think to speak her own language with people of a similar age could be helpful.'

He heard the sigh at the other end. 'I'll see what I can dig up, Edward, but it may take a while.'

'That's fine, no hurry; it's just a kindness. So you've retired now, Jim?'

'Yes, about five years ago. Oh, I see, is that your way of reminding me I don't have anything else pressing?'

Edward hadn't meant it that way, but it made him laugh. 'No, nor would I suggest it,' he said, feigning soft indignance. 'I hope you're enjoying life?'

'Not in winter but I love the garden in the summer and Shirley and I have a time share now in Cornwall, so we like to get down there as often as we can.'

'Good for you.'

'What did you say this woman's name is?'

'Kassowicz.' He spelled it.

'Well, I used to know those files intimately and I can tell you there are no children of that name that I recall.'

'I didn't expect there to be. She can account for her four siblings,' he said. 'None of them survived.'

'That's . . .' Jim struggled to think of a word that conveyed how he was feeling. 'Just terrible.'

'Hence my hope that we can link her up with some survivors.'

'For sure . . . I will look, but I'm just thinking that the person you should talk to is Lilian Jeffers.'

Edward frowned. 'Why's that?'

'Well, she was on those transports with the children. She was on the ground in Prague and her famously brilliant memory when I last met her – not even two years ago – was still as keen as ever. She knew those files better than all of us. But the reason I mention her is that she might be able to think of someone who would fit together with your friend. I can only give you names but as these children were mid-teens, I think she'd be better placed to be helping with such an emotional connection. Lilian can probably give a better fit, if you catch my drift.'

'I do. Jim, that's a good idea, thank you.'

'I'll have to find her number. I'll call you back – same place?'

'Yes.'

Two returned calls later Edward sipped his cooled tea and felt the best he'd felt all morning. He had made surprising progress. Marco assured him he would be calling back with proper news shortly but he had put enquiries into motion, plus Edward was now staring at the residential number of Lilian Jeffers. Two leads that made the fitful night and no sleep worthwhile.

Katerina had watched the city skyline edge away into countryside as she drifted into sleep. She'd bought a first-class ticket to avoid the general noise of people and she shared her carriage with a single gentleman who had been lost in his morning newspaper moments after taking off his overcoat, bowler, scarf and gloves.

'Good morning' were his only words and she matched them with an identical pair.

Beyond that she hadn't turned his way but had stared out at London's sky while it dissolved into daybreak and then sleep had found her. She woke at the screech of wheels and the harsh sound of a whistle pierced a dream she couldn't touch again now that she was stirring and instead she saw only Edward Summerbee's generous mouth shaping to whistle for a taxi.

She blinked into full consciousness. 'York . . . already?' she said, her voice raspy.

'I'm afraid so. You were sleeping so soundly it felt almost cruel to wake you, my dear,' her train companion admitted. 'I knew the train guards would do it for me with all their noise.'

She returned the kind smile and gathered up her belongings, pulling on her coat quickly. 'I would offer to help you down with your luggage but I see you have none. Good day to you.'

'Good day,' she echoed and followed him out of the carriage a minute later.

Milena Biskup was away in Durham; convenient, actually, as Katerina hadn't wanted to work through a detailed explanation for the surprise trip north beyond the excuse she'd given over the phone that she had to see a special piece for the museum. She had a key to the house and it wasn't much more than a five-minute taxi ride to the little home she'd helped set up for the woman she'd always viewed as her step-in mother. She spent the day quietly preparing, not just putting together her plan but mostly in preparation for the next day – for the confrontation she was torn between dread and excitement about. Katerina had insisted that a telephone be installed in Mrs Biskup's house, and was grateful for that now as it saved her a walk to the garage.

'The car we have for hire is a Morris Minor, miss.'

'That's fine. Is it available tomorrow?'

'It is.'

'Excellent. May I pick it up at ten?'

'Yes. We'll have her ready for you. Are you touring, miss? It's just, those roads through the moors can be quite narrow and twisty.'

'I'm headed towards Whitby,' she said, deliberately vague. 'Not sightseeing. I'm working, so I won't be going down any minor roads,' she lied.

'I can give you a map if you need the most direct route.'

'I know I sound foreign, Mr Williams, but I lived up here for several years. I know my way around these parts.' She made sure it came across as cheerful and not prickly.

'Oh, that's good, then. Sorry, I just wanted to be sure. Some tourists underestimate the geography.'

'Thank you. I shall be fine. And the weather looks clear for the next day or two. I'm in luck, I think.'

'Yes, no rain forecast. Not that it means there won't be any.' He chuckled.

She gave a soft laugh for his benefit. 'I'll see you tomorrow, Mr Williams.'

All she needed now was to dig out some appropriate clothes, and she supposed she had better think about food. She could see some pea soup was left over in the fridge but after last night she was sure her mood would turn it sour in her mouth. No. There was bread, some eggs, a slice or two of bacon. That would do. And there were coffee beans. She lifted the tin's lid to inhale their toasted, sweet aroma and smiled; she could always count on Milena Biskup to have good coffee ready to grind.

The ritual to brew her coffee began. It would soothe her for what she faced. She was in no hurry. The person she was to meet had a long journey to make.

───────────

Edward was finding it hard to concentrate. He had no briefs for today and no appearances in court. Perhaps he could take some files and work more productively at home. The low headache he'd developed might have been the lack of breakfast but he suspected it was more likely that an unfamiliar anxiety had descended. It took Miss Bailey by surprise but he didn't give her much of a chance to protest during his rapid instructions. He was in a taxi back to Lancaster Gate within fifteen minutes of making his snap decision.

He was just sighing into the chair behind his home desk when the phone rang.

'Hello again,' Edward said, snatching up the receiver.

'Right,' Marco said with no introduction. He'd obviously been redirected by Miss Bailey to Edward's home number. 'It seems this Körbel and Associates has been swallowed up by a bigger firm – a Swiss-French law firm. I called one of the partners and promised him a bottle of malt whisky from your cellar, Edward, for calling so early.'

'You Swiss rise rather late.'

'It's not the rising, my friend. Some of us have families and lives to attend to.' Edward heard him sip something and sigh. 'Anyway, Pierre says there are archives and he'll have his team look into it straight away for you. I'll need a name.'

'Thank you. Tell him he's hunting the last wills and testaments of Samuel and Olga Kassowicz.' He spelled the names for Marco. 'He was a reputable glass manufacturer in Prague. Died October 1941, but I gather their final wills were written in 1939.'

'All right. We should have an answer later today.'

'That's excellent. Thanks, old chap. I'll have a bottle sent over for him. And one for you.'

Marco chuckled from afar. 'You're welcome, Ed. I meant what I said. Come visit.'

Edward replaced the receiver, scribbled a note to himself not to forget to organise the liquor for Switzerland and decided he should call Lilian Jeffers while his mind was preoccupied with all things Kassowicz. He dug out the number he'd carefully placed in his wallet and waited while the connection was made. He let it ring for a long time, imagining that the woman would now have to be in her seventies. It was finally answered. She sounded out of breath.

He introduced himself. 'Are you all right, Mrs Jeffers?'

'Yes, yes. I ran in from the garden, actually. I thought my husband was indoors but I think I can hear him clumping around in the attic.'

'Ah. I'm sorry to have made you hurry. I wonder, could you give me a moment or two of your time, please?'

'A London solicitor, you said? I can't imagine how I can help but yes, you've got me indoors now, the rest of the leaves on the lawn can wait for my husband to rake them up.'

He chuckled. 'Thank you. I'm actually looking for some advice connected with the *Kindertransports* of 1939.'

'Good grief. How on earth have you tracked me down?'

'It was Jim Leyton, actually. Do you recall him?'

'Yes, of course. It's been a while and we never actually worked together.'

'Well, it seems your reputation lives large in his mind.'

She laughed, and he could hear her breath coming more easily. She sighed. 'Here, let me sit. All right, now. How might I help?'

'It's an odd request, I realise, but I've come into contact with a lovely woman originally from Prague who miraculously survived the occupation, the round-ups, the camps. I gather she was on the receiving end of generous help from some good people – a German included – who got her out of Czechoslovakia when she was in her mid-teens. Unfortunately, the rest of her family – three sisters and both parents – were not as lucky. They all perished. Her infant brother died of a fever coincidentally around the time of the last rescue trains.'

He listened to her pained silence. Finally, she sighed. 'Her family's plight is not unusual, but her story of survival is.'

'It's a wonder, for sure. Her father was desperate to get his children, especially the son, out. But Katerina said her mother refused for any of the children to be separated and then the boy passed away and it all went badly from there on.'

'Pity.'

'Indeed. Anyway, the reason I contacted Jim and he put me on to you was the slim hope that you might have some recollection of children around Katerina's age who might have been sent to families in and around London.'

'Oh, I see.'

'Well, she's incredibly alone in her pain still, and I was thinking that perhaps if she could be put into contact with other Prague Jew

survivors of a similar age that she might just form some helpful
friendships.'

'She's a client?'

'No. But I met her recently through working for one of my
clients and her plight just struck a chord. Don't get me wrong,
Katerina is neither helpless nor self-pitying. Frankly, I think she
would be irritated to know I was meddling, but I also don't think
she would resist being able to talk to some folks – even one person –
who know her city of birth, remember the times that she recalls . . .
I just think it could help. It's up to her, of course.'

'Well, let me think now. So she's in her mid-thirties by now?'

'That's right. She's actually based in Paris but she works in
London from time to time.'

'She sounds accomplished.'

'She is.' Edward noticed he'd been doodling Katerina's name
repeatedly on his pad and blinked in annoyance with himself. 'She's
a curator of antiquities – she has a specialisation in jewellery but
she's been seconded to the British Museum recently to help
with some of their items. You know, checking the authenticity with
regards to stolen Jewish jewellery and reliquaries.'

'I still have my old files in the attic. I'm happy to dig them out
and see if anyone might suit. Did you particularly want names
of women?'

'Not necessarily. I think anyone in their thirties would be great;
it's just they would have grown up in a similar timeframe so the
memories would dovetail. Talking over even simple things like their
favourite haunts of times past might bring some cheer.'

'Oh, I couldn't agree more. I do recall a sister and brother who
might have been around the early to mid-teens when they left
Prague, but I just can't remember where they were sent. I have a
feeling it was to Sussex, but let me check. I think they might suit
your Katerina very well as they were both from a well-known

family from the city. I think their father was a manufacturer of sorts – can't remember what he produced.'

'Mmm, sounds promising. Katerina's father was a reputable manufacturer too – glass, I'm told – quite senior in the Jewish community and well known too as a businessman.'

'Well, glass from Bohemia is the best, isn't it?' she remarked.

'I think the Irish may disagree with you there, Mrs Jeffers.'

She giggled. 'Maybe not. You know it was a Czech immigrant who effectively got the Waterford glassworks operational again, using crystal specialists from Europe.'

'I didn't know that!'

'I collect glass, so I know a little about its history.'

'Good for you. Well, I think Mademoiselle Kassowicz will be happy to know —'

'Kassowicz?' She paused, as if pondering the name. 'As in Samuel Kassowicz?'

He sat forward in his chair, knocking his knee on the leg of his desk. He felt stunned at her mention of Katerina's father and he barely noticed the grimace of pain. 'Er . . . yes, indeed, that's her father's name.'

'Oh, good heavens! *His* daughter?'

Edward frowned; he couldn't make the leap she needed. 'What am I missing, Mrs Jeffers?'

'Nothing. It's just that I met him.'

'Really?'

'Several times, actually. He was one of the familiar faces at the railway station during those traumatic days; he came to see each of our trains off and I saw him comfort many a weeping Jewish family as they handed over their most precious people.'

'I can't imagine that sort of despair.'

'No, you can't. The heartbreak was devastating for everyone. Even for us, knowing we were keeping their children safe from potential harm, it was hard to wrangle our emotions. We had to look grave – I'm sure they were angered by our blank expressions, seemingly lacking in sympathy, but it was the only way to cope with the feelings of physically separating mothers from babies, fathers from daughters, only sons from families. I have to say I think Mr Kassowicz was the most composed of all the fathers when we took his son.'

Edward had been nodding, already beginning to tune out from the conversation, which he thought had been winding down to a polite close of small talk, but his gaze snapped open again. The headache that he'd thought had been receding splintered back into sharp focus. He swallowed. 'Just a minute, Mrs Jeffers. No son of Samuel Kassowicz boarded one of the *Kindertransports*. Katerina said her infant brother died.'

'Then this was probably another brother.'

'One she'd forgotten?' He hadn't meant to be sarcastic. 'I'm sorry, I didn't mean that to sound like an accusation. I was thinking aloud at how preposterous it would be that she'd overlook this. No, I'm certain, Mrs Jeffers. She is still incredibly attached to the family she lost and only speaks of three sisters younger than her and a single brother, still an infant when she was a teenager.'

'How odd. Well, I must assure you that I certainly took a child out of Samuel Kassowicz's arms. A little boy. I can still see his face as plainly as I can see the leaves on my lawn, Mr Summerbee.'

Edward felt the headache fizz into a full throb. 'Forgive me for how this sounds, but could you be mistaken? I mean, could Kassowicz have been helping another family with their child's handover?'

'I'm not mistaken – this particular child listing remains vivid in my memory because the Kassowicz boy was a replacement for another boy whose mother simply refused to part with him at the moment of handover. It was all very last minute and highly dramatic, to tell the truth. I felt extremely uncomfortable about it at the time because the replacement boy's mother was not present, and while Samuel Kassowicz said she'd understand, I never believed she would.'

'Bloody hell! Oh, forgive me.'

'No, that's all right.' She told him everything else she recalled. 'You see, there was no time to produce fresh paperwork. The Germans were sticklers and we needed nothing to hold up that rescue train.'

'So his was a spur-of-the-moment decision, you're saying.'

'As I recall, yes. It was a damned-either-way moment, to tell the truth. There was a panic – lots of families suddenly offering up their children – and my colleague was desperately trying to explain that it had to be specifically an infant boy under two who could travel on the other child's papers. If we deviated, that's all the excuse the Germans would have needed to disrupt our train – we might never have got those carriages away if we'd presented a three-year-old girl, or even a boy who didn't fit the profile of those papers. There were even photos, and luckily all babies rugged up tend to look the same so it was my colleague who suggested to Mr Kassowicz that we take his son.'

'Mrs Jeffers, this revelation has enormous consequences. Katerina, to my knowledge, has no idea that this occurred. And either there is a secret brother that she never knew about, or . . .' He could not bear to say it.

Mrs Jeffers did. 'Or the parents lied to their daughters about their brother, letting them believe he died.'

'Appalling either way, although we can't walk in their shoes. There would have been a good reason in their minds, presumably.'

'No doubt.' She paused. 'Hmm. Let me just think.' Edward waited, unsure of where Mrs Jeffers's mind was tracking, but he was still shocked enough at the discovery to value the quiet moments. 'I'm trying to recall the name of the child that her brother travelled under. It's . . . eluding me. All right, can you sit tight, Mr Summerbee?'

'Yes, of course.'

'I want to catch Bob before he clambers down from the attic.'

He smiled. 'Let's not waste time exchanging my number. I'll call you back this evening, around eight. Is that sufficient time?'

'Perfect. Talk soon.'

Edward put the receiver down, filled with a double rush of dismay and excitement, like parallel rivers coursing around him. He'd need irrefutable proof, of course, but it was surely thrilling that he might shortly have the pleasure of delivering the most joyous of news to Katerina that not all of her family had perished during the war. Of course, then there was the revelation that her parents had lied about her baby brother. They might never learn the motivations for the lie but he would ensure she remained focused on the momentousness of being reunited with Petr.

He tapped upright fists on his desk in a brief show of triumph. He could demonstrate to her that even with his hands tied legally regarding the Pearls, he didn't lack empathy and was prepared to help her in other ways; the notion made him feel jittery with anticipation. Her final scathing look at him had lost none of its intensity overnight and he needed to see her smile again – just for him. And out of this sleuthing he would seek her forgiveness, but also be able to deliver her a victory from the tragic mess of her early life. Edward knew he mustn't get too far ahead of himself; Petr was yet to be found and there was the question of how, if he could be easily located, he would feel about discovering an adult sister and learning that everyone else in his family was dead. It would be horribly disruptive for a person who had presumably grown up in ignorance, given he'd been an infant when he was handed over to foster parents . . .

It all felt suddenly big and overwrought. Edward wasn't used to cases that involved so much emotion. He deliberately forced himself to get lost in other work, refusing himself a break for lunch. Instead he remained productive at his desk, switching on his lamp by three, and by four realising that the housekeeper was calling her farewell with reminders that the range was on and his dinner was in the oven. He heard the front door close and her footsteps receding. As shadows stole across his room, the radiators began to fill the house with a reliable warmth, and once again he was reminded that central heating was the new catchphrase . . . another project for another year. He closed the files on his desk, glad he'd cut through a lot of the legwork on the Thornton-Dray case; he could brief the QC with confidence now and was certain the judge would find in favour of his client. Edward stood and took a long stretch to straighten his spine, realising he was parched; he'd ignored the pot of tea his housekeeper had tiptoed in with earlier in the day, and his belly was rumbling.

He would change first. Edward let the dogs out for a sniff around the garden and took the time to nip upstairs and swap his day clothes for comfy pyjamas. At the bite of a cool night that rode in on the draught as he let the grateful dogs back inside, he was glad that the housekeeper had taken Violet and Pansy to the park earlier in the day.

He moved into the parlour, recalling with a prick of regret the pleasure of having Katerina Kassowicz share a bowl of soup with him here only yesterday.

'I wish I could change how it ended,' he said to Pansy, who paid serious attention to his words. 'I wish I could kiss her again, actually, and assure her that I could make everything all right.' Pansy frowned deeper, then stood and wagged her tail.

As he tipped his head back to give a long, satisfied yawn, he heard a soft tap at the window. In astonishment at seeing a face pressed against the glass, he recognised Daniel Horowitz. He frowned as Katerina's friend put a finger to his lips and thumbed towards the door.

Feeling a tug of vexation in his mind, Edward wondered what drama was about to unfold for him now.

25

Edward opened the back door to Horowitz, who wasted no time with pleasantries.

'We must speak.'

'My office is —'

'Now!' Horowitz urged, his voice low. Edward frowned as the man glanced through the door and upstairs. 'Is she upstairs?'

The frown deepened as Edward tried not to show his hackles were up. 'My dog? Yes, this is Pansy, but Violet is usually still fast asleep at this time,' he offered innocently. 'Is Mossad spying on the three of us?'

'Mr Summerbee, her life depends on my spying on you and I'm not talking about your dog.'

'What the hell?'

'Sssh. Don't let her know. Pretend you're organising the rubbish bins.'

Edward shook his head in mock despair. 'I'm lost. I have no idea what you're talking about, Horowitz.' He laughed aloud when the intruder deliberately clattered the lid of the bin. 'Oh, that's convincing, well done,' Edward said. 'I was told you'd left for Paris?'

'I want her to think I'm there.'

Edward shook his head in exasperation. 'I'm putting the kettle on. You'd better come in.'

'No. I'll tell you from here.'

He sighed at the cold that was already roaming around the room. 'You do know the war ended nearly twenty years ago, Mr Horowitz.'

'Only for some of us, Mr Summerbee.'

Edward gave Horowitz a baleful look as he turned on the faucet to fill the kettle. 'All right, I'll bite, but come inside or stand outside and speak through the window. I am not giving all my paid warmth to a cold spring night.'

His guest reluctantly stepped across the threshold and was immediately advanced upon by Pansy, who sniffed his shoes.

'Right, tell me,' Edward said.

'Is there any danger of Katerina walking in on us?'

'No chance at all.'

'Are you sleeping with her?'

'Heavens, man! What business is it of yours?' Edward slammed the kettle onto the gas stove and struck a match to ignite the flame. The smell of sulphur from the match and then the fuggy odour of gas both dissipated quickly in the frigid air. 'Close that door.'

Horowitz obeyed. 'Answer me.'

Edward regarded his visitor as a tired father, home from a long day's work, might regard the naughty child that the mother had warned *Just wait until your father gets home*. He did not want to be having this hostile conversation, especially now that he could see, as hard as Horowitz tried to act nonchalant, that he was as captivated by Katerina as he was.

'No! I am not sleeping with Miss Kassowicz but if I were, I wouldn't feel obliged to keep you apprised of the fact!' He deliberately looked away from the grinding jaw of Horowitz that pumped with anger. Instead he focused on the tea caddy and ladled three teaspoons of tea leaves into the pot, becoming horribly aware that he was in his pyjamas and perhaps looking vaguely ridiculous at not quite six in the evening.

'Not even nearly professional,' the intruder finally choked out.

'Actually, Horowitz, not even nearly a client. The reverse, in fact. And before you start lecturing me, you know full well what an extraordinary situation this is. I can assure you I want nothing to do with a war criminal, and if I can confirm that this item is indeed stolen, then I'll wash my hands of the client. If I confirm that the person behind this temporary gift to the British Museum is the same Mayek who was involved in the atrocities against Katerina and her family, then I will help her to hunt him down and bring the full weight of the law against him.'

He watched Horowitz's lips thin. He seemed torn. 'She set out to get your help any way she could. I noted she followed you into the Café Royal.'

He folded his arms, leaned a hip against the sink and then remembered the pyjamas and adjusted his stance to tighten the satin belt of his paisley dressing-gown. Heaven help him with the impression he was giving. 'I doubt she'd stoop to the level you're suggesting, Mr Horowitz. Sad of you to think of her in that way.'

'She's desperate.'

'Then you clearly don't know her as well as I.'

'You've known her one day!'

'That's my point, sir.' It was one of those touché moments but Edward took no pleasure in scoring against his opponent, who looked instantly wounded. 'Mr Horowitz —'

'Daniel.' The fight had gone out of him.

'Daniel, you seem to think I know where Katerina is.'

'I thought she was here with you.' He sounded worried.

'No.' He could see that his guest wanted to ask if he was sure about this but refrained. 'Did you follow us last night?'

'My colleagues did.'

'I see. Then they didn't follow her back out of my home an hour or so later, presumably. She left rather angrily, I'm afraid. We . . .' He didn't think Horowitz needed to know the intimate details. 'We said goodnight on bad terms because I won't give her the details of who I'm acting for.'

'Even though her life is in danger.'

'Well, I didn't know that yesterday, although she had told me her tragic story, for which I have immense sympathy and would like to help in every way that the law permits me to. However, as I explained to Katerina, all I have is the name of an overseas law firm. I have no knowledge of the man she's described. And don't you think talking about life and death is a fraction dramatic?'

The kettle began a breathy whistle threatening to become piercing within moments. Edward switched off the stove, hearing the satisfying pop as the gas flame extinguished and the kettle wheezed down from its shriek. He poured the water into the pot and placed a tea-cosy on top. All he needed to be doing was humming a daft tune to complete the picture of domesticity.

'Mr Summerbee . . . Edward . . . I believe the reason the Pearls have emerged is in order to draw out Katerina. I happen to know the man behind all of her pain, and indeed mine, is not dead. I have been hunting him for the best part of my life. Until the day she saw those Pearls, either he knew she was still alive and wanted to finish what he started two decades ago – I'm sure you know the story by now. Or he has been cautious, using the offer to the museum as a way of testing the waters. Either way, I can assure you that Ruda Mayek is now well aware of her existence and I am now well aware of his.'

'You've seen him?' Edward's voice had a fresh, fearful quality to it.

Daniel nodded.

'Then let me assure you that I will put my whole life behind guarding hers,' he said, not meaning to stab a finger towards Daniel but there it was, midair, slightly crooked and pointing accusingly. 'I'll be back.' He tried to stride away with an air of superiority but his leather mules forced him to shuffle and he groaned inwardly at the slide and slap of the soles of his slippers on the lino.

He took a few minutes to change back into some day clothes before returning to the parlour. 'I'm going to have some tea before it goes tepid. Do you want some?'

'Got anything stronger?'

'Sherry?' At Daniel's scathing look, Edward grinned. 'How about a Scotch?'

His guest nodded.

Within a few minutes they faced each other at the kitchen table, Edward hoping – despite the floral cup before him – that he looked more rakish in front of the serious-faced spy, who sipped and savoured the liquor for a moment or two.

'You'd have preferred the sherry,' Edward offered into the silence.

He watched the man's countenance relax slightly at the soft jest. 'Thank you, this is superb.'

'Glenmorangie. You can't go wrong, laddie, with the spirit from the Men o' Tain.' His suddenly acquired Scottish accent did not appear to amuse Daniel. Edward cleared his throat with a swallow of his tea. 'All right, the floor is yours, Daniel.' He gestured with one hand for Daniel to proceed and watched him over the rim of his cup. 'What's our next step?'

––––––––

Daniel was unsure how to feel about Edward Summerbee. He seemed to be a man of layers. He'd already seen a couple of the faces that Edward could wear: the slick professional in his offices, the polite stalwart who kept his emotions in check until the right person came along to prise them out – Daniel had felt only heat when he watched Edward's controlled aggravation appear at being ambushed in his offices – and now here he sat with the benign version: self-effacing and humorous.

His mind flicked to Katerina and her relationship with the man he sat in front of. The master spy could tell instantly that Edward was covering the full truth of what had occurred between them. Daniel suppressed the claw of desperate envy that Edward had enjoyed any intimacy with Katerina by swallowing another slug of the excellent Scotch.

Edward was waiting for him to speak and Daniel was more than aware that he was in the presence of a sharp listener.

He was concise. He remained cool and emotionless as he told his story. He gave Edward all of it; this was no time for hedging or withholding truths – her life was at stake. A month ago that wouldn't have mattered to him, but now . . . she made his life feel the polar opposite of what he'd been living. He gave the solicitor everything except his desire for Katerina.

Edward spoke into the silence. 'I realise this is difficult for you, Daniel. What you need to know is that I haven't stolen her from you.' It was surgical, as though he'd known all along. Daniel felt the whisky burning in the pit of his belly, or was that his fury? 'I wasn't meant to meet Katerina,' Edward continued conversationally. 'I certainly didn't expect to see her again after the meeting at Lincoln's Inn, as I thought I'd been perfectly clear. I'd hoped our paths would not cross again. But she forced it, as you know, because you followed her; the choices were hers, not mine. We both know this is a woman in trouble. I could have been any one of those solicitors at Lincoln's Inn or indeed across London.' He shrugged. 'I dropped my guard and she hers.

We . . . Look . . .' He raked a hand through his already dishevelled hair.

'You misread me,' Daniel interjected.

'No, I don't believe I do. You see, I don't think any of us choose who we fall in love with. Most of us tend to accept that it's an emotion, or a feeling, right? But I personally don't subscribe to that. I think it's a physiological response to a drug we don't control – just like we don't control adrenaline when we're in a state of fear. It is released into our system without conscious permission and I think if we looked hard enough, we'd find a love drug in our bodies that is only released by the brain when it decides this is your perfect match.'

'A philosopher.' Daniel grimaced and the sarcasm felt vicious when he landed the blow.

But Edward, wearing his solicitor's smile, was not offended. 'Not at all. Just trying to make sense myself of how I could live the last couple of decades as an island, allowing plenty of women to visit, but always shoving them off the beach soon after. And then along comes one I haven't purposefully pursued and I end up helplessly hooked as though I've been snagged like a woollen jumper on a tree branch. And just like that unlooped thread, it stops you in your tracks and you stare at it with a sort of resignation that it's done now. Katerina feels as natural to me as the sun rising each morning. I didn't choose this. It's done now . . . I can't undo it.'

'You admit you're in love with her, knowing her for a few moments?'

'I don't know what I'm admitting. I feel rather foolish being so open. I am helplessly trapped by her and her trauma, though, and I've been discovering information today that could change how she feels about this mission of vengeance she's on.'

'Mr Summerbee —' He wanted to hate him, but in describing his experience of Katerina, Edward had essentially described

Daniel's. They were both her accidental victims; both snagged on her branch.

'You can't drink my Scotch and not call me Edward – please.'

'Let me set aside my personal feelings.'

'Are you sure that you can?'

'I am.' He began to explain his story, even though he had learned that Katerina had briefed Edward. Couldn't he have been a portly, ageing, married, soon-to-be grandfather? No, he had to be so excellent to look at as well as charming, well groomed . . . and, worst of all, he was clearly fascinating company for the one woman who found most men lacking. He even had a rakish cleft in his chin, for pity's sake! Daniel searched for flaws, settling on the widening arch of Summerbee's hairline at either side of his forehead. Daniel discovered that the more he shared of his backstory, the gentler Summerbee's gaze landed on him. Despite that, he could see all humour draining from the solicitor's expression. His eyes no longer crinkled at their edges and that generous mouth had flattened to reflect his growing unease.

Daniel stopped talking abruptly once he'd explained how he'd seen the man he believed to be Mayek watching Katerina's London flat.

'Good heavens, man! In London? So you lied to her about leaving for Paris because you suspected he might be here?' Edward finished the thought that had arrived.

'Correct. Well, that she was being followed, certainly. But suspicion was all I had. Even in retirement you don't lose what I call spy sense, and I had the feeling in Paris that she was being watched. I noted that in the gardens – where I first made contact with Katerina – a man was observing her.'

'Hardly surprising. She's a striking woman in anyone's estimation.'

'Agreed. Nor was his presence unusual. I saw him later too,

strolling by whilst we shared a coffee at a café in those same gardens. Again, it was hardly worth more than a mental note at that point, but it was noted nonetheless.' He gave a tight, brief smile. 'Habit.'

'And now he's in London,' Edward said. 'Wait a minute! Maybe he has changed sufficiently as he's aged. There was an odd man making Katerina feel awkward in a teashop yesterday afternoon, I'm told. Could that —?'

Daniel waved a hand to stop him. 'That was George. An old friend and fellow practitioner from MI5.'

Edward looked at him, stunned.

'Katerina has known Mayek since her birth and he left a deep impression upon her. I doubt she would ever mistake him, unless his disguise was so professional as to render him unrecognisable, including his distinctive eyes. No, all I could do was my utmost to control the situation by keeping us close to her so Mayek could not make any approach.'

'Why would you ever leave her in the first place?' Summerbee sounded vaguely exasperated.

'Because she wasn't listening to me. She regarded me as an obstacle to you. I realised I could achieve more and take better care of her if I was out of sight. She barely batted an eyelid at my departure. She had her prize. You.'

'Don't be absurd.'

'I don't mean it like that. You were her only link to Ruda Mayek and I needed her to make that link work. If removing myself made it easier – and clearly it did – it was a reasonable gamble. Nevertheless, I was certain we were being followed by then, so I took a precaution and had George follow Katerina from the moment I left her. I couldn't take a chance.'

'But surely she's gone back to where she was staying?' Edward admonished him.

Daniel made a bitter expression. 'No, she didn't go back to her London digs last night. And George being taken off surveillance was my fault. I figured she'd come home when I was watching the flat so she'd be safe when she returned, but then the fellow I was keeping her safe from left too, and I learned a few minutes later that she'd gone home with you anyway. I figured she was staying the night when George reported that you were both seemingly getting cosy over a meal in the parlour. I told him to head home himself.'

'You got it wrong, Daniel.' Edward sighed. 'The stars aligned against you. But why wouldn't she go back to her flat?'

'Perhaps it's a blessing she didn't, as he's keeping such a close eye on her.'

'A hotel?'

'Maybe.' Daniel shrugged. 'I'm hoping she'll call me.'

'I doubt she'll call me but I do need to reach her. How do you know for sure that someone is following her – I mean, from Paris and around London?'

Daniel snorted. 'Mayek needs some spy training. One of his early lessons would be the advice to change hats and clothes, not to wear or carry anything distinctive if he's going to tail someone – this is rudimentary stuff. To blend in and be so ordinary as to become invisible in the crowd. The man in Paris had a slight limp he couldn't hide well. We might have encountered him twice in the same location that one afternoon but then I was sure I spotted that limp on the Underground when we were first coming to Lincoln's Inn. So I tested it. I brought us a very long way around and Katerina had an idea something was odd, but of course she doesn't know London well and had none of the clues to piece together what might be going on, so I managed to pass off our route with an excuse.'

'And he was following?'

'I don't think he followed so much as knew where we were headed. Because he'd brought the Pearls into the open it probably felt as obvious to him as it did to me that the only way to backtrack to him was to follow the line from the museum. You were the next logical piece of the jigsaw. I pretended to take a photo of her as she stood at the old bookshop but really I just wanted to look in the reflection, and right enough, there he was behind us, appearing casual but watching us intently.'

'What do you think is Mayek's plan with all of this? He dodged the war trials and has obviously been living in comfortable obscurity. Why now? Why would he risk everything to hunt down the teenager he once knew?'

Daniel nodded, impressed. 'It's the question I've racked my mind to answer. Here's my theory. I think his move to rid himself of the Pearls is because he's seriously ill and I suspect he is putting his matters to rest, tidying up loose ends.'

'Tidying up —' Edward repeated and then stopped. He'd been shifting his chair back to stand and now sat down heavily once more. 'Put your spy talk into layman's terms,' he demanded.

Daniel lifted an eyebrow. 'Katerina is a loose end, Edward. He's been living his life somewhere safe. He's surely got a new identity, could be married, possibly has a family oblivious of his past. He has created a whole new way of life and I'm sure has convinced himself that his past is now buried in history and he no longer resembles the man he once was. But then he gets sick or realises an ongoing illness is now life-threatening and I would imagine that the only factor in his existence that can now link him to being a war criminal or simply to being Ruda Mayek from Czechoslovakia is Katerina's Pearls.' He paused to let that sink in.

Edward nodded. 'Go on.'

'How is he to rid himself of this distinctive piece? He could break it down, turn it into many items of jewellery, but frankly, most of the world remains supremely touchy about antique jewellery with no easily explained provenance. Even a bracelet made of those old pearls would be suspicious to any expert. He could never rid himself of the stone – that sapphire is far too special. Besides, he may not have the connections or the energy to set about remaking the Pearls into a series of unrecognisable pieces.'

'He could bury them.'

'Yes, he could. But then his family cannot benefit from them. I think he still holds faith that he can profit from them and he's devised a cunning plan to gift them to arguably the most powerful museum in the world. Working through agents – that is, overseas solicitors and then your firm – he has kept himself at a distance, can remain anonymous and give the impression this was an item acquired during the war years for which he has simply been a caretaker.'

'But then what?'

Daniel smiled. 'He's a gambler, I'm reckoning. He's playing the odds by risking that no one knows their provenance. Katerina told me this is a highly secret piece – her mother publically wore them once and her grandmother before that perhaps also only once. Katerina never did get to wear them properly. No one has seen the Ottoman Pearls in Bohemia more than twice since the turn of the century and most of those people would be dead now. Previous to that . . . well, you probably know the history that Katerina shared about their emergence in Russia a couple of centuries ago. They were probably never seen outside of the harem itself or the Topkapi Palace in Constantinople of the middle centuries. So there are no experts for this piece who would recognise them. Ruda Mayek would know this – he'd been around that family since he was a boy.'

'And he's presuming there's no one living who can recognise them and provide the truth,' Edward said with a dawning of realisation.

'Exactly. The last living person who knew those Pearls he believes he personally shot dead and laid atop the rest of her murdered family in deep forest in a tiny forgotten hamlet of

Czechoslovakia.' Daniel became suddenly animated, waving his hands, his voice rising. 'He was there! He fired the bullet! Heard her call out in the darkness . . . he heard her drop, watched her lifeless, blood-soaked body dragged back to that frozen pit in the ground and witnessed all of the Kassowicz family buried.'

His mouth twisting in revulsion, Edward nodded. 'So . . .'

'Even with this burning confidence he is taking the precaution of first dipping his toe in the water by offering them for exhibit by the museum. They would attract so much interest.'

'But surely people with expertise in antiquity might connect them to stolen property.'

'They might. But he will have a ready story for how he came by them – and now he wants to give them to the world to enjoy. Maybe he's even gone so far as to accept he may have to lose them, but he's going to try to profit from them.'

'So after a few years he'll come to the arrangement he has proposed to the museum.'

'Exactly, in five years or so, when those Pearls feel like a piece of furniture around the museum and it wouldn't like to part with them because they always attract interested patrons, they will officially acquire them. Dead or alive, Ruda Mayek gets his price and provides it to his family. If he had no family, I doubt he would be going to this trouble. If that was him I saw yesterday evening, then looking at him even in shadow I can say he's not going to live long enough to enjoy the proceeds.'

'Or maybe he's absolving himself of his sins.'

'He can't. I won't let him. Neither will Katerina.'

'All right. So he's flushed out Katerina.'

Daniel nodded. 'A huge shock, I have no doubt.'

'That's my fault, of course. Mr Partridge told me and I alerted my client and one presumes they alerted him.'

'You said her name?'

'I told them what the museum told me. A visiting expert from the Louvre claims that this is a piece stolen from her family in 1941 and that we would have to do due diligence now and explore that claim if she formalises it.'

'So she's flushed *him* out of hiding. He likely couldn't believe what he was hearing and needed to see for himself this ghost supposedly risen from the grave. By the time he arrives at the museum she's already fled to Paris. I'm guessing it took him a while to get on her trail because she wasn't officially back at the Louvre when she and I met. By the time he hunted her down, I was in the picture. And I didn't leave her alone for a second. She was too precious to me, especially as I had a feeling she was being observed. I spent one entire night in a doorway watching her apartment to be sure she was not disturbed, and then we came to London. Which brings us full circle. I think he made his way to Lincoln's Inn that day already knowing we'd show up. But I was looking for him by then.'

'Then I owe you an apology. You've been protecting her as much as admiring her.'

Daniel lifted a shoulder with a sad shrug.

'How can you be one hundred per cent sure it's Mayek?'

'I can't. Katerina is the only person who can recognise him for me. And I agree, there must be no doubt. I can't just approach this stranger in case it isn't him; if it's not Mayek, then this fellow could warn Mayek that we're onto him.' He sighed. 'My line of work is always cat and mouse. And a cat is interminably patient when hunting prey.'

'Tell me about last night's sighting.'

'I was close. I couldn't see his face fully because it was dark, although I caught an impression of it when he lit a cigarette, but the limp is now unmistakable. I heard his cough – he is not a well man; he is weaker than his age suggests. I heard his voice. Definitely European, despite the easy use of English.'

'Where did you see him?'

'Directly opposite Katerina's flat in Bloomsbury.'

Edward looked thunderstruck.

'He was hidden. But I was better hidden.'

'Why didn't you follow him?'

'I should have. It was a mistake not to. But the reason I saw him was because I was watching her flat to ensure she returned home safely.' He watched Edward finish the dregs of his cooled tea and he swallowed the last of the whisky, which hit his empty belly in a fiery cascade.

'So we've lost them both?'

Daniel lifted a shoulder. 'For now. Don't forget, he's the scared one. He's rethinking carefully laid plans on the run; he needs to be sure that this is Katerina Kassowicz and not an impostor.'

'How would he recognise her?'

'How many people do you know that have eyes like Katerina's?'

Edward sighed in exasperation. 'Indeed. How stupid of me.'

'He only has to walk close enough to her on the street to mark her. He's followed her to Paris so he's had plenty of opportunity to confirm it's the woman he thought he'd never see again. Now I suspect he's watching her, planning carefully, so he can make his move.' Daniel nodded. 'He's having to be so careful not to be noticed by her and he's lucky he didn't give himself away in his shock at realising his nemesis was alive.'

'Daniel,' Edward began, standing and running both hands back through his hair. 'We know he's prepared to kill. Do you think he's going to make another attempt on Katerina?'

'Yes, of course I do.' How naive was Summerbee? But then this was Daniel's world and few understood it.

'You should know that I will not permit you to use Katerina as bait.'

'I won't have to.'

'Good.'

'She'll not wait for him to come to her, Edward. She's got every intention of finishing this part of her history on her own terms and neither you nor I will have any say in it.'

He could feel the solicitor's vexation like a third person, stalking around the kitchen. 'This is not going to happen. Tomorrow I am going to alert Scotland Yard and no doubt Interpol will be brought in —'

'You have no evidence and you have no suspect, Edward.' He watched his companion begin to bluster. 'Mossad will take care of this. He is our prize. He has always been my enemy and I will deal with him. What I need you to do is to help me prevent Katerina from doing something ill-advised.'

'Ill-advised? You mean a revenge murder?'

'I believe that's her intention, not that she'd know the first thing about how to plan a kill.' He spoke on, ignoring the fresh look of disgust on the solicitor's face. 'But together we will not let that occur. I will give you my promise that no blood will ever be on Katerina's hands if you promise to keep silent.'

'So Mossad can put him on trial?'

Daniel stood and looked away. 'Something like that.'

'If you can be sure this is the monster Ruda Mayek, then frankly I don't care what you do to him.'

'Then we agree and you don't need to know any more – just keep the British authorities out of this. As to your client, we can work that out later. Katerina can follow the right protocol to put in a claim.'

'She doesn't want the Pearls.'

Daniel shrugged. 'I don't care either way. What I need is for Katerina to recognise Ruda Mayek for us.'

'I thought you'd just take over now and hunt him down —'

'No. She intends to have her chance to look him in the eye and show her defiance, her contempt for him. This is why she is now in mortal danger.'

Edward raised a finger. It was levelled at him. 'And you've let her out of your sight.'

He resisted saying *So did you*, because Edward was blameless. Instead he put a hand on his heart and nodded, ashamed.

'If she hasn't gone home, how are we going to find her?'

The notion of teamwork wasn't lost on Daniel. He was glad Edward now felt accountable too. 'We wait.'

Edward stood, flustered. 'For all your clever spying experience, that's your best suggestion?'

'It's the only course. We'll watch her flat tonight and tomorrow. If he's hoping to trap her, we'll see him first. Remember, he doesn't know where she's gone either and he certainly has no clue she was with you last night.'

'She left just before ten.'

Daniel nodded.

Edward began thinking aloud. 'Where does a foreigner go at that time of the night, if not the one place she calls home?'

'A hotel.'

'Fair enough, but why? She's not suspicious that she's being followed, right?'

Daniel shook his head.

'Then she's moving to a new plan.'

'Such as?'

Edward threw up his hands with a gusting sigh. 'I don't know, I'm not a spy. But given it was a cool, somewhat clinical end to an otherwise warm conversation, she's given up on me, so tell me what other options she might have.' He suddenly looked at his watch. 'Oh, hell. I have to make a call.' At Daniel's bewildered expression, he added, 'It's for her. Might be the single item of news that could change her direction.'

'What are you talking about?'

'Give me five minutes. Help yourself to another Scotch.' Edward disappeared.

Daniel didn't want another drink. He wanted a clear head. He stood while he waited, prowling Summerbee's parlour, helplessly admiring the pale green kitchen range that was keeping the downstairs so toasty. He could see a chicken casserole was bubbling on the stove; no wonder sitting here had made him feel sluggish and hungry.

Edward pushed through the door again; his face was flushed and he was half smiling.

'You look like you won first prize,' Daniel remarked.

'I have news.' He told Daniel about the *Kindertransport* discovery.

'Katerina's brother is alive?'

Edward frowned. 'Well, I do need to confirm that, but there's every chance, yes. Presumably he would be in his early twenties. What we do know for sure, though, is that Petr Kassowicz did not die in Prague in 1939. He was put on the *Kindertransport* in a pressured decision to take the place of a boy around the same age called Hersh Adler. Heaven only knows why her parents kept this secret but the point is, he arrived here well and in the arms of Mrs Jeffers, whom I've just spoken to.'

'Hersh Adler,' Daniel repeated. 'Do we know where he was sent?'

Edward grinned and shook a page ripped from a notepad. 'I'm going to find him for her.'

Daniel smiled with wonder. 'This is what she needs.'

'I also hope to know by tomorrow about her father's will.' He briefed Daniel.

While he spoke, Daniel felt a shadow of guilt steal into the room and loom over him. While he'd allowed himself to waste energy thinking badly of the solicitor, it was clear that Summerbee, for all his naysaying, had been busy trying to help in ways that could improve Katerina's life. Edward might just deliver to her a brother and the Pearls in the space of a few days. Meanwhile all Daniel could bring was grim news that shifted her deeper into the mire she had spent a lifetime trying to escape. He swallowed his shame at thinking so poorly of the man from Lincoln's Inn. 'You've done well, Edward. Truly.'

'Well,' he replied, his tone modest, 'let's reserve judgement until I can deliver. What's your next move?'

Daniel shrugged. 'I'm going to wait for her call. She's obviously angry, running away from you, from me; perhaps she needs time to think. I doubt she'd return to Paris . . . not yet.'

'Why?'

'Because she's determined to find him and deal with him.'

Edward shook his head with disgust at the notion.

'No, she'll remain in England, I suspect, and —'

'North!'

'Pardon?'

'She mentioned that she . . . wait, how did she put it?' Edward reached for the memory. 'She quipped that she knew Yorkshire – had lived there – but gets lost in London.'

'Yorkshire?' Daniel looked unsure. 'Who's there for her?'

'The Czech woman who helped her escape . . . can't recall the name, although I want to say Mrs Biscuit.'

Daniel nodded. 'I see. You know more than I do in this regard. Well, now, that may well be where she's headed. We can take some heart that she's probably safer there than here. I feel sure she will phone me. Remember, she thinks I'm back in France, so I'm no threat to her plans.'

'All right. Will you call me?'

'Yes.' He retrieved a card from his pocket. 'Here's a number. Ring it any time – day or night. They'll find me.'

'Thank you. Let me give you the number for here. Leave messages if you need with Miss Bailey at the office. What now?'

Daniel checked his watch. 'I'll relieve my colleague watching Katerina's flat.'

'Why not just grab him if you see this man you suspect?'

'Because when we do grab someone, Edward, it's for real. There's no turning back from it, no apology, no second chance for him. So we have to be one hundred per cent sure it's the war criminal we're hunting. Only Katerina can mark him for us.'

'You're going to kill him?'

Daniel shrugged. 'Gladly. However, he should face trial as a war criminal.'

His companion looked relieved.

'Good night, Edward. Good luck finding the brother. Let me know if we can help.'

Edward offered a handshake. 'Night. And listen, Daniel, I'm sorry about —'

His companion gave a grimace. 'I had my chance. I'm not her type.'

'She's yours, though?'

Daniel sighed. 'In my line of work being single is a blessing.'

'I thought you were retired.'

'Spies never retire.' Daniel found his sad grin, shook Edward's hand and slipped silently out of the back door.

26

Katerina pressed the button on the ignition and the bluish-grey Morris Minor coughed into life. She hadn't driven in a few months, and not in England for a long time. Nevertheless, Otto had assured her years ago via one of his annual letters that while the skill may go rusty, she'd never forget how to drive.

'Just remember, left side of the road, Miss Kassel,' the garage owner reminded her, hearing her accent.

'I won't forget, I promise.' She smiled, giving him a gloved wave. 'I'll have this back to you by this evening.'

'No one's queuing for it and I don't want you hurrying on my account. You've got a full tank of petrol too, so I doubt you'll need to fill her up again.'

'I won't. I'm not going very far.' She grinned as she wound up the window and despite an initial jerky take-off, she was smoothly into third gear by the time she'd left the vicinity of New Earswick, the comforting smell of the car's red leather seats vaguely reminding her of happier days of childhood.

By the time she'd negotiated her way out of York and was feeling the rush of pleasure at being in open countryside, she began to allow her thoughts similar open rein now that she was hurtling towards Otto Schäfer. She was excited and daunted at once.

Uncharacteristically, she'd changed outfits three times and she was secretly glad she'd not had her full wardrobe at her disposal. Katerina had finally settled on the simplest outfit she could muster, which she knew probably echoed the publicity shots she'd seen of Audrey Hepburn in the forthcoming movie *Charade*, but this was Yorkshire and spring hadn't fully found it yet. It felt cold enough to dress for the slopes. She had a furred hat to add to the ensemble if needed, but for now a patterned headscarf in a houndstooth design was her only elaboration to what was essentially a fine study in neutral. Close-fitted casual slacks were tucked into short boots and over this she wore a loose but heavy knitted cardigan that had a cape-like shape. It was last year's design but it hid her figure and it was the warmest piece she could find in the few garments she had to choose from.

She pushed open the triangular window near the steering wheel for a moment and inhaled the sharp air as she steered the trusty Morris up the slow incline of the north Yorkshire moors. A small pang of regret caught in her throat that this wasn't summer, when these vast tracts of moorland were a breathtaking landscape carpeted with the richly pink needles of tall heather. Oh, how she'd used to admire it. The moorland in that season could look like a prehistoric beast slumbering as the northern winds stirred its pink fur. She'd heard somewhere that almost all of the world's heather moors were in Britain and most of those were in the northern half. An old farmer had once nodded sagely and remarked to her that a sheep could wander from Egton to Bilsdale without leaving the moor. She knew it had been meant to impress but she hadn't known either of those places; nevertheless, she'd given a look of wonder that had him nodding still more and saying the best time to enjoy the moors was at dusk when the landscape deepened to purple.

'Best honey from bees on the heather,' he'd finished with a tap on the side of his nose before strolling off, a small terrier in close pursuit, from where she'd been picnicking around the Hole of Horcum.

She was in Levisham Beck now and about to pass that same spot where local legend had it that a giant scooped up a handful of earth to throw at his wife during an argument. She smiled as the deep cauldron known as the Hole of Horcum, with its green felt-like surface, came into view on her left.

She pulled onto the roadside to stretch her legs and emerged from the pleasant warmth she'd built up inside the Morris to gasp as the cold air hit her lungs. Hunching deeper into the scarf at her throat, she moved to stand at the edge of the valley. The heather, so resplendent in the warmer months, was now a scorched, rusted brown and she could pick out the bright anorak colours of walkers, like insects in the distance, moving along the tracks deep into the Hole of Horcum, or sketching out its rim. The sun had broken through the clouds and seemed to shine a pillar of light to the far left, directing her attention almost to the valley floor, where there was a tiny cottage. It looked so fairytale-like, bathed in light with its chimney puffing merrily, that for a moment Katerina wished that was her home, where Ruda Mayek would never find her.

Katerina glanced at her wristwatch. She was making good time. The meet was planned for noon at a tiny hotel only known to outsiders because in 1935 J Arthur Rank shot his first feature film there, *Turn of the Tide*, about warring fishing families. She'd made arrangements for them to have lunch at Wainwright's Bar. By her estimation she would arrive at her destination of Robin Hood's Bay with maybe half an hour to spare. It would give her time to loosen out her limbs on the beach and gather her thoughts in the process because right now her mind felt blank . . . and perhaps that was a blessing.

Just over an hour later she was sighing with pleasure at the familiar sight of stormy seas from the top of the hill where she parked the car. The road into the village she knew to be frighteningly narrow as well as steep; it wasn't that she didn't trust the Morris, more that she didn't fancy her rusty skills were up to the challenge. Besides, the walk down would clear the miasma in her mind that was part fear about Mayek, part anticipation about Otto and part confusion about her feelings for Summerbee. If she was honest with herself, it was the last that was causing much of the bewilderment; she wanted him out of her thoughts, gone from her mind and her life. Yet the memory of that gentle gaze, the crooked hands that cupped her face so sweetly, the generous mouth that liked to smile and kissed with passion, wouldn't allow her to forget him. The more she tried, the harder Edward clung. It made no sense. He had let her down; she wanted to hate him.

Locking up the Morris a little harder than she meant to because of her vexation at Edward had her looking around self-consciously in case people were watching her after slamming the car door. She needn't have worried. Hers was the only parked car at the top and there was not a person to be spotted dodging behind net curtains in nearby cottages.

Dragging her gloves and scarf back on, she carefully moved down the familiar hill, past the soaring hulk of the grand Victorian seaside hotel built in the previous century to encourage holiday-makers, and onto the cobblestones of the street that led to a maze of even narrower lanes and into the village's heart. In amongst the labyrinth were whitewashed fishing cottages – she recalled how delightful they looked in summer with small brightly painted doors and their windowboxes of overflowing blooms. For now, though, the decoration came from a few early daffodils, the tips of crocuses pushing through, and the spheres of translucent glass fishing floats, some in nets, some standing in neat piles near sheds. Thin sunlight helped their blueish-green to echo the colour of the sea they normally bobbed in and leak into the small hotchpotch of streets.

Robin Hood's Bay was mostly deserted. She counted two locals doing some grocery shopping but she imagined the sensible ones were indoors and not far from the coal fire if they weren't out at sea or working in nearby fields. Crab pots were stacked on most street corners, attesting to the lesser action of these weeks, and the single seaside novelty store that doubled as a sweetshop and newsagent had obviously grimly opted to open its doors through the early spring. It had a small offering in its window display of the popular, if curious, English confectionery known as seaside rock. They sat like sticks of dynamite in the familiar radioactive pink that tended to turn the tongues of its young consumers fuchsia. And then that sticky, vague rose colour, smelling of peppermint, that clung to clothes and fingers – oh, she remembered it well from years back. She nodded a greeting to the woman who stood at the shop threshold, inhaling the last drag on a cigarette that had burned to its butt.

'Tide's out,' the woman said, taking in Katerina's appearance.

So . . . she didn't look like a beachcomber, but she'd done her best to dress down. Still, there was a glint in the woman's eye that hinted towards a sneer.

'I figured,' she replied in a breezy tone. 'I thought I'd take a walk around the rockpools,' she added, deliberately accentuating her French accent but giving just enough information so that the shopkeeper understood she knew the region.

'Mind you don't slip,' the woman said, seemingly determined to have the final and slightly sarcastic word at the helplessly fashionable boots she glanced down at.

Katerina smiled; they were her oldest pair, relegated to York. 'I'll be mindful,' she said.

The wind wasn't a gale and certainly not howling but it

whistled with glee around the snaking ginnels – as they were known in this part of the world – and she suspected once she hit the slipway, she might feel the brisk force of the North Sea. Katerina arrived on the steepish angle of the boat ramp and that wind wanted to rip her silk scarf from her head. Tying it tighter still beneath her chin, she looked back at the tall Norman seawalls that had once fortified this region and felt the thrill of history seeping into her consciousness. This was her comfortable world, touching the deep past. Above her the Bay Hotel stood out in whitewashed glory, black paint outlining its window frames and capped by a flint roof. It clung to the cliff edge, looking ready to topple over those seawalls at any moment, as houses had done in the past.

She turned away and cast her glance across the expanse of sand and glistening rockpools. There was only the barest hint of blue above; the sky looked as if it had been frightened to white, while low-hanging, smoke-coloured clouds hung like ghostly battleships. The cliff border curling around gave the impression of a brooding dog, selfishly enclosing the bay between its paws. One person stood amongst the rockpools, staring into their shallow waters where tiny sea creatures lurked and the world beyond the sea was reflected in their mirror surface. She was astonished that he was here first and recognised his shape immediately despite the overcoat and hat. Still tall and straight, he blended into the landscape not just in his charcoal garments but in the mood his lonely figure seemed to cut on the deserted beach.

'Otto.' She murmured his name like a chant.

It was as though he heard her whisper in his mind and he turned, looking directly across the yards that separated them, and lifted a gloved hand. His features were lost behind a scarf and in the glum light of the day. She found herself helplessly on tiptoe, waving back enthusiastically; she was a teenager again. And then, hardly caring about the impression it might give to any onlookers, she began to run. It wasn't a gallop but no one could mistake her eagerness, and her long stride covered the distance swiftly.

'Be careful!' she heard his lovely voice warning but she gave no heed and suddenly she was in his arms again, wrapping him tightly in a hug as though she were a long-lost child. 'Oh, my darling Katerina,' he said and they held their embrace without stirring, with the plaintive mew of gulls wheeling above them the only sound. Finally, he pulled her back to look upon her. 'Look at you.'

'Look at you,' she echoed, lost for what to say in the moment. 'New beard too! I didn't want to disturb you; you looked at ease.'

'I was. I was staring into that pool of water – its own little microcosm of life and activity.'

She smiled. 'Shall we walk?'

'Yes.'

She noted he didn't let go of her hand.

'Well, I don't have to ask how you are. I can see you are every inch more beautiful than the last time I set eyes upon you.'

She sighed, self-consciously but privately delighted; his compliments mattered while few others did. 'And you're still the dashing doctor I recall . . . even more handsome with the grey at your ears.'

He grinned. 'My wife calls it my debonair streak.'

She smiled, the reference to his wife not lost on her. 'What do you think of this place?'

'Wild, wonderful . . . wintry.' He shivered to make her grin widen. 'A lonely spot, typical of you.'

'Oh, it's beautiful in summer. We used to come here regularly for picnics. This beach can be quite crowded.'

'I'm afraid you can't convince me of that,' he said. 'Although I'll agree, its beauty is raw and magnificent.' He paused. 'Did you visit Durham before you came here?'

She shook her head, without guilt, feeling the rush of pleasure at hearing his voice for real and not just in her mind as she read his birthday wishes or a rare letter. 'No, I was in a hurry. Soon, though. Milena's visiting at the moment.'

'I thought I'd call in to the university on my way home.'

'Good.' She nodded. 'It will be a lovely surprise.'

A silence settled around them that again only the hovering gulls could pierce. They walked in that peace until she sensed they both felt more comfortable.

'This region is famed with fossil hunters. You'll normally see them walking around with small hammers to crack open likely stones. You don't even have to look too hard to turn one up that within its depths will house the skeleton of some ammonite from four hundred million years ago.'

'Stop showing off,' he said, his tone of wonder belying his words. 'What is an ammonite?'

She laughed, full-throated, thrilled to impress him. 'An extinct group of sea molluscs from the Devonian period. Just imagine something squid-like from a very long time ago.'

He grinned. 'I'm presuming you've fossil-hunted with —'

'Oh, many times,' she interjected. 'Actually, once we got past our fossil period, we moved into our Whitby jet period. We used to find bits of it on the beach . . . not any more.'

He frowned at her, amused.

'Whitby jet,' she repeated with emphasis on her dismayed tone at his ignorance, 'is quite the find in these parts. They used to carve it into stunning pieces of jewellery – still do, but I think we're past its heyday. The Victorians loved its black shiny depths for mourning jewellery. I have an exquisite brooch I'm particularly fond of.'

'So it's a gemstone?'

'Fossilised wood, actually, compressed over millions of years and prized for its, well, its blackness. It's particularly adored by jewellery designers for its lightness and smoothness, making it possible to shape into lavish designs that reflect as well as any mirror.'

'Well, then, I must look for a piece made up. Nice present to take home. Our daughter Elke, who has recently turned twenty-one, only wears black at the moment.'

'Oh, she'll love it. Visit one of the Hamond salons in Whitby, York, Leeds – that's the most famous jet jeweller in these parts. Of course, jet is found in many places around the world, but they say the very best is sourced in England's north. Queen Victoria made Whitby jet *de rigueur* in her court after her beloved Albert's death.'

'So, lots of reasons to choose this incredibly lonely place. I felt like I was travelling to the ends of the earth. No, I think I am at the end of the earth,' he jested.

'Yes, sorry. I was being cautious for a number of reasons, mostly out of respect for our pact.'

'Thank you. You've always been understanding of my situation.'

'I didn't want you to feel trapped into obligation, but thank you for coming.'

'How could I not? You've never asked before and on the phone you sounded frantic.'

'I am.'

'So . . .?'

'Not yet. Let me just enjoy these happy moments with you again.'

He lifted her gloved hand and kissed it. 'I'm always here for you, Katerina.'

She couldn't look at him with damp eyes and wanted to hug him again and feel the comfort of his long arms around her but that would be unseemly. She couldn't rely on the helpless teen of years gone. He had never been hers; she'd lived with the regret of her fascination for him for long enough now to know how not to dwell upon it.

'So, why do they call this place Robin Hood's Bay?' He turned her so they could walk the length of the rocky beach away from the ramp.

Katerina was glad to let out the sudden tension with a laughing sigh. 'I don't think he was ever here, but some say he kept escape boats around these parts, although it's surely too far north. Popular myth suggests that Robin Hood and Little John were involved in an archery tournament at Whitby and their arrows were shot so keenly they landed on Baytown's beach.'

'Nice story.' He smiled. 'Tell me about your work.'

She knew what he was doing and was grateful for his still impeccable ability for helping her to relax and he remained her favourite listener; even better than Daniel. He asked intelligent questions about her role at the Louvre and sounded impressed when he listened to the projects she'd been working on at the British Museum.

'Your father would be so proud of you using all those skills he helped you to acquire in childhood.' They were the right words; just enough praise with the perfect sentiment to make her feel for a moment that she was floating. And then, in typical Otto style, he didn't allow the emotion to spill. 'Shall we head back?'

She glanced at her watch. 'It's later than I thought. Yes, we'd better or we risk missing lunch.'

They turned and the small village made a picturesque backdrop with mainly terracotta and some slate-tiled rooftops stepped up the cliff. It was pretty despite being so grimly lit, although perhaps that was the charm . . . one of mystery. The village nestled within a natural dip of hills that looked like green velvet from this distance.

'The guidebook told me this was a smuggler's haven and I think I can see why,' he ventured.

'Oh, indeed. Many tunnels. Some of the houses have fake doors that connect to secret passageways. I've booked a table at the Bay Hotel in its bar. It's been around since the late 1800s as a happy smugglers' rest, no doubt. The local fare is wolf and chips.'

'Pardon?'

'Atlantic wolf-fish, which over the years has garnered the nickname of wolf, but the crab is great in this region too. And chips with everything, of course.'

'*Frites!* My favourite,' he admitted, dodging a pile of slimy, long-tentacled seaweed.

They reached the stones of the ramp and made the ascent up the slipway again and then a flight of stairs into the hotel itself, moving into a happy fug of warmth that the main bar had promised. A fire burnt with bright coals at one end and at the other the bar with its distinctive barrels beneath the counter enclosed what was a tiny and once again deserted space.

The fire guttered at the cold wind they brought in with them and Katerina had to dig in her bag for a handkerchief. She blew gently into it while Otto sniffed back on his runny nose. 'Just us today?' Katerina enquired of the woman behind the bar as a way of starting a conversation.

'No one else around, love,' the landlady said. 'Wednesdays aren't our busiest, anyway, outside of summer.'

'So we can sit anywhere?' Otto asked politely, and Katerina noted he was masking his German accent.

'Wherever you like, love. Where are you folks from?'

'France,' Katerina said, to save Otto the guilt-ridden conversation she was sure he felt the pain of each time he moved through England.

'Oh, and you thought you might escape the weather here, did you?'

Katerina laughed. 'No, I'm involved with antique jewellery

and have come to this region to admire the jet. That's a lovely piece you're wearing.'

'Ooh, thank you, love. My old man gave me this on our wedding day. My granny said it was good for nowt but mourning jewellery. But I've always thought it bonny. Anyway, what'll you have?'

'Er, a weak shandy, please.' She knew from experience that suggesting a glass of wine in these parts would earn her a scathing look. 'Beer for you, doctor?' She was sure this would impress the lady behind the bar . . . better than the name Otto, anyway.

'Lovely,' he said. 'A half pint of whatever's local, please.'

'I'll bring them over – you go get yourselves warm by the fire. Here we go, take those menus too.'

Katerina smiled and joined Otto at the table furthest from the bar, closest to the fire and next to the small picture window that looked out over that ancient crenelated seawall of north Yorkshire stone, onto the bleak seascape below. The stone had weathered to golden toffee, unlike its cousin in west Yorkshire that blackened with age. It seemed to take an eternity pulling off all the extra outdoor clothes and piling them on the bench seat nearby. 'I actually love it here in winter,' she shared, gazing out onto the restless North Sea with its foaming breakers that would soon roar back in to shore.

'I have to agree that it's deliciously atmospheric,' he said. 'Katerina, you are still too thin but very beautiful. It's wonderful to see you in the flesh again.'

This was her first opportunity to look upon him properly face-on. Maturing twenty years made no difference; annoyingly, he was still as handsome as she recalled from her youth. 'What's with the new beard when the rest of the world is becoming relentlessly clean-shaven?'

He shook his head. 'Lazy, perhaps. I've had it for years.'

'Suits you.'

'My wife doesn't think so.'

'And you don't go out of your way to please her?'

'In so many ways!' he answered, feigning despair. 'But I lead a busy life at the hospital and in my clinic, and with three children to run around, it's hectic. My personal grooming comes last behind the dog walks in our household.'

'Three children?'

He looked guilty. 'We adopted a Polish ten-year-old last year. I haven't had a chance to tell you. The child of refugee parents who both rather tragically died having somehow survived the worst years; it's a long story, but she's wonderful. Turned our lives upside down, including those of her older sister and brother, but she's quite the princess.'

'That's lovely, Otto . . . I like that you're still taking lost little girls under your wing. Even so, the guilt is not all yours to bear.' She reached out and squeezed his hand but didn't linger. The warmth of his skin remained with her, though.

He nodded. 'Her name is Lili,' he said as their drinks arrived. 'It's Marie she's closest to . . . even calls her Mama.'

'Here we go, loves. Now, food? It's just I promised the cook we'd close up early – we usually do in the cold weeks.'

'Oh, yes, of course, that's not a problem,' Katerina said. 'Erm, let me glance at this menu.'

'I'll have the fish and chips,' Otto said, keeping it simple.

'What's the soup for today?' Katerina enquired.

'The cook calls it fish chowder. I can vouch for it.'

'I'll have that and steal some of his chips.'

The woman grinned. 'Won't be long, then.' She left them to it with only the sound of the fire hissing behind them.

Katerina glanced at the motley collection of fishing ephemera across the cosy main bar. Everything from old storm lanterns and coppers to mugs with inscriptions and small pieces of carved drift-wood. The low tin ceiling was pressed into a familiar shape and felt like it was squeezing in on her suddenly.

The hour of magic was over. The bubble that she'd allowed herself to move in burst as he finally framed the enquiry she could hardly avoid.

'And so, Katerina. Why have you brought me here under a cloud of worry? I can see you are well. Do you need money? Is Milena ailing, or perhaps it's —'

'Otto, I haven't asked you for money in seventeen years and Milena is in robust health. No, it's not any of us.'

'All right . . .' He frowned, waiting.

'It's him – Ruda Mayek.'

Their meals arrived in a bustle of Yorkshire bonhomie to break the tense moment as the kind landlady laid out their meal.

'Soup's hot, love. Watch you don't burn your mouth,' she warned and then left them to their food.

'Eat,' Otto instructed, remembering a holiday chalet twenty winters ago in a snowed-in forest. 'And tell me.' He noted now that Ruda Mayek's name was spoken Katerina's face had lost its excited tension at their reunion and relaxed into what could be compared to a waxy mask.

She ate mechanically but he watched each mouthful of soup and bread that she chewed slowly. It was true that he could barely taste his food since she'd spoken that devil's name; freshly filleted fish, fluffy log-like chips unlike the thinner versions in Europe, oozy tartare sauce, buttered bread . . . it all tasted the same, like slightly soured cardboard because of Ruda Mayek.

Katerina spoke uninterrupted and in her usual manner kept her information factual, her words spare.

She looked up from the half-finished bowl of soup. Silently she scissored out an arm to hold his hand; he pushed away the thought of how now, as much as back then, he could wish to kiss those beautiful angles this moment, make her life feel safe in his embrace, but it was too late. They had begun their walk down this dark path once again.

'I couldn't think straight when Edward refused to help. I needed space to work out what to do next. But I was also terrified all over again – I had to find a safe place. He must never find us —'

'Sssh,' he soothed softly. 'This solicitor, Summerbee; tell me about him.'

She told him what she could.

'So it's not that he *won't* help you; you can see that legally his hands are tied.'

'It's as though he's deliberately hiding behind the law.'

'Hardly hiding when the law demands he follow it. From what you've said, I think he's behaved not only reasonably but generously. If I'm not mistaken, you effectively ensnared him with your letter —'

'Which he didn't read!'

'Which he certainly did read, according to you, because you waylaid him at a swanky London restaurant, brought his evening with his date to a sharp close – imagine the embarrassment – then forced him to hear you out . . . again. He sounds like a scrupulous lawyer, which I admire, and a good man because he relented and took you into his home, agreed to read your letter against all his better judgement, fed you, listened to your whole story and then tried to give you the best advice he could.'

'I wanted a single name and place . . . he wouldn't give me that.'

'Would you give up the single name and place of your secret?'

Her gaze narrowed in fury.

'No, you wouldn't. Well, he's in the same situation. A client is – in a legal framework – his most *treasured person*. And please, let's not ignore the fact that he's representing another law firm, not the original client.'

She blinked that memorable fierce, damaged stare in consternation and he knew she was angry with him for taking the wrong side. 'Summerbee isn't the enemy.'

'I know,' she suddenly relented, filled with a tone of exasperation as she lowered her gaze to stir her soup angrily.

'Yes . . . I think you *do* know that.'

She cut him a look of enquiry. 'What does that mean?'

He drew a breath and put his cutlery down. 'I'd take a solid guess that you're fonder of Mr Summerbee than you want to admit.'

'Otto! Where do you get such an idea?'

He grinned. Even her accusation sounded high and false. 'When you speak of him there's a softness about your tone. You fidget at his name.'

'Don't be absurd.'

'I'm not. Look at me.'

She did so awkwardly.

'This is me, Katerina, your friend. Someone with no guile who truly loves you. Tell me you have no affection towards Edward Summerbee? Be honest.'

She hesitated and ran a nervous tongue quickly over her bottom lip. 'I don't hate him. Actually, he's very easy to like and we've . . .' She trailed off, sounding embarrassed.

His eyes widened with only a small flash of jealously; mostly he was excited for her. 'You've what?'

'He kissed me . . . he probably felt sorry for me.'

'I doubt that. You wouldn't let someone get that close unless you invited it.'

'All right, all right, *we* kissed.' She blushed, pushing her bowl forward in disgust at herself. 'It was a weak moment for both of us and changed nothing.'

'Oh, Katerina, it changes everything!'

'A kiss?' she accused.

'For any other person I'd agree, but not you.'

'Don't, Otto. This isn't helpful.'

'It is. We've avoided it. Katerina, I'm turning sixty this year.'

'I know,' she sulked.

'And you're a vibrant, brilliant 36-year-old with a great life ahead of you.'

'Not if Ruda Mayek is still alive and trying to enjoy the proceeds of my family's property.'

In spite of their reason for coming together today, he was glad they had finally broached the topic that had sat between them like a third person since they'd met, and yet a thought struck at her remark that sent all of that skittering to the side.

'Katerina, you're making it sound as though Mayek is hunting you?' He reached for her as her skin, so warm and blushing on the beach, gave up that colour like water draining to leave only the cold white enamel of a sink. He was sure her breath was held, as if that intimate part of her didn't want to absorb the air around his words, let alone the words themselves. She shrank from his touch. 'Forgive me. It suddenly occurs to me that maybe he does know how to find you . . .' He sensed his own healthy colour blanching at the thought.

'How could he know?' She stared at him for help.

Otto felt his forehead tighten into a frown. 'Well, the museum contacted your Mr Summerbee, who quite rightly would have contacted his client. And, if you're right and this is indeed Mayek probing to see what response the Pearls can provoke, those international solicitors would have contacted him. He would surely have asked for the name of the person making the claim.'

Her lips seemed to bleed out their colour. She looked cold in the cosy bar. 'So he could be following me . . .' She trailed off her words, scowling with dark thoughts.

He reached to reassure her. 'This is supposition, Katerina. We don't *know* this.' But he could tell she was no longer hearing his reason.

'He'll hear them utter the name of Kassowicz and shock or not, he'll know I'm alive. He'll discover that I'm on loan to the British Museum and attached to the Louvre. Who knows what enquiries he might have already made?' She was fully distracted now, her gaze dislodged from him to the sea and beyond. 'I have to ring Daniel.'

'The spy?'

'Yes.' She reached for her bag, dragged out her purse and began rummaging for change. 'Excuse me?' she called out to the lady behind the bar. 'Is there a public telephone nearby?'

'Just through there, love.' She pointed. 'All done with your plates?'

'Yes,' Otto said, emptying his pockets of change. 'Here, I don't need pennies and shillings to take home with me.'

Katerina gratefully took his money. 'I'll be back.'

27

'Daniel?' Her dry mouth convinced her she could taste the soil of a grave. The demon was out again.

'Katerina.' He sounded relieved but as usual controlled. 'Where are you?'

Did he already know she was no longer down south? 'I'm safe.' Katerina decided she would lead this conversation. 'I'm sorry I left London without word; I needed to get away and think.' She sensed he knew not to push. 'I'm with Otto,' she relented.

'Schäfer's in England.' It wasn't a question; his quick mind had clearly already calculated hers wasn't an international call. Nevertheless, he couldn't entirely hide his surprise.

Katerina wasted no time with further explanation. 'He just asked me if Mayek could be following me.'

When Daniel didn't answer immediately, she knew he was getting those complex thoughts of his in order, perhaps running ideas for how to soften an inevitable blow. He couldn't. He answered bluntly. 'I believe he is, yes.'

Not that he *could be* . . . but instead certainty. She felt years of security dissipate like smoke into the wind, reminding her that the life she'd built under a false name had always been a smokescreen and she had never been safe. 'You're sure?'

'No. Not one hundred per cent. Let's say ninety-nine, though; it's why I need you here.'

'So you found him in Paris after all,' she said, feeling sick at the thought of him roaming around her home city.

'He *was* in Paris, and now he's in London.'

She inhaled sharply and tumbled a fresh pile of coins into the phone. 'You've seen him?' She nearly gagged on the words.

'I've seen the same man I now believe to be Mayek several times and I'm convinced he's following you. Tell me where you are.'

She covered her mouth to prevent any sob or sound of terror escaping. Katerina forced herself to breathe and tried to recall her fighting spirit, not just from the night of the forest but in Paris when she'd promised Daniel that she wanted a confrontation with Mayek. 'No. Not yet.' Her breathing was hardly slow but it wasn't audible and she was regaining control of emotions that had felt like a whirlwind across the landscape of her mind.

'Let me call you back. Give me your number.'

'No, Daniel. I know how smart you are and the tools you have at your disposal. I don't want to be found just yet by anyone.'

He sighed. 'What about Summerbee? I'll admit he's desperately worried too.'

'You've been with him?'

'Much of last night. You might even call us friendly.'

And there he was in her mind: lovely, principled, incorruptible Edward, gazing softly at her, concern crinkling his forehead, pinching those lips she had enjoyed too briefly. She really wasn't being honest with herself about Edward; even Otto had seen right through her. She wanted to taste those lips again . . . and again.

At her hesitation, Daniel took this as his cue to explain what he knew. Her breathing slowed further as he spoke, and while she felt even colder to hear that Daniel had seen Mayek outside her flat in London, the chill brought with it that rigid strength she had learned to count on. It spread like frost covering a windowpane: beginning at the edges, crystallising inwards. She feared him, yes . . . but not the challenge of finally dealing with him. She was an adult now. More level terms. She felt that same wintry anger that she'd experienced in Paris when she'd made her promise to Daniel. The ice was back. She knew what had to be done now and she knew how.

'Katerina?'

'I'm here,' she mumbled. 'Does he know about Edward?'

'Of course he knows of Summerbee, being the solicitor handling the matter of the Pearls.'

'I mean about Edward and me?'

'What does that mean?'

So Edward had said nothing. 'Being at his home,' she replied, quickly covering what she'd meant.

'No,' he said, sighing, as if talking to a wayward child. 'I don't believe so.'

That was a relief. She didn't want Edward in danger too. She slotted the last of her change into the telephone. The money wouldn't last long. 'When did you get back to London?'

'I didn't leave.'

'I thought —'

'It was a ploy . . . And before you get angry, it was to protect you from panicking about something I wasn't sure of until the night you disappeared. My internal radar was stirring in Paris and I took the precaution of shadowing you just in case but in London I became suspicious we were being followed. I couldn't be sure by whom and needed to make certain I wasn't imagining it . . . because I cared about you so much.' He cleared his throat. 'So I pretended to leave. I wanted to see what he'd do. He'd even have seen me enter the railway station and buy a ticket if he'd bothered to follow me, but he is only interested in you. I'm presuming he thinks we're lovers and I'm no threat, especially if he can get you alone. I doubled back to keep you close . . . keep you safe.'

'Thank you.' What else could she say even if she did despise the fact that he had lied, that Daniel had followed her, had followed Edward, knew her every move? 'So where is Mayek?'

'Right now, I don't know.'

She gave a hiss as criticism, which he ignored.

'So we have to draw him out,' he continued.

'How?'

'With you.'

She swallowed. It felt powerful to talk about wanting to look him in the eye again, to defy him, to show him that she had survived and was now going to bring him down. That was certainly inspiring and motivating but talk was hollow; it suddenly felt like she'd eaten old snow, as though her belly were full of the grimy slush that gathered at the side of the road.

'Katerina? You do want this, right?'

She moistened her lips to be sure she could speak. She thought of Otto Schäfer's courage in the face of certain death; she thought of Mrs Biskup risking everything for her. And she found her own bravery from nearly two decades of hate and despair; it was within her reach now to challenge him again. 'I do. But you have to promise to give me some time to say something important to him.'

'What?'

'My business. It doesn't affect anyone else. But I must confront him, or my wounds will never heal.'

'Then stay brave and get back to London – are you within direct train distance?'

'Yes.'

'All right. Call me again in a few hours when you know what train you're on and I'll meet it.'

She put the receiver back and returned to Otto. He was already rugged up in his coat, holding hers.

'I've paid. I thought you might like some air, cold though it is.' She nodded and he helped her on with her coat. 'There's a hotel at the top.'

'The Victoria.'

'How about a slow walk up the hill and we can share a farewell pot of tea. The sea looks as stormy as you do . . . might be a good idea for us to start making tracks.'

They called out their thanks to the landlady and moved out into the narrow lane. Already the sea water was surging back in.

'They said in the pub that the water will be in here, at street level, in the next day or two,' he said. 'Hard to believe, eh?'

'I've seen it nearly hitting the steps in January.'

He raised an eyebrow and with a gentle hand on her elbow guided their path back up the incline of the narrow King Street and past the post office in a tall Georgian building of the same toffee-coloured stone she'd admired earlier. The cobbles felt slippery as they passed the Men's Institute on their left and the lights of the Dolphin pub halfway up were already glowing through its many panes of Georgian windows. They walked slowly, pausing at lookout points from tiny laneways of cottages. Time passed as Katerina showed Otto every inch that she could of this favourite holiday spot of hers. They deliberately did not mention Mayek, both presumably gathering their thoughts about him, about her dilemma, and the people around her who could be affected by his presence.

'Down there is Bow Cottage . . . dates back to the early 1600s. It probably has a smuggler's tunnel.'

He gave a sad grin. 'I must return some time.'

'We'll take you fossicking,' she jested.

Chimneys were smoking and she could hear people behind the

houses busy in their coal scuttles, shovelling up the fuel to take indoors.

'I like the smell of coal,' she remarked, trying to keep her mind away from where it wanted to track.

'It's surprisingly pleasant in a . . . well, in an industrial sort of way,' he said. 'As you know, we tend to burn wood in Europe, so this is a novelty. Seems to burn longer, brighter.'

'I prefer it. I stopped enjoying wood fires . . . I guess I can smell the forest too strongly in it.'

He nodded, and she knew he was all too aware of what she meant. 'Ah, nearly there,' he said, looking up to see the Gothic structure of the Victoria Hotel looming ahead.

'This is the worst bit, though,' she admitted and shortened her stride to haul herself up the steepest part.

'People must stay fit and healthy around here.'

'Apart from coaldust in the lungs,' she replied, just to keep talking about anything other than Mayek. It wouldn't last. She could feel the questions about to burst out of the doctor but he was too wise to pressure her too quickly.

The sprawling red-brick hulk of a building crouched atop the hill with sweeping panoramic views across the rocky beach. They arrived at its portico, breathing hard and uncomfortably warm given the pinch of cold at their cheeks. Katerina dragged off her scarf and unpinned her hair, convinced the low headache that was forming was because of how tightly she'd tied it back. She followed Otto into a corridor of busy tessellated tiles of black and tan, a mix of Grecian and geometric shapes that echoed their footsteps towards reception, which opened up to a soaring timber-clad ceiling. The accommodation was on two open levels with neat bannisters encasing them. She heard a door close distantly above.

A man looked up from behind the counter. 'Hello, folks. It's getting colder out there . . . and darker. Welcome to the Victoria.'

'Is your tearoom open or still closed until the start of summer?' Katerina enquired.

The person behind the desk smiled from beneath a series of blunderbuss rifles that were hung on the wall like trophies. Better than the dead animal they killed, Katerina thought, as the gentleman pointed to their right. 'Of course . . . these days we're always open. Just over there.'

They retreated from the steep staircase of dark mahogany that angled its way through the levels, lit by oddly medieval-styled electric wall sconces. She suspected the old hotel had seen better days. It could use a designer with a keen knowledge of Victorian seaside properties to lend their services and return the establishment to its heyday of catering to the new railway station that welcomed thousands of holiday-makers.

They found the tearoom deserted, save for an old couple who looked to be local and were preparing to leave. Starched tablecloths hung low over a mix of round and oblong tables. Otto led her across the scuffed and worn narrow floorboards towards one of the tables alongside the satin-papered walls of buttery cream. Tall sashed windows punctured the floral design of the wallpaper to let them glimpse the cliff dropping away sharply to the beach. A chandelier glimmered above the table he chose, as though they were the favoured guests. Katerina seated herself and gazed out past the reflection of the chandelier in the window onto the darkening scene as light failed over the dramatic curve of Robin Hood's Bay and the tide began its inexorable sweep back into shore. It looked desolate, mirroring how she was feeling since speaking with Daniel.

A waitress arrived. 'Welcome to the Victoria.'

'Er, thank you.' Otto beamed. 'I think just a pot of tea for two, please.'

'Any cakes?'

He glanced at Katerina and she shook her head. 'No, thank you.' After the waitress left, he remarked, 'Tell me what happened with Daniel.'

She told him as the light fell further around the bay and his expression darkened in tandem. Their pot of tea arrived and in traditional Yorkshire fashion it was – in her experience, anyway – hotter and stronger than the offerings of tearooms of the south. The steam from Otto's cup as he lifted it reached in soft curlicues towards him and she watched his mouth, hidden behind his moustache and beard, pucker to sip with care.

'Don't say I didn't warn you,' she said at his slight wince at the heat, doing her best to sound cavalier in spite of what she'd just explained.

'I'm worried.'

'Don't be. I have Daniel. He won't let anything happen.'

'Well, you must promise me that you will keep him at your side. Or I refuse to leave you and then you'll set up a world of new problems for me. However, I didn't do what I did twenty years ago only to allow you to walk straight back into the clutches of the devil again – knowingly.'

'I promise Daniel will be close.'

He continued on his mind's path. 'As Mossad, he's got unquestionable skills. He's also got hardened colleagues who can —'

'I know, Otto. He's told me.'

He nodded, indicating he'd said his piece. 'And Edward?'

She sighed, stirring her tea aimlessly. 'What about him?'

'Give him a chance.'

'I did.'

'Katerina. I mean, give a man a chance with you.'

She glared at him. 'I did.'

His expression simmered; old angers were being allowed to surface. 'Do you want to do this now?'

'No.'

'I think we should.' He spoke over her grimace and how she clattered the teaspoon into the saucer at the base of the cup. He reached for her hand, would not let her whip it away. 'I am not the man for you. I never was. You were still a child, although I know a new teenager rarely sees herself that way. I was everything you needed in that terrifying period – someone in a position to and prepared to keep you safe at all costs . . . Perhaps it was an error to look at you with affection, but —'

'I think you Germans don't really understand what affection is, Otto. You never laid a hand on me,' she accused him. 'Hardly affection.'

'That's because I resisted, Katerina. Many times I wanted to hug you, to make you feel comforted by a show of endearment, but I could tell it was dangerous to the emerging young woman whose feelings were far too vulnerable. You wore them so openly that I'd need to be a dullard not to recognise you were developing a fondness that was unhealthy and downright dangerous to me given our ages.' Now their eyes held each other to account. 'So I had to love you in the right way . . . from the appropriate distance and with a fatherly attitude. You were too young and inexperienced to even know how to handle the emotions you were coping with and you were injured, damaged, traumatised. A single touch from me could have given all the wrong signals to a frightened, impressionable teenager. But you're no longer that girl and it is surely time to let a man of the present into your orbit – not a dream of the past – who can give you a real life. What you have – even though you tell yourself it's enough – is not enough. You deserve to be loved, you deserve to be cherished as a woman, not only as a m—'

'Stop it,' she said, not much above a whispered whimper. 'Please, don't.'

He sighed. 'I love you, Katerina Kassowicz, as my dearest friend, as a daughter, as a woman I am so proud of. Never wonder about that . . . just not —'

'I know.'

He released her hand so she could find her handkerchief.

'I'm sorry to make you cry.'

She shook her head.

'I've wanted to say that year upon year but I dared not write it down . . . it would have come across harshly on paper.'

It did hurt to hear it but it resonated with all that she knew in her heart. 'These are old tears, I promise. I won't ever stop loving you, Otto, but I want you to feel safe that it's an old candle and the flame never goes out. It doesn't burn fiery . . . it just . . . you know, makes me feel safe . . . a comfy blanket. I'm sure every woman looks back fondly to her first crush of teenage years.'

He smiled sadly. 'But what you've surely done with that blanket in the meantime is tuck it so firmly around you as to not allow anyone to – how shall I say this?'

'Share my blanketed bed?' She dredged up a smile for him.

He gave a sad gust of brief amusement. 'My point is, Mayek took so much from you and you're in grave danger of allowing him to steal your potential future happiness . . . but only if you let him. There are good men – perhaps Edward Summerbee – who can show you a new life that doesn't let go of the old but embraces a fresh future.' He waited, clearly not wanting to lecture.

'I have no intention of letting Ruda Mayek have any more of me than he already has. His time of reckoning is here.'

She could see that Otto wanted to ask what she meant by that but she distracted him by suddenly gathering up her things.

'What time is your train? I'm presuming you came by rail into Robin Hood's Bay?'

'Didn't you?'

She shook her head. 'I drove up from York. I wanted to enjoy the moorland. But it's getting on, so we'd best be on our way.'

'Are you taking the train home this evening?'

'I'm booked for the first one tomorrow.' She checked in her purse. 'Yes, I leave at the ghastly time of seven in the morning. But it doesn't stop everywhere. I should be in London by around ten. And you?'

'Mine's at four. It's just a few minutes from here.'

'It's on my way and then you won't have to hurry. I could drive you to York, you know?'

'No, I want to connect through to Durham this evening.'

Otto wouldn't hear of her paying for the tea and as they left the hotel he handed her another palm-full of change. 'For when you call Daniel at York railway station as promised.' He covered her fingers over the money. 'Don't fail to do so.'

She nodded and pointed towards where the Morris Minor was parked.

'Why does such a tiny place have such an impressive train station?' he said just a minute or so later when they clambered out in front of the grand building.

She grinned and shrugged. 'I think it had a royal visitor back in its day . . . and this whole region in the previous century was incredibly popular with Victorian daytrippers and holiday-makers; they needed all this to cope with the new visitor traffic to Scarborough, Whitby, even here.' She glanced at her wristwatch. 'Come on. You've got just under ten minutes.'

They spotted the senior couple from the Victoria Hotel huddled in the waiting room; they had obviously made a day trip into the region.

'Let's go onto the platform,' Otto said.

They emerged into a new fresh breeze picking up. Katerina could taste the salt riding on it from the coast. It made her think of tears and how this may be the last time she saw Otto for the next score of years.

'Shall we try and not avoid each other, Otto? I promise you it's not dangerous to be in the same city . . . the same room as me.'

His forehead creased in thought, no doubt pleased that the difficult conversation they'd always avoided had now been shared and a firm line drawn, invisibly and yet as clear as the two of them standing there on the frigid platform. 'Why not? Maybe it's your turn to come to Salzburg? Bring Mr Summerbee.'

She gave him a sighing smile. 'Then invite me properly. I'd like to meet your family. I feel I know them, although Lili is a surprise.'

'Next summer. Come and meet everyone.'

She hugged him, long and hard, savouring it but realising something had changed. The awkward conversation had shifted the fragile balance and she suspected their correspondence would take a newer, hopefully easier tone. Deep down, though, she suspected she'd miss the tension of Otto's normally carefully chosen words, looking for the subtext, feeling like their letters were secrets.

'Will you definitely go to Durham?'

He nodded.

'I'm glad. Maybe we'll all come next year; Milena too! She may not love the beard either but for what it's worth, I do.'

He chuckled into his scarf. 'I won't shave it before you come. You're all welcome.' The distant scream of a train and the rails below sounding their metal vibration pierced their cosiness. 'Well, I need to know what's happening, so I'm going to insist you not only call Daniel but you call me too. I shall be home by the day after tomorrow. Will you do that?'

His question was lost momentarily, engulfed by the steam that billowed around them as the train drew in with all of its noisy bluster, bringing with it the smell of coal, iron and an industrial age that was fast disappearing.

'These won't last,' he said, admiring the huge engine dragging squealing carriages.

She shook her head. 'There's talk of rationalisation. I doubt this line will survive it. Look, there's only three of you getting on and the train is already empty.'

'Pity,' he replied. 'But then sometimes letting go of the past is for the best,' he added, looking deep into her face.

She saw the grey in his beard; he was superbly handsome but he was moving into his seventh decade. Yes, it was the right moment for her to let her childish crush go. 'I hear you, Otto,' she said.

He pulled her close and was still tall enough to kiss the top of her head but then he kissed both of her cheeks gently. 'You make me very proud.'

Her eyes misted again as he turned away to board, wrenching open the heavy door. She waited until he found a seat, removed his hat and coat and reappeared at the door to let down the window.

'Katerina, I'm not sure why you brought me here. I'm glad that you did, but I can't tell if I've been any help to you.'

She reached up to hold his hand and held it close to her cheek. 'Just seeing you has reassured me, made me feel strong again.'

'Promise me you'll stay safe.'

She nodded. 'I promise.'

'Don't let Mayek get anywhere close to you,' he warned.

'I'm going to take his power away, Otto.'

He frowned, looking suddenly frightened. 'What do you mean?'

'No more running. I think I know how to finish him.'

The guard blew his whistle and it was too late for Otto to do much more than stare at her with terrified regret.

'Katerina!' The train wheels turned, metal screeching against metal. A billow of steam blew back as the iron serpent rolled forward.

'I'll phone you when it's done!' she cried into the noise and the vapours.

Calling him had been an uncharacteristic and panicked reaction to being stonewalled. If she'd given herself a day, she might have reached this same decision and dear Otto would not have needed to make a mercy dash. And yet perhaps it was because of him; the emotion of seeing him, having his balanced view, just clearing her head with a Yorkshire gale, maybe, had given her clarity . . . given her direction.

She would explain to him when it was over that he had made a difference by coming, but for now she watched with guilt as Otto was drawn away unhappily and she waited until the final carriage disappeared from sight.

Yes. She knew now exactly what she was going to do.

28

⦾ ⦾ ⦾

HAMPSTEAD

While Katerina was navigating a rocky beach in England's north, Edward Summerbee was walking from Hampstead Station towards a grocery store that he hoped still existed at the address he had been given. Relief and excitement trilled through him as he stepped into the corner shop. The bell jangled above him and the floorboards sighed an aged creak as he stepped aside to hold the door for an older woman bustling out with a leather trolley rolling on a slightly wonky wheel behind her.

'May I help you with that?'

'Thank you, young man,' she said, not noticing his chuffed grin, and allowed him to pick up the trolley and place it on the pavement for her. 'You look a bit posh to be from around here.'

'Just down from the city for a few hours . . . er, visiting my aunty,' he lied and then instantly regretted it to see her frown forming the next inevitable query about who that might be. He lifted his hat – 'Good afternoon, madam' – and hastened into the shop.

It was a reassuringly old-fashioned sort of store, just a few shelves in the centre with tins and bottles of products, but mostly people were browsing to kill time while waiting to be served at the counter for everything from cheese to flour. Hampstead was not yet consumed by the novelty of supermarket fever that was overtaking the south; he was no fan, preferring to step onto the sawdust and taste the metallic smell of a butcher's shop to have the aproned man behind the counter talk him through the best cuts. Every now and then he liked to shop for food with the same pleasure he shopped for clothes or a new umbrella. He loved the toasty, comforting smell of a bakery with its blocks of burnished 'high tins' or feeling smug at walking back out, having resisted the urge to buy a glossy strawberry jam tart. His favourite, though, was the local coffee shop that roasted its beans daily in small batches and ground them for customers. The fragrance could instantly lift his mood. And he could smell it now, above the slightly sour tang of wheels of cheese and the sugary promise of biscuits in tins waiting to be lifted off their greaseproof paper and into brown paper bags. His belly rumbled; buttered toast and thickly cut marmalade – not his first choice – from early this morning would not keep him going all day. This reminded him he had run out of Marmite and so he stepped into one of the two aisles and hunted down a jar. Good. That gave him an excuse for arriving at the counter.

'Yes, sir?' the woman said, wiping her hands on her apron. 'Sorry for the wait. What can I get you?'

'Er, just this, please,' he said, placing the squat jar of yeast extract on the counter. She looked surprised and he privately admitted it was an odd purchase for a man in a three-piece suit who looked like he belonged in the city. 'Did you know the originators of this product in Staffordshire believe it helped win both world wars because it was mandatory in rations?'

The woman chuckled and his appearance was forgotten. 'My son assures me it is named after a French casserole, which is very strange, don't you think?'

His turn to grin. 'Hence the shape of the bottle – an attempt at an earthenware casserole, perhaps? Even more intriguing is the discovery that it was invented – quite by accident – by a German scientist in the previous century.'

'I'm sure most British don't know that!' she said, ringing up the pennies on her till.

He found a sixpence in his coins and handed it to her.

'And your change,' she said, handing him back heavy, silken coppers that spoke of constant handling. 'Shall I put this in a small bag?'

'Thank you. Er . . . do you mind if I ask if you're Helen Evans?'

She blinked. 'I am, yes.'

The shop was now mercifully quiet. Her husband strolled over. 'I'm John Evans, the owner.'

Edward held out a hand in greeting. 'Mr and Mrs Evans, my name is Edward Summerbee. I'm a solicitor and I've travelled up from London today on a mission – a mercy mission, you could say.' It was suddenly a lot more difficult to face these people than he had anticipated and he found himself clearing his throat, half from embarrassment and the other part of him cautioning that what he was about to do might cause them suffering.

'Oh, yes? How can we help?'

He took a breath. Damned either way. He decided in that heartbeat that he would never live with the regret of not trying to find Katerina's brother. The boy had a right to know his living family, surely?

He gave a tight smile. 'Er, this is awkward, please forgive me. It's not my intention to cause any disruption to your lives but information you could give me might change the life of a friend of mine for the better.'

They both frowned, casting a worried glance at each other.

'What's this all about?' Helen Evans said. 'You're making me anxious.'

He shook his head and raised a palm to appease her. 'No, please don't fret. My friend is a war refugee.'

'Oh, yes?' John Evans said. He looked interested but no less troubled.

Edward pressed on. 'Her name is Katerina Kassowicz.' They waited. The Evans couple were patient – he'd give them that – but he'd better hurry or risk being asked to move on as new customers arrived. 'She believes all of her family – that includes four siblings – were killed during the occupation of Czechoslovakia.' Now the Evans exchanged a fresh look of distress; they were beginning to guess what might be coming. He hurried on. 'She has no idea that her brother survived and that he was sent on one of the *Kindertransports* to London. I believe that your son is —'

The bell jangled its interruption behind him and he wanted to yell for the customer to leave and just let him finish.

Helen Evans's worried expression relaxed. 'It's Summerbee, isn't it?'

He nodded.

'Mr Summerbee, I'm sorry that your friend is alone in the world but I can save you a lot of trouble. Henry – that's our boy – did come from Czechoslovakia, but he doesn't have a name even remotely like your lady friend's.'

'Nevertheless, his name when he arrived into your care was Hersh Adler, right?'

The woman blanched and her lips thinned with distress.

'Now, look here,' her husband began.

Edward gave them no more time to interrupt. 'I can tell you the date he arrived. I can even tell you the colour of the blanket he was wrapped in. I can certainly give you the name of the two people who delivered Hersh to you here in Hampstead. And I can assure you, his name is not Hersh Adler. It's Petr Kassowicz.'

'How dare you barge in here and make accusations!' Helen Evans said, hysteria creeping into her voice.

Her husband squeezed her arm to calm her. 'Be right with you, Mrs Shephard,' he said tightly towards the canned food.

'No hurry, darlin',' she called from behind the aisles, no doubt eavesdropping, Edward thought.

'Please leave now,' John Evans murmured in a strangled whisper.

'Please, this is not an accusation. It's the truth. May I just speak with your son?'

'No, you can't! They've had years. We've raised him since he was not much more than a baby. He's my son. He doesn't need to know about his family. Someone told us that if we hadn't heard by a decade after the war, they were likely dead. Now I feel badly for those folk, really I do. But while he may not be our flesh and blood, he's our child in every other way. Don't you bring all this trouble into his life.' Mrs Evans was pointing a finger at him. 'My husband asked you to leave.'

There was no point in lingering. He raised his hat to them. 'I'm sorry for the distress but I do have to speak with your son. He's over twenty-one and has a right to know, as indeed his sister needs to know he survived.'

'Get out!' Helen Evans had lost her manners and Edward knew it was best to retreat.

'My sincere apologies.' He hurried towards the door.

The jangling of the bell behind him echoed how his nerves suddenly felt. A couple of children about nine years old, he reckoned, skidded to a halt on bikes.

'Penny for the guy, mister?' one of them asked, nodding his head towards a sad pile of clothes to the right of the shop, near some bushes. They'd stuffed arms and legs to achieve a poor semblance of a figure and his face was depicted with a vivid green mask, the colour of shamrock. The familiar masks could be purchased in red or green for a ha'penny in most corner shops.

'You're joking, aren't you, lads? We're still in April – you're seven months ahead.'

'We just want to get ahead of our competition, mister.' One of them grinned mischievously.

He found a penny and tossed it into the tweed cap on the ground next to the slumped dummy of Guy Fawkes. 'Boys, do either of you know a Hersh Adler?'

They shook their heads. 'Nope.'

'He works here. His parents own the shop,' he pressed.

'D' you mean Henry?'

'Er, yes, I do.'

'Henry said he'd help us choose the best fireworks in November.'

'Did he? Good. Where can I find Henry?'

'He's a lifesaver. He works up at the Ponds,' one of the boys continued, flicking a thumb in no real direction.

'The Ponds?'

The door opened and John Evans loomed. 'Go on home, boys. I don't want to see that wretched Guy Fawkes outside this grocer's until next November, do you hear?'

They mumbled they had.

'Still here, Mr Summerbee?'

'Just leaving,' he said. He walked on up the hill, wondering how to find out what the boys had meant, when he saw a familiar figure struggling up ahead. He hurried to catch up. 'I had no idea you were going to drag your trolley so far. Do you need help?'

'You again, eh? Are you following me?'

He laughed. 'I'm not. My name is Edward Summerbee and I'm lost, actually.'

'On the way to your aunty's? Well, that shows how often you don't visit, eh?'

She'd trapped him so he changed tack like any good solicitor. 'Are you sure I can't help?'

'Quite sure, young man. I do this walk each day – good for me, the doctor says.'

'I'm too early for my aunt. I'm looking for somewhere called the Ponds . . . would you know what that —'

'The Swimming Ponds?' She pointed. 'Follow your nose. Who's your aunty, then?'

'Thank you.'

'Go on with you,' she said. 'Stop pestering me. Take her some flowers.'

He lifted his hat with a polite grin and set off. Right enough, he soon emerged onto the Heath and felt rewarded by the sprawl of countryside and copses that breathed for London on the doorstep of the metropolis. Within moments the air felt cleaner and Edward found a fresh bounce in his tread. He'd been too long in the city without a break. When all of this was done, he was going to plan a few days away – striding the moors in the north, perhaps?

He could see the first of the lakes – one person braving the depths. He recalled now reading about the swimming ponds that were said to be fed by iron-rich springs and good for the health.

It was astonishing that anyone would want to glide around in the dark waters while he was rugged up against the cold. A sign pointed him to the mixed ponds and he opted to head that way, skirting the leafy lane down which was a secluded lake for the use of female pond swimmers only. He doubted he'd find a young male lifeguard there.

He arrived at the mixed pond, which had, by his count, six swimmers doing slow laps. He spotted two lifeguards and made his approach; neither of them looked young enough to be the man he sought and he felt his belly dip with disappointment.

'Will Henry Evans be around today?' he asked one.

'He already is. Over there,' one of the guards said, and Edward's attention snapped around in the direction in which he was pointing to a man in a lifeguard's uniform crouched talking to a swimmer, whom Edward could now see was a young woman in a bathing cap. 'Are you swimming today, sir?'

'Er, no. I have a message to pass on to Henry Evans from a family member, if that's all right?' Stick to the truth, he decided.

The man shrugged. 'It's a free country. But he's known as Hersh around here; prefers it. But it's good you've come – you can drag him away from that girl he's all moony about before her brothers and uncles do it for him.' He swept a hand across the scene. 'These are the men in her family, keeping an eye on her.'

Edward couldn't be more confused . . . so not Henry. He raised a hand in a greeting: 'Hersh?' The fellow heard and turned his way. He watched the young man say something to the girl before he straightened. She swam away from the bank towards the other side. 'Hersh Adler?' Edward asked again.

'That's me,' he said, approaching, and Edward was struck by the unnerving gangly similarity to Katerina, in spite of his darker hair and features; he had a similar loose-limbed, angular quality. *Or am I imagining it?* Edward wondered.

But as the man called Hersh Adler, who was also known as Henry Evans, drew close, Edward could sense his pulse accelerating. He could feel the normally silent, suddenly thunderous sound of his blood rushing beneath his ears, as though the gate of a weir had been opened. A moment of dizziness left him with a rising sense of euphoria. There was no mistaking this man; instantly all his doubt about himself and his decision was washed away, like detritus down a street drain in a big downpour. His conscience was clear; he had stuck to the law, not broken any of his code, but he had something far better – surely? – to give Katerina now. He knew he had found Petr Kassowicz because it was written in the man's features: the cat's eye! The mark of the Kassowiczs was on him. The secret behind the supposed death of Petr and his equally secret escape from the Nazis was yet to be explained – might never be – but now all Edward cared about was bringing the two survivors of this tragic family back together.

'You go by the name of Hersh Adler?'

The strange-eyed man regarded him with understandable suspicion. 'And Henry Evans when I'm not at the Ponds.'

Not secretive, then. 'So I gather from your parents.'

The young man frowned in consternation.

'Is it because you're unsure of which best suits you . . . or perhaps feels like you?' Edward wondered.

'Amongst other reasons. Who are you, please?'

Edward kept it brief but explained he was a London solicitor trying to help a friend, a Jewish survivor. 'Would you care to join me on that bench?'

'So you're a solicitor. Why do I matter to a friend of yours?'

'Because I think in helping me to help her, you might also solve a puzzle of your own.'

'How so?'

'Because I can tell you your real name and what happened to your family in Prague.'

───────────

The grocer's boy, yet to learn that he was the son of a much-admired European glass manufacturer and art collector, stared at the solicitor as though he had just walked up and told him he was from a planet called Mars.

'What are you talking about?'

'I think you know what I'm referring to but I can understand this is a shock. I'm sorry that I couldn't give you more warning of my visit. It's unfair but life hasn't been fair to your Czech family, and finding you could right the balance.' Edward hated how bitter he sounded. He just desperately wanted the discovery of Petr Kassowicz to make a difference, and for the boy's sister to regard him with anything but that cool loathing in the expression she'd left him with.

'Let me think about it first.' The youngster looked shocked but spoke to Edward in a tone that landed on Edward to make him feel like a travelling salesman offering cut-price curtains or furniture on hire purchase.

'Young man, please understand. I know who your family is. I can connect you to the people you have probably spent a lifetime wondering about.' He wasn't ready for the tall youngster to suddenly bend as if doubling up in pain.

Edward was at his side. 'Henry . . . Hersh . . .' He swallowed. Damn it, say it. 'Petr?'

A low sob escaped from Katerina's brother. 'Please be real; don't lie to me.'

It was heartbreaking to hear the pain in his voice. 'This is no lie. You have living family.'

Later, when they'd excused themselves from the worried onlookers, he sat next to Petr on one of the Heath's benches. He noted it had been donated by a family with a surname as whimsical as his own: Cinnamon. It was even in memory of a man called Edward. He smiled to himself but regarded the 24-year-old who was now slumped over, holding his head.

Since that single sob he'd made no sound as Edward had shared all that he knew, how he'd found the truth of that snap decision in 1939 as Petr's father had handed him over to be carried under a different name and how the woman who had taken him from his father had never forgotten.

There were tears but they were slow and silent; not many but enough to hint that a life shift was occurring within the fellow formerly known as Hersh.

'I don't know why your siblings were told you'd died but there would have been a reason that was justified in the minds of your parents, I'm sure. Perhaps Katerina might be able to offer up some thoughts on that when you meet.'

Edward paused for the boy to speak, waited while he dragged the back of his hand across his cheeks.

'I've been coming here most days of my teenage years in the hope of finding a connection to my birth family. I almost gave up hope but thought to myself I'd give it one more summer.'

Edward smiled. 'Sounds like our meeting was meant to be.'

His voice carried wonder. 'I have a sister,' he said, finally straightening. He sounded awed.

'You had four of them. I doubt Katerina is ever going to let you go once she hugs you. She's a beautiful woman and you both look alike.'

Petr grinned self-consciously. 'How did she survive? You haven't told me anything about how she escaped death or the clutches of the enemy.'

'It won't be an easy story for her to tell, or for you to hear, but let it come from her lips. It's her tale and it's traumatic and courageous and only she knows what your household was like without you in it. Your mother . . . well, Katerina can explain all of this.' He sighed. 'What about your parents – John and Helen? How will they feel about you learning about your past? I feel badly going behind their backs when they expressly warned me against it. However, you're an adult and you deserve to know the truth of your family and Katerina deserves to enjoy a relationship with you. The *Kindertransports* were not designed to separate you all for good – simply to keep the young safe – and the hope was always to reunite the families.'

'Mum's frightened she'll lose me. Dad wants me to take over the shop, maybe turn it into one of those new supermarkets and get on with my life as *their* son. I can't blame them. They just want me to be happy, normal, married, living close by . . .'

'Perfectly understandable. Your parents will find it difficult not to like her, you know. Besides, she's like an older, female version of you – there's no denying the family resemblance. Tell them what you've learned. They won't be delighted initially because it means change is coming to your life – to their lives too – but it's good change. I guess you'll have to decide what you want to be called now that you know your real name.'

'I like Petr more than Hersh . . . or Henry.'

'Well, take your time. And don't rush your parents. Their fear is because they love you.' He gave the boy his card. 'Here's how to reach me . . . any time, don't hesitate.'

He nodded. 'When can I meet my sister?'

Edward paused. 'When I find her,' he confessed.

29

Katerina rang Daniel again. Now there need be no guilt; she'd kept her promise.

She wasted no time on pleasantries. 'Answer me this: can we find him again using me as bait?'

'Surely we can.'

'Where would we do this?'

Daniel didn't hesitate. 'Your London flat.'

She hadn't expected that. Somewhere so personal – intimate, even. She'd anticipated a hotel lobby, a restaurant, maybe, even an outdoor café in one of the city's parks. 'Why?' Her voice sounded leaden and she'd wanted to come across with more verve.

'It's quiet. Contained. Top floor. It has a fire escape. What's more, it's familiar territory to you, not to him, so that puts you in a position of power. It has a side alley that backs onto the garden. The people in that bottom flat are presently away.'

'How can you know this?' She couldn't help her astonishment.

'Katerina,' he began with a tone of injury.

'Don't bother,' she said, waving away whatever he was about to say. 'Why is the side alley or fire escape relevant, anyway?'

Now he just didn't reply.

'Best I don't ask that question either, I'm gathering.'

'My guess is that Mayek intends to come to you, anyway. He thinks he's in control so while he will plan carefully, he's not feeling particularly vulnerable at this stage.'

His logic was solid. 'Bloomsbury, then. Do you know if he's still spying on me?'

'He's not outside the flat, but I suspect that's because you haven't been there.' Daniel didn't mask the accusation in his tone. 'Our presumption is that when you return, so will he.'

'Then he's obviously being more watchful than you give him credit for if he can respond that swiftly. Be warned, the man I knew was horribly cunning. It amuses him to watch suffering.'

'Thank you for the warning. Where exactly have you been?'

'In Yorkshire. Daniel, I want to be alone with him.'

'Yorkshire . . . must be freezing.'

'Daniel!'

'I know what you desire and you will be alone with him, initially. But we shall only be moments behind.'

A worrying thought arrived. 'Do you think he carries a gun?'

'No. My men have already bumped into him to check.' Katerina gave a sound of disbelief. 'We're thorough.'

'All right, but he *has* pointed a gun at me in the past . . . and fired it to kill.' She let that reminder sit for a couple of heartbeats. 'So if he threatens me with a knife, then you'll what – rush him?'

Now the spy chuckled at her attempt at jargon. 'Something like that.'

Katerina bristled. 'Daniel, he's coming to do me harm, isn't he?'

'He is. But I suspect he'll attempt something . . .' He thought about it and settled for an odd word. 'Elegant.'

'What does that mean?' She inserted more coins into the telephone.

'He can't risk screaming, a scene, any sort of noise that might attract attention.'

'So he'll strangle me?'

Daniel cleared his throat. 'He may attempt to,' he qualified, adding, 'skin on skin.'

She wished he hadn't.

Staring at the chipped paint of the red telephone box she was shivering in, she tried not to succumb to feeling momentarily dizzy at the thought of Ruda Mayek's hands on her again.

'But I will not allow him to get that close to hurt you again.'

'He couldn't hurt me any more if he tried. To be truthful, I'm more fearful of not confronting him. It will set me free to look upon him again and show my contempt.'

'And killing him?'

'I will, but not in the way you presume.'

She could picture his sigh of relief although she didn't hear it. He was ever the professional. 'You have nothing but my admiration for your courage. Realise this, though. You're remembering a big, hale, younger man. The Mayek I've seen is not well. He's weakened by whatever illness is attacking him. But listen to me, Katerina. When I tell you to leave, you do just that – not a second longer. Whatever you have to say to him, you must get it out of your system and then you are going to leave that flat in Bloomsbury and not look back. No ifs, no buts, no questions or demands of me or my men. Once you turn your back on Mayek, he is our prisoner to deal with. Agreed?'

'Agreed.'

'Good. What time am I meeting your train?'

The train had left York and soon she would be back in London. That was the sum of her present: not twenty years of compressed anxiety but now just under three hours in which to make what were arguably the most critical decisions of her life. The solitude of another empty carriage would give her the space she needed to sort through her crowded thoughts, which were queuing impatiently to be heard, like a line of picketing workers. Placards in her mind stood out: trapping Mayek, having time to confront him, keeping the people she loved safe. And there was a fourth that seemed to be picked out in flashing neon lighting. A single word. *Edward*. It felt wrong that this thought seemed to be demanding – and achieving – equal weight in a mind already burdened with pressing problems. But there it was and she had been denying it since it had arrived.

As angry as he had made her, she wanted to see him again . . . not just again but often; perhaps always. She could see now that he wasn't the root of the anger; it was the law that was protecting Mayek, not Edward. Getting him to break the law would have only corroborated what she had already known in her heart, her gut, her soul – that Ruda Mayek was roaming her life again. And now Daniel had confirmed it. Edward's knowledge was not an obstacle to Mayek but a gateway . . . perhaps . . . to a different life.

So now the loudest of the dissenters – an image of Ruda Mayek – stepped firmly in front of the others, although it was Daniel's voice she heard in her mind:

Do you remember how much you hated him in that forest? Touch that memory now! Remember how if you could have reached one of those guns you'd not have hesitated to pull the trigger on him? Remember how you thought of nothing but delivering a violent death to him when you were so young – still yet to be kissed, and he took that from you? He thieved your most precious of properties . . . your purity that was yours alone to give . . . and not just that but your innocence of life. And then he stole still more that was yours – all those lives that belonged and were golden to you.

She closed her fists in her lap, glad she still wore her gloves, and focused on her breathing, slowing it down. Katerina let the voice speak again.

Finally, he took your heritage, claimed it as his; perhaps his wife wore it for him . . . perhaps it became a gift for a cherished daughter, the wife of a beloved son?

There was no mirth in the slow smile that stole across her as the idea bloomed. Was she really going to do this? Would she panic at the moment of confrontation?

The notion of how to hurt Mayek had begun to circle in her mind when Otto had defended Edward. 'Would you give up your most precious secret?' Otto had demanded. The notion had stirred, then coagulated and firmed over the afternoon. Slow and evil, it came together, feeling to her like the time Ruda had showed her what viper venom could do to blood. She'd never been scared of snakes in the forest; she'd seen them time and again and known them to be timid rather than aggressive. But Rudy's demonstration had frightened her as a child; the image of the blood losing its scarlet viscosity to become lumpish and purple had never lost its chilling effect.

That's how it felt now as her dark idea clotted and darkened but she'd need to be fearless when the moment came and the real serpent was there to test her. And that sense of purpose had given her the courage to lie to her friend.

'What time am I meeting your train?' Daniel had asked.

'I've decided to come back tomorrow morning,' she'd said, not even blinking as the fib slipped out.

'I thought —'

'I know. But I think I'll spend today in York. I'm quite tired, actually, Daniel. I'll stay overnight and catch the first train in the morning.'

'But I can hear that you're calling me from a railway station.'

Damn him! 'I've taken the precaution of buying the ticket today, so there's no queuing or running late tomorrow.' Though her excuse was lame, she sounded confident and then added a yawn. 'Excuse me. I'm weary. I've been driving long distances, doing a lot of walking and thinking on the moors. It wears one out if you're not used to it.'

'So the morning train gets in at 10:38,' he said. 'I've got a printed timetable.'

'Well, that's the one I shall be on,' she lied, refusing to feel guilty that it was today's first train she was about to board.

'I'll see you then. Be safe, Katerina.'

As frightened as she was, she was going to do this alone; most would call her a lunatic but she needed time with Mayek – not long, just enough that no one else would be privy to their conversation. She didn't trust Daniel to let her have that privacy; everyone was so understandably worried about Mayek not getting within an inch of her that she would likely never have the opportunity to do what she now felt was essential if she was ever to break the spell he had over her.

Katerina knew it was being bull-headed; she accepted the danger and the terrifying reality that she may not come out of this confrontation unscathed – or even alive – and still her moment with him felt more important.

So she'd let Daniel think she was going along with his plan, but she was using their conversations to discover everything he knew about Mayek. Now she'd learned he was frail and that he likely wouldn't use an obvious weapon. So she needed to be fast on her feet – no heels, then – and to keep her distance, despite the flat being small. Leave doors and windows open so he would be scared of any noise, maybe have water freshly boiled, a kitchen knife hidden, something heavy in case she needed to defend herself and bludgeon some pain his way. Her intention was to confront him and then run for it. Daniel and his henchmen could hunt Mayek freely then and do whatever they wanted with him.

She allowed her loose idea to roll around in her mind, and as the steam train gathered momentum, so did her plan.

She was going to return to her flat and look busy, as though packing it up to leave London. That activity, she hoped, would speed his action; give him a deadline to confront her. She was avoiding the obvious: that he likely meant to finish what he'd begun in the forest. He planned to murder her.

The first-class carriage became suddenly claustrophobic, like a coffin might feel if you'd been buried alive . . . like when you were the only soul still breathing but you were buried beneath the earth anyway.

She leant in against the fear, felt it as a heavy load . . . like a car she was helping to push, and the satisfaction of feeling the wheels beginning to move.

By the time the train slowed its way into King's Cross, she no longer permitted herself to worry about how she would get away from his clutches; maybe she wouldn't. Maybe this was the end of her journey. But she hoped she would be looking upon a man so ruined by what she had to share that she would be able to leave him behind to his own trauma. And then Daniel and his spies could have him – and if she lived through this, she would never think about Ruda Mayek again.

―――――

The phone buzzed on his desk. 'Yes?'

'It's a Mr Daniel Horowitz, sir. I'm sorry to interrupt but he says it's urgent.'

'That's all right, Miss Bailey. Put him through,' Edward said. He waited for the inevitable click. 'Daniel, what news?'

'I've spoken with her.'

It annoyed him in that heartbeat at how excited he felt to hear that she'd been found, and he found himself lost in thoughts of her.

'Did you hear what I said, Edward?'

'Yes . . . yes, sorry, I'm very pleased to hear it,' he said. 'And I've found Petr.'

'Peter?'

'Petr Kassowicz – her brother.'

'You're joking!'

He liked that he'd shocked the spy. 'No jest. I met him yesterday at Hampstead, where he lives with his foster parents. Apparently, Samuel Kassowicz got him out on the *Kindertransport* in 1939, but he's never known his true name . . . until now.'

'Bloody hell!'

'Indeed. Anyway, time enough for all that. Tell me where you found her.'

'She found me. Telephoned me a few minutes ago. She's been in Yorkshire, as you'd guessed.' He explained what Katerina had shared.

'So she met the good doctor. How did she sound?'

'Committed.'

'What does that mean?'

It was Daniel's turn to explain.

'Wriggling bait on a hook?' Edward spluttered.

'More like an irresistible lure that is full of cunning and ready to trap our prey.'

Edward stood, stabbing the air with a crooked finger. 'Over my dead body,' he said. 'No.'

'It's her idea.'

'Horowitz, this is the man who raped her and slaughtered her family in front of her . . .'

'I'm more than aware of his sadistic tendencies,' came the calm reply.

'And still you'd tie her up like a goat for slaughter and invite him to dinner.'

'He will never get the chance to touch her, Edward. I will make him have to kill me before he can get close enough to Katerina to do anything to her.'

Tension was like a kite flying around them now, caught in the updraught of the heated conversation.

'Where is she now, for heaven's sake?'

'Still in York. She'll take the train down tomorrow and I'll meet that train and shadow her every move. Listen to me, Summerbee. I don't think we should even pretend to understand what is motivating Katerina right now. She is going to do this with or without help – but at least this way I can throw a ring of protection around her. Let me tell you what she wants to do.' Daniel explained the plan.

Edward frowned. 'Is anybody at her flat now? Watching, I mean?'

'No, but there will be by the time Katerina arrives.'

'And where will you be?'

'I can't risk him recognising me as he's seen me in her company, so I will approach over backyards if I have to and use the fire escape, enter her floor, and then I'll go up onto the landing that accesses the loft of the house. He won't know I'm there but I'll know he is. I will have three other men watching and they'll come up to the flat too, seconds after he enters her building.'

As Edward took a breath to ask a question, Daniel pressed on doggedly. 'I shall have Katerina arrive by taxi, or maybe even on foot from the direction of the museum to remain plausible. I'll brief her not to look around or to act suspicious of anyone; just to be lost in her thoughts as she normally appears. I imagine he'll knock at the door . . . and we'll encourage her to play along, not to make him in any way wary that she might be expecting him. In fact, I'll suggest she act terrified or resigned – he'd enjoy either. All she has to do is stay out of his reach for thirty seconds.'

'You make it sound simple.'

'It never is. But if we keep the situation as predictable as possible, my men know what they're doing; as I said, she wants time alone with him but I don't trust him within arm's reach of her – she can speak to him when he's trussed up and I feel she's safe.'

'You lied to her?'

'For her safety. She'll still have her time with him but I have to know she's safe and out of reach within moments of his arrival.'

'So I have to trust you even though you lied to her?'

'Yes.'

'What should I be doing?'

'Sit tight and by the phone. I'll have someone ring you the moment she's safely out of the flat.'

'How about you have Katerina ring me?' Edward said. 'Then I can breathe easier.'

'That's a promise. I will be picking her up at King's Cross just after ten tomorrow morning. I can't tell you when this is all going to happen. It could be in the afternoon, through the night, the next day or in the next few days.'

'Right,' he said, frowning. 'Yes, I suppose he's hardly following our agenda.'

'He may want to watch her for a few days. Katerina might have to be patient and we can't have you in the frame. Stay accessible. Home or office – we'll reach you.'

30

Katerina had taken the Underground to Oxford Circus. She would walk the rest of the way to the flat in Bloomsbury because she wasn't in the mood to run into any of her colleagues from the British Museum and needed to pick her streets to zigzag there. Of course, it would have been easier to go straight to Tottenham Court Road or Holborn but the risk of being spotted was real. There would be too much explaining to do, although her guilt over leaving her friend Catherine without a word added to what felt like a tangle of worms in her belly. She would make it up to her as soon as this was done. Go for dinner, maybe make up a foursome with Edward and Daniel; oh, it was pleasant to daydream like this. What was she thinking! *Focus, Katerina . . . you could be walking into a trap.* And still she pressed on, feeling she had no choice now but to see this plan through to its conclusion – whatever that was to be.

She emerged from the Underground into the busiest tube exit in London. Soon massive works would begin in the summer for the new Victoria line that people were talking about. The notion of connecting Brixton in the south with Walthamstow in the north-east via the West End was exciting; it would run for its entirety below the surface of London. But for now the congestion would continue on the Piccadilly line and around Charing Cross in particular. A few weeks ago the chatter around the museum, the newspaper articles, even the posters in the Underground warning travellers of the city works had been academic to her, but as of this morning it mattered. Since her visit to York she'd made another decision: to make Britain her home again and for keeps. The realisation hit her mind as though she'd just taken a big sip of an icy drink, causing a momentary brain freeze.

She noticed the crush of women in the main street as they went about their shopping, pouring out of offices to navigate the crazily busy intersection of Oxford Circus. Katerina turned towards the nearby tobacconist, which curiously had only one person at its counter; she stepped up and as she waited for the customer in front to pay, she noted a few men in overcoats dodging their way through the clamour of hats and headscarves to join the queue behind her for their cigarettes. She'd chosen the Argyll Street exit beneath Western House and J Leon & Co was the tiny kiosk that wrapped itself around the corner.

'Polo mints, please,' she said, pointing towards the peppermints she figured might help if the nausea of fear returned. She'd suck mints all the way to Bloomsbury.

'Tuppence, please,' the man said.

She handed over a couple of pennies and took the foil roll of mint sweets with the green and blue wrapper that she favoured; she'd learned during her time in London that there was something about the hole in the middle that made them easier to melt silently in the museum. Katerina regularly took the unspoken British challenge of being able to suck the Polo without breaking it. It was an unimportant yet prideful pleasure to feel it disappear on the tongue. Katerina pulled at the foil and eased out one of the small round mints. She slipped it into her mouth and tossed the packet into her handbag. She'd decided her aim for the next hour was to buy some clothes. She felt she needed to arrive at her flat as if it were from a day at work at the museum.

As people pushed past she wondered if she could be bothered to walk halfway to Marble Arch for Selfridges when John Lewis was so much closer. *Make the effort!*

Katerina moved across Oxford Street with the stream of pedestrians and dodged her way down the broad street to the massive edifice that was the American-designed grand department store of Selfridges. Every inch of it she recognised as the Beaux-Arts style and, she noted, not without a strong influence from the British Museum's renovations of a few years earlier. The store had opened in 1909 with soaring Ionic columns creating a similar classical frontispiece but with a vast walk of huge display windows that she enjoyed peering into. Only Harrods was a larger store in Britain. She mused that she'd heard somewhere that the US Army had used the basement of Selfridges for its secure signal corps during the war – safe from bombing and close to the American embassy.

On the ground floor she purchased a few items, wishing that the Mary Quant range of cosmetics were already available. Without doubt her favourite London designer was Quant and the style that had won this year's 'Dress of the Year' was already on Katerina's wish list; it struck her that it might even be in the store by now. She went in search of the slim, mannish pinafore design of grey wool softened by a cream chiffon blouse with a pussy bow. To her astonishment the staff in ladies' wear were delighted to tell her that the outfit had arrived only that morning on the mannequin. They cooed that she was the first customer to try it and Katerina knew immediately that it would not only fit but she was in love with it. Changing into the outfit helped to keep her distracted, as did hunting for the black boots she wanted to team it with: calf-high with heels, as Quant had intended.

Inside the change rooms she pulled out the few items of make-up she'd purchased earlier and worked quickly to dab on some light foundation and a bare dust of powder and then smeared the lipstick with care as rouge before a careful, single sweep to her mouth. She rolled her lips together, making a soft smacking sound as she pulled them apart for a matte finish. Perfect. Now the eyes: fractionally bloodshot from stress, maybe. Oh, well, it all added to her tale; she would tell Mayek that she'd been staying over at a friend's place – a male friend. She wanted him to think her life was full, flourishing, romantic. That was assuming, of course, that Mayek turned up today, she thought. It could be days of pretence in the flat, she real-ised. Katerina frowned, concerned that Daniel would be back in the frame if that occurred, but she would have to adjust her options – change them on the run and demand time alone with Mayek. For now, she'd set events in play; she had no more control and so should press on with her plan. She finished applying eyeliner and mascara before stepping out feeling like a new woman. After paying for her purchases, glad that she'd taken the precaution of grabbing the emergency cash that she'd hidden in the York house out of habit, she adopted her vacant expression of distraction. With her chin high, the boot heels clicked her progress.

Despite her confident air, the packet of Polo mints was already four down. And by the time she turned into Bury Street the myth that peppermint could stave off nausea was, as far as Katerina was concerned, proven to be a lie. The adrenaline high of being in motion to her own plan had dissipated with each street she had drawn closer to her own, not helped by a blister from the new boots. The reality of facing Ruda Mayek clawed at her belly like a vulture at carrion. She chose to cross her street so she could approach her flat from the opposite side, giving her the widest range of view to spot a stranger without looking like she was trying to.

Walk purposefully, she told herself, *but not too fast. Rein in the nerves! They mustn't show if he's watching. No! Don't look. Act normal. Find your key, let yourself in, do all the usual stuff.*

She was almost in line with her threshold when she heard a whistle and turned, stopping by the doorway opposite hers. With dread she turned but was pleased to see Billy from the pub.

'Looking very fancy, miss.' He winked.

'Always, Billy,' she quipped, digging up a smile. She knew how to do this. *You haven't forgotten how*, she pleaded with herself. *If he's watching, he has to believe you don't know he's here.*

She went deep inside to find her mettle and grinned again over her shoulder at the youngster waving goodbye; it took every ounce of courage not to scan the street for someone who might resemble Mayek. Katerina held her poise steady and anyone watching would have seen only a confident woman step off the pavement to cross the street to Museum Chambers.

Katerina fiddled in her bag for keys, suffering a momentary panic that she had lost track of them since she'd met Edward, but the giveaway jangle in a zippered section reassured her. The sharp tug of panic in her throat now made her want to look around for Mayek and she let a curse fly beneath her breath. *She could have had Daniel and his men here! What sort of lunacy was this?*

Once again, fighting with all the emotional strength she could muster, she squashed the inclination to flee by deliberately pressing the key much too hard into the lock and twisting it. The door opened and she stepped in. After closing it, she leaned back against its solidity and took some long, slow breaths. She had begun to perspire – so unlike her. Annoyed that she was making her new blouse damp, she talked herself away from the cliff edge of panic. Katerina knew she needed to rid herself of this overwhelming anxiety or he'd already won.

Get upstairs and get ready for him, her inner voice of strength urged. She obeyed, pushing away from the door, finding some calm in the memory of Daniel's voice: *You have nothing but my admiration for your courage.*

She would not permit Ruda Mayek to hurt anyone again. But she was going to hurt him.

Katerina began to ascend the interminable stairs that led to the top floor. It reminded her that if Mayek was as weakened as Daniel assured her, he'd be fatigued from climbing these stairs. She made a mental promise that if she could, she would leave the door ajar after answering it. Nevertheless, something snagged in her mind as she took the stairs slowly to the top floor. She couldn't quite get a purchase on what it was that was poking at her thoughts and the relief at being inside her flat washed away the vague prick of alarm that the niggle was creating. She let out a sigh now everything was in place. Despite her ruse, Daniel, or one of his men, was probably somewhere watching. And that being the case, they'd not let Mayek be alone with her for long.

She took off her coat and put it on a hanger in the short entranceway. Pulling off the new boots, Katerina gave a soft groan of pleasure as her feet were released from the pinch of new leather and could now be flattened against the smooth floorboards. She immediately opened the windows in her bedroom and the main room as a precaution; she wasn't sure why, but it felt safer to know the world outside was blowing in.

That relief aside, she was still feeling on edge about something and couldn't shake the thought. A coffee was needed. Then her thoughts would clear, she promised herself. She was pleased the beans were still fresh enough to use. She took her time, going through her deliberate ritual. Of a normal morning she'd dress as her coffee came to its gurgling boil but with no reason to be doing anything else she leaned against the stove listening to it percolate. For reasons she couldn't immediately fathom, the bubbling pot that normally heartened her didn't soothe. Today the bubbles sounded like a death rattle, the last wet breaths. The aroma that normally woke up her taste buds now made her feel distantly ill.

What was it? What was wrong with this picture?

She switched off the flame of the gas stove abruptly and as it went out, a different death groan sounded as the coffee's previous excitement died. It was ruined but that was the last thought filling her mind right now. Her internal alarms were shrill; the most piercing of them insisted, not from the rim of her mind any more but right at the fore, that there was something she'd seen and had registered as odd, yet she'd overlooked. There was a fierce klaxon in her head now.

The flavour of mint tasted like old toothpaste and what was rising through the nausea and her increasingly rapid breathing was the memory of a colour: dirty orange. Where had she seen it? Katerina bit down on her fist, forcing her reliable mind to recall it.

The memory came and she gasped.

The cigarette packet!

As she had turned to greet Billy in Bury Street, her gaze had lighted briefly on the distinctive orange packet in the doorway opposite her own, where she stood. It was crushed, discarded, but she had noticed it as young Billy had whistled, distracting her with conversation. But that cigarette packet was the clue she'd missed. The cigarettes were German, identical to the packet from which a cigarette had been smoked in her presence when she'd still had teenage dreams and plans.

Her life was in dark danger now because she'd not paid attention to the instinct that had protected her for all these years.

Surely not! He couldn't be!

Katerina was facing the stove, still leaning against it, but now she whipped her head around as dawning hit and she saw him.

'Hello, Katka.' He smiled.

Miss Bailey arrived with a pot of tea. 'I just popped in to finish that document for the Ryan case, Mr Summerbee.'

'Mmm?' He looked up. 'Oh, thank you. Er, that's right, you are taking the day off. You really shouldn't have come in.'

She smiled. 'All right if I leave now? I'm going to a matinee.'

'Oh, marvellous. Of course, hurry off. Which show?'

'*Half a Sixpence* at the Cambridge Theatre.'

'I hear that Tommy Steele is quite the star.'

She smiled. 'Can't wait. He's very handsome.'

Edward grinned. He hadn't heard Miss Bailey accuse anyone of that . . . ever. 'Enjoy yourselves. Oh, wait.' He stood and removed some notes from his wallet. 'Take this and please get a taxi to and fro, and buy your sister and yourself a flute of champagne from me.'

'Oh, Mr Summerbee, I couldn't.' She looked delightedly shocked.

'Yes, you can. You've been very understanding of my mood of late, Miss Bailey. There's a difficult situation I'm dealing with and it's leaving me quite distracted, I'll admit.' He came around the desk. 'Please. It's my pleasure to do this and I hope you have a splendid time.'

The phone rang at his desk.

'Oh, I've flicked it through. Shall I get that, sir?'

'No, no. I'll get this one,' he said, waving her away and moving back around his desk. 'Put on your hat and coat and leave or you never will, Miss Bailey. Enjoy!' He picked up the receiver as he glanced at the clock. It was past two already. 'Summerbee and Associates.'

'Er, good afternoon. I'm looking to speak with a Mr Edward Summerbee, please.'

'You've found him.' He grinned farewell as Miss Bailey tiptoed out the door, closing it behind her.

'Oh.'

It was odd that he was answering calls. He pressed on without explanation. 'How might I help?'

'You don't know me.'

'I rarely do know new clients.'

'I'm not sure I'd describe myself that way but my name is Schäfer.'

Edward blinked. He knew the name and the accent confirmed it. 'Is this Dr Otto Schäfer?'

'It is.'

'Then I do know you, sir. Or at least of you.'

'Good, so I don't have to waste time explaining. Do you know that I have recently seen Katerina?'

He wasn't wasting any time. 'I do.'

'She's spoken with you?'

'Er . . . no. We're not that close.'

Another slight pause. 'That's not the impression she left me with.'

'I don't know what to say to that,' he replied. He sensed the man on the other end was smiling.

'I do have a vested interest in Katerina, as I'm sure she has mentioned.'

'She has. She is incredibly loyal and I'm surprised she contacted you because she mentioned how she deliberately hadn't seen you since she left Czechoslovakia.'

'That's correct. But I suspect this is the measure of how frantic she is since those wretched Pearls emerged. Promise me that you will be honourable. She needs no further pain.'

'Did you ring me to play a father figure, Dr Schäfer?'

'No. I'm ringing you because I don't know who else to turn to.'

'That sounds ominous.'

'I'm sure you're aware her life is in grave danger.'

Edward pursed his lips momentarily. 'You must forgive me. I cannot divulge the name —'

'That's not what I mean, Mr Summerbee,' the doctor interjected. 'This is not about your client. It's connected with what I suspect Katerina is about to do.'

'What do you mean?'

Otto explained. 'It just struck the wrong chord with me as we parted. I don't trust that she's going to do what she said she would . . . or rather, I don't trust that I'm hearing all of the truth.'

'Well, let me put your mind at rest. She did call Daniel Horowitz as she promised. And he's meeting her from the train tomorrow morning, as I understand it.'

'Tomorrow?'

'Yes. Why?'

'It's my understanding she was leaving *today*. In fact, I suspect she's already in London.'

'That can't be right.'

'It is right. She was leaving at some unearthly hour to be in London by ten this morning!'

'Well, she told Daniel tomorrow . . .' he repeated, feeling stupid for it, but the spark of fear was beginning to fizz in his belly. 'What does this mean?'

'It means she lied. It confirms my fears. She's going to confront Mayek alone.'

'She wouldn't risk her life.'

'She's got more to lose than you probably fully understand, Mr Summerbee, but watching her yesterday I felt like a shroud had descended. It was the same Katerina I remember when she emerged from her shock all those years ago. There's a will of iron in her. I don't think she's considering her life right now. She wants him finished and no longer able to reach her or those she loves.'

'And risk death?'

'She's faced it before several times.'

'But this is 1963, not wartime! What can we do?'

'I can't do much from up here in the north of England except panic, and that helps no one. Where is this Horowitz she spoke of?'

'I don't know. I can try to find him but he usually calls me. We left it that he would telephone me tomorrow when the trap was laid and done.'

'What trap?'

Edward summarised it succinctly in his well-honed solicitor's manner. 'She did say to Daniel that she wanted to confront Mayek – needed to, in order to let this all go.'

'This is so much worse than I even dreaded. She's deliberately given us all false information so she can confront him alone.'

From all of his experience working in the world of the law, Edward knew better than to ask why. The why, he knew, no longer mattered. 'I can't promise I can easily reach Daniel Horowitz. So, Doctor Schäfer, write this number down. Got a pen?'

'Yes. Go ahead.'

Edward gave him the number. 'I got this from Horowitz. It's Paris but I suspect they can reach him. Make them contact him. Tell him to go to Bloomsbury or send his henchmen immediately. Now, forgive me, please, but I'm going to fling the telephone down and get to Katerina's flat as fast as humanly possible.'

'Just go. I'll get hold of Horowitz. Summerbee, just remember Mayek is dangerous.'

Edward's features had settled into a grimace. 'So am I!'

31

Her mouth was too dry, her throat too choked to respond. He could surely tell this and was enjoying her shock. In spite of the panic, her mind was taking in information clearly.

It was as though nothing else mattered but her and him. They were in a bubble of the past but Rudy hadn't aged well. His face was deeply lined, no doubt a canvas of stories of the pain and torture he'd inflicted in his time. She was reminded of the wood carvings she'd watched the artisans make during her childhood. The designs were achieved by deep grooves being dug into blocks of soft wood before paint was rolled over them and they were placed down repeatedly onto paper or fabric. That's how his face appeared to her now: as if a tool had been taken to it to etch out the lines. Wrinkles were sketched haphazardly across his cheeks, bags hung beneath his eyes. His mouth was still meanly thin, still amused. Those watery-pale eyes seemed dirtier, rheumy, their once fierce outline now smudged. His gaze did not regard her from a clear white background but stared from a nest of spidery bloodshot capillaries and puffed lids. His chin was furred with white, like his hair which had grown out past his ears. The blond had become cloudy white. It was thin but he was not balding and it flopped loose and unkempt with two distinct cowlicks at the top of his forehead. In days gone, he might have smoothed those lank flops back with hair cream. Now he just looked old. Ill.

'You spoiled my surprise,' he said, his tone conversational. He was enjoying himself. 'What gave me away? I was careful not to wear cologne or anything that might smell distinct. I switched on no lights. I made barely a sound.'

'How long have you been here?'

The lips pouted in a sort of shrug. 'Since the evening you didn't return home. I was going to take a taxi back to my accommodation but I decided I should simply wait for you to reappear. And here you are. I enjoyed sleeping in your bed, Katka: smelling your perfume on the pillow, lying on your invisible shape.'

She began to tremble with revulsion but mostly with fear.

'You haven't answered,' he continued. 'I'm intrigued. I know you guessed in those few seconds before you turned and saw me; what was it that clued you in?'

She swallowed. 'Ernte 23.'

He frowned, a half smile forming. 'Cigarettes?'

'Your brand. German. I remember them from when I was little.'

He shook his head, puzzled. 'I haven't smoked in here.'

'But you smoked outside,' she replied. 'You discarded the packet.'

Mottled hands came together in slow, mocking applause. 'Very good, Katka. That's impressive. And still you came upstairs.'

'I . . . I was distracted.'

'By the young man. Yes, I noticed. Is he in love with you? I'm sure any man who meets you falls for your cool poise. I've watched you for weeks now, trying to find the right moment. You're incredibly beautiful – far more . . . ethereal, I think is the word, than any

of us might have imagined. You always promised beauty – but this?'
He swept a blunt hand in the air in front of her. 'Magnificent . . . even
barefoot.' He chuckled and the sound was ugly.

She had no reply for him. Instead her mind was reaching to
Daniel; he would have no idea that Mayek was already with her
so no one would be coming to save her. She needed to give a sign to
the outside world that she was in trouble; maybe one of his
men . . . anyone – Billy? – would see.

'I can see your mind working, Katka. Are you imagining
a plan? Are you thinking to scream?' In a blink he produced a
knife – a thin-bladed stiletto – and it was at her throat. 'Don't
scream, Katka.'

So it was a knife, after all, she thought redundantly.

Her throat felt locked anyway, so screaming would be impossible. He led her into the tiny sitting room. She walked like a doll
might, with stiff legs that had no joints. His hand was clasped
around her neck, easily closing around most of it. She was reminded
of Daniel's fateful words *skin on skin* and gagged.

'Sit.'

She obeyed.

He sat next to her on the small couch. It was intimate. 'This is
satisfying, to be back together again after all these years, eh?' He
chuckled at her silence. The thin blade was poised now near her
belly. She glanced down at it, imagining the damage it could do.
'My, my, but you are truly delicious. Where were you these last
days?'

She tried to speak but it came out as a mumble.

'Say again?'

'With a friend,' she repeated.

'A friend you spent the nights with?'

She took a deep, silent breath. No one was coming to save her;
no one knew he was here. So what was left to her? To die sobbing?

To die resigned and complacent as her father and the rest of the family had? Or to die fighting? Cursing his name, even trying to turn his own weapon on him?

Fight, Katerina. You've fought for your life before; fight again for yourself, for Daniel's sweetheart, for your parents and sisters . . . for Edward.

That kiss. Its delight returned to remind her of everything she'd missed out on in life because of Ruda Mayek, and everything she might potentially have if she outmanoeuvred him one more time.

She let go of the kiss; she would have another with Edward! She didn't stop shaking, she didn't stop being scared, but Katerina found her voice and her defiance once again. If she was going to die by the hand of Ruda Mayek, then she would give him no satisfaction and she would say to him what she had intended. She would take her last breath enjoying his pain.

'More than a friend, actually,' she said, careful not to sound overconfident. 'My lover.'

He didn't like that. 'The man from Paris, I'm guessing?'

'Daniel? No. Daniel is a friend. My lover is called Edward Summerbee . . . You know him; he's handling the Pearls you stole from my family.'

If the way his amused expression bled to confusion could be termed a triumph, then Katerina felt momentarily like a winner.

'From Lincoln's Inn?' he said, in a voice full of disbelief.

She nodded; she couldn't be flippant because she sensed his grip hardening around the blade.

'You are sleeping with my solicitor?'

'I am,' she lied.

'I feel betrayed.' But he shocked her by laughing. 'And I thought I was your man, Katka.'

'The first. Mercifully not the last. At least I've had the chance to know a good lover.'

His smile, like an illustration of evil, widened. 'That's good, Katka. Try and hurt me before I hurt you.'

'You can't hurt me, Rudy. The pain from you is done. All that's left is the killing, so you might as well get on with it.'

He didn't enjoy this remark. Clearly, he wanted her squirming, perhaps pleading. Well, she wouldn't give it to him. Her mind was reaching to Durham but perhaps it was a divine defence mechanism that reined it back. *Don't go there. Only weakness awaits if you go there.*

He too regained equilibrium. The sneer was back to accompany the tsking sound he was making, as though reprimanding a child. She recalled it well. 'That's such a pity.' He began to draw the stiletto across her belly. It was sharp enough to score the fabric; her pinafore began to split. 'Imagine what I can do with this blade against your pale, perfect skin.'

She stared at him, hoping her flawed eye would unnerve him again.

'Or what if I poked it into that eye of yours? Hmm? We could make that mark uglier still.'

'What a sad man you are. What a pathetic bully. Looks to me like you're dying anyway, Rudy. What's the illness?'

'Diabetes and some other complications, like cancer.'

'Oh, I'm thrilled. I hope it all hurts?'

'I need insulin. I've become rather deaf, amongst other oddities. I've lost some toes.'

'Well, I hope you lose sensation in all your limbs before you're taken. I hope you die screaming in agony from the cancer, with the doctors unable to give you anything but an overdose of morphine . . . but that would be too kind, in my opinion.'

'Spirited.' He nodded. 'You impress me.'

'I don't want to impress you.'

'How will Mr Summerbee feel when he sees you lying here dead?'

'I'd like to spare him that, but if it is Edward, then this thick fabric will help cover some of your mess, won't it?'

'Not if I undress you first. Perhaps have one last go with you. One part of me still works.'

She grimaced. 'You might as well do it after you've killed me, Rudy, because a corpse is the only way you'll have me compliant. I don't fear your blade.'

He threw his chin up to laugh. She wanted to slash the throat that stretched before her but he'd pulled the blade away; she couldn't get close.

'I'm not ready to kill you just yet. I'm astonished to see you alive and so well. We haven't even discussed that yet, have we? How you dodged my bullet, how you appeared so very dead in that forest. We even buried you. I'm trying to imagine you climbing out of the grave. Were your family stiff with death by then?'

She knew her features betrayed her. He'd hit his mark and he laughed again.

'Ah, there you are, little Katka. I like it when you tremble. Now we're talking properly. Who helped you, I wonder? How could you have escaped my notice? It had to be someone with influence. Tell me.'

'It was. A better man than you, although that's not hard to achieve, is it?'

He ignored the barb. 'A man. Did he fall in love with you?'

'I was fourteen.'

'Oh, Katka, you really had no awareness of yourself, did you? Tell me his name.'

'Never.'

'A local?'

'A German. A real one. Not like you . . . always pretending. *Volksdeutsch*.' She said it in a tone filled with insult. 'You have to smoke German cigarettes and do the dirty work for the Nazis to make yourself feel German. And yet you were born an impoverished, reluctant Czechoslovakian. At least I was proud to be from Prague. Proud to be a Jew.'

He hit her. She had expected it but didn't see it coming. Her head snapped to the side and she thought she heard a soft crack. He heard it too. Sharp pain shot through the side of her face, heating it instantly.

'I like the sound of your bones breaking. Your exquisitely shaped cheekbone is depressed. Shame. I didn't want to mark your face.'

She wished she could resist but it was instinctive to place her hand against the pain.

'Hurting? Let me get you something for it.'

He hauled her to her feet and while holding her tight, dug around in her icebox. He pulled out the tray and placed a tea towel on the kitchen bench. He banged the metal container and a few cubes fell out. He banged again, until he was satisfied. 'Wrap them up, put them against your face.'

'Why?'

'Because I say so. I don't want you too bruised. You know they remain after death?'

'Only you would know. You must have seen enough bruised, dead bodies beneath your hand.'

He laughed. 'Put it against your face.'

Again, she obeyed, wincing at the double pain now of the pressure against the injury and the freeze. It was like pressing against her sister's dead body again. The memory brought anger and with it a fresh surge of courage. He led her back to the room with comfortable chairs.

The Paris office had called London and Daniel, bemused, dialled a number for a Durham guesthouse. He was surprised to find himself talking with Dr Schäfer. He did indeed have a gentle voice, clearly European but not instantly identifiable as German, and no doubt deliberately smoothed off to lean towards the Austrian city he lived in.

The doctor wasted no time with introductions. His first words were: 'Katerina lied to both of us.' He quickly explained what Daniel had feared.

'You mean Mayek is there? My man moved into place at noon. He would have seen him arrive.'

'Well, your man might already be too late, Mr Horowitz. She may well have walked into a trap. What if he's already in there, waiting for her?'

Daniel experienced the rare spangles of true fear, making his limbs feel weakened and creating a twisting sensation in his bowel. He needed to think. Adrenaline was being released so fast and hard a low headache began.

Schäfer was still speaking. 'I'm helpless up here in the north. Summerbee has gone to the flat and has urgently requested you do the same. Don't be shy, Mr Horowitz. Smash that door in if you have to.'

'On my way.'

'Ring me . . . please!'

Daniel Horowitz took that call in a nondescript office in the gods of a tall, red-brick Victorian building in Harewood Place. This was London W1, and although only a few hundred yards from the chaotic Oxford Circus, it was not only a peaceful enclave that opened into tranquil Hanover Square, but the offices themselves throughout the building were all but silent due to being a mix of mainly accountancy and legal firms. It was little wonder then that people emerged to discover who it was from the top floor that was yelling orders as he descended via the fire stairs, in too much of a rush for the single slow lift. If they had looked out of their windows fronting narrow Harewood Place, they'd have seen the normally reserved gentleman from the import and export company on the top floor all but exploding from the main entrance, leaping into a revving car and instructing the driver to 'Go!' before he'd even shut the passenger door.

———

'Be seated.' Mayek gestured, pushing her back into an armchair. She could feel strength still existed in him; she wouldn't win if she tried to physically hold him off. 'It's been two decades. I'd hoped you'd have more to say to me.' He sat opposite her this time, his back to her bedroom.

Freshly emboldened, she began. The time was right. Whatever happened now she no longer cared, so long as she struck this final blow.

'Where have you been all this time?' she began.

'Why? Have you been searching for me?'

'No. I have deliberately not thought of you for all these years. I locked you away, Rudy. You weren't worth even my vaguest consideration.'

He showed no offence. 'Until now . . .' He chuckled at her.

'Yes, now I am thinking about you and I do have something to say.'

His pleasure deepened, horrible eyes twinkling with mischief. 'I'm pleased to hear that. I've been living in Britain, Katka. I came here as a refugee in 1946. I go by the name of Josef Beránek. I stole it from a Gypsy in one of the camps.'

She gave a sneer of disgust and nodded. 'Suits you.'

He laughed aloud, taking great delight in her restraint.

'I hope you're dying?'

'We're all dying.' She stared at him and he shrugged. 'Perhaps I am.'

'You seem strong.'

'Don't try testing me. I may not be the man I was twenty years ago, little Katka, but I can snap you in two; there's not that much of you. I could wish for better hearing, I suppose, but my eyes are still functioning well enough. Lots of other complications, as I say, from my illnesses, but I'm wealthy enough, I'm alive, I've found you. Life's being kind.'

***

Edward had run, moving at a pace he didn't think was possible for him, and casting away all of his inherent politeness, he didn't give a single glance at the people he shoved aside. He ran out of Lincoln's Inn with no hat or coat, but idiotically he'd grabbed his brolly like any sensible Englishman. It was now fear and determination he wore, strapped on like armour. Down the busy street he hurtled, moving fast as though he'd just grabbed the elliptical ball on the rugby field and was going it alone towards the touchline – in this case the Underground, where a queue of people were patiently waiting to step into big black taxis.

'This is life or death!' he yelled as he shouldered his way to the front and hauled back the man who was just easing into the cab, a barrister he recognised.

'Oh, I do say, Summerbee, this is outrageously rude.'

'Bill me, Smithers!' Edward snarled and leapt into the taxi, shutting the door against people's angry calls. Mr Smithers QC irritatedly tapped the glass with his umbrella as though that might change Edward's mind. Another person shook a fist at him. Edward looked away to the driver, who was grinning.

'Looks like you're in a hurry, mate,' the taxi driver observed.

'I'm trying to stop someone getting hurt' was all he could say, still out of breath from the running. 'Bury Street, Bloomsbury,' he said, recalling the address from her letter. 'Hurry, man, hurry.'

'Do my best.'

'How long?'

'Fifteen minutes, I reckon.'

'I'll give you double if you can halve the time.'

The man grinned. 'Righto, we might have to break some rules and it's not going to be pretty.'

'Do it,' he said, grimly nodding.

The taxi driver floored it as best he could, and although the huge car was hardly agile, he drove it like he was riding a stallion in the Grand National. He deftly dodged and wove his way around the restless London traffic, using a labyrinth of streets that Edward barely knew, avoiding the lumbering buses, the crush of pedestrians and the narrowing river of vehicles that often simply and inexplicably stopped. He avoided traffic lights as much as he could, and while it felt like the long way to Bloomsbury, Edward could see they were cutting out precious minutes all the same.

His mind was like a dropped bottle of milk: glass shattered, contents rolling inexorably away from the main spill of his thoughts, breaking away in little rivulets to all corners.

'What number house in Bury Street?' the driver asked.

'Actually, what's the road behind?' The driver told him. 'Drop me there, anywhere.'

He could see the man's expression in the rear-view mirror; the driver wanted to ask why but perhaps a lifetime of driving strangers around told him it wasn't worth asking. 'Another minute at most.'

Edward remembered what Daniel had said about how he would approach Katerina's flat from over back gardens, using the fire escape and silently climbing into her flat. He couldn't be sure the Nazi would even be there but he was not leaving it to chance, and he would not make a ruckus approaching the more convenient way and knocking on her door. Edward had learned to be fleet and light on his feet from his sport as he'd already demonstrated. Now he had to be all about stealth – like the wing, his favourite position, stealing the ball from the opposition or being fed a stolen ball and then flying down the edge of the ground, so the players barely knew he'd captured the prize.

He was going to steal into Katerina's flat, and if she was alone, apologise. And if not? He had no idea. But the sport of rugby was full of unexpected dramas and split-second decisions. So was court. So many times he'd had to change his brief on the fly and in front of the judge. Focus was required.

Focus and a weapon, perhaps? All he had was his umbrella, and he closed his eyes momentarily at the ridiculous thought that surfed through his mind that he was *not* going to lose another one and would have to carry it with him!

32

She put the ice down so she could breathe out her despair. 'Do you still have your family?'

'Yes. I loathe my wife. She was a convenience – made me look good, holding the hands of my twin children as we stumbled into Britain as helpless, needy folk.'

'Twins?'

His sinister smile crept back across his face. She could read what was coming before he said it, so she was prepared. 'Just like your pretty little sisters. Beautiful girls, they are. Not at all like their ugly mother. Blonde and blue-eyed. Perfect.'

'Except you're their father. Hardly perfect,' she remarked and watched his smile widen. 'How old are they?'

'Mid-twenties. They're like English roses except there's only German blood running through their veins. I've taught them the language in secret. People are still touchy, you know.' He laughed horribly and then began a tirade of coughing.

'That doesn't sound good.'

'It will take me,' he admitted. 'But not yet, not before I've secured the girls' future.'

'With my Pearls, do you mean?'

'Those included.'

'I watched you steal them, you know.' She explained.

He put down the blade to clap again, knowing full well the layout of her family's garden. 'Oh, Katka, if only I'd known. Up a tree, then, wounded by a bullet? Amazing!'

'I didn't think I could hate you any more on that night but you surprised me. Of course, I don't care about the Pearls.'

'No?'

Tingles crept through her body, sparkling at the crown of her head like a halo of disbelief as much as relief because, impossibly, she glimpsed the figure of a man peeping from around the bedroom door with his finger to his lips.

Ruda Mayek followed her line of sight and looked around but the intruder had already stepped back silently. 'What is it?'

'Nothing,' she said, astonished by her calm at the surprise of seeing the shiny white knight she needed in her life right now. Impossibly, here he was, and she was almost sick with relief that she'd opened that bedroom window on arriving in her stuffy flat. 'I felt a bolt of pain through my face. It made me nauseous.'

He turned back to look at her, then twisted his head again to check . . . just in case . . . but there was nothing behind him. Now she must not look, not even once, past Rudy's shoulder. It was going to take all her courage, all her willpower not to give him away.

She picked up the ice again. 'I don't know why I'm bothering.'

'Because we both want you to die beautiful,' he said. 'Where were we?'

'I was telling you that I really couldn't care any less than I do about the Pearls. You can have them.'

'I already do.'

'Unless Edward finds my parents' original wills, of course, Rudy. You do know they exist, don't you?' she goaded him. She sensed a shadow in the bedroom doorway but she wouldn't look.

Don't step on the creak, she pleaded. *And come forward slowly. A snail's pace* – she would keep Rudy talking.

Her mismatched stare was fixed on the man she hated. Suddenly it seemed she might have something extra to live for; her plan was crumbling around her but Rudy didn't know that. He was frowning at her.

'You're lying.'

'I am not. But we shall see . . . or rather, *you* shall, when the police come knocking at your family's door. The girls are going to get quite a shock to find out that their father is a war criminal.'

'I'm not falling for it, Katka.'

She shrugged again. 'I really don't care how you feel about it, but I hope Edward finds what he's hunting for. He will know later today from his colleagues in Switzerland . . . and I suspect so will you. You see, my father's best friend was a lawyer; perhaps you never knew this, but do you recall him speaking of a man called Körbel?' She watched with intense pleasure as Rudy's face twitched, blanching. He couldn't hide that he recalled the name and the man's profession. 'Well, before he died at the hands of the Nazis, his friend sent my parents' wills to his firm's branch offices, I gather. So it's just a matter of time. You'd better tell the girls to get packed if you plan to go on the run again.'

Although she forbade herself to look at him, Katerina was aware that her potential rescuer was now halfway between the bedroom and the chair where Rudy sat. He was on the rug. No creak. She was counting on her torturer's poor hearing letting him down but she couldn't rely entirely on that. She needed to keep him engaged and distracted so the rest of the distance could be travelled on tiptoe without discovery.

'Rudy, I told you I did have something important to say to you.'

'What is it?' He was testy now, rummaging through thoughts of what she'd just revealed. Without her knight she would probably only have a few more moments of life.

Katerina began the story she had wanted to tell Ruda Mayek for over twenty years. 'You used to boast to me about the son you wanted. How you would teach him to fish and to hunt. How you would raise him in your own way.'

Rudy sighed. 'You have a good memory.'

'Do you regret not having a son?'

'I don't regret my daughters, if that's what you're asking. They're —'

'That's not what I'm asking,' she said, enjoying cutting across his words.

He blinked. She waited, forcing him to respond.

'It is true that I regret not having a son. I will admit only to you, Katka, that I was deeply disappointed when both my children turned out to be girls. I was angry with their mother. If she weren't needed for feeding the children, I think I would have done her some violence.'

She nodded. 'I'm convinced you would have too because you have no respect for anyone, Rudy, especially women. So I pity your daughters, no matter how much you claim you love them. They probably love you and it is fortunate they do not know that what they have for a father is the devil.' His face set like concrete drying out. He was no longer amused, no longer prepared to play along. But Katerina continued. Edward surely had only a couple more stealthy steps to make, although she had no idea of his plan. She wouldn't look at him, would not give Ruda Mayek even the slimmest chance of dodging his fate. 'I don't wish them pain and that's the truth, but I don't care a whit about them or you, so if they have to suffer in this discovery, so be it.'

He sat forward, pointing one of his blunted fingers at her. 'What are you talking about?'

'Me.'

'They will never find out about you because I have hunted you down, Katka. You are the last remaining person, I believe, who can identify me.'

'Are you sure? Are you also sure that you're not the one being hunted, Rudy?'

He sneered, and in one fluid movement Edward was finally close enough to smash down the handle of his umbrella across the man's wrist and on the weapon that sat idly menacing her in Mayek's palm. In an equally fast action he lifted the brolly and smacked it now across Mayek's face. The double shock of a potentially broken wrist and a definitely broken nose shifted the power in the room and Katerina leapt towards the stiletto blade, which had been sent skittering across the floor. Mayek tried to struggle to his feet, out of instinct, it seemed, because he was unsteady, disoriented, and Katerina watched in amazement as Edward punched Mayek with all his force. Her captor's eyes bulged with surprise and rage at her for barely a heartbeat before he dropped like a boulder from an avalanche, collapsing onto her couch.

Edward was flicking his hand around and grimacing at the pain. 'That's what we call a king hit in rugby circles,' he said. 'Bloody hell, it hurts to deliver it, though.'

Katerina crouched on the floor with the stiletto, ice scattered around her. Curiously, with all of the terror surrounding this scene, she gave a mirthless laugh, stretched taut by her nervousness. 'I thought you wielded that umbrella with great dexterity.'

He pointed a finger. 'Don't jest. What were you thinking?'

Before she could answer there was an explosive sound of timber being broken as her flat door was smashed in and Daniel ran in, wide-eyed and dishevelled.

'He's here!' Daniel exclaimed.

Katerina knew he would have hated such an obvious response to the scene but it was true even Daniel couldn't control his shock in this moment.

'He's out cold,' Edward assured him, moving to help Katerina to her feet. 'And she's hurt.'

She lifted a trembling hand to her face, amazed she hadn't fully noticed the pain until now and dropped it again, determined not to seek sympathy. 'I'll live, thanks to you.' A look passed between them that spoke of intimacy and she knew he understood they would discuss everything later. She turned to Daniel. 'This is him, the man you've hunted.'

Daniel hadn't shifted his gaze from the slumped Czech but he took the stiletto from her before moving to the window and giving a signal. He was back at Katerina's side in a blink. 'I'm so sorry for failing you. We didn't know he was already inside.'

She shook her head as his gaze searched her forgiving expression. 'It never occurred to me and I lied to all of you. I brought this on myself. But you're here now . . . both of you.' She pressed a hand to Daniel's cheek to impress upon him her gratitude.

She thought she felt him shiver beneath her touch – a leaf's tremor – and experienced a surge of sorrow for this broken man. She shared grief with him. Yes, they were like dried and fallen autumn leaves, tumbling over each other in the wind: helpless but driven by a force bigger than they. Except she had been lucky. Her leaf had recently become caught, trapped on something solid and immovable in Edward, while Daniel must roll on, at the mercy of his sadness.

He covered her hand with his and took the opportunity to lean his head into her caress. It was a poignant pause in an otherwise ugly scene and she felt they would always be connected through their sorrow and the prisoner that was slumped opposite. Katerina kissed his other cheek gently. 'Thank you,' he whispered at her tender forgiveness. He let her go and the bond was broken. His expression told her he knew he would never touch her like that again or be kissed in that careful yet intimate way either. 'Keep ice against your face. Edward, are you all right?'

'Tore my bloody pants on the fence I had to climb over,' he replied with dismay at the flap of gaberdine revealing a knobbled knee.

She knew he clowned deliberately to make her smile and she did and so did Daniel. It lifted some of the dread.

'You did well, Edward. Let me deal with him.'

They watched Daniel fetch duct tape and rope out of a bag to bind the unconscious Mayek's ankles and wrists. He was taping Mayek first over the sleeves of his pullover, presumably so that the rope would not leave marks. Men arrived. She recognised both now; one of them was the annoying chatty one from the teashop. She found herself privately marvelling that they had obviously been circling her movements around London since she and Daniel had first arrived; there may have even been more of their colleagues conscripted to guard her. They nodded in her direction, both with fleeting expressions of guilt because they could see she had been wounded. But the debt was hers. They had all likely saved her life more than once during these past days, maybe weeks, and she had been none the wiser of Daniel and his team's care.

Daniel picked up the discarded stiletto, which he put away in the same bag and now withdrew a syringe, fully loaded.

Katerina's hopes were dashed; she was not going to be given her chance to say what she needed to impress upon Mayek. Her thoughts collided, torn between relief at him not having his way with her again but dread that she would continue to carry the burden of grief. If she could just have a couple of minutes, she just knew her life would be shaped differently . . .

'Daniel?'

He shook his head at her as their prisoner began to stir and made a sudden sound like a growl; an animal cornered.

'Don't even twitch, Mayek!' Daniel warned and in his voice was a tone she'd not heard before. It was pitched softer than most men's, yes, but gone was the pleasant note, the patient note, even the affectionate one she knew he possessed. It was all threat now. It frightened her that he could be capable of sudden violence and yet so calm. 'You're trussed like the beast you are.'

Despite the warning, Mayek roared and struggled against his bonds. For his trouble, he instantly had duct tape plastered across his mean mouth. So instead mean eyes bulged over the top of the dull grey seal. Within his rage, trying to hide but not entirely able to disguise itself, was fear. She was sure she'd spotted it because she knew the feeling all too well. There it was; she saw it again reflected in those angry windows when his dead-eyed stare glanced her way, unintelligible words being hurled at all of them.

While Edward moved to her side, Daniel stepped back to join his colleagues, all of them dressed similarly in monotone. They would blend easily into the City of London. She even had time now to imagine umbrellas and briefcases and no doubt long overcoats that were probably cast off in her small hallway. No one would pick them as anything but office workers.

'Daniel, let me introduce our prisoner to everyone,' she said, and it was not a question.

The spy gestured for her to go ahead. 'In English, please, for the ease of my colleagues,' Daniel suggested. He glanced at Edward too.

'Don't worry, I refuse to speak German for his benefit.' She kicked an ice cube aside and cut her gaze to Mayek, who still stared at her alone; he'd stopped struggling and had become quiet. 'Rudy, standing next to me is Edward Summerbee, the solicitor who is representing you, via that other third party, to the British Museum.

It was his umbrella that I hope has broken your wrist and mis-shapen your nose. I do hope you're in a lot of pain from both injuries.' She smiled and hoped it appeared cruel. 'Perhaps more importantly on this occasion, I'd like to introduce Mr Daniel Horowitz, whom you don't know but might recognise from being by my side in Paris and more recently in London. I'm sure you can guess from his name much of what you need to know about him.'

She watched the small eyes regarding Daniel in a vicious gaze.

'Mr Horowitz has been looking for you since 1948, but he knew about you four years earlier. You should know you've been in his thoughts for every day of those many years.' She paused, frown-ing as though gathering her thoughts, although she knew precisely how to strike the next blow. 'Oh, Rudy, forgive me, I failed to men-tion at the outset that he's Mossad,' she added conversationally. She couldn't remember a moment more satisfying than this one when she heard the click of Rudy's breath becoming trapped in his throat. His breath had become her prisoner now. It would know no free-dom while she spoke.

She sensed most of what she said now would become irrele-vant to him, of course, for the mere mention of Mossad had said everything and would have struck the deepest of chills. She under-stood he would be contemplating his death . . . his thoughts no doubt reaching to his daughters. She couldn't fathom her own cruelty as she continued, but then this was Ruda Mayek, and he deserved all the emotional pain she could inflict. Her tone remained cordial, almost friendly, as she continued.

'He's a committed Nazi hunter, Rudy, and as you are one of that twisted ideology's most faithful followers, he is particularly thrilled that you are nonetheless stupid enough to come out from wherever you've been hiding. It must be your illnesses that have clouded your decision-making because while I have always hoped your arrogance would be your downfall, I never thought idiocy was one of your qualities and didn't think to rely on it.' She smiled. 'Anyway,' she added brightly, barely feeling the regular bolts of pain at her cheek, 'it's pertinent that this is personal for Mr Horowitz. He's not just Mossad tracking one of the most cowardly of war criminals, but he is a bereaved fiancé of a woman you took private pleasure in torturing, abusing and slaughtering.'

She held up a slender hand, shaking her head briefly, dismissively, like a tutor admonishing a naive student. 'No, please. It's no use protesting. There's proof. And, Rudy, he plans to take his revenge not just for the woman he loved but on behalf of all the women I loved that I watched you murder, and for the deaths of all the women and men of Europe that have your vile fingerprint on them. We don't need to be specific. You are a mass murderer and a war criminal who does not deserve life or the love of a family. Again, I pity your daughters, but they really are better off without the devil in their lives.'

At this Rudy began to struggle again. There was a moment – a heartbeat – when Katerina believed he might just break free of his bonds and lurch at her, but the tape held and Ruda Mayek was not the strong man he'd once been. Life's ravages had reduced him and she could see he didn't have the strength in his legs to launch himself again off the spongy sofa.

'Mayek?' It was Daniel. 'Be quiet. And pay attention.'

Rudy stilled.

'I refuse to discuss with you the woman to whom Katerina refers. Her name no longer need be associated with yours from here on. Moving on, I am giving you a choice. Generous, eh? We can deliver you to Israel. Our courts there will be pleased to put you on trial for your mass crimes.' He put a finger to his lips to hush the new protest that began to rage with nonsensical words behind the tape. 'Do not think about the logistics. That's my problem. Rest assured we can get you out of the country and into Israel with just a few phone calls and help from friends.' He sighed. 'Alternatively, we can deliver you to hell – which is where you're going anyway, even if you do take the scenic route via Israel.'

He held up the syringe, which Katerina watched Mayek notice for the first time with a wide-eyed whimper. 'Quick, simple, hard to detect and painful, I hope, but I can't be sure about that last one. It will stop your heart in an instant, so even if there is some pain, it will be fleeting.' Daniel swept a hand in the air. 'You will be found in this empty flat, with no sign of its previous tenant, who, even her work colleagues will attest, had left her job weeks ago. And she will have an alibi, anyway, provided by us. People will wonder at the smell and a helpful call from one of my men in a fortnight to ensure we muddy the day and time of death will alert police. We'll make sure you'll look like a squatter . . . an old, sick man taking shelter in a vacant flat. Your family need never know the truth of your past and this is the only kindness I will show you because I agree with Katerina – they don't need to know the devil was amongst them. They're the innocents and we will allow them to remember you in their way.'

Her breath came so shallow she wasn't sure she was breathing. It felt like a gap was opening in her thoughts, slicing through her mind, and she was angry to sense it filling with sympathy for Rudy and his terrible decision ahead. What a cruel choice . . . but then the gap became a pit and the pit became a grave and from the grave stared her dead family. Their eyes were open but they saw nothing; their naked bodies were too thin, too pale, and she could hear her screams dulled by the canopy of a forest she had once loved. She could also hear laughter and it belonged to Rudy. And in her mind she watched him close one eye, take aim with his pistol, hold his breath and squeeze gently. 'She's down,' she heard him say. 'Drag her back and throw her in with the other filthy Jews.'

Her eyes snapped wide again and back at Rudy. She swallowed

her pity and found the hatred she shared with Daniel. It was like a taut, invisible cord that tied their psyches. She could almost sense hers reaching out, curling around his and wrapping together for strength.

Daniel's voice was thick, hard. 'Decision time, Mayek.'

Ruda Mayek looked at her again, then back at Daniel, and his sigh seemed to collapse him into himself. He looked like death would take him soon anyway.

Daniel pointed to the syringe. 'I'm guessing this one?'

Rudy nodded once.

'The wise choice,' Daniel sneered. 'But first, I believe Katerina has something else she wishes to say to you.'

Her breath now caught in her throat as she watched Daniel gesture for one of the men to use more duct tape to secure Mayek to his death chair, wrapping it around his shoulders. 'Just for a few minutes so we know she's absolutely safe.' He glanced at the men; they seemed to understand and filed away. 'Katerina?'

She looked at Daniel.

'We are just outside.'

She breathed out, shocked that she was still going to have her opportunity to kill Ruda Mayek in her own way.

'Katerina?'

Again she lifted her gaze from Mayek to Daniel.

'Don't remove the tape around his mouth. Don't let any of his filthy words touch you.'

She nodded. The men left and she turned slowly to Edward. 'You may not want to hear this.'

He had been silent, like a shadow lurking in the corner of her room. 'How can I know?'

'You can't.'

'I shall remain because I don't intend to leave you ever again. Say to him what you have to say.'

For the moment, at least, Mayek seemed intrigued for the stay of execution.

'Rudy, the plea in your expression has no effect. I am not your judge. The Mossad is. You should have left the Ottoman Pearls in their box and never allowed your greed to overcome that once horribly sharp mind of yours, or I'd never have found you again. But now that we're here I do want to tell you something. I just never thought I'd get the chance.'

She paused, taking stock, feeling the tension trapped in her chest like a caged bird, desperate to find an escape. This was it; this was the encounter she'd only allowed herself to dream she might one day have. This was the moment she'd told herself would give her the release she needed to rid herself of the dark and finally climb out of the grave she felt she'd lived in all these years.

Say it, she commanded herself. Katerina looked down, drew a slow, deep draught of air into her lungs, forcing her to square her shoulders to their full sharp angle. She lifted her chin, despite the pain it pinged into the rest of her face, and let her gaze fall fully with hatred upon Ruda Mayek, hoping her cat's eye continued to offend him.

He watched her intently, unsure.

'You always wanted a son, Rudy.'

Creases formed at his forehead; the remark had taken him by surprise.

'Well, I want you to know you fathered one. A golden-haired boy came early into the world in 1942. He was born not far from the forest in which you raped me.' She refused to look at Edward but she sensed he was appalled. 'I gave birth to him cursing your name and refusing to give him one, especially not yours.'

She was sure the words were scalding her lips as they stepped out of her mouth. This was her most guarded secret. She waited to see the effect on the father of her son. He was staring at her with so much disbelief in his gaze that she sensed he no longer felt fear over what was coming. In a few heartbeats he had become a famished man, hungry for any morsel she might offer on the child she knew meant more to him than either of his daughters. This fact alone sickened her and made her tone deepen, her resilience stir and strengthen. She felt no more the pain at her cheek as she pressed on, emboldened, aware of the seconds leaking away before Daniel would return.

'He was beautiful . . . like you were as a child, Rudy. He would grow up in your image – of that I was sure. He was weak, though, from his early arrival. As I gave him no name, I also gave him no milk. I refused him all nourishment from my body. I watched him wither. And then . . .' She faltered, horrified that she began to weep. 'I helped him to die and I pretended he was you.'

Rudy roared behind his bindings, his eyes glazed with tears and rage.

'And when your son was dead I followed your lead and I buried him directly in the soil of an unmarked grave in the forest; he was naked, tiny, helpless. With each spadeful of dirt I threw over that small body, I found strength. And then I walked away from him . . . from you . . . from my past. Until now, of course. But I'm glad I could share this with you. I'm glad your son died unknown, unnourished, unloved . . . and I'm relieved that you will be dead this day too.'

Her heart felt hard and cruel as she watched the tears cut channels down his fleshy cheeks.

'Goodbye, Rudy. May your dark soul rot quickly.'

She could not look at Edward for fear of what his silence and expression would reflect. Katerina Kassowicz sniffed away her helpless tears at the mention of her baby and she refused to listen for another second longer to the anguished wails that erupted from the man who had haunted her life.

Still ignoring Edward, Katerina opened the door to the surprised but silent enquiry of Daniel. 'I imagine he'll go quietly for you now,' she remarked. 'I doubt it can come quickly enough.'

Daniel couldn't help himself. He gently grasped her elbow. 'What did you say to him?'

She shook her head. 'No one will ever hear such a thing again.' She was still glassy-eyed with tears. 'Are you going to do this?'

He nodded and glanced towards Edward, who looked nearly as ashen as the grey-faced man on the sofa. 'It looks like you've already killed him . . . but that was your intention, wasn't it? We will take care of everything. A woman resembling you has already purchased train tickets to York at King's Cross a few minutes ago and made a slight scene so she'll be remembered . . . just in case we need an alibi.'

She was surprised but heartened by his precautions. 'A boy called Billy from the pub up the road saw me today – he recognised me and wished me well.'

Daniel shrugged, unbothered by this. 'As far as anyone is concerned, you packed up and left your flat today. My men will remove everything of yours.'

'It's just that suitcase in the bedroom – I don't want anything else.'

He nodded. 'So you left, leaving the keys inside on the counter here before you closed the door for the last time. May I?' He held out a hand.

She dug into the slashed pinafore's pocket to retrieve her keys and gave them to him.

'The same lady impersonating you will telephone the rental agent later to say as much. Given they have your rent up-front and it's not to be vacated for a fortnight, I doubt they'll be in a hurry to visit. And if they do, you are safe, Katerina. This is an old man you don't know who died in your flat after breaking in through the fire escape. I'll leave his trail, please don't worry.' He paused. 'Edward?'

The solicitor finally moved and Daniel led them both to the doorway so they didn't have to look upon Ruda Mayek.

'I'll take her home with me,' Edward said, putting a proprietorial arm around Katerina's shoulder.

'Of course.'

The men shook hands.

The awkward pause was upon them before she could fill the space.

'I don't know what to say,' she admitted to Daniel.

'Kiss me goodbye and walk away. Words are not necessary. We both know all has been said.'

She knew what he meant. 'Daniel, when I feel ready to explain, I will write to you at your Paris apartment. I want you to visit me wherever I am.' She glanced at Edward but he was not looking at her, still no doubt turning over what he'd learned. 'And I will tell you what you want to hear.'

'I shall be back in Paris in a few weeks. I thought I might visit my family first.'

She smiled. 'Cleansing.'

He gave her a smile in agreement. 'Before you ask, no, I feel no guilt. I will feel only elation that a monster is no more.'

She nodded. 'Me too.' She leaned in and gave him a gentle kiss on his mouth, pulling away before he could misinterpret it. 'I love you, Daniel . . . you are now officially my best friend, and I've never had one of those since childhood.'

The face that struggled to smile seemed to find the right combination of levers and pulleys to achieve a warm, clearly heartfelt grin that she would have sworn he couldn't pull off. 'That will do me, Katerina.'

Her eyes misted. 'And there's another friend I want you to meet. Her name is Catherine. She's English, pretty, fun, with no painful wartime backstory. She'd be good company for you . . .'

He hushed her with a hug. 'Not yet, but maybe. Take her somewhere safe, Mr Summerbee.'

She intensified the hug. 'Thank you for looking after me.'

They parted and the smiles were sad this time.

He squeezed her hand. 'Go make a life. You deserve it.'

She turned and didn't look back, although she sensed Daniel had gone inside to watch her and Edward walk down Bury Street until they had turned the corner and left this place and the unpleasantness that was about to unfold there.

33

* * *

They sat in a frigid silence in the taxi all the way to Harley Street, where Edward introduced her to his doctor, who apparently could see her at short notice. Amazing what money could achieve. His estimation was that no bones had shifted; it was a minor fracture and bruising would likely occur. Nevertheless, she was to be taken to a private hospital of his choice for X-rays. Phone calls were made; the men muttered between them.

'What did you tell him?' she said on the way to the hospital. It was their first exchange of words since her revelation.

'The truth. A madman hit you.'

'You're not very good at lying, are you?'

'I'm rubbish at it.'

'I'm excellent at it.'

He frowned, obviously unsure of what she meant.

Once in the care of the staff, she suggested that he leave and she would come to his house later.

'Absolutely not. I'm not letting you out of my sight.'

'I know we need to talk.'

'Well, that's an understatement, but firstly I don't think I want to talk about today's events and particularly what I had to listen to, for a while. I need to think on it all. But you need to be looked after in the meantime. You have no one in London, I'm guessing, so let me do that much.'

She nodded; she didn't feel like fighting him.

It was four hours or more before they were back on their way to Kensington.

'Edward, I'm sorry you had to hear what you did.'

He shook his head. 'You gave me the option.'

'There's more to it.'

'Don't. Not now. What happened happened a very long time ago. It was war. It was life and death every day. What you told him was horrific but I can't swear that I wouldn't behave identically given what that man did to you.'

She left it at that. He wasn't ready to hear the rest of her story. He might never be, but she was rid of the darkness and for that she could only be grateful.

'I need to get hold of Otto.'

'He's in a Durham guesthouse apparently but didn't say why.'

'I know why. I even know which guesthouse.'

———

Edward wasn't curious; he was in shock. Shock at his violence, terror at the execution that was likely already finished in Bloomsbury, and trauma listening to what Katerina had done to a newborn twenty years earlier. He desperately didn't want to be judgemental. He hadn't been there; he hadn't lived through any of her desperate years, he hadn't been raped or subjected to the cruelties that she had. But a child? A helpless baby? He needed to come to terms with it; either find somewhere in his heart to forgive, or find somewhere to bury it in his mind . . . or simply to walk away from Katerina Kassowicz.

That last one seemed the most difficult of all. He wished he could. She seemed to read his mind as he held the door of his home open to her once again. Both dogs this time came clattering across the parquet flooring and then the housekeeper emerged.

'Oh, you have company, Mr Summerbee. I didn't realise.' She smiled warmly at Katerina, no doubt used to the comings and goings of women who were strangers, but then she frowned. 'Oh, my dear, you're hurt.'

'This is a close friend of mine, Mrs Lawson. Katerina will be staying.'

'Of course.'

'Is a guestroom ready?'

'The Shell Room is made up.'

'Lovely. Thank you.'

'There's food in the oven, Mr Summerbee. Always plenty for two, and I've fed the dogs. They'll need their walk, of course.'

'That's fine. Why don't you head off early?'

'Ooh, I won't say no, sir. My daughter's down from Harrogate.'

'Off you go. We can manage.'

'I won't be in tomorrow, sir, don't forget,' she reminded him, fetching her coat.

'That's fine. I shall survive.' He grinned. 'Thank you.'

After the housekeeper had left, he turned and regarded Katerina. They both seemed awkward about what to say.

'You shouldn't be with me,' she murmured.

'No, I shouldn't. But there is something addictive about you, Katerina. I think we both felt it the other evening and I'd be lying if I didn't admit that today has only made me feel more involved in your life.'

'I'm sorry.'

'Don't be. I have things to tell you, too, that I've discovered since we were last together.'

'Edward?'

'Yes?'

'Can we not talk about me, my past, my family, Mayek? I too am still trying to come to terms with what happened today. Just for the rest of today, can we just . . .'

She looked at him still so shocked, face bruised, palms turned out in a sort of helpless plea, that he reacted on instinct. The sensible, measured solicitor once more gave way to pure intuition and he hoped the reflex was the right one. 'Can we just do this?' he wondered, stepping towards her and pulling her close.

She wept. The tears were mostly silent but they shook her body and his heart, which had felt hardened at hearing her capable of murder, melted. He still couldn't get to grips with that tragic story; he couldn't yet discuss it either.

So he let her cry against him. She was tiny, really. Tall but so slim it felt like he could snap her if he pulled her too hard. Finally, feeling like they were in a movie, he decided to pick her up and carry her upstairs. His chivalrous act only lasted halfway up before he had to stop and lean against the banister. It was the strangest of moments because she seemed to find amusement in the ridiculousness of his failure. She laughed through tears.

'I so wanted to impress you with a Tarzan-like gesture,' he admitted.

Her chuckle was a balm. 'I can walk, you know.'

'You could have said so,' he accused her, faking an injured tone. 'I thought you needed rescuing.' He allowed her to stand.

They looked at each other on the stairs, too high up to turn back.

'You did rescue me.'

'Come on, let me show you where you can put your head down and sleep for as long as you want, uninterrupted.'

She let him take her hand and lead her up the stairs. He pointed. 'My room is just down there. You're here.' He opened a door into a bedroom bathed in soft afternoon light. The dying western sunlight created a warm, golden glow against thick striped wallpaper in a custardy yellow. Honey-coloured pine furniture added to a sense of cosiness and the bed was dressed in white with a checked rug of toffee and pale grey.

'I hope this is all right for you. The bathroom is through there. I'll get you some supplies; we'll worry about clothes tomorrow. Hold on, let me get you something to sleep in.'

He disappeared for a couple of minutes and returned with a pair of his pyjamas. 'Will these do?'

She hugged them to her. 'Thank you.'

He led her to the bed. 'Sit before you fall over.'

She did.

'Now, what else can I get for you?'

'Nothing. You're being so kind. May I tell you something?'

He looked unsure but nodded.

'Edward . . . when I first caught sight of you in the flat today, you were the knight in armour all girls dream about.'

He shrugged, embarrassed. 'I thought Daniel was the hero, crashing through the door like that and sorting out Mayek.'

She shook her head. 'It wasn't Daniel who saved my life. It was you. I still don't know how and I'm not ready to discuss it but you are my hero. And I have so much to say to you and it begins with an apology for dragging you into all of this.'

Edward sat on the bed and took her hand. 'I was always involved, whether I liked it or not. The Pearls were my responsibility from the moment I accepted the brief.'

'Yes, but I'm sorry for ambushing you and then stalking you – then when you were trying to help I made all sorts of accusations . . . and then I ran away. I'm a nightmare.'

'You are.'

She looked at him and all he could see was the livid bruise forming and his heart gave in fully.

'But . . . for an inexperienced lover, I can't forget how addictive your kiss is.'

She blinked, clearly not expecting this response. 'Do you want to remind yourself about it?'

'Your cheek?'

'Wouldn't you like to kiss that pain away?'

'Yes, please,' he murmured. He kissed her cheek but then also her neck, her ears; he buried his face in her hair, which smelled of her perfume – he wanted to know what it was. Never did he want to stop inhaling the heady mix that was Katerina. He wanted to watch her spray it on her skin each day and he wanted to be the only man who ever had the pleasure and privilege of seeing that bare skin, of touching that skin . . .

She lifted his head and let her lips tell him everything that he knew to be true about Katerina. He didn't for a moment feel like he was kissing a murderess and so he gave in to the passion and would wait until she felt herself ready to explain the rest of her story. He tasted all the possibility of love with a relative stranger and yet someone whose life he knew much more about than those of most women he had slept with. She kissed him back as deeply as he had ever allowed a woman to kiss him and he enjoyed letting it last until they both needed to part . . . to draw breath . . . to pause and consider where this led.

'Would Violet and Pansy approve if I asked you to get into this bed with me?' She shifted her embrace so she could look at him and he noted she appeared coy.

'Well, now, this is a room that Miss Violet chooses to doze in of an afternoon, hence the scratching at the door.'

She listened and smiled.

459

'So why don't you let me take you to my room?'

She didn't hesitate.

Recklessness had overcome her. A need to feel abandon and disconnection from what had recently occurred clearly seemed important. Katerina stood.

'You should know I've never undressed in front of a man before,' she admitted as they entered his bedroom.

'Let me put you at ease . . . neither have I,' he said, reaching for a cabinet as she laughed and winced at what that did to her injured cheek. The lid lifted to reveal a turntable. He selected a small stack of records – sixty-fives, as he called them – and hung them off the arm of the record player. He bent down and blew on the stylus. 'No one likes a gritty needle,' he remarked before pushing the small lever that activated the first shiny black disc of vinyl to drop and the arm that held the needle to move across and plonk itself down onto the record. There was a momentary scratching sound before a slow tune from a vibrato-rich clarinet oozed around the bedroom and Edward swung around and sighed. 'Recognise this?'

She shook her head.

'This is Mr Acker Bilk and his huge hit of last year called "Stranger on the Shore".'

'Haunting,' she admitted.

'Exactly.' Edward began to undress, slowly, using the music to time each button being undone.

Helpless, she began with an embarrassed grin and soon moved to chuckling aloud, her hand helplessly against her cheek to ease the pain, as he seemed to have no shame. By the time the moody instrumental had finished, Edward was all but naked, clothes strewn carelessly around him, as though he'd shed his skin. He gave her a pirouette to make her laugh properly.

It seemed they were both deliberately using humour as a counterbalance. It was the necessary distraction to allow their emotions to settle from what they'd witnessed and been a party to.

'Shameless,' she remarked, keeping in the spirit of the mood he'd created.

'But beautiful, surely? Don't you admire my body, as though sculpted by Michelangelo himself?'

She snorted a soft laugh, understanding this self-effacing humour was all for her benefit and comfort. 'You're holding together very well for a . . .?'

'Forty-four next birthday,' he admitted.

That was a surprise. 'Extremely well for someone heading towards their sixth decade.'

He mock-glared at her. 'That's a terrible way to describe a man who is still in his early forties,' he admonished her. 'I'm hoping you'll forgive the not quite so firm belly as I could claim at twenty-five, my frightened hairline and, according to others, no bottom to speak of, with legs like a flamingo.'

'Flamingo?'

'Pink and thin . . . and a bit too long for my body.'

The pain be damned. She was lost to him, laughing without further care for his feelings, for surely he couldn't care any less about them.

'And still you're trim, you look strong, and that pot belly you mention is not authentic. You are deliberately forcing out your tummy, I can see. As for your hair, you are not balding. You're fair and it's probably been thin since childhood. You'll be years watching it disappear into a soft, white frame for your boyishly handsome face.'

'Is that backhanded pity you're showing through your kind words?'

'Well, let's reserve judgement until you're fully unclothed,' she said, nodding at the boxer shorts he still wore. There was something ridiculously sexy about him standing there allowing himself to appear vulnerable and yet she sensed that Edward likely felt anything but threatened. She was delighted by the arousal she felt pinging around all corners of her body, half horrified that she'd be naked shortly too but in equal measure excited that Edward would reach for her.

She wanted his hands on her body. She wanted someone to love touching her and to feel his excitement against hers. She could forgive herself this behaviour and to hell with the fear of not knowing how to have sex.

The needle scratched against the record, refusing to budge.

'Gosh, that annoys me. I must either get a new copy of my favourite song or a new record player.' He dropped the next disc at the same time as his boxers, turning around to face her, now wearing only a rakish grin, as Chubby Checker told Katerina to twist. 'Dance with me?'

At her open-mouthed hesitation, his grin widened and he began to swivel his hips and she began to convulse with silent laughter at what this did to the one area of his body she was trying not to focus on and he was doing everything to make her focus on.

'. . . and it goes like this,' he sang, dancing as if he had no care in the world. 'Get your clothes off, Katerina. Let's dance. It's the best distraction to a troubled mind and the best foreplay!'

How could she refuse him? She undressed, casting her inhibitions away as carelessly as she tossed her damaged outfit, which she never wanted to see again. All she knew in this moment was that Edward Summerbee was the most generous, delicious and guileless person she'd ever met and she wanted his fun around her; she never wanted to lose it. Was this love? She exploded into fresh gales of amusement as Edward grabbed her hand and twirled her around, then twisted his hips in an ever-more suggestive and dramatic fashion. He began scissoring his knees in the way of the dance called the Twist to lower himself closer to the floor and then straightening, all in fluid movements, never losing the beat of the music. For a moment she had to accept that this deranged behaviour of theirs was perhaps the only defence they had against the concurrent execution of Ruda Mayek.

And she felt herself falling deeper for the silly, funny person who seemed to have multiple versions of himself: the serious, correct man in his solicitor's office; the flirt over dinner; the teen in his bedroom; the hero who had cast all his conscience away to come swinging in with little more than an umbrella and essentially saved her life.

She didn't know she could dance with such wanton laughter or with the sense of recklessness she felt right now with Edward, who was singing along and looked for all the world to be entirely abandoned to the music and to her. Chubby Checker sang the last note and they laughed and fell together, *skin on skin* – of the best kind – his fresh arousal thrilling her. She was nervous but not anxious; she was filled with the knowledge that at another time, with a vastly different man, in another place, the very act that was about to take place was horror-filled, whereas now she couldn't wait to cling tightly to this man with her arms, her legs, her mouth, her body . . .

The record player miraculously began to work again and another record dropped as they breathlessly collapsed onto his bed. The smoky voice of Ella Fitzgerald embraced them in a slow burn of 'My Funny Valentine'. Edward remained silent for a while, smiling affectionately as their breathing slowed to meet the pace of the new song that would carry them out of the hilarity and into the new mood gathering around them.

'Thank you for this,' she said. 'I needed it.'

'So did I. What's going on behind that frown?' he wondered aloud.

She took a moment to think on it in this bedroom that was dominated by a vast black closet with gilded adornments and brass handles. The wallpaper was embossed – the style was called Lincrusta, she knew – and it was painted the richest of creams that in the soft lamplight glowed towards a buttercup. This was the Edwardian part of the house he spoke of. She was letting her thoughts ramble in preparation for what was about to occur and yet she didn't feel frightened by his hardened, needy body pressed against hers.

'I'm reflecting on how comforted I feel right here, right now.' She paused a beat. 'Or as comfortable as anyone might be who hasn't a stitch of clothes on in the arms of a naked stranger.'

He smiled. 'I wasn't prepared for you, Katerina.' He sounded wistful. 'My world is sorely disrupted now,' he said in a tutting tone. 'But I'm concerned about what occurred with . . . I don't even want to say his name.'

'Don't,' she warned. 'I will not permit him to share this.'

His voice was as gentle as the fingertip that caressed her shoulder. 'Nevertheless, he *is* here. He damaged you in ways that are incalculable. I would be lying if I said I wasn't frightened to go further . . . and I don't ever want to lie to you.'

She touched his cheek gently. 'I like that word *ever*.'

'Are you frightened?'

'A little.' Honesty might kill the mood but she sensed he would prefer the truth in this tender moment.

He watched her, not moving any more, and their faces were so close that it was if he were breathing only the air she allowed him. Ella's sultry song deepened their connection. 'I'm sort of horror-struck, Katerina. I didn't imagine there would ever be anyone special enough to trap me.'

'You are free; I have no intention of imprisoning you because of this.'

His frown intensified. 'You misunderstand. I am the proverbial moth to the flame, the fly to the spider's web, the bee to the honey pot, although I have to say that bees are attracted to flowers and their nectar, not honey per se.' He rolled over and she began to laugh again beneath him; was he being amusing again to ease their tension? He let out a sigh of exasperation. 'I'm not explaining myself, am I? The point is, cast your spell, I want to be in its thrall; never release me.'

'Did you just accuse me of witchcraft?'

'I have no other explanation.'

'There have been so many other women,' she teased.

'Loads of them. I'm a dreadful Lothario.'

'I believe you.'

He shrugged, tracing the angles of her face with a finger.

'Out of nowhere you arrived and it's been drama ever since, including me believing myself in love with someone I have spent the sum total of about four hours with.'

Katerina kissed him gently for his honesty, enjoying the fresh tendrils of desire this prompted instantly between them. She could feel the pull of that arousal deep in her belly and lower, tingling at her nipples, pinching her skin to gooseflesh.

'You are now officially my drug,' he murmured in between soft, wet kisses.

'Then love me, Edward. Don't worry about either of our pasts. Just let's both live in this moment. The memory of two decades ago must submit to the present; this is my life now. I've never chosen to be with anyone but I'm choosing you. Just – go slow . . .' She trailed off as if unsure of what she meant but he didn't need her to explain, it seemed.

Edward Summerbee proceeded to kiss every inch of Katerina Kassowicz that night in an achingly tender demonstration that he was in no hurry. To the sound of a scratchy needle that refused to lift from the end of Ella's record, he took their lovemaking at a glacial pace. Expertly, Edward built her need for him over what felt to Katerina like hours, so that by the time he made a move to finally join their bodies, she felt the novel – and for her, incredible – surge of desire to have a man inside her and only because it felt like the most natural step. She wanted this man and she was secure in the knowledge this time that he adored her. There was discomfort but it passed and her body received him as easily as if they were crafted for each other.

And with their bodies linked, a new, restless energy overtook them; she was not prepared for this either but she gave herself over to the pleasure that forced her to close her eyes at first before squeezing them in a sort of agony that she never wanted to let go of. Then, together, they sighed and they reached, moving in delicious slow tandem like making an ascent until it was Edward who let go with a soft and apologetic gasp and moments later she felt herself sink into a delicious shuddering that rippled through her body. Deep within the spangles of intense pleasure Katerina felt a seam of pity open that she had missed out on so much loving for twenty years.

They finally lay quiet, their breathing the only sound they made within while the odd car horn or distant voice came from beyond . . . a different world, she decided, to the special safe world of Edward's arms. They were both still as if glued, but the truth was Katerina didn't want to move, didn't want to ever leave this haven.

'I think I'm suddenly jealous of all those women you've slept with.'

He dipped his golden head to face her, his look suddenly serious. 'Don't be. I slept with them but didn't love them as I do you.'

'Edward, I don't want you feeling obligated because we've —'

'I don't. Presumptuous or not, I feel as though we've skipped all the traditional phases of friendship and that you're mine now and your pain of the past is also mine. We both have things to share. Let's leave it for a few days. Let's make a promise not to talk about any of this for forty-eight hours . . . time to heal just a little.'

'I like that plan. So what shall we do for the rest of tonight?'

'Ah, yes. Well, for the rest of the night, I think I can take care of that . . .'

34

Two days later, they were wending their way through the narrow cobbled streets of old York.

'The joyous cacophony of bells seems to be calling to us,' Edward noted.

'They're from St Wilfrid's, which stands in the shadow of York Minster,' she explained. 'They're calling parishioners to Latin mass. Mrs Biskup is Roman Catholic and goes to that church. But our destination is the largest Norman cathedral in northern Europe. The Normans decided to build their grand place of worship on the site of the old Roman basilica. The beating heart of this region of England for the last' – she wobbled her head, trying to make up her mind – 'two thousand years or thereabouts.' She grinned. 'But right now we're in a cluster of streets in the walled city known as Petergate. It's where Guy Fawkes was born, by the way.'

Edward nodded, impressed.

'Formerly known as Via Principalis when the Romans built their fortress. Now, as you can see, it's a mix of medieval and Georgian architecture – it used to be the way into York from Scotland.'

'My darling, you would make a fine tourist guide.'

'I *am* boring you,' she said, sounding disappointed in herself.

'I swear not. I suppose I'm only just discovering this brilliant, historical side of you.'

She looked appeased. 'Minerva.' She pointed to the corner of the streets at High Petergate, not far from the small bed and breakfast they were staying in above some tearooms at number 52. 'Goddess of wisdom and drama – note with her wise owl nearby, and leaning on her stack of books. When we first came to York in December 1949 she became my lucky talisman. She makes me feel safe.'

He leaned in and kissed her non-injured cheek. 'You are safe, although I'm worried others might think I've done this to you.'

Katerina tightened her arm around his. 'I know you didn't and if they ask I shall tell them that Sir Summerbee, the Knight of Lancaster Gate, rescued me from the person who did this.'

He turned towards Henry Hardcastle's Jeweller & Silversmith, which seemed to offer everything from regimental mess plates to wedding gifts.

'Antique silver is this fellow's specialty. I've spent many an afternoon staring into these windows.' She smiled.

'You obviously liked it here.'

'Oh, I did. I was a creature of winter, and coming from Czechoslovakia the cold didn't trouble me. The city oozed history all the way back to the Romans and the Vikings, the Normans, the Tudors . . . it's a historian's playground, really. And I was anonymous. I could start my life again, plus culturally England was so different that there were no reminders of my past. Especially not a German accent or a swastika in sight.'

He smiled sadly. 'So maybe you could be persuaded to remain in England?'

She leaned into him against the spring chill. 'I'm here, aren't I?'

'Don't stay just for a while. Stay forever.'

Katerina sighed. 'Nice thought.' The light reflected from the silver in the windows lit her face in all of its exquisite angles but highlighted the bruising she'd done her best to conceal. It hurt his heart to see it, but he was glad that the fracture was thin and hadn't depressed the sweep of her elevated cheek structure he admired.

'Marry me, Katerina,' he said.

The words slipped out before he could consider what he was suggesting. It was a rush of emotion but not a hollow one. He'd kept his romantic nature in check for too many years. Now there was a reason to let go.

―――――――

Her head whipped around in disbelief. She'd heard the expression 'the world stilled' and for the first time she understood it and experienced it in a situation that was not about her demons but genuine delighted shock. She felt her lips part to respond but words failed her. She frowned; she needed to be sure she'd heard him right and so she replayed his question in her thoughts.

'I mean it,' he reinforced. 'I don't want you to ever leave me and I don't want to be with anyone else. You've killed Lothario.'

She stared at him in a mix of shocked bemusement. 'Edward, you hardly know me.'

'I know more about you than any other man alive and I don't need to know more to believe we should be together for keeps . . . I . . . well, for pity's sake, Katerina, I love you. I need you.'

A helpless smile broke and it felt like sunshine arriving into night. Perhaps it wasn't right to feel this happy and yet she couldn't deny the wave of pleasure that moved through her like a tide surging to the shore.

'Shouldn't we talk about what we're not talking about first?'

'No. Nothing you say will change my mind. What happened

occurred two decades before I knew you. You were a teenager and had suffered more than most adults ever will in a lifetime. I want us to put it away and never talk about it again.'

'My darling, we must talk about it. In fact, we are going to talk about it today, but it might be easier if I just show you.'

'Is that why you brought me here?'

She nodded.

'All right. We shall confront whatever you want but give me an answer first. Will you marry me?'

He was summer in every sense to her winter. 'Yes,' she said, hardly daring to believe this was happening. 'I would love to be your wife, Edward.'

He gave a brief whoop of joy that made her grin like a loon. 'I want to marry you immediately. This month! I want to hear you called Katerina Summerbee. I mean this with no disrespect to your family but perhaps the sooner you disconnect with the dark past, the easier it will be for you to look forward.'

She nodded; it was harsh but it was a kindness that he had aired what had often floated around her mind about cutting free of death, of rape, of murder . . . of survival. She needed to become a new version of herself, an open individual who shared her world with others and let her heart be filled with life. Edward was her chance for all of this.

'How does next week sound?'

The thrill through his lovely features amused her further and he held her shoulders as she laughed. 'Kiss me. Seal it. Or I refuse to move,' he threatened.

With no care for tutting observers, she wrapped her arms around his neck and kissed him briefly but with such tender affection he could never be mistaken that this was real.

'I love you,' she whispered and regarded him through misty eyes. 'We'll celebrate properly later.'

'On our squeaky guestroom bed,' he murmured and they shared the intimate laugh of lovers as they opened an umbrella against the new drizzle and headed across the slick paving stones of Minster Yard.

'Come on, we can't be late,' she urged.

———————

Inside, shaking out their brolly and slightly out of breath from hurrying, they stepped, not quite on tiptoe, down the grand cruciform design of the York Minster.

'Widest Gothic nave in England. Look at this magnificent sweeping chancel with its vast ceiling.' She sighed with pleasure to see the vaulted design overhead, a pale background with its ribs picked out in gold. 'I'm humbled by the beauty of Christian churches.'

'I don't think I've ever been in here before, not even as a child when we travelled north. This is stunning.'

'We have seats reserved,' she whispered and guided Edward past the choir screen of stone that depicted regal figures. 'Fifteen kings of England from William I to Henry VI.' She cut him a grin. 'Just say if you're bored.'

'No, I can see how this all thrills you. Besides, how could I be bored listening to you, my fiancée?'

Katerina enjoyed the sound of that word, and squeezed his gloved hand.

'But, I'm just wondering why we're here?'

'To hear the organ recital,' she said, suddenly distracted by looking for their seats.

Other church visitors were finding places in the pews, whispering to one another.

'How did you swing this?' Edward murmured as she led him up the small stairs and into the choir stalls.

'All will be explained,' she said, gesturing for him to be seated.

He did so, removing his coat and gloves, giving a soft sigh that said he was glad to be off his feet after all the walking around old York.

'This is a lovely idea, actually,' he murmured just above a whisper. 'When do you reveal why, though?'

She lifted a single eyebrow at him with an expression of mystery.

'Because, my love, any day of the week I can take you to a superb organ or choral recital in London. We don't have to come up to the freezing north to do this.'

'We do, though,' she assured him.

'So secretive. Will I be pleased?'

She frowned. 'I hope so.'

They shifted their knees as apologetic people squeezed by them to sit in the same carved choir stall, which stepped up across three levels.

'Now.' He drew a low breath. 'I have an admission.'

She raised an eyebrow in enquiry.

'I have a secret to share with you too. In fact, I'm so excited to do so, it's bursting out of me and I reckon on top of the news that you will marry me I could now sing soprano with the choir if asked.'

She chuckled, hushing herself for fear of their jolly conversation being frowned upon by purse-lipped couples feeling they were disrespecting the cathedral's atmosphere. 'Please don't,' she whispered. 'What secret?'

'Later. Coming to York this weekend made it awkward but I couldn't hang on to my surprise a day longer, so it's required some organisation, but I can tell you we're meeting someone at Terry's later.'

She nodded. 'I know it. Why there?'

'Well, I'm warned that Betty's can be horribly busy and noisy while Terry's seemed like an easier – but still central – place for this person to come to. I doubt he knows York at all.'

'He? Daniel?'

'No. I spoke to Daniel last night, actually. He's back in Paris – didn't spend long in Wales but is returning shortly. Sends his love. Impresses for you not to dwell on *stuff*.'

'Why did you speak to him?'

Edward tapped his nose. 'Be patient. In your words, all will be revealed.'

Other voices hushed and theirs fell silent too as the choir of St Peter's School filed in. This was the revered Chamber Choir from the famous school.

'You're going to tell me something about the schoolboys now, aren't you?'

She shook her head. 'Well,' she began, 'only that Guy Fawkes attended their school. Fourth oldest school in the world, I gather. Did you know this glorious cathedral was once a simple church of wooden structure back in AD 627?'

He looked at her in wonder as she nodded back.

'Today it has the highest proportion of medieval stained glass of any cathedral in Europe and its rose windows – the ones you admired – they're known as the Heart of Yorkshire.'

Again they had to become silent as it appeared proceedings were soon to begin, but Katerina had another, far more pressing and heart-squeezing reason to fall quiet and still. She instinctively looked up towards the Grand Organ above the quire screen at a row of vertical pipes, resplendent in rich colours and glittering with gold that the choir stall candles picked out. She looked for a soft glow emanating from where the organist sat and she saw a shadow pass across the space.

There he was! He turned, looked for her and a crooked smile lifted at one corner of his mouth, disappearing as quickly as it came.

Over the next hour Katerina was lost in the music; it didn't matter to her that she was in this Christian cathedral. She had long ago subscribed herself to being part of the church of the world. Religion had no divide any more for her; she was convinced that prayers could be offered anywhere, any time, and that lives would be judged by their actions, not on how many times they were seen in their places of worship. The soaring voices of the choirboys lifted the audience to cheering point by the end of the concert but still the proper English clapped politely but loudly for the angelic, pink-cheeked youngsters who made her flesh goosepimple with joy at their high, haunting notes. But it was the rousing pipes of the organ, whose notes she could feel booming through her chest, that she came for. Only three years earlier the organ had been renovated so its massive sound could reach out more widely into the nave and she felt that effect now, marvelling at the agile fingers and feet of the organist as he pulled out the stops and worked the pedals to make her teary.

Afterwards, they stamped their feet outside the minster as people rushed to find warmth after locating their family members.

'We're waiting why?' Edward bleated. His nose looked as though it had turned red with the frosty night air, although the light was too low for her to be sure. She grinned at it and then she saw who she was waiting for, passing beneath one of the lamps around the front court of the cathedral. He raised a hand and hurried towards her. She knew she was ambushing poor Edward once again but it was easier to show than tell.

Katerina caught her breath. He looked like a man suddenly; these last three months since she'd seen him, a change had occurred. How could she have missed it? Even the once fluff-ridden chin seemed to have settled into the shadowy outline of a real beard. So he would be shaving properly now. Emotion choked her. He was lankier, broader, and his once white-blond hair had darkened to nut brown, which he'd allowed to grow past his ears. And he was wearing the sweater she'd bought for him in Paris that day she'd met Daniel at the gallery – it seemed like a lifetime ago, but it was only a fortnight.

'That lad seems to know us . . . you, I mean.' Edward looked at her, puzzled.

'It's him we're waiting for.'

He arrived, his smile faltering at the realisation that Edward wasn't just a passer-by.

'Peter,' she said, her voice breaking on his name, and uncharacteristically threw herself at the young man and hugged him tightly, stroking his long hair, kissing his stubbly cheeks, staring into those eyes ringed with a navy outline. 'My handsome Peter.' She finally pulled herself away and looked at the puzzled Edward.

'Peter, I'd like you to meet the man I told you about. He's very special and important to me. This is Edward Summerbee. Edward, this is the organist we've been listening to.'

'Good grief. You were amazing. What a sound, especially that rousing number that led us out.'

The younger man's pale eyes reflected the smile that showed small, neat teeth. 'Pleased to meet you, sir. Yes, we're given free rein on what to play when the audience is leaving and I always enjoy playing something they recognise and feel like singing along or clapping to,' Peter said, extending a hand that was long, his handshake deliberate.

'Well, I'm impressed. Good to meet you, son. Mmm, firm grip. Do you play rugby?'

'I do, sir. I prefer cricket, though.'

Edward nodded as if to say *Fair enough*. He cut a look back at Katerina, waiting.

The moment was here. She let go of her final secret. 'Edward, Peter is my son, named for the brother I adored who died.'

Edward's happy, interested expression faltered. He seemed to want to speak but no sound came out; it was obvious that he was struggling to process what she'd just said and for a heartbeat or two she regretted springing the surprise.

'Your son? But . . .'

Peter cut her a look of soft recrimination. 'I'll be back in a moment,' he said generously – as usual – giving her a chance to explain. 'I just need to catch Mr Clarke.' He shot the last few words at Edward, who could only nod.

She nodded too without looking at her child, her gaze firmly on Edward, who had blanched in his shock. Peter extricated himself from the tension that had formed around his mother and her companion like a rubber balloon, stretched to its limit.

'You said you —'

'I lied.' She shivered but not from the cold. 'I couldn't let Rudy know his son was alive.' She filled in the blanks for Edward. 'He was born in 1942 after we fled the hospital. I told you Otto made sure I got to Switzerland safely. Mrs Biskup came with me. She delivered Peter for me. I didn't have a clue what I was doing . . . I was only just fifteen by then. We discovered I was probably four months pregnant by the February and so we had a deadline to get me out of Czechoslovakia. The attempted assassination of Heydrich gave us an impetus to go sooner rather than later. Luckily, I barely showed. We stayed in Switzerland until the end of the war. We found our way into France as refugees and Mrs Biskup and Peter remained an hour or so north of Paris, while I worked in the city, until Peter was four. I decided I would give him the very best education money could buy but in a place no one like Ruda Mayek would think to look. I thought if Peter grew up with an English accent, he would be less conspicuous.'

'Does Peter know who his father is?'

She shook her head. 'Nor will he ever know, nor that he has

stepsisters . . . for their sake as much as his. I told Rudy what I did to hurt him in the only way I knew how. I told Peter his father was my nineteen-year-old sweetheart killed just before our wedding during the war.'

'He resembles Mayek.'

She nodded. 'It used to be more obvious and I had to fight that repugnance daily, but look at him now – his hair colour has changed irrevocably and even his eyes are now far darker than Rudy's.' She squeezed Edward's arm for emphasis. 'He is also nothing like his father in character. He's finishing law at Durham but he won a special organ scholarship through school – he's been playing since he was a little boy, learning on a small upright that Mrs Biskup's local priest had in his home. Music is in Peter's soul, as it is in mine. I think he'll choose to follow his music but if he chooses the law . . .?'

'Then he'll have me,' he finished for her.

Her eyes watered at his generosity. 'You're not upset?'

'No. How could I be? Surprised, shocked, definitely relieved and slightly unnerved.'

'Unnerved?'

'That you love another man as much as you do me.' He smiled, recovering himself. She knew his excuse was simply a cover but she also knew Edward would find his way through this knot. His next words confirmed it. 'But that's my problem, not yours. He seems a fine young man and I know now how you survived all of your pain.'

She nodded. 'My life this past twenty years has been about Peter. Raising him, keeping him safe . . . I completed some study in Switzerland to complement my passion, which properly qualified me to get my role at the Louvre and that meant I could earn sufficiently and independently to give him the life I wanted for him. I can't help who his father is . . . was . . . but neither could I hold his birth against him. I loved him with all of my heart from the moment I held him, in spite of how he came to be.'

'You amaze me with all this love you've kept hidden and still you were able to say those horrible things to Mayek about the boy you love.'

'Pure hate helped me to do that. If it were to anyone else I could not have spoken about Peter in such a terrible way. But while I knew I could never end Rudy's life, I knew I could kill his evil spirit, and I forgive myself for using the child I love with all my heart to do so. Peter will never know. You, Daniel, me – our secret. From childhood I was aware that Rudy wanted a son so badly that it felt empowering to make that dream come true and then destroy it in the next breath. I don't regret it, Edward, but I don't ever want Peter to discover my ploy. Will you keep my secret?'

'Of course,' he soothed, hugging her. 'Does he ask about his father?'

'He used to. Not any more. Will you be all right about this?'

'Katerina, I love you, which means I want to know everything about you but I'm now wondering how Peter must feel about you having someone else.'

'We've talked about it over the phone and we'll talk more, I'm sure. The truth, though, is he's happy for me, especially now he's moving into adulthood and carving out his future. He must be feeling relieved that the burden of being the sole focus of two women is about to ease. Besides, he needs a man in his life. I can't think of a finer one.'

He grinned. 'He's coming. Er . . . Katerina, are you comfy that we're taking Peter to Terry's, where there's another surprise waiting?'

'I shall share it with both of you. It is a happy one, isn't it?'

'You could say it's of the same magnitude as the one you've just landed on me . . . I think you'll weep with pleasure.'

'Don't exaggerate. Come on. Let's walk to St Helen's Square before we freeze to these cobblestones.'

She linked arms with Peter and Edward, unable to imagine herself any happier than she was in this moment and so wrapped in the pleasure of her release from the torment of years gone by that she only had room in her heart for optimism. She couldn't imagine who Edward was going to introduce them to, but quietly assumed it was someone senior in the art world who was perhaps going to offer her a role that would allow her to continue to work in her specialist field in England, now that it was going to be her home.

En route she loved Edward a little more – if that was possible – for the way he engaged Peter in conversation about his studies, about Durham University, about the contacts that he could connect Peter to . . . and the Beatles, of course, as he'd quickly worked out this was the fan to whom she'd referred in the taxi.

'If your mother doesn't take you to their next concert, I will,' he promised.

'Be warned, he sings and dances along . . . badly,' Katerina cautioned.

They arrived with laughter around them at the sweep of windows that was the main Terry's Chocolates Salon and Tearooms, proclaiming it offered everything from bridal cakes and confectionery to the famed chocolates and jellies. A four-tiered wedding cake teetered in the main window.

'I think we should order that,' Edward whispered in jest.

'Sssh, no one knows yet,' she admonished him but without heat.

Peter held the door for them to enter the steamy warmth and Katerina led them up the few stairs and into the tearooms. It was just closing in on a quarter to six but the place was full and happy voices echoed around the salon, which was a merry mix of Victorian counters and Art Deco ceilings.

'It keeps evolving, obviously,' Edward said, looking around as he made himself comfortable at a corner table, then held up a hand. 'No more history, please, Katerina.'

Peter laughed. 'Oh, it's your turn to suffer, I'm afraid.'

This prompted a gust of laughter between the men and she loved hearing it; she wanted to pinch herself.

The waitress who had got them seated returned. 'Sorry about that, folks. Whew, it's busy tonight. There must be something on at the minster. My name is Jean. Would you like to peruse the menu while you wait for your guest, sir?'

'We would, thank you, Jean,' Edward agreed. Large menus were handed around. 'He shouldn't be long. We arranged to meet at six . . . a few minutes more.'

'I'll be back shortly.'

'Edward's keeping our guest all very cloak-and-dagger,' Katerina explained to her son. 'It's a surprise.'

'For both of you,' Edward added.

Katerina got busy unpeeling her coat and gloves. She smiled as Edward continued the conversation they had been having earlier as they entered pretty St Helen's Square and the jolly scene of Terry's and Betty's lit up for their patrons.

'Human rights? It's a fabulous area of the law, and the more bright young minds we can have applying themselves to this still rather cruel world we live in, the better. I know some barristers you may like to have a chat with.'

'Oh, thank you, sir. That's brilliant. I do have to make a decision about my music, of course.'

'Call me Edward. I've asked your mother to marry me, so we're going to be family.'

Peter's mouth opened and Katerina held her breath. She hadn't intended her son find out like this or so soon. She herself was still in the rush of novelty at the idea. 'Edward!'

'What?' He didn't even sound defensive to her; he was a maestro of polite directness. 'Listen, Peter. This is a night of pleasant shocks. I love your mother more than rugby. More than a Sunday afternoon stroll through Kensington Gardens. More than a . . . a Terry's hot chocolate. I want to keep her safe and adored. And I want us to be a family. I know it's something she probably wanted to ease you towards but I'm all for up-front honesty, while your mother is more a shades-of-grey kind of person. Plus . . . you don't have to fret about her. I'll keep her happy while you get busy building your career.'

'Mum, I think it's wonderful.' The young man regarded them, his gaze moving between them with a smile that lit his eyes. 'Congratulations to you both. I've never seen my mother look this carefree.'

'Well, I hope she has good reason now.'

She reached across the table to squeeze her son's hand. 'Family. That has a nice ring, doesn't it?'

'My Granny Biskup will have to give you the all clear, of course, Edward. She's fearsome.'

Katerina laughed. 'He's right, she is.'

'Right, I'd better ask her permission then too. She lives here?' Edward asked.

'Yes. Milena lives on the edge of York. Peter used to get a weekend release from St Peter's boarding school in York to live with her on Saturdays and Sundays. She likes the city.'

'She doesn't like that I'm in Durham and you're in Paris, though,' Peter admonished her.

'Well, soon your mother will be living full-time in England so you can all spend more time together,' Edward said. 'Oh,' he added, looking over their heads and moving his chair back to stand. 'Our guest has arrived.'

Katerina followed his gaze. The dark-haired stranger had his back turned as he shrugged off his coat, and then her view got blocked by moving waitresses.

'I'll just be a moment,' Edward said and left the table.

'Mum, who's this?' Peter asked conversationally.

'Honestly, darling, I have no idea. That fellow can't be much older than you, can he?'

Peter shook his head and craned a look. 'A couple of years at most, perhaps.'

She sighed, not wishing to stare.

Her son looked back at her. 'He looks nervous.'

She glanced across. 'So does Edward. I guess we'll find out soon enough.'

Edward led the youngish fellow with the dark looks towards them. Their guest was in a suit and he straightened his tie in a freshly nervous gesture as they drew close.

She watched as the man stepped out from behind Edward and what she saw in his face made her breath catch. Suddenly there was only their table, only their quartet; everything else in the busy tea-room felt as though it had gone as still as her chest, which trapped her voice. Emotion tumbled around her thoughts like rocks rolling down a hillside, gathering speed. Her vision seemed to close in until all she could see were the stranger's eyes like the colours of the lake near the villa, and in one was the haunting mark . . . an oddity . . . a mote that marked him.

She heard Edward's voice as though he were speaking from the depths of that lake. It reached her nonetheless. 'Katerina, this is Petr Kassowicz, your brother.'

She stared at the man as though she was looking at him through a window pane in the rain because she was helplessly weeping as Edward threatened she might, while he told her that her father's will had explained that Petr had been sent away on the *Kindertransport*.

'I found him through the Red Cross and a wonderful woman whose keen memory recalled that a child using the name of Hersh Adler was actually Petr Kassowicz of Prague, whom Samuel Kassowicz handed over as a substitute when the Adler family panicked and would not give their son up.'

'Our mother knew, apparently. It's in the will documentation that Mr Summerbee unearthed,' Petr said, in a voice that sounded so reminiscent of her father's that she had to cover her mouth for the sobbing.

She nodded, trying to get past the shock. 'It explains so much about our household now.'

'Mum, people are beginning to stare,' her son remarked. 'And how marvellous; looks like I've gained an uncle,' he said kindly, standing to shake hands and then surprising Petr with a hug.

'Let them stare,' Katerina said, openly weeping, and reached for the brother she had mourned for too long.

EPILOGUE

LONDON

1964

Katerina Summerbee stood at the entrance to the dining room of the house at Lancaster Gate where everyone she loved had gathered. Edward had insisted on Christmas festivities, despite her Jewish ancestry, as a simple way to celebrate the end of a special year for Katerina that was free from fear and had produced Amálie, their daughter.

'What do you think? It means beloved,' she'd explained to Edward when he'd held his daughter for the first time in the hospital.

'I think it's an appropriately beautiful name for the most beautiful creature I've ever laid eyes on. Sorry, Katerina, I have to tell you, I love another girl as much as I love you.'

Lavish decorations cut a sparkling trail of wreaths and acorns, holly, ivy, red berries and silver tinsel from the fireplace to the glinting candelabra above the polished table around which laughter erupted. She mentally hugged herself at the doorway, holding a fresh tray of poppyseed cakes she'd made with Milena Biskup, faithfully following a familiar recipe from Prague. Was this really her household? Look at them all talking over each other, breaking bread together, laughing so much!

Her Christmas Eve guests included Daniel meeting her old friend Catherine for the second time, and they seemed to be getting on rather well, she thought. She hoped it might develop . . . Her son Peter had introduced them to Laura, his girlfriend, both finishing a big year at university, and Katerina liked that the woman Peter was so soft-eyed over seemed to be her own person. She was presently holding a serious conversation about American politics with Daniel. Good for her.

Hilarity erupted as music suddenly boomed from the record player. It was the Beatles; John Lennon was suggesting a girl please, please him. And Edward was all over it, leaping around, demanding that Mrs Biskup dance with him. This had put her son into convulsions of laughter to see the woman he considered his grandmother shaking a leg in the grand dining room with his new stepfather. Meanwhile, Katerina noticed that Catherine was showing her brother how to sip an advocaat without pulling a face that it contained egg yolk.

'No, don't eat the cherry straight away, Petr. Save it for last,' she was telling him.

Peter stood to take the tray of small cakes. 'Here, let me, Mum.'

She smiled as she handed them to him. 'If anyone wonders, I'm just going out for a cigarette.'

He nodded. 'You've got a few more days,' he warned. 'And then you stop. Think of Amálie.'

'I promise. Can you check on her, darling? I know she's sleeping but just while I'm outside.'

Trailed by Pansy, her affectionate new companion, she stepped out into her garden via the back door of the parlour. She shivered, regretting not grabbing her coat, and lazily lit up, convincing herself she'd only take a couple of drags. She didn't need the nicotine; she just wanted to savour the moment in her mind that life had changed so dramatically for her. She liked the way the moon's glow lighted on the string of pearls around her, which that she could see reflected in the darkened window nearby. An early Christmas present from Edward.

'I want you to have your own precious heirloom to enjoy and hand down to our daughter,' he had murmured as he placed the cool orbs around her to fix the clasp. He had kissed the back of her neck. 'There.'

She'd raised her slender fingers to them, loving immediately how their serpentine quality laid a blushing trail over her clavicle to hang with a heavy pleasure in a double strand just above the rise of her breasts. She could only imagine the cost, for their nacre even in artificial light was dazzling. She touched them again now, knowing that apart from her simple wedding ring she would never need or want another piece of jewellery.

She watched a robin land on a tree, admiring his proud scarlet chest for the seconds he perched . . . and then he was gone.

Katerina turned at a sound behind her. It was Petr, smiling shyly and carrying a coat, which he helped her into. 'You shouldn't be out here. It's freezing.'

She linked arms with him. 'No, I like it. Reminds me of home.'

'Does it? I wish I knew it.'

'Let's go.'

'What?'

'I want to take you. It's time I returned. I've been thinking I need to go back. I marked their grave, you know.'

'Back to the forest?' She'd told him the terrible tale of his family.

'Yes, especially there. We'll have to get approval from all the right departments in the communist government but we must exhume them; lay them to rest properly. But also we should return to the villa, to the house in Prague . . . just to see them again.

Edward has been busy looking into how we might settle them back into our joint names and I'd like you to see where you were born. It won't be the same, of course, with the new government, but . . .' She flicked away the cigarette.

'I wish I'd known them.'

'They're here, Petr,' she said, placing a hand on his chest over his heart. 'You were the most beloved child in the family.'

He looked down smiling. 'I can't imagine it.'

'We all adored you. You were a bit poorly so you cried a lot but oh, when you laughed, we all laughed. You haven't lost your dimples either; I can still glimpse the baby brother beneath this grown-up face,' she said, giving his cheek a tug.

He sighed. 'You've met my foster parents —'

'And there's no doubt how much they love you,' she reassured him. 'I wish they'd come down to London tonight.'

'They will. They're coming around and no longer feel threatened. And the name change came through.'

She frowned. 'Are you struggling with it?'

He shook his head. 'No, I love my real name. It fits me in a way that Hersh never did. Odd, isn't it, that even as a youngster I didn't feel that name belonged to me. Do you like Nissa?'

'She's adorable.'

'I'm going to ask her to marry me.'

She kissed the side of his head. 'Nissa's a wonderful girl with a superb family. You couldn't do better. Let's visit Prague and together we'll build those lost years for you and then we will build a new life together. Now that I've found you, I will never let you go. We've got family again, Petr . . . we belong, not just to each other, but to all those people in there who love us and the ones not here – your parents, Nissa.'

Edward appeared. 'There you are, darling. Are you both all right?'

They smiled, nodding.

'There's a phone call for you. Mrs Lawson took it so I'm not sure who it is.'

'Right.' She frowned. 'Petr, tell Edward our plans for Prague. See you boys inside.' She kissed Edward as she passed.

She walked back through the parlour where Mrs Lawson had reappeared.

'I thought you'd take it in the study, Mrs Summerbee.'

'Do you know who it is?'

'He said it's a surprise.'

'He?' She frowned with a smile. 'Thank you. Maybe tea and coffee soon?'

'Coming up.' Their housekeeper beamed.

Katerina strolled to the study, intrigued. Who could be calling her? Maybe it was Mr Partridge trying to convince her to join them as a part-time staff member again at the museum. She was still considering his offer, now that she knew Amálie and Mrs Lawson were near inseparable and she could spare some hours to work again.

She picked up the receiver. 'Hello, this is Katerina.'

'Hello, Katerina.' The mellow tone triggered a feeling as though her insides had decided to do a collective somersault.

'Otto!'

'I hope you don't mind me calling. Your husband contacted me.'

She smiled, tearing up. 'It's so good to hear your voice. Did you receive my card . . . with the photo of Petr holding Amálie?'

'He's a fine young man and she's beautiful. I'm so thrilled for you all. How's Milena?'

She laughed. 'Currently dancing around the dining room with my husband and drinking advocaat.' Katerina delighted in the sound of his gentle laughter at the other end. 'Are you calling from Austria?'

'No, our family is holidaying in Switzerland this year but I thought it was high time we kept our promise to have a reunion. I want to formalise our invitation – do come and visit us in Salzburg – and Edward has asked us to visit London in return; insists we all stay with you, although he will live to regret that with all the women I bring.'

She laughed. 'Promise me you will – all of you. And we will come early next year before the snow disappears.'

'I promise.'

There was a pause.

'He's finally gone, Otto. I mean, out of my mind completely. The Pearls are now on permanent display at the British Museum – a donation from the Kassowicz family to the world.'

'I'm proud of you, Katerina, and there's a little gift under the tree for you from me. I know you don't celebrate Christmas but your husband does and he said he'd be delighted to have it wrapped up.'

'Oh, you didn't have to.'

'I wanted to. Anyway, don't let me keep you from your family and festivity. We shall see each other in the new year, for sure.'

'I will hold you to that.'

'Well, lots of love to you and yours,' he said. 'I really am so very happy for you and this lovely life ahead.'

She didn't want him to know she was crying to hear his tender voice. 'Thank you,' she managed to ease out without her voice breaking.

'Bye, Katerina.' The line went dead and she stood there for a second, gathering herself back from memories.

She felt arms around her waist and a soft kiss at her neck. She turned in the embrace to face the man she loved now and always would.

'Thank you,' she said, 'for contacting him.'

'I thought it right that the man who saved you should share in all this. He sent this for you.'

She took the gift; she could tell it was a book.

'We're going to play pass the parcel, so hurry back in. And I like to win, so it's going to get ugly,' he warned, wagging his crooked finger with a wicked grin.

She blew him a kiss as he left. Katerina undid the wrapping and knew what the title of the book would be before she fully revealed it. It was Daphne du Maurier's *Rebecca*. When she opened it she could tell it was an original edition and that it was Otto's personal copy of the book . . . creased and well-thumbed from many readings. It linked them again in a private way, and while she sensed that she had become his Rebecca, haunting his life, she refused to believe it was sinister.

She could hear music starting and then stopping, followed by raucous laughter. She didn't think Edward would ever grow out of his childish joy of making people happy, and she would see to it that he never did. As she wrapped her book back up with a promise to keep it as a treasured item in her private study upstairs, Edward reappeared.

'I'm coming,' she said, turning to see him cradling Amálie in his arms.

'Our precious girl woke up and Mrs Biskup said she uttered the word "Daddy",' he said with a wry smile.

'Edward, you terrible fibber; she's not talking yet and you know it.'

'Well, she's thinking it,' he assured her, kissing his child's forehead.

Peter peeped around the door. 'Come on, we started the game and now we're all waiting.' He bent down and kissed his infant sister's head. 'And Mum, Daniel's cheating.'

Katerina felt in this moment as though her world had fully

righted itself. This was where she was meant to be: surrounded by family and friends, in love with all of them and finally looking forward to life rather than simply existing. 'Let me take her before she realises she's hungry.' And as Edward placed their child into her arms, he kissed their daughter first and lingered for a longer kiss with her mother.

'I've never been happier,' he whispered.

'Neither have I,' she replied.

AUTHOR'S NOTE

From as early as 1935 Hitler's discriminatory laws and government policies had begun to regulate and radically change the lives of all Jews in Germany. These edicts covered a range of harsh new rules regarding everyday life as the purity of the blood became Hitler's slogan. Amongst other humiliations, German Jews were no longer considered citizens but subjects. Restrictions tightened drastically over the ensuing years. When news of the feared *Kristallnacht* – Night of the Broken Glass – broke in the summer of 1938, and members of the Reich openly attacked and murdered Jews in Germany, Europe was collectively shocked. The violence was triggered by the killing of a German official in Paris by a Jewish teenager desperate to bring the plight of the Jews to the world's notice. It was the eruption of the volcano that had been threatening to blow since Adolf Hitler became Chancellor to a simmering Germany that would not heal from the humiliation of the Great War. Thirty thousand men in Germany alone were arrested the morning after the slaying in Paris simply for sharing the same spiritual belief as the boy killer. As a result, Jewish children from Germany and greater Europe began being moved to safety within weeks of the looting, burning of synagogues, trashing of homes and killing that followed in retaliation for a teenager's crime. Rescuers worked all hours to remove endangered children via what became known as the *Kindertransports*.

Czech Jews knew their days as citizens were numbered and it was a British stockbroker, Nicholas Winton, who came to the rescue of as many of their children as he could get out of the region to the safety of homes in Britain. During 1939, as the provinces of Bohemia and Moravia fully succumbed to become a protectorate of Nazi Germany, he raised the funds, found the foster families and organised for nine *Kindertransport* trains to leave Prague. The first left on 14 March but only eight made it out successfully. The final one, carrying two hundred and fifty children, was stopped at the last minute due to the outbreak of World War II. Records show he rescued six hundred and sixty-nine children. They never saw their families again; their parents and elders mostly perished in the round-ups and Nazi death camps.

ACKNOWLEDGEMENTS

There is usually a host of generous people behind each of my stories and *The Pearl Thief* is no exception.

Notably, Alex Hutchinson has become my firm research buddy, and she is in the pages of this novel walking alongside me through most of the research done in England. She sat alongside me in the Jewish Library and studied book after book. Without Alex I doubt I would ever know where that secret door in the British Museum is, and when I was pondering a location not too far out of London for some scenes, Hampstead Ponds was her inspiration. It was Alex who suggested Robin Hood's Bay when I needed a particular sort of wild and lonely setting, and it was she who made me put on my beanie and get out of the car on the freezing Yorkshire moors to see the Hole of Horkum. She even bought me my own hammer so she could show me how to hunt fossils for ammonite on a rocky beach, and she taught me about Whitby Jet. She is also responsible for most of the hilarity we share on our research trips and I am delighted that, over the course of this book, Alex has been picked up by a major UK publisher and contracted to write a series of period novels. Her first, *A Quality Street Christmas*, will be out for Christmas 2018 under the pen name of Penny Thorpe. I hope she enjoys all the success she deserves.

My thanks to Kay Hyde and the Tourism York team for their help while I was up in the north, and I'd like to give a nod to our lovely guide, Mrs Zuzana, in Prague for helping me to hunt down the location in the forest where, arguably, this book's most powerful scene takes place. It was so important to get the setting right and she took her brief seriously and got it bang on. I am grateful.

William Altman, one of the top tourist guides in Paris who we have used in the past, will wave away the idea that he did much, but without his wisdom my Paris of 1963 would lack the richness he brought to it. His help came just at the right moment.

Thank you to the Wiener Library in London for all of its helpful research tools that I go back to time and again when I am writing about the Holocaust.

The team around me at Penguin Random House seems to expand with each book and I am so grateful to each of you but especially to my publisher, Ali Watts – who always helps me to be better – and to Lou Ryan, Chloe Davies, Rebekah Chereshsky, Amanda Martin, Louisa Maggio, Saskia Adams and Penelope Goodes. The sales team . . . you're brilliant, thank you.

Booksellers of Australia and New Zealand – you are powerhouses of resilience, and long may your shops be the secret worlds we will always want to escape into. Thank you for your support and excitement for this novel. The world really is a better place with your magical spaces.

And the counterbalance to our booksellers are the readers. Without you, there are no books worth writing, and I am the lucky recipient of one of the best audiences any novelist could be blessed by, full of mischief, fun and a hungry need for more stories. Love and thanks to all those wonderful people out there who buy books and borrow books from our marvellous libraries – thank you to the enthusiastic library teams nationwide. Don't ever stop reading! And thank you to my audiences for all the fun when I'm touring – you bring out the best and the wicked in me.

Writers need to be alone . . . it's just how it is. But when I emerge there's always a fun, affectionate family waiting for me. My thanks to my beloved gang, who make life a happy one – especially sons, Will and Jack, and my husband, Ian, who I think we should call Mr Spinach because over the course of this book he grew fields of the stuff! For the next adventure I have a feeling we may have to call him Mr Broad Bean.

Fx

BOOK CLUB NOTES

1. In the prologue, Samuel Kassowicz puts his son Petr on the *Kindertransport* against his wife's strong wishes. Do you think he made the right decision at the time?

2. In what ways has Katerina's work as a jewellery curator prepared her for the challenges she later faces in her personal life?

3. What do you think Otto means when he tells Katerina, 'There are rules to war'?

4. Daniel describes Ruda Mayek as 'the devil . . . a monster that walks this earth in plain sight'. Do you agree with this assessment? How else might we perceive him?

5. Katerina tells Daniel that 'perhaps life was preparing me for this hunt'. In what ways do you think this is true? And in what ways does she feel she needs to become a new version of herself to track down Mayek?

6. Katerina was determined that she had no susceptibility to being romanced, or to falling in love. Why did she feel this way? In what ways did Edward manage to prove her wrong?

7. Otto is described as displaying 'love of the most generous kind'. What does this mean, in your eyes?

8. Katerina was prepared to risk her own life in order to end Ruda Mayek's. Do you see this as a weakness or a strength in her character?

9. Can you appreciate the attitudes of Petr Kassowicz's adopted parents?

10. Did Katerina do the right thing in keeping her baby, despite how he was conceived?

11. Which character changes the most throughout the course of the story?

12. Do you think this book has a happy ending?